THE COLDEST WINTER

BRITTAINY CHERRY

THE COLDEST WINTER

Brittainy Cherry

By: Brittainy Cherry

The Coldest Winter
Copyright © 2023 by Brittainy Cherry
All rights reserved.

Published: Brittainy Cherry 2023

Editing: Emerald Edits, Lawrence Editing, Virginia Tesi Carey,

Editing: My Brother's Editor, Editing4Indies

Sensitivity Editing: A Book A Day Author Services

Cover Design: Murphy Rae

❀ Created with Vellum

To anyone who has lost themselves and fought like hell to find their way home.

This one's for you.

AUTHOR'S NOTE

This story came from a place of love and the utmost care. It is a tale about honoring the different stages a person might go through when grieving the loss of loved ones. I wanted to create a raw and honest story to show that the path to healing differs for each individual traveling down said road.

For those reasons, I'd like to note that parts of this story may be sensitive to a few readers due to the subject matter, which includes substance abuse, depression, illness, and the topic of death.

PROLOGUE

Eleven Months Ago

My world,

The first year is the hardest.

That's what I remember from when I lost my mother. I remember feeling as if the world were moving in slow motion, yet somehow spinning wildly out of control at a wicked speed all at once.

It was as if every little thing triggered me in some way. Even happy occasions felt depressing because I realized she wasn't there to celebrate the big moments with me. What was worse was that she wasn't there for the small moments. The small moments sometimes felt even more important to me than the big ones.

I'm sorry I'll be missing out on the moments. The

1

big ones. The small ones. The in-betweens. I'm sorry I won't be there to give you the pieces of me you'll need when the world gets heavy.

I'm sorry our goodbye came sooner than we'd hoped.

But I do want to leave you with something. A gift of sorts. It's my recipe box. You know how much this means to me, and I want to pass it down to you. Hundreds of my favorite meals I've made for you throughout your life are within it. If you ever feel inspired to cook a meal, I want you to have this. I hope this helps you feel me when you lose your way. I hope you taste my love in every single bite.

I love you always. And then a little bit more after that.

Find me in the sunrises. I'll always be there, waiting to shine on you.

Con amore,

Mama

CHAPTER 1

Starlet
January
Present Day

*T*he day I turned fourteen, I created a life plan. I knew what I wanted and saw the roadmap to get everything I desired. Step one was to graduate from college with a degree in education like my mother did. Step two was to get engaged to my boyfriend, John, by graduation. Step three, start my teaching career and land a fantastic job. Then to have kids by twenty-three always seemed right.

I knew what my life was supposed to look like, and as I entered the second semester of my junior year of college, I was sure I was on the straight and narrow path to my dreams coming true.

I prided myself on being levelheaded. If there were a word to describe me, it would be perfectionist. I always did the right thing because I had an irrational fear of failure. I wasn't one to step out of my security box, as I knew all the angles of said box. I knew the ins and outs of my protected walls of stability. I had no problem staying on the right path—I liked my safety net.

That afternoon, I stood in front of the full-length mirror of my shared dorm room, smoothing my hands over my white A-line dress. Beside said mirror was the vision board I'd created with every item I planned to accomplish. Many people updated their vision boards yearly, but I was lucky enough to have the same precise vision since I was a teenager. I knew who I was. Therefore, I knew what I was becoming, and that afternoon was bringing me one step closer to my happily ever after.

It was my twenty-first birthday, and my boyfriend, John, was going to propose to me that evening.

John wasn't very clever when it came to surprises. When he told me I should get my nails done for my birthday and wear a white dress, it became clear what was happening. Plus, when I was at his dorm the other night studying for our physics exam, I'd opened the top drawer in his desk to find a pen and saw the ring box.

The timing couldn't have been better, seeing as I wanted to be engaged for at least a year before marriage. If things went according to plan, we could have our first child by age twenty-three—only one year older than my parents were when they had me.

To say my parents' love story was my inspiration was an understatement. Even though my mom passed away a few years ago, Dad still talked about her as if she were the greatest gift to the world. He wasn't wrong about that, either. My mother was a saint.

In almost every way possible, I'd been my mother's daughter. Every decision I'd made since she passed away was created with the idea of what she'd think about me due to said choices. I received perfect grades because I knew that would make her proud. I never cursed because she never did. I went into education because she was one of the best educators I'd ever known. I wore red lipstick and high heels because those were her two staples. I also wore her jewelry. Every single day, a piece of her rested against my body.

My mother was a beautiful Italian woman with a Mediterranean skin tone and dirty-blond hair, the opposite of mine. My father was a handsome Black man with deep-brown skin and the kindest eyes known to humanity. I had black hair that used to match Dad's when he had hair on top of his head, and my dark brown eyes resembled Mom's. Dad always said my skin was a golden sun-kissed tone, the perfect blend of my parents' DNA. My hair, though, was mostly wild in its natural state. My curls were a daily task I had to deal with that neither of my parents ever experienced. Mom had mastered learning how to care for my hair, though, and before she passed away, she taught me all her tips and tricks.

When I missed her, I straightened my hair so I'd see her looking back at me when I looked in the mirror. I straightened my hair a lot. She would've scolded me about doing it so much because she loved my natural curls, but all I ever wanted was to be just like her.

I saw her in my eyes as I finished getting ready to meet John. The thought of what would occur that night sent a wave of butterflies throughout my system.

I wish you were here, Mom.

I wished I had been able to call her after the engagement took place so she and I could've gone into wedding-planning mode. Missing her during the big moments felt extremely unfair.

Mom would've liked John. He was like me in many ways—structured, stable, and safe. He knew what he wanted from his life and where his road map led him.

I was supposed to meet John at his dorm room in an hour so we could head out to dinner, but the nervous flurries shooting through me made me head over an hour earlier than I was meant to arrive. My mind was in a tailspin as I wondered when he'd propose. Would it be before dinner or after? Would it be after I drank my first ever sip of alcohol—which would be a glass of prosecco—Mom's favorite? Or would he wait until late at night and do it on our walk home from dinner, on the steps of Rander Hall, where we'd first met our first year of college during our History 101 class?

The excitement of the possibilities made the upcoming proposal that much more thrilling. I knew it was coming, but I didn't know how.

As I reached John's dorm room, I could hear music blasting in his room. It must've been his roommate, Kevin's music blasting. John wasn't one to listen to rap music even though I told him some of the most lyrical geniuses came from rap music—I got that trait from my father.

I turned the doorknob to walk inside as I always did, seeing how the boys never locked their room, and I froze in place as I stared forward at John on his bed completely naked, with a girl between his legs giving him a blow job.

His blue eyes widened as my chest tightened from the lack of air circulating through my lungs when he saw me. Panic began to build second by second as I stared at my boyfriend and the girl on her knees before him.

"Oh crap!" John shouted, shaking the girl from his bottom half.

"Sorry," I blurted out. Dazed and confused, I quickly rushed out of the room, shutting the door behind me. Did I apologize for catching my boyfriend cheating? My eyes stung with emotions as I shook my head, utterly dumbfounded by what I'd walked into. I started down the hallway quickly because I felt on the verge of an emotional breakdown.

"Starlet! Starlet, wait!" he shouted behind me.

I glanced over my shoulder and saw John hurriedly stepping into the left leg of his sweatpants, still shirtless, racing toward me.

My eyes bugged out at the sight of him. The hallway had a few other guys walking through it, and their eyes all moved over to John's and my situation.

"It's not what it looked like!" John said, sending a wave of anger shooting through me. But I didn't showcase it. The last thing I needed was for the strangers in the hallway to know that I caught my boyfriend getting a blow job from another girl. Many people have different fears in their lives, and public mortification was high on my list. The last thing I needed was to start sobbing in front of others after learning that John was a cheater.

I picked up my pace, shooting over to the elevator. I tapped the button repeatedly as if that would cause the elevator to appear magically. Unfortunately, it didn't, and John caught up to me. He was out of breath and panting by the time he reached me, but to be fair, he was panting in bed with her. Her. Who was she? Did it matter?

No.

It didn't.

It didn't matter who the cheater was cheating with—all that mattered was that he was cheating.

The elevator opened, and I hopped inside as John followed me.

"Leave me alone," I shot his way, hitting the first-floor button nonstop.

"Starlet, it wasn't what it looked like," he urged. My eyes widened with shock at his choice of words. He pinched the bridge of his nose and sighed. "Okay, it was what it looked like. But you don't understand. She and I were studying for a math exam at first and—"

"And let me guess, one plus one equals your penis in her mouth?" I cut in. "I bet you love those types of equations." The tears at the base of my eyes began to fall as he looked at me with remorse. Did he feel bad that it happened or that he got caught?

"I'm sorry, Star," he whispered, his eyes flooding with tears.

What a jerk! What kind of person started crying when he was the one who got caught in the act of being unfaithful? On my birthday of all days! I would've done what she did to him later on and probably done it better! As I said, I was a perfectionist.

"How could you?" I cried, feeling ridiculous that he was getting to witness my breakdown. "It's my birthday, and you were going to propose to me!"

His eyes narrowed. "You knew I was going to propose to you tonight?"

"Of course." I held my freshly painted red nails in the air. "I did my nails!"

He scratched at the back of his head. "I was still going to propose to you tonight. On paper, you and I are a great match, Starlet. My parents like you. They think you're good for me, unlike Meredith. She's wild and fun while you're...you."

"What's that supposed to mean?" I asked, offended by his tone. He sounded as if he was mocking me.

"You know. A bit boring and predictable. In a good way, of course!" he remarked. "I like that I always know how you're going to act. You never step out of your box. That's very good. You're like Cheerios—slightly basic but good for the heart. Meredith is like a sugary cereal that leads to diabetes or something. I mean, it's good— *it's so good*—but like...bad for you. But you're Cheerios. I like Cheerios. My parents like them more, but I think I'd be a bigger fan with age. I'd probably like you so much in our thirties."

Was he comparing women to cereal right now? My best friend, Whitney, would have a field day with that one.

The tears kept falling, and my heart kept breaking. I wished I could've shut off my emotions. John didn't deserve them, yet they were on public display for him to witness. I bet his cocky ego loved to see how he was affecting me. Whitney once told me that certain low-quality men got off on seeing how they'd hurt a woman's feelings. I didn't think that would ever be John, but I had no real idea of who he had been at the end of the day.

"Who's Meredith?" I asked.

"Oh, that's the girl who was giving me..." His words faded off. He shrugged. "If it makes you feel better, I'd never date Meredith. She's sort of a slut and gets around."

My jaw dropped as I began to bat him with my purse repeatedly. I didn't know if I was hitting him for Meredith or myself. Either way, I was going to pound-town on his arm.

"You're scum!" I screamed, feeling disgusted by his words. The elevator doors opened as I cried and beat him with my purse. "You're scum, John, scum! And I never want to see you again!" I shouted. As I turned away from him, a group of people stood in the lobby staring at me during my breakdown.

Public mortification.

Great.

Just great.

Happy birthday to me.

* * *

I WAS STILL GOING to propose to you tonight.

John said that as if it were a compliment, and I should've been thrilled by the concept of it.

If I had a time machine, I would've warned past Starlet about the risk of walking into her boyfriend's dorm room when he didn't know she was coming over.

Catching John cheating on my birthday wasn't one of my resolutions for the new year. I knew he was a lousy gift giver, but this had to be the worst present ever.

You knew you were down bad when "Angel" by Sarah McLachlan was repeatedly blasting through your dorm room, and you had *Bridget Jones's Diary* on standby to watch, followed by *He's Just Not That Into You.*

He's just not that into me!

There I was in my room, emotionally spent and not engaged. I was single as a Pringle in the bottom of the can.

Alone.

Lonely.

Pathetic.

Happy birthday, Starlet Evans.

If swimming in one's feelings was an Olympic sport, call me Michael Phelps.

"Oh my goodness. Where is the sad, starving puppy asking for a money donation?" Whitney asked as she walked into our room.

There I was, in all my glory, sitting on my bed with mascara rolling down my cheeks in complete distress. Since I used it as a handkerchief, my white dress was smeared with my makeup.

"It's me," I sobbed. "I'm the sad, starving puppy needing your donations."

She quickly shot over to me and wrapped me in her embrace, stepping firmly into her best friend role. "Nope, nope, nope. I refuse for this to be a thing. You can't be sad on your birthday. That goes against all the rules of life. What happened?"

"John was getting a blowie from another girl when I went to his dorm room!"

She narrowed her eyes. "Seriously?"

"Yes. Why would I lie about that?"

"No, of course, you wouldn't. I'm just a bit shocked, seeing how he's John."

"I know." I nodded in agreement. "Because he's so loyal normally."

"No, I mean because he's ugly. How did he find a girl to go down on him?"

"What?" I gasped. "He's not ugly."

"Oh come on, Starlet. He's med-ugly. There's no denying that. And you can't defend him after he did that to you. On your birthday!"

"On my birthday!" I cried, tossing my hands up in the air. "He is med-ugly!"

"So med-ugly."

"What's med-ugly?" I dramatically sobbed.

She snickered at my theatrics. After living with me for the past three semesters of our college career, Whitney wasn't too fazed by me.

"It's a person who isn't completely ugly, but medium ugly. Med-ugly."

I huffed and puffed. "John is so med-ugly."

"And you're hot. Like hot-hot. Maybe not right now with the whole exorcist girl makeup look you have going on, but baby, you're a knockout. You were doing charity work, sweetie. But the problem with a hot-hot dating a med-ugly is that most of the time, the med-ugly gets cocky thinking he's hot because he got a hot-hot, you know?"

"You should teach a college course on this topic."

"I would save millions of women from heartbreak. The worst thing in the world is being heartbroken over a med-ugly guy. You probably had to convince yourself to date him in the first place. If anything, you're probably feeling embarrassed right now that out of all the penises in the world, it was *that* one who hurt you. He had no right to hurt you, looking like that."

"Because I'm hot-hot?"

"Yeah. All women are hot-hot. Most men are med-ugly. But they are just cocky jerks who dated hot-hots, and now their egos are out of control! It's alarming, and I blame the patriarchy. This is a tale as old as time. Do you know why Napoleon was such a dick? Because some hot-hot girl probably told him he wasn't that short, and BOOM! The rest was history."

I snickered a little, and Whitney's eyes lit up.

"That's what I like to hear, laughter," she sang. She hurried over, hopped onto my bed, grabbed my phone, and shut off the song.

"Hey! That's a great song," I called out.

"No. Do you know what a good song is? Anything Lizzo right now. Or 'Flowers' by Miley Cyrus."

"Maybe Sza?"

"No! No Sza right now. There's a time and place for Sza, but it's not during a breakup."

Fair.

She grabbed a hair tie from my nightstand, then bundled my hair into a bun on my head. She then wiped away my tears with her thumbs. Cupping my face, she locked my brown eyes with her blues. "You know what we're doing tonight?" she asked.

"Eating Ben & Jerry's and going through old pictures of John and me?"

She gave me the "don't make me smack you upside the head" look.

I sighed. "What are we doing?"

"We're going to a frat party." She wiggled her hips against my bed and clapped her hands in excitement. "We're going to a frat party to celebrate your birthday!"

"I don't go to parties."

I was the opposite of the "go to parties" type of girl. My college life was wrapped around class, class, and class again. Then I'd sit in my dorm room and study for hours. I didn't let anything distract me from my goals, particularly partying. Who had time for hangovers, drama, and dressing up while pursuing their dreams?

Oh gosh. John was right. I was Cheerios!

Whitney placed her hands against my shoulders and shook me. "Starlet."

"Yes?"

"We're going to this party. You are going to drink cheap, bad alcohol, and you are going to flirt with men who aren't med-ugly. And I swear, if I see you with a med-ugly, I will shout MU at you."

"What if the guy is hot?"

"Then I'll tip my invisible hat your way, and you shall proceed cautiously. Hot men are assholes, too."

"Remind me why we like guys again?"

"We were programmed in our youth to find the opposite appealing, which led to us gaslighting ourselves for years to come due to society's drive to push the past social norms onto our plates to make our parents and grandparents feel as if they didn't waste decades of their lives not living in their truth, which, in turn, led to them wanting us to remain in their lies."

Whitney always had the most long-winded answers for the simplest questions.

I shrugged my shoulders. "And here I was thinking it was because we liked penises."

"Oh yes." She nodded in agreement. "We do like the penises. Now, get showered and get dressed. We're going out in a few hours."

* * *

I STOOD in the kitchen of a dimly lit fraternity house, feeling completely out of place. My hair was still slightly damp from my shower, and I wore a black tank top with tight black jeans. The jeans were Whitney's, and she swore they'd make my butt look amazing. I'd never worn such tight jeans, but my behind did look pretty plump when I glanced in the mirror before we left.

Sadly enough, Whitney didn't allow me to bring a novel to said party because I was on a mission to be social. She even stole my headphones so I couldn't sneakily listen to my audiobooks. I was told to engage with others instead of being my regular hermit crab. Still, I didn't know how to speak to those in that house. My hands kept rubbing up and down my arms as I took in my surroundings.

The number of alcohol bottles littering the tables and countertops of the kitchen amazed me. Along with those were a few kegs of beer and two massive coolers with what people were calling "magic punch." I'd never seen so much booze in my life. Music blared through the space, creating a slight ring in my ears as people gathered around, laughing and chatting. A handful of men flirted in corners with women, and many make-out sessions were going on, too.

Whitney came back over and handed me a red Solo cup. "Here you go, drink this," she urged. "It's the magic punch."

I sniffed the drink, and my nose scrunched up. "What exactly is magic punch?"

She shrugged as she took a big chug of hers. "That's the magic part of it all—no one knows. But rumor has it that by the end of your second cup, you'll be on your way to Hogwarts."

"Splendid." I semi-chuckled.

She held her cup in the air toward me. "A toast. To the birthday girl. May tonight be a night she's never experienced, filled with fun, laughter, and hot-hot guys!"

"Hear, hear!" I cheered, tapping my cup with hers before I took a sip. The second I tasted it, I spit it out. "Oh my gosh, what is that? Rubbing alcohol?"

"Look at that. Your first sip of alcohol." Whitney smiled widely and placed her hand over her heart. "My little girl is growing up."

"Yeah, look at me. I'm living, and I'm vibing. I'm doing the thing," I said, trying to act cooler than ever. "John was wrong when he called me Cheerios."

She arched an eyebrow. "He called you Cheerios?"

"Yeah." As I thought about his words, my eyes began to wash over with tears. "Because I'm boring and basic!"

"Oh my gosh, what a dick. Screw him. He's a lying jerk who didn't deserve you."

"You're right," I said, leaning against the kitchen counter. As soon as I felt its stickiness, I leaned forward. I was already daydreaming about my steamy shower once I made it home. "This is the perfect time to prove John wrong. I'm not boring. I'm fun! I'm wild. I can be just like Meredith."

"Who's Meredith?"

"The blow job girl."

"Oh. Screw her, too!" Whitney remarked. "The jerk."

I frowned. "I don't know if she's a jerk. I don't know if she knew he was in a relationship because sometimes guys lie, and the other girl might not have known she was a home-wrecker. And can a woman wreck a home, or was the home already wrecked before she arrived? Sigmund Freud once said—"

Whitney grimaced and placed her hands against my shoulders. "Sweetie, please don't tell me you're about to quote philosophers because that would be a buzzkill for me. You can't be that kind of drunk tonight, okay?"

"What kind of drunk am I supposed to be?"

"I don't know. The kind of drunk who dances on tables, gets wild in a good way, and makes out with a stranger. Just not Freud quoters."

"Right. You know, I wasn't even going to quote Freud. That was me being in a silly, goofy mood."

"Star."

"Yes?"

"You're my best friend, my roommate, my ride or die, so believe me when I say I know you were about to quote Freud."

Fair.

He was fascinating, though, and had great thoughts.

"I do think it's nice that you aren't shaming the girl, though. That's very kind of you," Whitney pointed out. "I'd hate both of them."

"What can I say? I'm a girl's girl." I sighed, thinking about what had taken place not that long ago.

I still couldn't get the image out of my head of walking into John's room. Dad told me that John wasn't the right one for me. His reason? He had terrible tattoos. My father owned one of Chicago's most famous tattoo parlors and judged people based on their ink—maybe not all people, but John, nonetheless.

"I'm going to dance on tables and find someone to make out with," I told Whitney, puffing my chest out. I wasn't going to let that boy ruin my birthday. I'd just turned twenty-one, and the last thing I wanted was for John to mess up what was supposed to be a very exciting night for me.

"Good! I want to hear that because it's your birthday, and we will not let little pecker John ruin it!"

"John's pecker isn't little." I sighed.

"How many peckers have you seen before, live in action?"

"Only his."

She shook her head. "Then trust me, John's pecker is small."

"How would you know?"

"That man oozes small dick energy. Remember when he picked a rose for you, called it a rosy with a baby voice, and placed it in your hair?" She gagged. "Instant ick detected. I played nice for years because I loved you, but he's a total small dick *dick*. You're better off."

"I know."

If only my heart could believe that, too.

"Anyway, to me!" I cheered.

"To you!" she celebrated. Whitney downed her drink and then smacked my butt. "That's my girl."

"I'm going to find a boy to make out with tonight." I said the words, but I hardly believed them.

Whitney shook her head and locked her blue eyes with mine. "No, dear friend. You go out there and find a man to make out with. Not a boy, a man."

"Yes," I said, hopping back and forth like a boxer about to enter the ring for their first match. "But before I go, can I tell you the Freud quote?"

She smiled. "Of course."

"*Out of your vulnerabilities will come your strength.*" I smiled. "Freakin' Freud, am I right?"

"The man, the myth, the legend," she agreed, snickering as she shook her head. "Never change, my weird friend."

I wasn't sure I could even if I wanted to.

15

Whitney headed off to probably dance on a table, leaving me to dump out the cocktail in my red Solo cup. I hurried over to fill it with the fruit punch juice on the island. Maybe I wasn't drinking that night, but I made it to a party. That had to count for something. As I turned around, I stumbled sideways after stepping into something sticky and losing my footing. Before I could crash and fall, a person instinctively reached out and wrapped his huge, calloused, firm hands around my upper arms, steadying my position. The heat from his hold and the roughness of his hands sizzled against my soft skin. The contrast of the warmth and roughness of his touch to my smooth skin heated my blood. My eyes inquiringly studied his hands on my arms before I tilted my head to take him in. As my eyes met him, cataloging every inch of his being, he swiftly released his hold on me, tucking his hands away.

I didn't stop my observation because I couldn't. My heart rate intensified as our eyes locked once more. He was the most attractive person I'd ever seen, with eyes packed with such sorrow. I wondered if he knew that his eyes looked like that—so painfully sad. Still, he was beautiful—the kind of beautiful I'd only seen in magazines.

The mysterious rock-hard man might've been one of the most striking individuals I'd ever seen in my twenty-one years of existence. He dressed like midnight and moved like stone. Everything seemed concentrated about him. Even though his touch was warm, his spirit felt ice cold. It took a few moments for me to realize I'd spilled my juice against his shirt, but once I noticed, I couldn't stop staring. His damp black T-shirt hugged his chest tightly, showcasing his toned arms. He towered over me, easily at least six-foot-three, and had the kind of mouth that looked as if it never crafted smiles, only grimaces or frowns. His beard was perfectly trimmed, too, making the grimace even more pronounced.

His lips were full, though, and his skin was flawless. Either he had a fantastic skincare routine or he was one of those lucky jerks who never had a day of acne.

Then there were his eyes.

I'd never met a gaze that hypnotized me, yet I felt frozen in place.

Those eyes sent a flurry of sensations straight to the pit of my stomach, creating a pool of heat as they locked in on me. Green orbs with sparks of brown intertwined within them. Or maybe they were brown with dashes of green. It was hard to tell with my semi-tired mind and my semi-broken heart. All I knew was I liked looking into them, even if they seemed cold.

No, not cold.

Maybe dejected?

Dejected eyes had a way of appearing somewhat chilled.

His looked like they were hurting as much as my heart.

You noticed that in people when you were hurting yourself—how their pain mirrored your own.

"Crap, I'm so sorry," I stuttered.

I placed the red Solo cup on the countertop and then, without thought, rubbed my hands up and down the strange man's chest, trying to remove the spill from his clothing. He stayed motionless, as dark and foreboding as a gargoyle statue on a parapet, his eyes locked on me. His stare was penetrating yet oddly aloof. Like he could see my every thought but didn't wish to.

I discovered his rock-hard abs as my fingertips caressed his chest. I wasn't helping the situation, yet I couldn't stop wiping him down for some reason. My hands weren't a drying machine, yet I moved them across his body as if the quickness would result in dried fabric.

"If you're going to rub me down, you might as well lower your touch." His voice slipped through his mouth with such ease and certainty that I almost missed his inappropriate commentary.

My hands froze against his chest as I tilted my head to meet his eyes. "I'm sorry, what?"

"If you're gonna rub my chest, you might as well rub my cock, too."

I pulled my hands back from him, completely flabbergasted. "Huh?"

"Did I stutter?" His voice was smooth like whiskey, with the same tingling sensation when his sound hit my ears. It was low, with bass, and stable without an ounce of doubt. I didn't know voices could be

17

that strong, that sure when they spoke. It wasn't as if he was demanding power. He was powerful without even trying.

Definitely not a boy.

Definitely a man.

A hot-hot man.

"Uh, no. You didn't stutter."

"So?"

I raised an eyebrow. "So what?"

"Are you going to rub my cock, or will you move out of my way so I can get a beer?"

"Are you always this crude?"

"I'm not crude," he said. "Just straight to the point."

"And what is the point, exactly?"

"You rubbing my cock."

"Stop saying cock." I grimaced.

"Stop asking me my point, then," he replied.

I placed my hands on my hips and shook my head in disbelief. "Is that what you guys do? Does that work for you? Just asking women to touch your penis?"

"My penis?" He huffed, and his mouth slightly turned up into a devilish smirk. "So formal, so proper," he mocked.

"I could've said phallus."

He leaned in slightly, his hot breath melting against my face. "You can suck my phallus if you'd like. Along with my testicles for shits and giggles."

"What's wrong with you men and blow jobs? Anything for a blow, I swear!"

He shrugged his shoulders. "I'm a giver, too."

"What's that supposed to mean?"

"It means you can sit on my face."

My jaw dropped as my eyes widened. "Oh my goodness!"

He cocked an eyebrow. "Sitting on faces makes you bashful, huh?"

"What? No. Psh, please. Not fazed at all." I shifted around in my shoes. "I'm cool with that. I'm fine. I'm hip." *Freaking Cheerios, Star.*

"Hip?" He almost laughed, but I wasn't sure his voice could make such a noise. "How old are you again?"

"Oh, shut it. I don't go out of my way to meet strangers who tell me I can sit on their faces."

"I'm sorry to hear that. I hope this year brings you more face sittings. That's my New Year's resolution for you. By all means, I'll be your first chair."

My cheeks heated. "Stop it."

"What? I was offering you a seat. What do you need? A wedding proposal?" he joked.

That wouldn't be so bad, I thought to myself.

"No offense—" I started.

"You're about to be offensive—"

"I said no offense."

"That's what people say before they are about to be offensive. But continue."

I shrugged. "You're kind of an asshole."

"My friends call me Dick."

"What's your actual name?"

"Doesn't matter," he said, flicking his thumb against the bridge of his nose. "Because by night's end, you'll be calling me a dick or riding my dick. Either way, it's Dick to you."

"Oh my gosh, are you always this explicit?"

"Depends. Are you always such a prude?"

"Do I look like a prude?"

His eyes moved up and down my figure several times before he met my stare again. The curve to his lips almost made me blush. He didn't hate what he saw. Hips and all. "You look like a woman who should be sitting on my face."

I laughed and shook my head. "I'm done with this conversation."

He crossed his arms over his broad chest and leaned in. "I get it, but I'm just trying to help you with your New Year's resolution of sitting on some faces."

"That wasn't my New Year's resolution. That was yours for me."

"What can I say? I want what's best for you."

I hated to admit it, but I was enjoying our back-and-forth banter. John never bantered with me. Ugh. John. *Screw you, John—stupid boy.*

I turned back to the man. "I think this is where we stop talking now."

"Yes. Less talk, more sitting."

I parted my mouth to speak, but my mind shut down as I stared at him.

He tilted his head and narrowed his eyes as he seemingly grew more captivated by me. He studied me as if I were the *Mona Lisa—* something unique yet foreign to his mind. He stared as if he were trying to collect clues to a mystery I hadn't known I'd been a part of. Why was he studying me like that? And why did his eyes on me make me feel both panicky and protected all at once?

Walk away, Star.

But I didn't. I couldn't.

We stood there, neither of us speaking as the beat of the music pulsed around us. The chatter of the other partygoers buzzed in my eardrums as we stayed in place.

Why was he still looking at me?

And why couldn't I look away?

I pushed out an awkward smile. "Okay, well, this was...odd. Okay. Yeah. Goodbye." I started walking past him. My arm brushed against his, and once again, I was met with the same warmth of his touch as his hand landed against my forearm.

He tilted his head and narrowed his eyes. "Do you want to forget?"

Butterflies fluttered in my stomach. "Forget what?"

He moved in closer, his mouth landing near the edge of my earlobe. His hot breaths melted against my chilled skin as he whispered, "Everything."

My stomach rumbled with nerves as I looked up to meet his green eyes with specks of brown once more. I saw it again—the flash of hurt in his eyes. It was short-lived, but it was there. Hidden behind secrets and stories he'd never shared with another. A part of me almost thought I made it up, but no. It was there. I swore it was there. I felt his sadness traveling through my system as he kept his hold on me. It was as if his intensity was exploding throughout my soul. Not only did I witness his darkness, but I felt it through his touch.

"Who hurt you?" I asked in reply.

His eyes flashed once more. There it was again—the sorrow. There was no way I'd mislabeled it.

His eyes hardened as he replied, "No one."

"Liar."

"Liar," he agreed. "How about we lie together as we...lie together," he offered. His hand was still on my forearm, and the heat it sent through my system flustered my mind. I liked his touch of warmth. I liked his blinks of pain. I liked how he reminded me of a roller coaster —terrifying yet thrilling and worth the price of admission.

I also liked that he smelled like oak trees and lemonade.

As I looked past him, my eyes locked with Whitney. She raised her eyebrows and nodded as she mouthed, "HH," in my direction.

Yup. A hot-hot man.

At that moment, I knew I had two choices. I could've been the safe, boring Starlet who always did the right thing. The one who always made the brain-forward choices. Who always thought about the future and the consequences of life. Or I could be unhinged Starlet. The girl who shut off her brain and stepped into her wild side. The one who let go and let herself be free—the one who wanted to climb that man like a tree and take a proper seat. I didn't want to be Cheerios anymore. I wanted to be the bottom of a box of Frosted Flakes where all the excellent stuff settled. Sugary, fun, and delicious.

My stare fell to his hand and then rose to meet those eyes again. "Okay," I breathed out.

He arched an eyebrow. "Okay, what?"

"I need a chair."

He gave me a devilish smile.

I liked that, too.

I flipped my hand around so I was the one now holding his wrist and began pulling him toward a room.

CHAPTER 2

Starlet

*O*nce we found a bedroom, I closed the door behind us. My back turned to Dick as I locked the door, shutting us into our fantasy. The anticipation of it all increased once that bolt clicked into place, making it more real. As I pivoted around on my tiptoes to face him, I found him watching me, taking me all in as his breathing grew choppier as his hands clenched at his sides. He stayed patient and in place as if waiting for me to give him the go-ahead to touch me.

I grinned shyly, biting my bottom lip. I felt slightly unnerved to be the center of his attention. I'd never had a man look at me like he did...as if he were a hungry beast ready for the biggest feast of his life. He stalked over to me, pushing me up against the chilled door. My back fell against the wood softly, and his big hands cradled my head to stop me from hitting it against the door.

His lips hovered over mine briefly, his nose brushing against mine. My lips parted as his breaths fell against my mouth. His exhales became my inhalations seconds before his mouth crashed against mine. His tongue plundered into my mouth, discovering my taste.

His hand rode up the back of my tank top, caressing my skin as he deepened the kiss. My mind spun as the thrill of his taste grew increasingly addicting. My hands wrapped around his neck as his body pressed against mine. A quivering sensation fell between my thighs as his other hand wrapped around the back of my neck. My body arched toward him, unable to remember what it felt like before our bodies were tangled. I felt dirty, but I craved for him to make it messier. I wanted him to destroy me in all the best ways. Against the wall. On the dresser. Laid up against the bed. I'd never felt this way before—high on kisses.

Was this what kissing was supposed to feel like?

Powerful? Ravenous? Euphoric?

Was this what being wicked was all about?

Was this why people threw caution to the wind?

My body began to pulsate from his hold on me as his hands kept exploring my body. My hips, my thighs, my curves... His mouth traveled down to my neck as his left hand unbuckled the belt on my jeans.

He growled against my skin as he tasted me, making me arch my neck to the side to trail his tongue down to my collarbone, which he did, tasting every piece of me.

Once the belt was removed, he unbuckled the jeans and slid them down. I stepped out of them quickly after kicking my shoes to the side of the room.

He paused, placed a finger beneath my chin, and tilted my head to lock my stare with his. There he was again, piercing into my soul and reading the newly crafted pages dipped in the ink of trouble and written cursively in sin.

Everything slowed.

My breath caught as he reviewed me.

He was so intense without even trying to be.

His eyes searched mine deliberately as if he were looking for something, searching for an answer within my browns.

"Okay?" he whispered, grazing his mouth against mine.

My heartbeats intensified as realization set in.

He wasn't taking from me; he was honoring me. He wasn't only hoping to please himself, but he was asking permission. For some reason, that only turned me on more.

"Okay," I breathed out.

With that, his lips locked with mine one more time. His kisses made me high. My brain was fuzzy, and my heart thrilled. I liked how he felt against me. I loved it, in all honesty. He felt like heaven intermixing with hell, like a fallen angel who could still somehow soar.

When his lips finished against mine, he pulled up the edges of my tank top and tossed it to the side of the room. His hands cupped my bra, and his mouth lowered to trail kisses along the curves of my breasts. Then he lowered himself more and more, his mouth tasting every piece of me as he inched closer and closer to my panty line.

"It's my birthday," I choked out. I didn't know why the words left my mouth. Or why my mind was trying to move to the forefront and push my desires to the side.

Those brownish-green eyes found my stare again. He tilted his head in confusion, waiting for me to provide more details.

I cleared my throat. "My boyfriend cheated on me today. On my birthday."

"That dick," he growled, almost in a protective manner.

I snickered. "I thought that was your name."

"Trust me, it is." He thumbed his finger against the thin fabric of my panties and kept his eyes locked on mine. He slid them down my thighs and allowed me to remove them. Then his hands fell to my hips, and he lifted me.

"Wait!" I shook my head. For a split second, I became too self-conscious. I wasn't ashamed of my curves, not in the least. Yet I worried I might not have been featherlight like some other women he was used to hooking up with. "You're going to hurt your back. I'm a little curvier than the average co-ed. You can't lift me like—"

"I see you," he said, his hands roaming around my curves, against my skin, against my stomach. "I want you," he whispered, his mouth kissing the parts of me that John avoided. He massaged my skin before he wrapped his hands below my buttocks, lifted me into his arms without effort, and carried me to the bed. I was almost certain that was when the first orgasm of the night took place.

"You're mine tonight," he swore, his voice low and dripping with want and need. "Now, grab the headboard," he instructed, positioning me on top of him. "And let me feast."

The overthinking part of my mind shut off when he lifted my two-hundred-plus body into the air and sat me on his chest. He grabbed my waist and raised me onto his face as I lost sight of reality. His tongue slid in and out of my core, forcing me to cry out in pleasure. My hips rocked against his mouth, against his beard that was now dripping with my essence.

My hands gripped the headboard, and he fed on me as if I were his last supper, lapping his tongue against my clit, sucking it, swallowing every drop of me. He drank me as if lost in the desert, and I was the first to quench his thirst. I felt how he craved me as much as I did him.

"I'm going to...I'm..." I breathlessly whimpered as the sensation of an orgasm increased with every passing second. My nails dug into the headboard as he buried himself in me.

Yes, yes, yes, please...

His tongue quickened as if he could hear my thoughts begging. I arched myself back, grabbing his upper thighs, moving as if his tongue were the rhythm and my core were his favorite melody.

I fell apart against him, the shaking orgasm causing me to cry out loud. The moment it felt like too much, too powerful, I began to move away, yet he wrapped his hands around my thighs and said, "Not yet," before he pulled me back for more. That was when it got good. That was when I truly hit the mark. I would've pleaded for more, but he gave it freely, unselfishly, with instruction. He made me feel like a queen and worked as if he were nothing more than a peasant trying to earn my good grace. Yet I rode his face as if he were a king, and I wanted to be his humble servant.

As I arched backward, lying against him, I could feel his hardness flicking across my back. He was fully awake and ready to play. Feeling him pulsate against my spine only made me want him more.

Once I finished, he lifted me onto his stomach. The look of pleasure in his eyes made my cheeks heat as a wave of shyness hit me. His beard glistened with my essence before he wickedly wiped his hand across it. His smile matched Hades, and I craved to be his Persephone.

"Happy birthday," he whispered, pulling me down to his face and kissing me with my taste. "You're amazing. Every piece of you."

The praise hit me in a way I'd never felt before. I'd never been with a man who admired me in bed with his words. It only increased my confidence.

With him, my body did things I didn't know it could do. I didn't know it could respond so well to the right words, praise, and touch. Not only was he physically transforming me but mentally, too. He had me basking in my womanly curves, exploring myself in a new way.

His hands flipped me over effortlessly so I was lying on my back, and he hovered over me. I liked how he did that—how he moved me around like a rag doll as if my weight was an imaginary concept that only existed in my flawed insecurities.

I didn't know I could feel that much confidence being naked with a stranger when my previous partner hardly looked at me when we were intimate. Sex felt like a chore with John, something we had to get out of the way before returning to our other tasks. That night, though, it became an adventure—a voyage of discovery.

As he hovered over me, I couldn't stop staring. He felt so familiar, yet I knew we'd never met. He felt like a memory my mind had somehow forgotten along the way. A lost dream that was finally being reimagined.

I pulled off his shirt and then he unbuckled his jeans. An audible gasp slipped from my mouth as he slid down his pants and boxers.

The size and girth of his member should've come with a caution sign and a fair warning.

Warning, consumer. Choking hazard. Swallowing this item might result in a stiff jaw and swollen lips. May lead to death if one does not come up for air. Viewer discretion is advised. Explore at your own risk.

My jaw ached looking at it, but a fair trade was a fair trade.

I started to lower myself, and he chuckled a little, shaking his head.

"It's your birthday," he told me, laying me back down and kissing my neck. "I'm the one giving the gifts, not you," he whispered against my earlobe as he spread my legs apart and lowered himself against me. He hurriedly grabbed a condom from his trouser pocket and slid it on before returning to me. His hardness rubbed against my core as his hand moved behind my back. He unhooked my bra with what seemed like a snap of a finger.

My mind turned to mush as his lips fell to my left breast, and he began to flick his tongue back and forth against my nipple in a rhythmic way. He took his huge length and rubbed the tip over my clit several times. I felt the build up of anticipation as he teased me by gliding his length back and forth against my saturated lips. The want and needs of him inside of me were driving me wild as I begged him to take all of me.

"Please," I breathlessly muttered. "I want all of you..."

His lips danced across mine as if they'd always belonged there. His tongue slipped into my mouth as he plunged inside me with one beautiful, hard thrust.

"Yes, yes, yes," I cried as he entered me.

My back arched as he deepened himself. He was initially slow, each inch feeling like a mile. My hands landed against his rock-hard chest as he lifted my legs on his shoulders. He folded me like a pancake and picked up his speed. My legs quivered against him as my hands flew over my head. I pushed the palms of my hands against the headboard, loving his pace, his thickness, his everything.

Yes, yes, yes...

He placed one hand at the base of my neck, not squeezing tightly but holding on enough to intensify my sensations more than I thought possible. That was new, and I liked that... I liked being choked by him.

His mouth lowered to mine, and he licked my lips from the bottom to the top before whispering against them. "Who's the good birthday girl?"

His eyes dilated, and my heart felt sprung as I whispered back, "Me," wanting nothing more than to stay lost in him for a while. He held me tight, too, as if he cared. He caressed every single piece of me, both physically and mentally. He soothed the loudest parts of my insecurities as he pressed against my mouth.

"That's right," he softly spoke. "You're my good birthday girl."

At that moment, I lost myself.

At that moment, he discovered me.

My legs trembled against him, and he growled in pleasure as I discovered another orgasm. He felt it, too—everything. As I trembled, he moaned in pleasure. I could tell he was fighting everything in his power not to join me yet in his final destination. He wasn't looking to stop the celebration anytime soon.

He turned me on my side, wrapped his legs around me, and slid into me from behind. "Oh my gosh," I breathed out, discovering that different angles hit different marks, and I loved every second of it.

His face pressed against my side as his words rolled off his tongue. "I like that," he told me. "I like that I can see all of you." His hands fell to my breasts, massaging them as he nibbled against my earlobe. "I like that I can feel all of you."

We stayed there with one another, losing time and every inhibition we'd held. I didn't know his hurts, and he hardly knew mine, but for those sacred moments, we felt like one. One strikingly beautiful mess.

He flipped me over to my back and met my stare once more. Those brownish-green eyes were addictive. He could've asked me for anything then, and I would've granted him his every wish. If he asked for a star, I would've found a ladder tall enough to reach the sky because that was how much I craved his pleasure. I wanted him as much as he seemingly wanted me.

"Come with me," he ordered as his tip rubbed against my clit. He thrust into me, keeping eye contact, holding his stare as if I were the only person he'd ever want to look at again. I did as he commanded of me.

He came inside me, and I came fast, hard, long, and freely.

Yes, yes, yes...

After we finished, he collapsed on top of me. "Fuck," he muttered, pleased. He trailed kisses down my neck before he flipped over to the side of me, completely drenched from the roller-coaster ride we'd ridden with one another.

"That was…" he breathed out.

"Yeah…" I agreed.

He tilted his head toward me, and a sly smirk found him. "Told you that you'd be sitting on my face."

I rolled my eyes, feeling slightly bashful. "Whatever."

A strange look found him as he stared at me. He narrowed his eyes, tilting his head slightly as he observed my face. The wicked smile that landed against his lips evaporated as he met my eyes. Then he hurriedly stood from the bed and gathered his clothing. He moved as if he'd just witnessed a ghost within my stare.

The sensation of his urgency sent chills of confusion down my back.

How could he look at me one second ago as if I were everything and then blink and make me feel like nothing?

I pulled the blanket over my body, hoping it would work as a shield to protect my timid heart. A flurry of nerves hit me as my mind returned to reality. An odd feeling of rejection settled in my mind when his warmth evaporated from my skin. Coming down from the highest high was met with the unfortunate aftermath of feeling lonely. He was still in the room, but he felt so far away. Maybe not physically, but mentally he'd somehow checked out the second his feet left the bed and found solid ground.

The whole situation left an odd taste in my mouth, but I tried to swallow it. What did I expect, anyway? I didn't even know his name. He didn't owe me anything, not even a goodbye. Logically, my brain understood that, yet my heart? It felt slightly cracked.

I bit my bottom lip. "Leaving already?"

His eyes met mine, and I saw it again—his rawness, his confusion. Something was eating at his mind and scrambling his thoughts. Maybe he was feeling as conflicted as I had been. Didn't he feel what I felt? That wasn't just sex. It couldn't have been. I'd never felt so personal with someone I knew, let alone a stranger. But maybe that was what one-night stands were—fake situations appearing real.

He paused for a fleeting second. His lips parted slightly as if he were going to express himself, but instead, he shut them tightly before continuing to get dressed. He was tossing on his clothes as if he were a paramedic racing out of the door to attend an accident scene. I'd never seen someone rush so quickly to get away from me. I would've asked what I'd done to offend him, but I doubted he would've been honest. I didn't know him, but I knew his eyes told the truth more than his lips ever had.

Guilt filled me up as I thought of what could've been wrong. "Do you have a girlfriend?" I questioned. Was that why he was rushing to get away from me? Was I his Meredith in this situation? Did he have his own box of Cheerios sitting back at home?

"What? No."

"Then why are you rushing to leave so fast?"

"What did you expect?" He grimaced, avoiding eye contact at all costs. "Cuddles?"

I didn't expect cuddles, but it would've been nice.

The way he avoided my stare was so odd to me. It wasn't as if he thought I was a plague of some sort, but more so like I was his favorite drug, and he'd been desperately trying to get sober.

"Hey," I called out, making him look once more. "Are you okay?" I wanted to examine his expression. To have a few more moments before he let go of whatever we'd just done. Yet this time, when he looked my way, he was different.

His eyes weren't as gentle as they were during our performance. That cold aloofness had returned, but I couldn't tell which was the real him. Was he the gentleman who asked permission? The one who sometimes looked like the saddest soul alive? Or was he simply a man who had one-night stands and felt nothing?

"I'm fine. This isn't some fairy-tale ending. We fucked. Now we leave," he told me as he pulled up his jeans. "Welcome to the real world."

"You're such a dick."

"I told you that from the jump. Happy birthday," he said. "Thanks for the sweets."

After he left, I stayed in bed for a few seconds longer. Emotions began pushing through my system, and I could not tame them. Tears flooded my stare, and I began to sob into the palms of my hands, realizing what I'd just done. I didn't know who I'd been that night and always had a strong sense of self. I was reliable. Responsible. Stable. The good girl who never did the bad thing. Everything that took place in that room was wrong. It should've never happened. I should've never been in that situation at all. Yet I wanted to relive every single second of it in slow motion. His hands gripping my waist...his tongue licking my neck...his lips against mine...

No, Starlet. This was wrong.

My mind and heart were at war as the tears poured from my eyes because I didn't understand.

How could something so bad feel so good?

CHAPTER 3

Starlet

I woke up without a single headache to be discovered.
It's a twenty-first birthday miracle!
I guessed that one sip of magic punch wouldn't have been enough to grant me a hangover.

The first thing that came to mind as I stretched my arms in my dorm room bed was how John cheated on me. Luckily, the second thought that crashed into my head was dick—both the person and the phallus.

My body still felt sore from how he flipped me around like a pancake.

Did I tell him I was a good birthday girl?

Oh gosh, Starlet. What a night, what a night.

After hopping out of bed, I headed to take a shower. One of the perks of no longer being a first- or second-year student in college meant you had a solid chance of getting a dorm with a shower attached. That sure beat sharing a bathroom with twenty other girls on your floor—the perks of advancing in school.

I had finished my shower and was drying my hair when Whitney stirred in her bed. She yawned wide-mouthed and then patted her stomach five times, as she did every morning.

"Morning, roomie," she stated.

"Morning, roomie," I replied.

She sat up and stretched her arms. "Hungover?"

"Not a lick."

Her eyebrow shot up. "Seriously?"

"Maybe I'm immune to hangovers." That, or I didn't drink a lick last night.

"Don't jinx yourself, dude. Remember that time I took twenty-one Jell-O shots?"

I shivered at the memory. "I do." She came stumbling back to our dorm as if she were made of Jell-O.

She smiled. "I ended up in the nurse's office being told my hangover caught up with me two days later. I'd never drunk so much Gatorade in my life."

"Let's just hope that's not my case." I snickered. "I'm feeling pretty good."

"Good. That's good, seeing how John was a total jerk. But then, based on the night you had..." She let out a sly smirk and wiggled her eyebrows. "We didn't even get to talk about the night you had after you ran off with hot-hot."

That was right. Whitney and I stumbled back home, giggling like schoolgirls over anything and everything. I mainly stumbled because of the bedroom activities, and she walked sideways due to the magic punch. We didn't even begin to dive deep into my adventures with Dick.

I felt my cheeks heat from the thought of the previous night. I was not super comfortable talking about my sex life, mainly because sex with John was pretty mundane and boring. But last night?

About last night...

BRITTAINY CHERRY

I sat down at my desk and pulled out a hairbrush. "Last night was...different."

"Did he have a big peter piper? Did he pick a peck of pickled peppers?"

I chuckled, shaking my head. "Why are you like this?"

"I don't know. My parents are weird. I think the gene transferred to me, too. Really, though, how was it?"

"It was..." I shut my eyes for a moment and swooned to myself.

"Oh my gosh." Whitney gasped, making me open my eyes. She pointed a stern finger my way. "He rocked your vagina!"

"He rocked my vagina," I echoed, shaking my head in disbelief from the previous night.

"Heck yeah! I'm so proud of you, roomie. So does it stand true now? Did John have a small dick?"

"I don't think we can even classify it as a dick anymore. It was more so a peanut."

"And Mr. Hot-Hot was a..."

"Elephant trunk."

Whitney tossed her arms up in victory. "Happy freaking birthday, Starlet Evans!"

Happy birthday indeed.

"I hope you can't walk straight all weekend long," she told me. "Speaking of... on a scale of one to ten, how basic are we feeling right now? Avocado toast level?" Whitney asked me as I tried to untangle the wet mane of hair on my head.

My curly brown hair was a comedy of errors each morning. The number of times I'd thought about shaving said hair was at least fifty times per day.

Saturdays to Whitney meant one thing and one thing only— brunch. It was her favorite way to sober up after her wild Friday nights. For the most part, my roommate was a book nerd who took her education too seriously, but when Fridays rolled around? She was off the clock as an educated girl and punched in her party wild child timesheet.

She called it the perfect life balance. After last night, I understood

34

why and was somewhat disappointed I'd missed out on two years of college parties because I was too focused on my studies.

"That sounds amazing. With a scrambled egg," I offered.

"Hard-boiled, grated with a cheese grater," she corrected. "And goat cheese with Mike's Hot Honey." She moaned in desire. "Can we go to Eve's Place for brunch? My treat for your birthday."

Eve's Place was our favorite brunch spot for two reasons; we could walk there from campus, and it included a menu the size of my forearm. If you wanted to eat like a health nut or drown in maple syrup and whipped cream, Eve had a food item for you.

After giving up on brushing out my hair, I tossed it into a messy bun that flopped on top of my head. "I can't do brunch, remember? I promised my dad he could have me all weekend for my birthday."

She cried out in despair as if I'd told her that London had fallen. "But what about our weekend brunch traditions?"

"The tradition will have to take a hiatus for one weekend. Unless you want to join us."

She narrowed her eyes in thought. "Eric is quite the looker."

I shivered. "Never mind, you can't come."

"Are you sure you don't want a new stepmom?"

"You disturb me daily." I chuckled as I picked up my sneakers and slid them on before grabbing my pink puffy winter coat, scarf, and mittens.

After I was bundled up and packed my backpack, I walked over to Whitney and kissed her forehead. "Have some avocado toast for me."

She grumbled and waved me off. "Tell my future husband I said hi."

I snickered at my friend before grabbing my laundry basket of clothes to wash at Dad's house. I headed to my car and hopped in to drive down to Chicago for the weekend. Going to school at UW-Milwaukee worked out nicely for me, seeing how it was only a two-hour drive to my dad's house. We'd spent every Sunday together for father-daughter time. It was the one day he didn't work at the tattoo parlor and the one day I'd spend doing all my laundry. Having

Saturday and Sunday with him that weekend would be nice. Day in and day out, I was a daddy's girl.

I drove straight to Inked, knowing Dad would be there Saturday morning. He lived and breathed that shop, and I was almost certain he and his employees would be working on some fantastic pieces. When I was a kid, I'd spend so much time sitting there watching Dad and his guys and gals ink up individuals. It was amazing how many people cried joyfully when they saw their masterpieces come to life.

If I weren't already on my career path and had a steady hand and a lick of artistic skills, I would've gladly spent my life working at Dad's parlor.

I parked the car around the corner from the shop and hopped out into the freezing weather. I rushed to the front door as my cheeks were hit with the chilled wind.

"Surprise!" the crew shouted, sending me into a complete frenzy of shock. The parlor had been decked out in birthday decorations. "Happy birthday, Starlet!" they sang.

One of the coolest things in the world was seeing a bunch of beefy, tatted biker men holding pink and purple balloons to celebrate me. The whole crew consisted of Dad's best friends, and I'd grown up surrounded by them my entire life. Nelson was the first to hurry over and wrap me in a tight bear hug.

"Happy birthday, nugget," he said, rubbing his fist over my curly hair.

Nelson was the definition of a rock star. He looked like a line-backer, too—effortlessly cool and effortlessly gigantic. Nelson was six-foot-four and at least two hundred and ninety pounds. He wasn't chubby, though. He was all muscle. He lifted me off the floor as if it were the easiest thing to do. His wife, Joy, was the next to come my way. Joy was a beautiful Black woman who was inked from head to toe. She had vibrant gray hair and shaved the sides of her head. She always wore high heels at least five inches tall and was still shorter than her husband.

I pretty much considered them my aunt and uncle. They were what Dad called his ride or dies. They surrounded us with so much love during some pretty dark days of our lives, and I honestly didn't think we would've made it through the tough days if they hadn't showered us with their light.

Harper was next to embrace me. He was an older guy in his sixties and one of the best tattoo artists in the world. People flew in from around the world to have Harper ink them. He was a cool, calm man in touch with energy and the universe. Sometimes, if he sensed a person was nervous before a tattooing session, he'd pull out his deck of tarot cards and do a reading on them, then follow it up with a quick reiki session. We called him our hippie guru.

"Bright greetings, our beloved." Harper smiled, pulling me into a hug. Harper gave the best hugs. He hugged someone as if he'd been waiting his whole life to embrace them. The kind of hug that made a person melt into his arms.

Next, Cole—the party animal. He was in his late thirties yet still celebrated as if he were twenty-one. Cole decorated his body with piercings, the newest being his dolphin bites right below his bottom lip. He was a slim man with shaggy blond hair and green eyes that sparkled. I'd never seen him have a bad day. Cole lived for the thrill of life. It shouldn't have been a shock when he walked out with a tray of shots lined up for everyone.

"Twenty-fucking-one!" Cole shouted while blowing on a party favor noisemaker hanging out of his mouth. "Happy birthday, bucka-roo," he said as he placed the tray down and kissed my forehead.

Last, there was Dad—the best papa in the whole world.

"Happy birthday, princess," he said as he hugged me. "I can't believe you're all grown up." He kissed my forehead repeatedly.

My father and I looked very much alike, though he had a few more tattoos on his skin than my naked self. He'd been trying to ink me for years, but I still wasn't ready for what I wanted him to create against my skin. One day, though. One day.

Dad was a handsome man with deep dimples that always show-cased when he laughed, which he did a lot. I had those same dimples. I had his brown eyes and his full smile, too. He stood at six-foot-two with a shiny bald head that everyone liked to rub for good luck.

"I thought the boyfriend was coming with you?" Dad asked.

I wrinkled my nose. "Let's just say that didn't work out, and I hope I never see him again."

Dad narrowed his eyes, debating whether to ask for more details, but then shrugged. "Good. He had shitty tattoos."

I smiled. "The worst of the worst."

"Shots!" Cole called out, shoving one into my hand.

I laughed. "Okay, but we can't get too wild. I have a big day on Monday, and I can't get too crazy," I warned.

Cole waved me off. "It's your twenty-first birthday. You're supposed to let loose."

If only he knew how loose I'd been the night prior. Just thinking about it made my cheeks heat.

"Don't worry, buttercup," Dad said. "I'll take care of you."

They all looked so excited that I couldn't let them down.

Besides, how bad could a shot be compared to last night's magic punch?

I took the shot from Cole, and we all cheered and tossed it back. "Oh my gosh!" I cried out. Worse. It could be much, much worse than the magic punch.

Joy snickered and patted me on the back. "Let me make you an actual drink. One that won't make you want to throw up. Trust me. This is coming from a girl who hates the taste of alcohol."

In Joy, I trust.

She mixed me a drink, which was a real magical punch because I couldn't tell there was a drop of alcohol in it.

I drank those mixed drinks like a sailor. We blasted music all day, dancing in the parlor with full freedom. I didn't know I could drink so much until I drank *too* much. The next thing I knew, it was Saturday evening and I was hugging my father's toilet while he held my hair back for me.

"I feel like death," I said after throwing up for the third time.

The hangover I thought I'd missed Saturday morning? It was kind enough to catch up with me Saturday night.

Dad snickered. "I remember my first ever hangover. I was fourteen and threw up in my dad's favorite pair of shoes."

"Fourteen?!" I gasped.

"Not everyone was a good kid like you, princess. Some of us made bad choices day in and day out."

"I'm never drinking again," I groaned as I sat back and leaned against the tub.

Dad sat beside me, and I laid my head on his shoulder. "That's what everyone says when they get sick from drinking. Then what do you know? Another night to forget happens, and the cycle replays."

"Not me," I swore. "I'm done."

He kissed my forehead. "You take a shower and put on some pajamas. You smell like ass. I'm going to make you some popcorn to help settle your stomach. You haven't eaten enough today." He pushed himself up to a standing position. "How about some Taco Bell? It makes all hangovers a little better."

CHAPTER 4

Milo

*M*y house was full of laughter and light when my mom was around. I'd wake up every morning with her dancing around the kitchen while music blasted as she made me breakfast before school. It was never a simple kind of breakfast, either. She'd always go above and beyond, making freshly baked muffins along with a frittata or some bullshit.

She'd make the biggest pot of coffee, drink just about all of it, and then try to engage me in her dancing, too. I never did, seeing how I was the opposite of a morning person. I got that trait from my father.

I never realized how much I took that for granted until those days disappeared. I hated that it wasn't a quick fade, either. When she got sick, the music never played as loudly as before. Then the dancing slowed. She couldn't make the fancy breakfasts, either. I knew it was hard for her, so I'd sometimes cook for her. I'd put on the music when she'd forget. I'd dance now and again to make her laugh.

Her laugh…

I missed her laughter the most.

She'd also make her big pot of homemade gravy for our Sunday dinner. It was a slow-cooking pasta sauce that tasted as if the gods had made it. Sunday dinners were a big deal at our house. We used to have dozens and dozens of people over for the meal, some of my friends included, and we'd laugh until the sun went down as everyone went apeshit over Mom's cooking.

I missed the taste of her love. I knew it sounded crazy, but it wasn't the ingredients she used but rather how she used them. Dad always joked that the magic was in her favorite wooden spoon that she mixed the gravy with. Now, the spoon just sat in the pantry with the rest of her cooking equipment, mostly left unbothered.

It was odd thinking about how lively the house used to be. Now, each morning was quiet, especially on the weekends. Most of the time, Dad was missing in action by the time I woke up, which was pretty early. Even though I wasn't a morning person, I usually woke up at the crack of dawn to catch the sunrises—something I started doing after Mom passed away. I had no idea where that man went. I just knew he wasn't at home.

When I'd get up on the weekends, I'd make my breakfast, crawl back into my room, and sit in the darkness of a house that once was a home. It was a house packed with haunting memories of how good life was before. On days when the silence would get too loud, I did one of two things. I used sex to distract me, or I'd hang out with my friends.

Sex was my main go-to since I'd lost my virginity a few years back. I'd had quite the reputation around my part of town. It wasn't some secret that I tried to keep. A lot had known me by many names. Some called me a manwhore, others called me Daddy, but most women called me Dick.

Like birthday girl.

Fucking birthday girl.

What was that about?

Last night didn't go as planned. Well, it did…until it didn't.

My mind kept thinking about the night at the frat house and the quirky and weird woman. Something about her unsettled me. She looked at me as if she could see the real me. The me that most people overlooked outside of my small core friend group. That bothered me a lot. Or it intrigued me—one of the two.

Plus, the sex…

That was one of the most enjoyable nights of my life, and I didn't even know her name. I'd slept with my fair share of people, but nobody made me feel like that woman did, and she hadn't even gone down on me.

She was chaotic, too, which was oddly amusing. I didn't feel that often, either—amused. Since we'd hooked up yesterday, she'd crossed my mind more than I would've appreciated. Usually after my hookups, the women never crossed my mind again. I'd never hooked up with the same girl twice. It left little room for emotions to get involved. But for some reason, I missed her taste on my tongue. The night we shared was almost too much for me.

The moment I left that bedroom, I hightailed it out of there. I couldn't explain what I'd felt. It was as if my world was knocked off-kilter. I felt like an ass as I tossed on my clothes and made a beeline for the exit, but I couldn't stay in there with her. Something about her eyes made me want to be real, and I didn't want that. I felt the unease of her soft stare building a panic in my chest because she felt so different from all the women before her. Most of them made me forget about life. She made me wonder.

Based on how I was reacting, she probably thought I was an asshole, yet she had no clue that my body was shutting down. My hands grew sweaty as she sat in that bed, looking my way. My eyes glassed over as a feeling of panic overwhelmed me. I've had many panic attacks over the past three years, but never after sex. Sex was the thing that tamed my anxiety, not reinforced it.

The panic attacks typically only presented themselves when I'd think about my mom too much. And trust me, when I was in that room, I was not thinking about Mother dearest. I had no damn idea why that woman pulled that level of unease out of me. I hoped we'd never cross paths again for my well-being. But still, I couldn't stop thinking about the sex. It was so good that I didn't feel like hooking up with another girl that evening.

Therefore, I had to go to the second thing that helped me when my mind was too loud and the silence was too much—my friends.

It was no secret that I'd been a shitty friend over the past few years, but they still let me hang around them. I guessed those were the people who mattered the most—the ones who saw you at your worst and still wanted to have you around.

Most of my friend group kicked it at Savannah's place on weekends. Savannah was my oldest friend. We'd known each other since before we could say our first words. Our moms were close friends. Savannah always acted like my big sister even though she was younger than me. Her instinct was to be motherly with our whole friend group and me.

Her parents were well-off and lived in an upscale neighborhood. You couldn't drive down the block without seeing a luxury car parked in every driveway. That weekend, her parents were out of town, so she had everyone over to drink and smoke a bit, which seemed to be what I needed.

Our main friend group was small at six, but we had strong personalities. We'd all met in elementary school, outside of the new guy, Tom.

First, there was Brian, the gamer. He always talked about what games were coming out and the hottest stuff on the market. I did not doubt he'd someday be the multimillionaire owner of a video game company. His knowledge was remarkable. He was also a year older than me and attended UW-Milwaukee for college. He was why I ended up at a damn frat party the night before.

Then there was Chris. He was pretty shy. Savannah and I met him in the third grade when two kids were bullying him on the playground. Savannah gave the two guys a black eye and told Chris to stick around us. He never left after that.

Bonnie was Savannah's girlfriend. They'd been going together for two years, and I'd never seen a pair more right for one another. Tom was the newest—he met Bonnie at their job at the local Target. I didn't know much about him because he met me in my emo era. He hadn't known me before my mom got sick, so he'd only seen my closed-off side.

The night was uneventful. We'd always ended up in the basement of Savannah's house because her parents told us if we were going to smoke pot or drink, we had to do it down there. That way, they knew we'd be safe instead of drinking and driving. It seemed odd that her parents were so okay with that fact. Rich people lived by a different set of rules. My mom would've never let that fly.

I was thinking about Mom again. I was too sober.

Chris, Tom, and Brian sat in front of the television, playing a video game, going back and forth about something. I wasn't listening closely enough to pick up on the conversation. I couldn't think of the last time I talked to them. Most of the time, I just showed up, smoked, and drank.

"Stop being a hog. Pass it over here," Savannah said, nudging me in the leg as we sat on her couch with Bonnie. I took another drag of the joint before passing it to Savannah. "You're being weird," she mentioned before she passed the joint to Bonnie. "Are you okay?"

That felt like a loaded question.

Savannah always asked me if I was okay. She constantly worried about me. With good reason, I supposed.

"I'm fine," I said. Same answer I'd always given.

"Rumor has it that you hooked up with a girl last night at that frat party," Bonnie mentioned.

"Is that the rumor?" I asked.

"That's the rumor," they said in unison.

"Then the rumor must've been true."

"We need you to find another form of coping, Milo," Savannah said. "Sexually transmitted infections are real. Speaking of, I hope you're still wrapping your dill pickle."

"Please don't refer to my cock as a dill pickle," I flatly replied.

"Yeah, Savannah. I'm sure he's more of a summer sausage," Bonnie added. "If he's a dill pickle, that means it's green, which means an STI is going on."

Savannah turned to me. "Is your dill pickle green, Milo? If so, we can help you with that. It's nothing to be ashamed of." She said it with such motherly care that it made me miss my mom.

I stayed quiet again because talking about a dill pickle green dick wasn't at the top of my to-do list for the night. Feeling numb was the only thing I was searching for.

Savannah nudged me again. "What's wrong?"

"Nothing," I replied.

She frowned because she cared. I hated how much she cared. All of my friends cared. They'd watched me go through the worst years of my life and stuck by my side even when I tried to push them away. I didn't deserve them. I didn't deserve much of anything from anyone.

"You're so weird tonight. Are you sure you're okay?"

No. I'm not, Savannah.

She wasn't wrong.

I was weird that night. Because while I was there, I wasn't *there-there*. My mind was elsewhere.

It's been almost one year, Mom.

One year without you.

Shit.

I was still too sober because my heart was still beating, and my thoughts were still thinking. I knew my friends wanted me to open up, but I didn't know how. Plus, I didn't need to talk about my sadness. I lived with it day in and day out. That seemed like enough torment on its own—no need to put words to it.

Ignoring my friends, I stood from the couch and headed to the bar. Reaching into the cabinet, I pulled out a red plastic cup and poured myself half a cup of Hennessy. I was almost to the point where I couldn't think about Mom, which meant I was almost blackout level.

I chugged the alcohol. It burned on the way down, but I hardly flinched.

I poured another cup full and downed it, too. I did that a few more times when no one was looking, and after a while, the noise in my head subsided.

"Hey, Milo. I have a question for you. I heard you and Erica Court hooked up before, yeah?" Tom asked me as he walked over and patted me on the back.

I had to give it to the guy. He didn't let my closed-off ways faze him. He was always kind to me, like he was nice with everyone else. He talked too much for my liking, but I thought everyone talked too much. Most of the time, I wished people knew how to shut the hell up.

I gave him bonus points because he always had a mint container with feel-good pills if anyone needed an extra boost. That, and Jolly Ranchers. He was obsessed with candy, both the legal and illegal kind.

"I don't know who that is," I replied.

"Erica Court. Cute girl who always wears high pigtails. She's into anime, sometimes dresses up with cat ears."

Oh, cat ears girl. Yeah. I'd screwed her. She meowed during the whole thing. "What about her?"

"Are you into her?"

I arched my eyebrow. "Into her?"

"Yeah. Since you two hooked up, I wanted to ensure I wasn't stepping on any toes because she asked me out. I didn't want to disrespect our friendship. I wanted to ask permission first."

Oh, Tom. Sweet, thoughtful Tom.

"By all means, go for it," I muttered, pouring another drink and downing it. I probably didn't need that one.

I patted Tom on the back. "I'm out tonight."

"What? It's still early!"

"It's two in the morning, and I've got somewhere to be tomorrow," I muttered, grabbing my keys and jacket from the back of one of the chairs. "I'm out."

I stumbled toward the stairs, running into a side table I didn't see. "Shit," I muttered, trying to shake off the throbbing pain shooting through my toe. "Fucking hell," I griped.

Savannah somersaulted from the couch and shot over to me. "Are you okay?"

"I'm fine," I grumbled, walking up the stairs.

"You're always running into stuff. It would help if you opened your eyes more. My blind dog sees better than you."

"I didn't see the damn table," I remarked as I continued to the front door.

"Where are you going?" she asked.

"Home."

"You're drunk and high."

"Thank you, captain obvious," I sarcastically replied. I was mean when I drank. As I said, I was a shitty friend. I made it to the front door, and she blocked my path. "Move, Savannah."

"It's not safe, Milo."

"I'm not safe," I echoed.

She placed a hand on my forearm, glanced around the room, and moved in closer to whisper, "Milo, I know things have been hard for you since your mom died, and I know the first anniversary is—"

"Don't," I warned. "Don't keep speaking."

Her blue eyes grew somber, but I didn't care. How dare she look sad when she had no reason to be. Her parents were still alive. They still celebrated birthdays with her. They were still able to get pissed at her for her bad choices. They still said "I love you" to her. She knew nothing about sadness and how it infected every inch of a person's soul. She knew nothing about the nightmares both during the daytime and at night. She knew nothing about what true heartache felt like. Hell, she still had four grandparents. The closest Savannah ever got to death was what she saw in the movies. I'd seen death up close and personal with the only person who ever meant shit to me. That didn't seem fair. Then again, who said life was fair?

"Milo—"

"Move, Savannah," I bellowed, drunk, rude, and heartless.

Her eyes flashed with more emotions.

She still wouldn't budge, so I did what I had to. I placed my hands against her arms, lifted her body, and removed her from the door.

I stumbled down to my car and slid into the driver's seat. My vision was fading in and out. I couldn't think or see straight, so I couldn't drive. I wished I could drive. All I wanted was to go home.

I hopped out of the car and looked up at the sky. It was dark and snowing. I couldn't see any stars, but I felt the snow. Mom loved the snow. Winter was her favorite season. Everything about it reminded me of her.

I walked over to Savannah's yard and let my body drop against the foot of snow that had fallen over the past few days. I spread my arms out and began to make a snow angel. Mom used to make snow angels with me when I was a kid. Then she'd make us homemade hot cocoa. She'd always add extra marshmallows to mine.

I loved the extra marshmallows.

I should've felt cold out there. I should've been shivering or something.

Maybe I was shivering. Maybe I was getting frostbite.

Perhaps I was dying.

That would be a plot twist.

My arms and legs glided up and down, making an angel in the snow before I blacked out.

I woke up the following morning in a random bed. The room was pitch-black, and it took a second for my eyes to focus. It was still dark out. I glanced down at my outfit, and I wasn't in my clothes.

"What the hell?" I muttered, glancing around.

"Morning, sunshine," a voice remarked. I looked up to find Tom sitting at the desk across from me. "Took you long enough to get up."

"Where am I?"

"In my humble abode. I found you passed out in the snow last night. I tossed you into my car and drove you here. Don't ask how I changed your clothes." He shivered as if he had chills. "I'm forever scarred from what I saw," he joked.

I was at Tom's house with a pounding headache wearing his clothing.

Either way, I wasn't dying.

Damn.

"You want breakfast?" he asked.

I arched my eyebrow, trying to determine the amount I'd screwed up the night prior.

"Nah. Going home." I pushed myself up from the bed, feeling next-level nauseous, but I didn't want to hang around too long.

I glanced outside and saw the sun.

Damn.

I missed the sunrise.

Sorry, Mom.

That was the problem with being fucked up—you missed out on the important things.

Tom drove me back over to Savannah's to pick up my car. I thanked him for helping me out, and he said anytime. It seemed like he meant that, too, which was odd. The guy didn't even know me but treated me like we were best friends.

As I pulled into my driveway, I sighed, seeing Dad's car in the garage. He'd left it wide-open and was parked on an angle. He hadn't drunkenly passed out in the snow the night prior. He must've thought getting behind the wheel was a good idea.

At least I didn't drive home wasted, I thought to myself as if trying to justify that I wasn't my father. Though, I would've driven home like my dumbass father if I could've. I was no better than him. I was him in so many ways that it left me uncomfortable. Mom always said I was a carbon copy of my father. I always felt that that was some insult, though she said it as if it were praise.

I hated the parts of me that mirrored him, and lately, those parts seemed to move in rhythmic harmony. Drunk, high, and disconnected from the world.

Like father, like son.

I walked inside the house, and the smell of something burning instantly hit my nose. I turned the corner into the kitchen and groaned. "What the hell, Dad?" I barked, rushing to the oven and pulling out a black-as-night pizza. Burnt to a crisp. Tasty.

The oven was smoking like wild, and I hurried to open the windows to air out the house. I wasn't fast enough because the smoke detector went off, echoing throughout the space.

I grabbed a newspaper and started fanning the detector to get it to shut off as the smoke cleared out of the space.

"What the hell are you doing?" Dad muttered, walking into the kitchen, still drunk, rubbing the sleep out of his eyes. He was wearing a suit, probably the one he had worn to work two days ago. I was shocked he hadn't been fired yet, but judging by his looks, that was probably right around the corner.

"Your pizza is done," I muttered, annoyed, angry, and sad.

"Shit. Forgot about that. I shut my eyes for a minute."

"You could've burned this whole place down. You gotta be smarter."

"Who do you think you're talking to like that?" he barked, scratching at his scruffy hair. "Don't forget who pays the bills here. Watch your tongue. Do you understand me?"

I didn't reply because I didn't care.

"Speaking about smart, I got a call from your uncle. He said you're failing your classes. What's that about?"

"It's not a big deal."

"It is a big deal. If your mother..." He paused as if he'd become frozen in time. The words rolling from his tongue seemed to work as a reminder that his wife, his best friend, was gone. He shook himself from the grief that sometimes choked him out midsentence. "You need discipline. It would be best if you enlisted after graduation. No question about it."

Here we go again.

My father's idea of parenting was telling me to become who he'd been, starting first with me joining the Army—the opposite of what I'd ever do. I was trying to run far from who my dad had been, not toward it.

"I'm not doing this," I said, walking past him.

I bumped his shoulder, and he swung me around to face him. "Don't do that. Don't brush me off. You need to enlist."

"I'm not doing this," I repeated. "You're drunk."

"Don't talk to me like that," he ordered.

"Don't talk to me," I dryly replied.

"Listen to me," he barked, gripping my arm. He locked his eyes with mine, and it happened again—the suffocation of grief. I knew why it happened to him. I had her eyes. I figured that was why he'd hardly looked at me over the past year. I might've had my father's asshole tendencies, but I held my mother's eyes.

He dropped the hold of my arm and averted his eyes. He moved over to the fridge, opened it, and pulled out a pack of beer. "Do your damn schoolwork and get your life back on track," he ordered.

You first, Father dearest. You first.

Over the next days, I knew the tension in the house was only going to get worse. We'd step on one another's toes, trying to avoid facing the fact that we were approaching the year mark of Mom being gone. He'd drink more, I'd smoke more, and we'd pretend we weren't falling apart until we ultimately crashed.

A ticking time bomb.

CHAPTER 5

Milo

Mondays were my least favorite days of the week. Especially the Mondays after I fought with my father. Those Mondays always sucked the most.

Last night, my father called me a depressed adolescent. I called him a drunken asshole who'd abandoned me. Both comments were true, but he only focused on my failures, not his own. I knew I was depressed. That was a given. My depression had lingered for over three years since Mom got her cancer diagnosis. It started with me crying in the darkness of my closet alone at age fourteen because I didn't want her to hear my tears. I knew that would only make her feel worse, so I hid my pain the best I could. I performed my best when I was around her and others. Everyone bought my act, too, except for Mom. She'd always notice the cracked parts of me that everyone else seemed to miss. She'd stare at me the same way birthday girl had—as if she were peering into the depths of my soul.

Most people thought depression meant lying in bed or sitting in darkness for weeks, but it wasn't that way for me. In the beginning, I'd laugh through my depression. And once I'd become sexually active, I fucked through the pain. I built a false sense of confidence that helped me find women who helped me forget for a little while. I moved through life as if I were a normal person, but it was in the quiet parts of me where the depression thrived. I only felt a crippling sadness or a complete indifference to everyone and everything around me.

Mom had me in counseling and on medication to help with my depression until she died. I stopped all of that after she was gone. The medication made me feel better mentally. It worked wonders, and I knew it sounded messed up, but I didn't think I deserved to feel better with her gone. I didn't want to feel better. I didn't want to feel anything. For the most part, I'd also wished I was six feet under. Because what was the point of life if you didn't have your best friend anymore?

Dad and I had that same mindset. We didn't discuss it, but I saw it enough in his drinking. He was trying not to feel, too.

I thought about the dead more than I did the living. I blamed my mother for that. My mind was a toxic landfill of negativity, and my soul swam in those poisoned thoughts daily.

I deflated into Principal Gallo's office chair, bored with his repetitive lecture.

His office smelled like chicken wings and protein powder. Not the most pleasant scent in the world, though it seemed the new norm every time I showed up for our weekly meeting. He'd remind me how I was weeks away from needing to repeat my senior year due to my failing grades.

Failure seemed to be one of my greatest talents. Just ask my father. He made sure to point out my shortcomings consistently. It was his favorite bedtime story each night. If only he knew my ability to zone out was at an ultimate high regarding his parenting styles. Besides, lately, he entertained the whiskey bottle more than me. He was never truly a parent—Mom took on that task. And now, with her gone...

"Milo. Did you hear me?" Principal Gallo asked, snapping his fingers.

I looked up from the coffee stain on his yellow carpet, the stain I'd focused on since being summoned to his office. No cleaning product could get that shit out.

"You should've soaked that up," I muttered, unamused by…everything.

He arched a bushy eyebrow. "What?"

I pointed toward the stain. "That's never going to come out. Your carpet is fucked."

He tensed up at my comment. I was a professional at stressing out Principal Gallo. "We're ripping the carpeting out in two weeks. Milo, are you—"

"Are you getting hardwood floors?"

"Milo—"

"A nice oak would do you good. Maybe some more paint on the walls and—"

"Milo!" he shouted, slamming his hand against his desk. "Focus."

Why?

I was in a hopeless situation, anyway. What did it matter if I focused or not?

"We have one of the best tutors set up for you. You'll meet with her each day down at the library after school. She's been tutoring students since she attended school here, and everyone she helped has passed their courses. She's busy with college classes, but I put in a good word for you."

"No." I began to rise from my chair. "Thanks, anyway."

"Milo," he barked. "Sit back down."

I considered telling him to piss off briefly, but Mom would've probably lectured me about disrespect.

Why did I care what my mom thought? She was dead. Her opinion didn't hold weight anymore. Still, I respected it.

Principal Gallo clasped his hands together. "You're seeing the tutor."

"Or?"

"Or you're flunking out."

"I'll take flunking for two hundred," I mocked him as if life were a game of *Jeopardy!*.

Mom's favorite show was *Jeopardy!*.

I'd watch it with her every day after school.

There I was again, thinking about the dead.

Principal Gallo sighed and pinched the bridge of his nose. "Milo, what would your mother—"

"Don't." I cut in with a slight headshake. "Don't talk about my mother."

"I get that losing Ana was hard for you. Trust me, I know."

"You have no idea."

"She was my sister, Milo. I lost her, too."

I looked at my uncle and felt a pit in my stomach. Of course I knew he'd lost her, too. It was why I showed up to his office weekly for the conversations about how I was screwing up my life. It was why I sat down in his uncomfortable chair. It was why I stared at his godforsaken carpet.

Because he had her eyes.

He had her smile.

He had her genuine concern, too.

I both hated and loved him for those reasons.

He took off his glasses and rubbed the bridge of his nose. That was how I always knew it was time to talk to my uncle instead of my principal. When the glasses came off, Principal Gallo became Weston.

"I'm worried about you, Milo," he expressed.

"I'm fine."

"You're not. Your grades are slipping, and you're failing three classes, almost four. Ana wouldn't want this for you. I don't want this for you. You need to take the tutor."

"What if I flunked out? Would that be the worst thing in the world?" I was tired of caring. I didn't have much energy left in me to care.

"You're not going to flunk out. I refuse to let that happen."

"Unfortunately for you"—I placed my hands on the arms of the chair and pushed myself up from it—"you don't get to make that choice for me."

I started walking toward the door to leave his office, and he called out to me, but I ignored him. He called again. I still ignored him.

"She left you a letter," Weston said.

The hairs on the back of my neck stood straight. I turned to face him. "What?"

"Your mom...she left you a letter."

"No, she didn't."

"Yes," he urged. "She did. I'm supposed to give it to you at—"

"Give it to me," I ordered. My cold, tired heart started rapidly pounding.

Weston shook his head. "I can't. I'm supposed to give it to you on your graduation."

"Who the hell cares? She's not here to control the timeline. Give it to me."

"I won't."

"Weston—"

"It was her dying wish to me, Milo. I'm not going to disobey her request."

"I hate you," I told him.

Weston nodded. "I know." He placed his glasses back on and sat straighter in his chair. He was now Principal Gallo again. Splendid. "You'll also have to attend all your classes to get the letter."

"Was that Mom's rule, or are you just being a dick?"

He didn't answer my question. "Your tutoring starts today, Milo— three o'clock at the library. Please don't give her a hard time. If you do, she'll report back to me."

Damn tattletale. Why did I get the feeling that woman would become the bane of my existence over the next few weeks?

As I was about to leave, I huffed. "Do you know what's two weeks away from today?" I asked him.

"Yes." He grimaced. "The first anniversary of Ana's passing."

Anniversary.

What an odd word to use for such a tragic situation.

He pushed his glasses on top of his head. "How are you handling it?"

I didn't reply because I wasn't handling it at all. I was mentally shutting down every single second that passed by me.

I walked into the hallway, into a tornado of students zipping past me, yet I felt as if I were moving in slow motion, treading through quicksand that sometimes I'd consider allowing to swallow me whole. I wondered if other people felt that way—as if they'd rather sink away into the earth, never to be seen again, than keep walking mindlessly through the fog.

She left me a letter.

What did it say?

Did Weston keep it in his possession?

That thought made me want to break into my uncle's house and flip the whole thing upside down in search of said letter. If I knew my uncle well enough, he probably had those things in a locked safe.

I wasn't in the mood for school that day, but honestly, I wasn't in the mood for school any day. Yet I was in the mood to get said letter from my uncle at the end of the semester, so I dragged myself to my English class.

"So nice of you to join us, Mr. Corti. I was beginning to think you forgot what this classroom looked like," Mr. Slade mentioned as I walked into class fifteen minutes late.

"You know me. Can't avoid a trip down memory lane," I muttered. I tossed my backpack to the side of my desk and slid into my chair, already disappointed that I chose to show up to class. My uncle got into my head about that damn letter my mother left for me.

"I hope you're caught up on the reading, seeing how we have a pop quiz today," Mr. Slade said as he picked up a stack of papers. The whole room groaned in annoyance. I was almost certain teachers got off on stressing students out with pop quizzes. It was probably the best high of their week.

"Do you even know what book we're reading, Mr. Corti?" he asked as he stood over my desk.

"Let me guess, *See Spot Run*?"

A few people snickered.

"I bet your future appreciates those jokes," Mr. Slade said. "Or lack thereof one."

I flipped him off when he turned his back to me.

Mr. Slade was a dick, but I was certain he felt the same way about me. I wasn't the easiest student to deal with, and there was a 99 percent chance I was about to bomb the quiz he'd set on my desk. He knew that to be true, too. I didn't care about his lack of faith in me, though. I didn't believe in myself, either. It seemed to be a universal belief pattern.

I went to dig in my backpack for a pen to butcher the exam when a person came rushing into the classroom.

"I'm sorry, I'm sorry. I got turned around, and there was traffic, which isn't an excuse because I should've left earlier, so I'm sorry about that, but I'm here. I'm sorry. Hi." The voice was packed with nervous energy. I didn't care enough to see who entered. I still needed a damn pen.

Mr. Slade cleared his throat. "No worries. You're right on time."

I huffed to myself, not looking up. Sure, she could be late, but I couldn't. Hypocrite.

I kept digging in my backpack, unable to find a damn pen. That was when Savannah reached out with an extra. Big sister to the rescue. I wondered if she was sick of my bullshit over the last few years. If she was, she never showed any signs of her annoyance. She kept checking in to make sure I was okay.

I nodded. "Thanks."

"Always," she replied.

Mr. Slade clapped his hands together like a toddler gathering our attention. "Class, I'd like to introduce you to Ms. Evans. Our new student teacher for this semester. She'll be shadowing me and taking over lesson plans occasionally," Mr. Slade said.

As I looked up to the front of the class, shock washed over me when I saw her standing there. Birthday girl.

"Fuck," I blurted out without any thought at all.

The muscles in my neck and shoulders clenched as all eyes shot in my direction, including hers. Her brown eyes that only a few days ago were locked in on mine. Her full lips that only a few days ago were moaning out for me. Her stunned expression mirrored my own.

My fingers fidgeted as a feeling of restlessness overtook me. I didn't like the sensation of all eyes on me. Especially hers, because they stared at me in such a distinct way.

I wrung my hands together several times before rubbing them against my pants. She shook her head, quickly averting her eyes from mine. She turned to Mr. Slade and pushed out a tight-lipped smile. It wasn't her real smile. I'd seen her real smile. It was a beautiful one. Innocent. Rare. It wasn't every day you saw someone's real smile. Yet at that moment, her grin was covered in anxiety and nerves. She was mortified.

Me, on the other hand?

Slightly uneased but intrigued.

Really damn intrigued.

"I'm looking forward to working with you all and forming great working relationships with each individual," she said, gesturing toward all the students.

Mr. Slade instructed us to start our quizzes as he pulled Ms. Evans over to his desk, where he'd talked to her about work or some bullshit. I couldn't take my eyes off her, and I could tell her stare was working overtime to avoid glancing my way. Her nerves were somewhat cute, and she was beautiful. There was no getting around that. I knew that the first moment I looked at her, from her long legs to her phenomenal curves. Her hair was straightened that afternoon, unlike when my fingers got tangled up in her curls three days ago. She looked good with straight hair, but I liked the wildness of her curls a little bit more. She wore a navy-blue top with a pencil skirt and tan high heels. She was completely covered from head to toe, but I could still envision what was beneath the fabric resting against her skin.

Her lips were painted crimson, and my eyes couldn't look away.

I knew this situation was killing her, but she had to remain professional. I had to give her some credit on that front. Most people would've run out in panic.

Ms. Evans.

The thought of calling her that in bed might've crossed my mind. Even though by the end of our night together, I found myself in the middle of a panic attack, the moments leading up to that had been some of the most satisfying times of my life. The panic attack was probably a once-in-a-blue-moon situation that had nothing to do with her. At least, that was what I was telling myself as I daydreamed about tasting her once more.

Ms. Evans.

Ms. Fucking. Evans.

Many inappropriate thoughts formed in my head at that moment, things I knew would've made her blush. I didn't know why, but that idea somewhat thrilled me. Seeing her professionally dressed in that skintight pencil skirt made me want to rip it from her skin. I wanted to bury my face between her legs, tugging at her panties with my teeth to pull them down her thick, luscious thighs. I wondered how she'd look bent over on the teacher's desk with me behind her, smoothing a hand over her bare ass.

Maybe I was wrong. Maybe I did like this school thing. With the right incentive, I could look forward to the lesson plans.

CHAPTER 6

Starlet

"What the heck are you doing here?" I barked toward the mystery man after our English class ended. I told Mr. Slade I would hurry to the bathroom between periods, yet truthfully, I was on a mission to catch a second with Milo to figure out what was happening.

Milo.

His name was Milo Corti.

I figured that out from the handy-dandy student list Mr. Slade provided me with. Gosh, what a name for him. It seemed smug, like his personality. I could feel his stares on me the moment realization set in for him, too. Almost as if he were proud of the surprising storyline to his and my life.

I felt sick to my stomach the moment I locked eyes with him. I needed to take the longest, hottest shower of my life to wash away what we'd done together.

He was a student! A high school student!

He stood with his locker open and glanced down at me. I hated that, too—that he had to look down at me. I needed to feel taller than him, or well, more in power of the situation, and that didn't come easy when he was peering down at me.

My eyes kept darting up and down the hallway to make sure no one was around to listen to our conversation.

"Listen, I'm as shocked as you are," he said, his voice still as strong and certain as when I'd met him.

"How old are you?!" I whisper-shouted.

"Nineteen," he replied. "I had health issues as a kid. Started kindergarten when I was seven. Why, Ms. Evans? Were you worried about something?"

My cheeks flushed at him calling me Ms. Evans.

Oh, I hated that.

I hated hearing my name roll off his tongue like that. Off the same tongue that rolled on me. On every. Piece. Of. Me. Even the parts I could hardly reach.

"You're in high school!" I scolded. "What the heck were you doing at a frat party?"

"Pretty sure I was doing you, so..."

I swatted his arm. "No. No. Don't do that. Don't joke about this. It's not funny."

"It's a little funny."

"No. It's not. How are you in high school? When we did that... that...*thing*...you didn't do it like someone your age would do it. I thought you were older than me! You were very"—my face heated as I grew flustered—"advanced."

He smirked, smug as ever. "I take that as a compliment."

"Well, don't. All I'm saying is, the things you did...those moves you had, were very *mature*."

His wicked grin grew. "Thank you, Ms. Evans. I'd like you to know that you taught me a few things, too. Like how you like to be choked—"

"Shut up!" I whisper-shouted. "*Shut up, shut up, shut up!*" Tears flooded my eyes, but I worked hard to keep them from falling. My nose stung with the overwhelming emotions due to my predicament at hand. My stomach bubbled with fear that everything I'd spent the last few years working toward was now in jeopardy. My hands were clammy and my jaw tight as I stared at him. I was seconds away from cracking completely, and the hammer that could destroy me was in Milo's hands.

He tilted his head as if he would say something sarcastic back, but he bit his tongue instead. He turned away from me slightly and then looked my way again. "I'm not going to say shit about it, all right? Don't do that."

"Don't do what?"

"Cry."

"I'm not gonna cry." Oh my gosh, I was so going to cry.

"Don't worry. I won't tell anyone."

My chest slightly untightened. "Swear?"

"You want my pinky or something?" he spat out.

Yes, well, kind of...

I shook my head. "No. It's fine. No more touching—ever. We'll be fine as long as we can stay professional and out of one another's realm."

"Yup. It's only one hour a day."

"Only eighty-six hours together until you graduate."

"Did you just do that math? Did eighty-six pop into your head?"

"I did it while you took your quiz. I needed to calm myself."

He arched an eyebrow. "Nerd."

"Don't call me a nerd," I ordered, crossing my arms.

"Okay, Ms. Evans."

"Don't call me that either!" I shivered. I wish it were a shiver from disgust, yet if I were honest, him calling me that sent a pool of heat straight to my core. The words fell from his mouth like a dirty sin, and I secretly loved how it felt against my ears. His deep, velvety tone held such confidence and ruggedness that it was painfully seductive. My body was overheating, and it felt like my system would self-destruct at any moment. But he couldn't know that. He'd never know that. "Seriously, don't. It's weird."

"What am I supposed to call you?"

Solid question. "I don't know—nothing. Call me nothing. Pretend I'm like the rest of your teachers. Pretend I don't exist."

"Easy enough."

"Good."

"Great."

"Splendid."

He grimaced and shut his locker. "Can I go to my next class, or were you going to walk me there?" he sarcastically remarked.

I stepped aside.

Before he could walk off, Principal Gallo called out to Milo and me.

"Milo, Ms. Evans. It appears you've already met one another," he stated, heading our way.

That panic that somewhat subsided from my chest began to return with a vengeance as the principal of the whole school approached me. Oh my goodness, did he know? Did Milo share what happened between us with another student? Did they rat me out? Was I going to prison? Oh my gosh, I looked awful in orange. It did nothing for my eyes.

"Uh, hi, Principal Gallo," I blurted out, uncertain what else to say.

Milo stood there with his backpack strap on one shoulder, calm, cool, and collected. I couldn't tell if he was nervous or just that laid-back regarding everything in life. He didn't seem as terrified as I felt.

Principal Gallo smiled, which threw me off. If he'd known what happened, a smile wouldn't be resting on his face. "Milo, remember the tutor I got for you? This is her. She'll be helping you out at the library after school each day. Thank you again, Ms. Evans, for volunteering to help."

Oh.

My.

Gosh.

No!

No, no, no, no!

I pushed out a grin and nodded. "Yes, of course. Not a problem at all."

Principal Gallo went on to talk, but my mind melted into a puddle of nothingness as a tiny grin found Milo's lips. After he excused himself and walked off, Milo's stare moved back to me. I caught his eyes darting up and down my figure, too, which led to me crossing my arms.

"I guess that's one hundred and seventy-two hours spent together, now, huh, Ms. Evans?" he said before walking off, leaving me dazed and confused.

Well.

It appeared he wouldn't need too much of my help with mathematics.

* * *

OVER THE PAST FEW HOURS, I couldn't stop thinking about what Mom would've thought about me, about my choices. I felt sick to my stomach when simply thinking about her disappointment in me. When I revealed to Whitney what had taken place, the guilt in my soul only intensified.

"*You slept with your student?*" Whitney blurted out; her eyes widened with nothing but pure shock.

I groaned as I collapsed onto my bed. "Don't say it like that. It sounds so bad like that."

"I think it sounds bad any way you slice it."

"I know, I know. Trust me. It's been a rough day. I'm also supposed to tutor him after school each day for an hour or two."

For the first time, Whitney was so blown away that she was silent. I didn't even know my best friend knew how to be quiet.

"Is it that bad?" I asked through clenched teeth.

"I mean, it's not good."

"You're supposed to make me feel better about this, Whit."

"Sorry, but, uh...you slept with your student! I'm pretty sure I read a romance book about this." She rubbed the side of her chin. "But don't worry, it ended with babies and a happily ever after."

"This will not end with babies and a happily ever after."

She arched an eyebrow. "That depends. Have you gotten your period since you went to bang town with a student?"

"Whitney! Please never say bang town again. And to be fair, he wasn't my student when it happened, and he's over eighteen, and—oh my gosh, I went to bang town with my student," I groaned, rubbing my hands over my face. That was what I got for listening to the devil on my shoulder that night instead of the angel telling me to cry and watch *He's Just Not That Into You.*

I blamed John for this.

I would've never been at that party if it weren't for him.

"What were high school students doing at a college party, anyway?" I groaned. "They should do ID checks at the door or something. That's a lawsuit waiting to happen."

"You put the poop in party-pooper. It's not a club, Starlet. It's a dirty, grim frat party. The bed you boned in probably had months' old dirty sheets that others boned in that night."

I shivered at the thought.

"Okay, okay, silver lining," Whitney started. She must've seen the panic in my eyes. "You're not sleeping with him ever again, and nobody outside of me, you, and him know about it, right?"

"Right. And he said he wouldn't tell anyone."

"Perfect." She patted her hands together. "See, as they say, 'all's well that ends well.'"

"Shakespeare knew what he was talking about."

She raised an eyebrow. "Is that Shakespeare? I thought it was Harry Styles."

"'As it Was' was Harry Styles."

"That's pretty much the same thing."

"That's not the same thing."

"Potato-potahto, whatever. Did you ever learn what his actual name is instead of Dick?"

"Milo Corti."

"Oh dang." She sighed. "He even has a hot name."

Tell me about it.

I shrugged my shoulders. "Okay, maybe frats don't need ID checks, but I do. From this point on, before I hook up with someone, I'll have to ask for identification."

Whitney giggled. *"Hi, I'm Starlet, and I'd like to go to bang town with you. But first, I'll need to see your license and registration."*

"Sounds good to me."

"You know what I've been thinking about this whole time while you told me the nightmarish story of your life?"

"Do tell."

"Tacos."

I smiled.

She always thought about tacos.

Me, on the other hand? I was thinking of everything that could ruin my life forever if, for some reason, Milo got pissed at me one day, went rogue, and told everyone I let him blow out the candles on my birthday cake.

But tacos were the second thought to cross my mind.

I sighed and dropped my hands into my lap. "Taco Tuesday?"

"Taco Tuesday!" she cheered, tossing her hands up in victory.

* * *

I ARRIVED at the high school the following day, ready to face my fears. I got there fifteen minutes early and sat in my car, waiting to go inside. My stomach's butterflies felt like they were in an intense war against dragons. My intestines felt as if they were in knots. The idea of seeing Milo again made me feel nauseous, and the fact that I couldn't simply avoid looking in his direction was driving me crazy, seeing as I was supposed to be the one tutoring him.

I'd considered asking Mr. Slade if I could switch to one of his other classes so I wouldn't have to see Milo twice a day, but I couldn't make it work with my college class schedule. Like it or not, I'd have to be around Milo Corti for two hours each weekday for the remainder of the semester.

I walked through the hallways of Brooks with my briefcase pulled tightly to my side. The day I bought the briefcase, I felt empowered and like a total badass for being professional. My dad took me on a shopping spree to buy teacher-appropriate outfits, and I felt as if I were killing the game. I called them my Michelle Obama power suits. When I tried them on, I was almost sure I could take on any room I entered.

The high school corridors were packed with students, all with their eyes glued to their phones, either taking selfies or watching some trending video. They hurried around on the hard tile flooring with backpacks slung on their shoulders and books stuffed under their armpits as their eyes stayed glued to their cell phones. Banners and festive balloons promoting the upcoming theater club's performance of *Hairspray* and the senior prom were plastered on the walls. The scents of a high school were very distinct. A mixture of intoxicating perfumes and Axe body spray with dashes of sweaty gym socks.

Maroon lockers lined up in groups of ten, separated by doorways leading to the classrooms. A few lockers had been adorned with stickers and decorations that reflected the students' personalities and interests. I couldn't count the number of Harry Styles, Taylor Swift, and Beyoncé decorations I'd encountered. Yet, nothing was louder and prouder than the love of BTS. I couldn't blame them. I was a proud member of the ARMY myself.

I moved through the high school hallways like a mouse trying to avoid lions. High school was scary when you were a student. I wasn't cool during my high school years. If anything, I was the awkward straight-A student who kept her head in her books and hardly had a social life. That was the level of nerdhood I'd lived in. But now, high school was fifty times more terrifying as a teacher. A student teacher, but still. Especially when you accidentally slept with one of the students.

"Hi, Ms. Evans," a deep voice said as I approached the classroom door. Those same shivers were recreated from his intoxicating sound, moving through my body and down my back.

"Stop calling me that," I whispered, looking up to meet Milo's stare.

I hated that he still smelled like oak trees and lemonade.

I also hated that he looked better today than he had the day before.

I wondered if he did that to irritate me or just looked better with every passing moment. I bet he'd be a silver fox in his sixties.

I went to walk into the room right as Milo did the same.

We bumped shoulders.

"Move," I ordered.

He tilted his head at me, seemingly amused. He stepped backward and gestured toward the doorframe with a slight bow. "After you, Ms. Evans."

I grimaced as I walked through the door, and as I did, I could feel his hot breaths not far behind me. Milo followed *very* close, pressing his front against my back. His heat saturated my power suit, throwing me completely off my stride. I picked up my pace, darting for my desk, trying to shake off his intensity. How would I survive being around Milo when it only took so little of him to cause such a commotion throughout my entire system?

Luckily for me, the first week of being a student teacher for Mr. Slade consisted of me observing from a distance. I didn't have to speak a word in front of the class or in front of Milo. I solely sat at the desk Mr. Slade brought into the classroom for me and watched as he instructed the class.

Still, I felt it—Milo's eyes lingering on me.

CHAPTER 7

Milo

"Showing up two days in a row, Mr. Corti. Color me shocked," Mr. Slade said as I entered the classroom.

"You and me both. You and me both," I muttered.

My mind was still on the student teacher's ass that guided me into said room. She was a good girl. That was given by how she'd almost burst into tears the prior day. But the trouble with her being a good girl was that I was a bad boy who wanted her to be my good girl. I still wanted to taste her against that desk, under the fluorescent lights, as she scolded me for not following the lesson plan.

After taking my seat, I looked at her and tried not to let my stare appear so obvious. She looked good that afternoon. Even better than she had the previous day. She was still teacherly, with her straight hair pulled back into a tight ponytail. I couldn't help but think what it would've been like to pull that ponytail a little while she was on all fours with her ass facing me.

Thoughts you shouldn't be thinking, Milo.

Her name was Starlet, not like the letter, but like the constellations in the sky.

I found that out with a quick internet search because I needed to know her first name, not only her last. Ms. Starlet Evans.

She didn't have much online regarding social media, and the accounts she possessed were private, which was unfortunate. All I wanted to do last night was dig deeper into who she was. I didn't even know why. For the most part, I hated people. No...hate was too strong of a word. I was indifferent to other human beings. I couldn't have cared less about them if I had tried. Yet the plot twist of Starlet ending up being my teacher and tutor was something I didn't see coming.

I had difficulty focusing on whatever Mr. Slade was talking about during the hour because I couldn't keep my eyes off her sitting at that desk, doing her damnedest to avoid looking my way. It was as clear as day that she was avoiding me. I couldn't blame her.

With how her conscience worked, she was probably beating herself up for the unfortunate events between us. But if I were honest, I saw nothing unfortunate about it. After we'd hooked up, I daydreamed about it for the longest. I hadn't even been with another woman since. I was still high off her. I'd never tasted anything like that, like her, before. Starlet tasted like heaven soaked in sin, and after I left that bedroom with her, her tastes lingered against my tongue.

With the way my conscience worked, I only craved more. That was probably why I was destined for hell, and she was made for heaven. We were the opposite of one another. Hell, I'd never even met a woman like her. Someone so timid yet sexy. Smart yet quirky. Thick yet so... Okay, there was no yet to that fact. I just loved how thick she was. Lifting her onto my face and having her hover on top of me was the highlight of my night.

And to think, I wasn't even going to attend that party, but it was either that or sitting at home alone with my thoughts.

She kept her eyes glued firmly on Mr. Slade. I couldn't help but smirk because I knew she was going out of her way not to look in my direction. I couldn't wait to have the chance to sit near her. Smell her. Be close enough to touch her yet knowing that would be forbidden. It was the sweetest kind of torture; one I couldn't wait to experience during our tutoring session after school.

Mr. Slade began handing out the graded quizzes from the previous day. As he laid mine on my desk, he shook his head slightly. "Not a shocking score, Mr. Corti."

I glanced down at the paper and saw the large red F written on the top. I swore Mr. Slade went out of his way to make my Fs big and bold. It was almost as if it were screaming, "fuck you, Milo, and your stupidity."

The joke was on him, though. I wasn't stupid. I simply didn't try. There was a big difference.

I glanced up from my failure and caught Starlet's stare on me. She didn't look away this time like she had for the past forty-five minutes. Instead, she tilted her head with eyes packed with curiosity. She must've overheard Mr. Slade's comment toward me.

For the first time that hour, I felt discomfort from Starlet. Her ochre-colored eyes were so soft, so gentle that they pissed me off. She stared at me as if she felt pity for me. I didn't need a person's pity. Most of the time, all I needed was to be left alone.

In our game of stare, I failed by looking away first. I didn't particularly appreciate how her misplaced care made me uncomfortable.

After the school day ended, I packed my things and headed to the local library to meet Starlet for our session. I picked a study room toward the back and slumped in the chair. I waited for a while, and my irritation built over time. We were coming from the same damn place. How was she late?

"Sorry, sorry," she muttered, entering the study room. The moment I saw her, I sat straighter. An odd sensation washed over me that I didn't recognize. Was that…excitement? Was it pleasure from seeing her show up? Or maybe just gas in the pit of my gut. Maybe I had to take a shit. Hard to tell, seeing how I hardly knew how feelings worked. All I knew was the discomfort was annoying as hell.

She pulled out the chair across from me, still talking. "I had to stop by the principal's office to talk to him about the tutoring and—"

"Already looking for a reason to quit?" I cut in.

I wouldn't blame her.

I knew a lost cause when I saw one, too.

She narrowed her eyes, confused. "What? No. I had to gather the books from your classes to keep up and ensure we were on the same page across the board."

Oh.

Right.

"And we are, right?" she asked, arching an eyebrow. "We're on the same page, correct?"

"Are you talking about school or about us fucking?"

Her full lips slightly parted as her jaw dropped. She shook her head. "Both. I'm talking about both, Milo. And please don't say it like that. It makes me feel dirty."

"You are a very dirty girl."

"Milo," she yipped.

I shifted in my chair. "You're uncomfortable with me."

"Yes. Especially when you say things like that and stare at me during class."

"Can't help it. You're up there."

"Yes, but..." She glanced around the library and sighed. "Did you mean it when you said you wouldn't tell anyone what happened between us?"

"Why wouldn't I mean that?"

"Because I don't know...you seem...I don't know..." She tugged her ponytail tighter. "I don't know how you seem. I don't know you. I don't know what to expect, or the type of person you are, or if you'd use that against me somehow if I piss you off or—"

"You think I'm mischievous and conniving."

Her doe eyes widened, and she shook her head. "That's not what I'm saying."

"It's what you're thinking."

"I..." Her words faltered.

It irritated me that she thought those things about me. She didn't even know me. She was judging my book by its cover, but if she had any sense, she would've looked harder and realized I didn't give a shit

73

about shit enough to be conniving or sinister toward a person. Yet her unease about me did tick me off slightly.

I hated this new realization, too. Most people didn't get under my skin, yet for some reason, Starlet was effortlessly doing so.

What's the deal with you, woman?

Why do you bother me so damn much?

I shifted in my chair and brushed my thumb against the base of my jaw. "Guess you'll just have to be on your best behavior, huh?"

A flash of panic hit her stare.

Almost felt bad about that, too.

"That's not fair," she whispered.

"Life's not fair. Welcome to the party," I replied. "Are you going to teach me something, or are you going to sit here and think about the night my tongue was so deep inside you that you came multiple times?"

Her jaw dropped, and tears flooded her stare.

"Not again with the crying. It was a damn joke. Don't tell me you're that sensitive," I grumbled but instantly felt bad. Her emotions did something to me that made me just as uncomfortable as I'd made her. A part of me wanted to soothe her nerves and wash them away because I wanted her to be relaxed. Why did I care about her comfort? She was supposed to be a distraction for me, a thing that kept me from thinking too much about my depressive state. Yet whenever she almost cried, my chest ached. It ate me alive that I was also the cause behind her pained expression. I knew I was an asshole, but I wasn't that big of an ass. At least, I didn't want to be.

"I am that sensitive," she expressed. "And it wasn't funny. This is my life, Milo. You're messing with my life."

"Wrong. Your nerves are messing with your life. And forgive me for taking offense that you think I'd hold that shit over your head to get what I want. I told you I'm a dick, but I'm not that big of a dick. Don't worry, Starlet. I'm not here to ruin your life. I'm just trying to graduate." That was true, too, because graduation meant I'd get a letter from Mom. That was the only endgame I had in mind.

"Right. Okay." She reached into her briefcase and pulled out a few notebooks. "Let's get started. I was told you need help with your English course, history, Spanish, and math classes?"

"And photography. That's based on one big project."

"Oh, sweet. Lucky for you, *hablo español*."

"I have no clue what you're saying. I don't speak Spanish."

She blankly stared at me and sighed. "Okay. This will be a process, but I'm not a quitter. Everything's gonna work out fine."

"Sounds like a quote a millennial would put on a mug and drink under their 'live, laugh, love' sign."

She smiled.

Screw her and her smiles. They felt like warmth in my chilled world.

My chest tightened. Shit. There it was again…the odd feeling of panic building up in my chest. I tried my best to shake the sensation away.

Just think about screwing her. Forget about her smile, Milo.

"My dad says it all the time," she said. "After my mother passed away when I was young, he'd say it to me every night before bed. 'Everything's gonna work out fine.' At first, I thought he was saying it to make me feel better, but I quickly learned he was saying it to make himself feel better, too. Ever since then, it's been our thing. It's like tattooed on my brain whenever I get overwhelmed."

My chest tightened more as her words replayed in my mind. My hands grew clammy as they formed fists under the table. The early stages of the panic were building second by second as I looked her way. I arched my brow. "You lost your mother?"

"Yeah. I was thirteen."

"How?"

"Car accident. A drunk driver hit her while she was riding her bike."

Damn.

At least I saw my mother's death coming with her illness. A car crash didn't give people a heads-up at all. Yet sometimes I wondered which was worse—knowing death was around the corner and dragging toward it daily or being completely naive to the fact.

Some days the knowing felt like a tortured clock that kept ticking louder and louder with every passing second.

I looked up at her, feeling an odd urge to divulge a piece of my heartache to her, too. I'd never met someone my age who'd also lost their mother. I wanted to speak, but the words wouldn't leave my lips.

My mom's dead, too. She's gone. Cancer. It will be a year since she's left in a few weeks. I miss her so much that it's hard to breathe. Everything around me feels dark, except when I look at you sometimes.

Instead of speaking my truths, I mumbled a quiet, jaded, "Sorry."

No person should lose their mother. Especially at thirteen.

How did she manage to be okay? To be the good girl she'd been? Part of me wished she could draw a road map of life after losing a parent to let me know how many stops I still had before I'd be okay like her. Most of the time, it felt like I'd never be okay again. The same went for my dad. We were a shell of the people we once were—an echo of our past lives.

She brushed a piece of fallen hair behind her ear. "It's okay. My dad and I...we're good."

"Yeah. Everything's gonna work out fine," I muttered, somewhat mocking her saying and somewhat hoping it held some truth to it.

She smiled again.

My tightened chest...

My clammy palms...

My twisted mind...

I shifted in my chair and tapped my notebook. "Where are we starting, Ms. Evans?"

She hesitated as if she would correct me for calling her that, but instead, she said, "English. Let's start there."

I nodded and pulled out the homework for the class.

"How did you do on the exam yesterday?" she asked.

I pulled out that paper and placed it in front of her. "Swimmingly," I mocked.

She frowned.

How was that possible? How was her frown beautiful, too?

"Did he tell you he's not surprised with how you did?" she questioned.

"Something like that."

"That's not okay, Milo."

"It's just my reality."

Her brows knitted together as she shook her head in disappointment. Only this time, she wasn't directing the disappointment toward me. "Is that the first time he's made a comment like that?"

"No. Doubt it will be the last, either."

"Milo."

"Don't cry again, Ms. Sensitive. It's not a big deal."

"It is a big deal."

"I gave him enough reasons not to believe in me."

"That's not his job," she said, slightly irritated.

Holy shit. This woman didn't have one bad look within her. Everything was remarkable. That was annoying.

"His job is to educate you, no matter what. Not ridicule you and make you feel lesser for flaws and mistakes you make along the way."

"If you want to kick his ass for me, by all means," I semi-joked. I was used to my friends caring about me, but having Starlet care felt extra personal. Having her stand up for me when she didn't have to did a number on my thoughts. I didn't know how to define my feelings, but seeing her riled up in my cause felt…good.

Yeah.

She felt good to me.

She chuckled. "I'll consider it. Or we can get you a passing grade and then prove him wrong repeatedly for the remainder of the semester. If anything, that would tick him off."

Well, I did like the idea of ticking off my teachers.

"You're supposed to read *Oedipus* for tomorrow, yes?"

"I'm not much of a reader," I confessed. My eyes would zone in and out on the words before me. My eyesight wasn't the best, both near and far. Half the time, I couldn't see what was on the whiteboard in front of the classroom, and when it was time to read out loud, I dreaded it. Teachers who made students read out loud in front of their peers deserved a special place in hell.

Here's looking at you, Mr. Slade.

I probably needed glasses, but I didn't care enough to get it checked out. My mom was a reader. She loved that shit. I didn't pick up that trait from her.

"That's fine," Starlet replied. "Let me see your cell phone."

"Are you gonna give me your number?" I joked.

"Yes," she said matter-of-factly.

"What?"

"I can't tutor you for all these classes within an hour each day. So we'll have to be in communication after school, too. Some days, we can meet at the library on the weekends to keep you up to date with the work. The first weeks will be hell, but we'll get through it."

I liked that she said hell. It sounded sweet on her lips.

"Oh. All right," I replied.

She tossed me a stern glare. "Don't misuse this number, Milo."

"Wouldn't dare to do such a thing," I lied. I was already thinking of the messages I could send her as she pounded her digits into my phone.

"Are you a podcast guy?" she questioned. "You seem like a podcast guy."

"I do the podcast thing now and again. Why?"

"Sometimes, when people aren't readers, they are listeners or viewers. We can't view the books you have to read, but we can listen to them. I'm downloading an app for audiobooks on your phone now. Since you're not a reader, you can listen to the book. Same concept, better outlet for how your mind works."

That was...thoughtful.

When I once told Mr. Slade I wasn't a reader, he told me to suck it up, buttercup.

"Thanks," I mentioned, a bit thrown off by how thoughtful she was being. Then again, I guessed that was her job. I wasn't getting special treatment or anything.

"Not a problem. Not everyone learns in the same fashion. It's best to find out what works for everyone and determine how to prepare steps to get them to the same finish line. I'll also be listening to the book, and each night you can give me a fifteen-minute call to discuss what took place in those chapters so you're prepared for anything Mr. Slade might present you with."

"All right. Sounds good." Truly, it sounded great. The idea of hearing her voice each night before bed felt like a gift of sorts. Something about the sound of her voice was so appealing. It held a breathy quality, coming out so gently with such a slow tempo. When we were studying, it had an extra dash of distinct assertiveness that I found wildly attractive.

Teach me, Ms. Evans. I like when you do that.

She continued writing a guideline to tackle each class without overwhelming me. That was something I dealt with, too. Sometimes— all the time—I'd let everything pile up so much that when I looked at how much needed to be done, I'd do none because it was impossible to decide where to begin.

Not only did Starlet make it seem doable, but she made it seem effortless. She even scheduled time for me to relax and have a life outside of schoolwork.

"Breaks are needed. That's when your brain can rest and recover so you can tackle things better. Therefore, Sundays are off for you. No work at all," she explained.

"You're shitting me," I told her.

"I am not shitting you," she replied. "It's important. Our hour is up, but please listen to the book's first two chapters tonight. You can text me to discuss it or call any time after seven in the evening. I'll be back in my dorm and finished with most of my work for the night."

"They must be paying you nicely to do this for me. That's a lot of your life taken away from you."

With a smile, she packed up her briefcase and stood. "They aren't paying me at all for this. I'm happy to do it for free. I'll see you tomorrow but hear from you tonight."

I saw why she wanted to be a teacher. She was good at it. Great, even.

As she left, my eyes followed her exit.

I picked up my phone and went to look at the number and name she had left on my phone.

Teach. Just call me Teach.

Shit.

I liked her sass.

That was going to be a problem for me.

CHAPTER 8

Starlet

*M*ilo: Did this guy screw his mom?

I giggled as I sat on my bed, reading Milo's text message.

Starlet: How are you that far into the story already?

Milo: Audiobooks for the win. No, really. Is he screwing his mother?

Starlet: Not on purpose.

Milo: There's no coming back from that. I hope he jumps off a cliff at the end. That's the only way he'd ever recover. Death.

I could almost envision his expressions in my mind as he was listening to the audiobook. The mere shock of what was happening was enough to make me laugh.

Starlet: So you handled the reading for this weekend already. See? Getting caught up won't be hard. Don't forget to write an essay about someone who inspires you. That's due on Monday. You can shoot it my way, and I'll proofread it. Get it done tonight or tomorrow. Remember, Sundays are off days.

Milo: I don't have a person who inspires me.

Starlet: Don't worry. I can help you pick a topic. It could be anyone. A teacher, a friend, your parents. Even a celebrity.

I saw the ellipses appear on the screen before they disappeared. They reappeared, then disappeared once more. Milo was trying to gather his thoughts, but he kept deleting them before I could receive them.

I placed my phone back down and went back to reading my novel, but my focus was a little off. I couldn't help but think about Milo that night. Was he still at home doing his homework, or had he found himself at another party? Is that why he didn't respond? What if he was off finding another woman to forget with for a while?

I felt jealousy as I tried to continue my normal Saturday night activities, which included face masks, books, and Chinese food. I tried to shake off the odd feeling. What did I have to be jealous about? And why did I feel like texting him to ask what his plans were for the evening? Was he staying in? Was he going out? Was he with another woman? Did she remind him of me?

Stop it, Star.

Behave.

The line of professionalism with Milo was drawn with a Sharpie, and it wouldn't be erased.

Still, I wondered where he'd been that night and who he'd been with. Did her kisses taste like mine, or did he miss the smoothness of my lips?

Hours later, my phone dinged again.

Milo: Do you still think about it, too?

My stomach knotted from his words. He didn't know it, but he made me so nervous. A flurry of feelings swam inside me whenever he said something that could've been taken the wrong way. The inappropriate way. I felt as if my desires were sins, and I couldn't stop them from heating with urges and desires strictly forbidden. His question could've meant anything, but my mind went straight to the night of the party.

Milo: How he'd screwed his mother?

The breath that caught in my chest evaporated slowly. Then he texted me again.

Milo: That's what you thought I was talking about, right? Nothing else crossed your mind, huh?

He was messing with my head, and he knew it, too. He was trying to get under my skin, and it was working. And why did I like it? Why did I like the teasing of his words? Why did they leave me so hot and bothered?

Starlet: Milo. Only messages about your schoolwork, please.

Milo: Yes, Teach.

Starlet: Thank you. Please forward me your math assignment from two weeks ago that I wrote out for you to finish tomorrow, along with your English essay, okay?

Milo: Okay, Teach.

Starlet: You're being a sarcastic jerk, aren't you?

Milo: Language, Teach.

This man was going to give me a migraine or an orgasm. One or the other.

I didn't reply, and he stayed quiet, so I figured that was the end of the conversation. I returned to reading my novel, though Milo kept swimming through my thoughts uninvited. A few hours later, my phone dinged right before I fell asleep.

Milo: I'll write an essay about my grandfather.

Starlet: Good. That's a good plan.

Milo: Good night, Teach.

Starlet: Good night, Milo.

Milo: I think about it, too, you know. How you let me be your chair that night. I think about that so much, and how I wish it could happen again.

I shut off my phone quickly, trying my best not to fall so deeply into the words he'd written to me.

For the love of all things righteous...

I should've known he wasn't going to let that go easily. The worst part of it all? I did think about it. At least once a day. Sometimes twice. I was officially screwed, and it was Milo Corti who was doing the screwing.

* * *

THE BATHROOM STALLS of the high school were an interesting sight to take in. The amount of scribbling against the stalls showcased exactly where a lot of the girls' minds were. In the third stall was a tally list of the hottest guys in the school, and sitting comfortably at the top of the list was Milo's name.

Did it surprise me? Not in the least. Milo was ridiculously good-looking. It was annoying how attractive he was. I had to hotwire my brain to disconnect from that fact after I realized I was his student teacher.

I want to sit on Milo Corti's face was written on the stall.

I couldn't blame the girl.

He made a nice seat.

Sometimes when I'd walk through the hallways, I'd notice the girls noticed him, but he never looked back. He seemed uninterested in the idea of anyone…except for me.

He and I would cross paths in the hallway, and his eyes would lock with mine. He refused to ever look away first, holding said stare until the nerves of it all overtook me. I'd break eye contact, but somehow, I could still feel the weight of his stare on me. I felt conflicted with it all, yet I never brought it up to him. I figured the less I talked about his stares, the better. Because it was clear he loved to push my buttons. When it came to him and his greenish-brown eyes, said buttons were easily pushed.

Though, over the past few days, he seemed a bit more distant than normal. During our sessions, he made fewer sarcastic remarks. A part of me wanted to question if he was all right. Another part understood it was none of my business.

CHAPTER 9

Milo

*E*very single day, I woke up to a world of darkness. Both figuratively and literally. Whenever I woke up, it took my eyes a second to adjust to the space around me. I had to blink away seconds of darkness before climbing out of bed. That had happened to me for as long as I could remember.

It didn't help that I woke up before the sun was up. I'd been doing it for a year now. Before the crack of dawn, I headed out my front door and went down to the park not far from my house. Estes Park was Dad's favorite park since he was a kid. It was where he and Mom first met. Within the park was a wooded area that led to the lakefront if you took a hidden path. Nobody really knew about it except my parents and me. Dad even bought a small bench for Mom with their initials carved into the wood that he set up there. It was Mom's favorite place in the whole world. The three of us used to fish there for hours.

Now, only I showed up, and that winter, the lake was frozen over. I probably shouldn't have even been out there with the freezing wind chills, but I swore I'd try to never miss a day standing in front of that lake every day, looking up at the sky.

Mom told me to find her in the sunrises, so I tried to make sure to catch every single one since she passed away, no matter the weather. Some days, the clouds blocked the sunrises, but I figured the sun was still there. I'd missed her extra that morning, and watching the sunrise didn't seem enough for my comfort that day.

Starlet had worked as a nice distraction for a short period. She kept me from overthinking about the day right around the corner for a bit, yet once that day came, my mind couldn't handle its pain.

It'd been a year since she'd been gone.

A year today.

Happy Death Day, Mother. Screw you for leaving me here on this planet.

Also, I miss you so much it's hard to breathe.

I watched the sunrise, feeling empty inside, then I headed home and got ready for school.

Weston's and my weekly meeting was the last place I wanted to find myself that Monday morning. The carpet was ripped out of his office, exposing an ugly hardwood floor that looked like shit. Weston told me his office renovations were in the in-between stages, stating that the new flooring wouldn't be in until the following week.

The floors looked like how I felt—like shit.

Weston sipped his coffee as he eyed me up and down. Truth be told, I didn't even know how I'd managed to make it into his office that morning. I hadn't slept all weekend. Mainly because whenever I shut my eyes, I'd be haunted by the memories of my past. And when that wasn't happening, I was haunted by the situation of my present day.

"Are you high right now?" Weston asked.

I glanced up from my chair and arched an eyebrow. "Who's asking? Weston or the principal?"

"Both," Weston stated, setting his coffee mug back down on the table.

"Well, I think you know the answer, seeing as how you're asking."

"It's seven in the morning, Milo."

"It's called wake and bake," I replied.

Weston shouldn't have been surprised. It was a crap weekend. Dad went on a drinking binge and decided to take it out on me when he came home smelling like a piss-covered sailor. Spending my weekend dealing with a drunk, grieving man who I had to force into the shower and feed wasn't my idea of fun. On top of me taking care of him, I had to deal with hearing how much of a disappointment I'd been. Then that morning marked a year since Mom's passing. So forgive me if I got high before school to try to deal with the shit going on in my head.

Weston frowned. I couldn't tell if he was disappointed in me or sad for me.

Maybe a mixture of both.

"You should've taken today off," he told me.

"You said I couldn't get the letter unless I attended my classes. So I'm here."

"You're here, but you're not."

I'm here, but I'm not.

He shifted in his chair. "Do you want to talk about her today? Maybe that will—"

"No." I cut in. There were a million things I wanted to do that day. I wanted to get high. I wanted to get drunk. I wanted to do anything possible to make me forget that today was a year since the worst day of my life. I wanted to feel less and disappear more. I wanted the hurting to stop and for me to feel like there was some chance that one day I'd be okay. I wanted to breathe again. I wished so damn much that I could breathe. But I couldn't. I chose not to, at least. It felt selfish of me to breathe when Mom couldn't do so any longer.

Grief was a complex creature. One day, you were sad, and the next day filled you with rage. On rare occasions, you'd be both. So aggressively angry, so depressingly sad.

"You should've known I would've been fine if you took today off," Weston mentioned. "Today, of all days, would've been okay."

"Yeah, well, maybe you should've mentioned that before you held that letter over my head."

"Milo."

"What?"

His mouth parted as the bell rang for the first period of the day. No more words came out of him, so I reached down and grabbed my backpack from beside my chair. "Can't be late to class, Principal Gallo," I muttered as I pushed myself up from the chair.

He called after me, but I didn't turn back to face him. I didn't feel like talking anymore. I didn't feel like staring into the eyes that looked like hers.

I headed into the busy hallways, moving through my quicksand, and went straight to Tom's locker.

He looked my way. "Who hit you with a bus?"

"I need pills," I said, cutting straight to the point. I didn't do small talk, and I was still feeling a bit too much for the day that was approaching. I knew I'd feel worse as the hours crept closer to three in the afternoon, the time when Mom took her final breath. I needed not to be functioning at that point. I needed to stretch out my high as long as I could.

"Well, good morning to you, too, sunshine," he mocked.

"Seriously, Tom. What do you have?"

"You start your period today or something? Snappy, snappy."

I stayed quiet.

He arched an eyebrow and grew a bit somber. "Shit morning?"

"Something like that."

For a split second, his eyes found a dash of pity for me. He quickly shook it away because he knew I wouldn't appreciate that. He reached into his backpack, pulled out a mint tin, opened it, and grabbed a pill for me. "This should make you feel...well...good. You'll feel good."

Perfect. "Give me a few more."

"Dude, I don't know if—"

"I'll pay you."

"You know it's not about the money."

"Tom. Please," I choked out. I wasn't one to beg for anything in life, but at that moment, I felt the need to.

That must've tripped him up. Without question, he handed me a few more pills. He then placed a hand against my shoulder. "Hey, man. I know we don't do that heart-to-heart stuff, but if you ever need to talk—"

"I don't." I tossed one pill into my mouth and slid the others into my pocket to space out throughout the day.

"Noted." He pulled his hand back and shut his locker. "With that said, have a nice trip."

See you next fall.

* * *

GOOD.

I felt good.

Great even. Shit, I felt great.

The quicksand of my movements had transitioned over the past few hours, and now I was floating through the hallways. Everything was heightened, all of my senses. My fingers stretched out, and I stared at the space between them. I could feel it. I could feel the air.

Holy shit, I was gone.

"Are you all right?" a voice said, breaking my stare away from my fingers. I turned to find Starlet standing in front of me with concerned eyes.

Wow.

She had beautiful eyes.

"You have beautiful eyes," I told her.

She glanced around the hallways and took a step away from me. "Never say that again, Milo," she warned, her voice low. "The bell rang. You should be in class."

I laughed.

Because things were funny. Everything was funny—Starlet, school, life, death.

She didn't see the humor in it, though. Maybe I was meant to show her the comedy in life.

I'd reached into my pocket and pulled out a pill. I held it in her direction. "Here, take this. It will make you laugh, Teach."

"Oh my gosh," she whisper-shouted, stepping toward me. "Are those drugs?"

"Well, it's not a spearmint."

"Put that away and get to class," she ordered.

The hallways were pretty empty, probably because she was right. I was supposed to be in a class like everyone else in the school. What class, though? What hour was it? Shit. The letter. I needed to get the letter.

"I gotta get to class for the letter," I muttered. My head felt a bit fuzzy, and my stomach flipped a few times. I went to pop the pill into my mouth, and Starlet hit it out of my hand.

"Milo, what the heck are you doing? You can't just pop pills in school," Starlet scolded. She was sounding more and more like a teacher. Bummer.

"You didn't want it."

"That's because I don't do drugs."

"But life would be so much better if you did, Teach." I stumbled a bit, and she caught me. Her eyes locked with mine, and I released a sigh. "You have beautiful eyes," I repeated.

"Milo. Stop it."

"I'm not feeling great, Teach."

"Yeah. That's clear."

"I can't fail. I can't. I need that letter. I need it."

She narrowed her eyes at me, confused. She wouldn't understand. No one would understand. She glanced around the hallway, then sighed. "Come on. We gotta get you sobered up." She began pulling me down the hallway and around a corner. We went down a flight of stairs, and she opened a janitor's closet. She pulled me inside and shut the door behind us.

"Sit," she ordered, pushing me to the floor. Next, she blocked the door with a broomstick so no one could get inside.

"Are we going to get naked now?" I murmured. Shit, I was messed up.

"What? No. Gosh, you're messed up," she muttered as she went digging through her briefcase. She pulled out a water bottle and held it out toward me.

I shoved it away. "No."

"You need to sober up, Milo."

"No. My father needs to sober up, not me. I'm fine. I'm good. I'm happy," I blubbered out, waving my hand in her direction. "I'm okay."

I looked up at her and saw the sad expression in her eyes.

"You have beautiful eyes," I repeated.

Her frown deepened. "You're going to be okay, Milo."

"I told you, I'm okay," I murmured, slouching over against a mop bucket.

She moved over to me, placed her hand under my chin, and held the water bottle to my lips. I could hardly open my eyes. Everything felt heavy and light all at the same time. Every movement felt like a chore. Through my hooded stare, I still saw her eyes. Those fucking eyes.

"Sip," she ordered.

"No," I said, pushing the bottle away.

"Sip," she repeated.

"I hate you," I grumbled, not wanting to drink.

"Good," she replied. "That means you still know how to feel. Now, sip."

Sip, I did.

"You're going to be okay, Milo," she said once more, and for some reason, that made my chest tighten even more.

"She's gone," I whispered, feeling myself seconds away from spiraling. "She's really gone," I blurted out before curling into a ball and losing myself. Starlet didn't say another word. She placed a comforting hand on my back and rubbed it in a circular motion. Every now and again, she'd make me sip the water. At one point, I fell asleep. Or I passed out. It was hard to say. All I knew was that Starlet's hand was still resting against my back when I came to.

Her words echoed like a lie in my head.

You're going to be okay, Milo.

You're going to be okay, Milo...

How?

How would this...how would I ever be okay again?

CHAPTER 10

Starlet

J was risking everything by sitting in that janitor's closet
with Milo. I didn't even know why I'd done it. If anything,
I should've reported his inappropriate actions to the front office and
had them discipline him. Yet something in my gut didn't want him to
be seen in that fashion. I didn't know him, but I felt it was my job to
protect him. To help him get through whatever he was dealing with.

Plus, the hurt in his eyes...

What are you doing, Star?

My whole future was being jeopardized, everything I'd worked
toward, for a mere stranger. If I were caught in the broom closet with
this guy, it'd be the end of any part of me that wanted to be a teacher.
My dreams would be tarnished within a moment's time due to a
rushed decision to shove Milo into a closet.

What happened to him? I knew he was a lot, and I knew he had a
handful of pain based on his brownish greens, but that day felt differ-

ent. Especially with the few clues I'd received about him mentioning his father's drinking. Was he in a safe situation? What struggles did he face alone, and why was he using drugs to push those struggles down?

I texted Mr. Sloan that a personal situation had arisen and that I wouldn't be able to make it to class that afternoon. Another bad decision. What was it with me making bad choices when it came to being around Milo Corti?

Stupid, stupid girl.

Hours passed as I gave Milo water to sip, and when he was good enough to sit up straight, I offered him a half grin. "You're going to be okay," I swore to him, hoping I wasn't making myself a liar.

His hand pressed to his forehead, and then he raked it through his hair. "Yeah, all right."

"I should get going before someone heads in here. You can leave a bit after me if that works?"

He nodded.

Before I stood, I placed a hand against his knee. "Milo, I know you don't want to talk, and that's fine. I'm not going to ask you or make you. But you do need to talk to someone soon. Confide in them because whatever scars you're carrying around with you, they aren't healing. They're raw and messy and harming you in all those different ways, and you don't deserve that."

"What if I don't deserve to heal?"

"Everyone deserves to heal. Especially you." I slightly squeezed his knee before I stood and smoothed my hands over my pantsuit.

"Hey, Teach?"

"Yes?"

"Don't tell anyone about this, all right?"

"Of course not."

"I mean it. I don't need the principal to know about this situation. It would ruin everything for me."

I smiled. "What, do you want my pinky or something?" I mocked how he'd asked me that same thing weeks prior.

The corner of Milo's mouth twitched up.

He almost smiled.

That made me breathe a bit easier, thinking he'd be okay.

As I left the janitor's closet, I rounded the corner and ran into Principal Gallo, which sent a wave of anxiety coursing through my system. I tried my best not to showcase said panic.

"Ms. Evans, there you are. I've been looking for you," he said as he approached me. "I wanted to talk to you about Milo. Can we go to my office for a bit?"

I swallowed hard, wanting to run away from the confrontation I was about to find myself in. My mind began thinking of ways to express my deepest apologies for what had gone on. That had to be why he was calling me into his office, right? Because he knew what had gone down with Milo that afternoon. There was no other reason. Especially with his somber expression.

We walked to his office, and he shut the door behind him. He gestured to the empty chair in front of me, inviting me to take a seat. I did as he requested.

Principal Gallo sat in his chair, swiveled a bit, and then paused his movements. "How are you, Starlet? How are things going with Milo?"

I wasn't sure if it was a trap he was trying to get me to walk into. "Good, good. He's been getting his work in, and I believe our study sessions have been going well."

"Good. Yes. Wonderful. I've spoken with a few of his teachers, and they said they've received old assignments, and he's been showing up to class."

Except for today.

Then again, I didn't show up, either.

I remained quiet, not quite sure what I was supposed to say to him.

He smiled before a weighted sigh fell from him. He removed his glasses and pinched the bridge of his nose. "Sorry, Starlet, can we just be real for a moment?"

"Yes, of course."

"Milo is my nephew, so this situation is quite personal."

Oh.

Well.

That added a few missing pieces to Principal Gallo's and Milo's puzzle.

"Don't get me wrong, I care about all of my students, but Milo has been through a lot over the past year, so I worry about his well-being. So if he gives you trouble at any point, please let me know. The last thing I want is to add any stress to your life. I should've written you about missing today's appointment with him, too, seeing how it's the first anniversary of his mother's passing today, my sister Ana."

There it was.

The reason for Milo's spiral.

My stomach knotted up as my heart somewhat shattered for him. I knew how hard that had to be for Milo. I wished I hadn't known, but I did.

"I'm sorry for your loss, Principal Gallo."

His eyes flashed with the same emotions as his nephew's had in the janitor's closet. It amazed me how different individuals could hurt, and the sadness still appeared the same in their eyes.

"Thank you," he muttered. Principal Gallo cleared his throat and clasped his hands together, shaking off his feelings. He sat straighter. "I know Milo's a hard one to crack, but he wasn't always so tough and cold. I do believe that beneath his harsh exterior still lives that sweet, kind boy who misses his mother."

"I won't stop tutoring him, Principal Gallo. Now that I know these things, I can tackle the situation from a different angle and make sure I'm making his life easier, not harder. I lost my mother, too, so I know how challenging that can be."

"I'm sorry for your loss, too, Starlet."

I nodded. "It's been a few years now, so I'm okay."

"I'm learning that time passing doesn't make it easier. Sometimes it just makes the grief quieter."

That was the truest thing I'd ever heard.

"I'll update you on how everything is going," I promised him.

"Please do. Day or night. Please."

Principal Gallo truly cared about Milo. I could see it in his eyes. It pained him to see his nephew struggling so much.

I nodded and stood. "Thanks again for meeting with me."

He stood, too. "Of course. Thank you, Starlet. Have a good afternoon."

I started walking off but paused and looked back at Principal Gallo. "I do have a question. Milo mentioned a letter...is that something I should know about?"

Principal Gallo blew out a sharp breath. "His mother left him a letter. I'm supposed to give it to him on his graduation day. I told him he has to attend every tutoring session and graduate in order to receive the letter."

"Thank you for explaining that," I said.

"Of course. Have a good afternoon."

After the meeting with Principal Gallo, I headed back to the janitor's closet to check and make sure that Milo was all right. When I opened the door, a slight ting hit my stomach.

He was gone.

* * *

STARLET: Okay?

I shouldn't have texted him that night, but for the past few hours, all I could think about was Milo. I could hardly focus on my studies because he kept popping up in my mind. Whitney was at her night class, which worked out well for me because if she had been in our room, she would've instantly known something was wrong.

I had no poker face. Every emotion, both good and bad, I ever felt was shown against my expressions. I got that trait from my mother. You always knew what she felt once you looked at her. Dad said it was the easiest guide to knowing when he'd messed up.

I stared at my phone for the longest time, seeing no reply.

My mind began to spiral. What if something bad happened to him?

What if he used more after leaving that closet?

What if he needed real help, and I made the bad decision of not reporting him to the principal?

I swam in a pool of guilt until I received a text message from him around eleven o'clock.

Milo: Okay.

I exhaled deeply for what felt like the first time that night.

Okay.

CHAPTER 11

Milo

I got home late after spending most of the day messed up. I felt sick to my stomach. That wasn't shocking. *What goes up must come down.* The crash was always the hardest. Tom was good enough to find me as I wandered the hallways messed up. He got me into his car, drove me to his house, and hid me in his bathroom until I was sober enough to make it home. As he dropped me off, I muttered a thank you.

"Milo, you know we're friends, right?" Tom said before I was able to climb out of the car.

"Yeah, sure."

"No. I mean it. I know I'm new to this town, and I know we're different in almost every way possible, but I do consider you a good friend of mine. So if you ever need someone to talk to or to just be quiet with, I got you. I might not be as quiet as Chris, but I can learn to shut up."

I looked over at him and nodded. "Thanks, T."

"T?" he gasped, slamming his hands to his chest. "Did you just nickname me? Are we on a nickname basis?"

"Don't make this a thing," I grumbled, opening the passenger door.

"It's totally a thing."

I climbed out of his car, and he rolled down the window and yelled, "See you later, Mi-Mi!"

Mi-Mi.

I hated that more than he'd ever know, but I was almost certain he'd call me it for the remainder of my life.

Dad's car was in the driveway, which was a good sign. I figured he'd be passed out at some bar or locked up for indecent exposure for pissing on the side of a building or something. Instead, I walked into the house to hear him in his bedroom. The door was shut, but I could hear him clear as day.

He was sobbing.

Choking on his inhales. Slicing through his exhales.

I didn't know his heartbreak could worsen my own.

We weren't close anymore, but something was damn painful about hearing your father cry. He spent most of my life being a strong, tough man who never showed any weakness. Now, to hear him falling apart felt so bizarre.

Without thought, I tried to turn his doorknob to check on him, but it was locked.

I lowered myself to the floor outside his room, placed my back against the wall, and bent my knees. My arms rested crossed against my kneecaps as Dad wailed in his pain.

I fell apart with him, sitting against that wall with my face buried into the palms of my hands.

Our pain was different from one another. He lost a wife; I lost a mother.

Still, we both shattered into a million pieces.

That was the thing about grief—it didn't discriminate. It simply made everyone drown.

CHAPTER 12

Milo

$\mathcal{I}$ spent most of the weekend trying to pull myself together.

I didn't often feel ashamed, but I sure did when Monday came around and it was time for my study session with Starlet after she'd witnessed my full-blown meltdown.

"I'm sorry about Friday. I wasn't myself," I muttered to Starlet as I sat down in the library study room. I tossed my backpack onto the table and grumbled from my aching headache. No amount of ibuprofen was easing up the discomfort. I probably should've drunk more water throughout the weekend, but I wasn't in the best frame of mind to take on those actions.

Starlet smiled at me. Her look held no annoyance, judgment, or blame.

"You're not pissed," I commented.

"No, I'm not."

"Why aren't you pissed? I could've gotten you in a shit ton of trouble."

"It's fine." She shifted around in her chair and then reached out and placed a hand against my forearm. My eyes moved down to her touch. I should've pulled my arm away from her, but the warmth was too addicting.

"Why are you touching me?" I asked.

"I spoke with Principal Gallo. He mentioned what Friday was."

Oh.

That explained it.

She was pitying me.

I pulled my arm back and placed it in my lap. "It was just a day."

"No." She shook her head. "It wasn't."

No, I silently agreed. It wasn't.

I shuffled in my backpack to pull out my math book and said, "I figured we should start with the math assignments and—"

"What's her name?" Starlet cut in.

I arched my eyebrow. "What?"

"Your mother. What's her name?"

My throat tightened as I froze in place. "Why are you asking me that?"

"Because I can tell she's important to you. I want to know about the things important to you."

She is important to you.

As if my mother were still around.

I hated how she said that.

I loved how she said that, too.

I grimaced. "No, you don't. You feel bad for me."

"I do feel bad for you," she confessed. "But I also do want to know the important things. Two things can be true at the same time."

"You're supposed to tutor me. Not ask about my personal life. So how about you do your job," I huffed.

Her eyes locked with mine, and she smiled, completely unmoved by my bad attitude. She crossed her legs and leaned back in her chair, not taking her stare away from mine. "My mother's name is Rosa. She's my best friend. Her favorite thing in the world was making homemade items. Soaps, lotions, and fresh homemade applesauce from the apple tree in our backyard. She was allergic to dogs but still always snuggled them whenever one approached her. She hated vegetables but pretended not to in order to get me to eat them. And she loved my father and me to her core. We loved her, too. Losing her felt like losing ourselves for a very long time. It took years for me not to cry when I saw a photograph of her. I still cry sometimes, but it's less. She once built me a bike, too. She built one for me, one for her, and we'd ride said bikes together down the steepest hills. I'd stretch my arms out wide, and she'd hold my hands in hers as she did the same thing, and we'd ride down the hill together."

"What are you doing, Star?" I whispered.

"Sharing a few of my scars to make you feel safe enough to share your own. If you don't want to share, that's fine. I won't push anymore, but I feel happy when people ask me about my mother. I love talking about her because it's like she's still here when I get to share. Most people say they're sorry and carry on with their lives. I don't want to do that with you, Milo. I want to know more."

I sat back in my seat, debating how to move forward. A big part of me wanted to get up and leave, never returning to school again. Yet another part of me knew Starlet was right. Most people offered their condolences and left it at that.

What's her name?

How did those words from Starlet rock me sideways?

"Ana," I confessed. "Her name was Ana."

"That's a beautiful name."

"Yeah. It was."

"What's her passion?"

"Cooking. She was a chef. She was Italian and lived in Italy until she was thirteen. She studied cooking her whole life and had a restaurant here called Con Amore."

"With love," she breathed out, translating the name. Her hand flew to her chest. "That was my mom's favorite restaurant. She was Italian, too. She said it was the most authentic Italian food you could find around our parts. We used to go there every Sunday for freshly baked rolls and ham. Your mother was very gifted at her craft, Milo. I'm glad I was able to experience a piece of her."

I wasn't one to cry, but that comment almost brought it out of me.

"How did she love to spend her weekends?" she asked next.

My tongue pushed into the side of my cheek as I tried to press down the emotions stirred inside me by Starlet's questions. No one had ever asked me that question. No one had ever given me the space even to share my mother's name.

I stared down at my hands and cleared my throat. "By the water. She loved fishing. My grandfather took her out on the water when she was a kid, and it became her favorite hobby. Every weekend during the summer, we'd go fishing down at Estes Park with my father. It's his favorite park and Mom's favorite part of the lake. We found a hidden area that people didn't know about, and we'd fish there for hours. We'd even go ice fishing up north during the winter. That was her and my dad's favorite time. I hated it. It was cold, and we'd just sit there for the longest time. But I always asked to go with them. It was kind of our thing. Now, I miss the cold-ass days on the ice, doing that with them."

"You don't still go with your father?"

My jaw tightened. "My father died the day my mom passed away."

Her mouth dropped in shock. "Oh my goodness, I didn't know—"

I shook my head. "No. He's still physically here, but what I mean is, the day my mom left, my father mentally checked out, too. He's like the walking dead."

"Milo…I'm so deeply sorry. I cannot imagine how hard that is for you."

I shrugged. "Tell me about your parents," I said, needing to shift the conversation.

Starlet smiled, but it felt sad. Still, she accepted my request. "I've never been fishing, but my parents love nature. We'd go hiking and biking every week when I was a kid. I haven't done it in so long, but that reminds me of my mom. I'm glad you have fishing to remind you of yours."

"I don't fish anymore because it reminds me of her."

"I don't ride bikes or hike anymore because it reminds me of her."

I stayed quiet. I didn't know how to process what I was feeling. Mom was better at explaining my own emotions to me than I was myself.

"What was her favorite candy?" Starlet asked.

The corner of my mouth twitched. "Reese's Cups. She'd eat the jagged edge off first before eating the inside."

"It makes sense. The peanut butter is the best part."

I smiled a little.

Only a little, but she noticed, and then her smile grew wider, too. She was good at that—smiling. Smiles were probably created mainly for people like Starlet. The two things went together very well. I was more into grimacing myself.

"What was your mom's favorite candy?" I asked.

She shivered in disgust. "Black licorice."

"I'm sorry to hear that your mother was a psychopath."

She laughed, and it sounded like something I'd want on a vinyl record so I could play it repeatedly. "Yes, she had her set of flaws, black licorice being at the top of the list."

I relaxed a bit into my chair. "What's your favorite candy?"

"Red licorice, but the rope kind that you can peel. Anything else is boring."

"So you're from a licorice family."

She leaned in and whispered, "Yeah, but I like the good kind, not Satan's flavor."

I smiled a little more.

She made that happen involuntarily.

"My favorite is Sour Patch Kids," I mentioned. She didn't ask, but still, I shared.

She gave me a devilish look. "Do you relate to your candy?"

"What do you mean?"

"Are you first sour, then shockingly sweet?"

I huffed. "No. I'm just like a pound of sour."

She laughed again.

Fuck me, that laugh.

"I like Sour Patch Kids. I lick the sour off the candy, though, instead of sucking them off in my mouth," she explained.

The thought of her licking the candy pleased me more than I'd admit. "That's weird."

"I'm a weirdo."

"Yeah, you are." I shifted and fiddled with my hands. "Can you do me a favor?"

"What's that?"

"Ask me more questions about my mother."

She did exactly that. She asked me what felt like a million questions, and still, they didn't feel like enough. We stayed at the library longer than planned. We talked about our moms as if they were still alive. I told her stories about my mother that I'd never shared with another. Starlet cried, but that wasn't surprising to me. She seemed the type to feel everything a little deeper than others. I wondered what that was like—to feel everything so deeply at all times, no matter what.

It wasn't until the librarian came and knocked on the study room that we snapped out of whatever weird world we'd created between the two of us.

"Sorry, the library is closing," they told us.

"Oh gosh. I'm sorry. We got carried away. Thank you," Starlet said as she gathered her things to leave. I did the same.

As we walked out of the library, she thanked me for opening up to her in such an intimate way.

"It's not a big deal," I told her. "But thanks for today. Even though we didn't study."

"You're right, we didn't," she agreed, "but we did learn a lot, and I think that's important."

"Thank you."

"For?"

"Asking about her." I didn't know how deeply my soul needed someone to ask me about my mother.

Her smile came back. "Thank you for asking about mine. I'll see you tomorrow at school."

"Yeah, see you."

As she rounded the corner, I stood there, a bit dumbfounded about what had taken place over the past few hours.

Her smile lingered in my mind that night. As I lay in bed, I replayed our earlier conversations nonstop. I couldn't remember the last time I stayed up thinking about a girl, but Starlet seemed damn near impossible to get off my mind. I couldn't even process how she'd made me feel alive. She did that to me—she made me feel a little bit more alive than I had the days before.

Damn...

She made me feel again.

I almost forgot what that was like.

After she had to deal with me and my being high the other day, I should've not made her life harder than it had to be. So I did my homework that evening. I figured that would make her proud or some shit.

CHAPTER 13

Starlet

For the past few weeks, Milo turned in almost 70 percent of his missing assignments. He showed up to our study sessions each day without complaint, too. He gave me some of his sass and sarcastic remarks, but I was learning that that was just who he was as a person. I liked the bark behind his comments because I knew they didn't hold any true malice.

Some days he'd share a few details about his mom, and others, I'd share about mine. It felt like a safe place for us to talk about things that many people our age didn't have to deal with.

After one of the nights I shared with him, he frowned, shook his head, and said, "No thirteen-year-old should lose a parent."

"You shouldn't have lost yours either."

"Life's a bitch."

Another day, he told me that for weeks after his mother passed away, he'd walk into the kitchen, close his eyes, and pray that once he opened them, she'd be back there whipping up his breakfast.

He didn't know it, but I cried in my car for him after he shared that fact. My heart ached for him and the things he'd lost when his mother passed away. He was a shell version of himself, which was heartbreaking. I wondered what he was like before the heartbreak. I wondered what it was like for him before he lost his way.

Starlet: I have an idea for your photography class final project.

Milo: Am I going to hate it?

Starlet: There's a good chance you'll hate it. But that's just because you seem to hate everything.

Milo: You're not wrong.

I smiled down at my phone as I sat on my dorm bed. Sometimes, I wondered if it was okay that I smiled the way I did when Milo's name popped up on my phone. Or I was playing a dangerous game that would end like a Shakespearean tragedy.

Milo: What's the idea, Teach?

Starlet: The assignment is to showcase an emotion or feeling. I want it to be as authentic as you are, and I want it to be your truth at this moment. I think that would be best.

Milo: Which would be...?

Starlet: Empty. Coldness. Closed-offish.

Milo: I'm glad you're discovering who I am.

Starlet: I'm a quick study. So your theme would be winter. We have plenty of snow around, and even if you wanted to travel up north for some photos, that's a possibility since they'll have more. I can go with you on these shoots to help you stage the photographs and whatnot.

Why? Why did I offer that? Why did I want that? Why did I want to find reasons to be around him when I wasn't supposed to be? Why did I wish for more days, more hours, and more minutes with Milo?

I waited patiently for Milo to come up with some sarcastic remark or tell me it was a dumbass idea. But all he said was...

Milo: Cool. I'm in.

Cool, I'm in.

Nothing more, nothing less, yet somehow it was a lot more than I thought I'd get.

He then sent a photograph of his completed math homework, which I looked over. Every answer was correct. I'd quickly learned that Milo wasn't unintelligent. He might've been one of the smartest individuals out there. He simply didn't apply himself. After learning about his mother, I understood him a lot more, too. I didn't want to learn those first few years after losing my own mother. I didn't want to feel anything. If it weren't for my father pushing me, I wouldn't have made it, if I were honest.

It felt good to be that person for Milo—the one in his corner. He was a gifted individual. He just had to find his way back home.

What I didn't expect was how protective I'd become of him. One afternoon when Mr. Slade handed out graded assignments, he set Milo's in front of him and said, "One day, I'm going to find out whose homework you're copying, Mr. Corti. Mark my words."

"He did it himself and earned that grade," I blurted out without thought.

Mr. Slade turned and looked at me with a raised eyebrow. "Excuse me, Ms. Evans?"

I swallowed hard, feeling all eyes falling on me. "I just think that's an inappropriate comment to make toward a student."

Mr. Slade's brows knitted, and he let out a short breath. He looked around at the students. "Everyone, open your books to chapter twenty-two and start reading for the remainder of the class." He then turned back to me. "Ms. Evans, let's speak in the hallway quickly."

He pulled me out of the classroom, shutting the door behind him. He then crossed his arms and gave me a stern stare as if I were the student he could discipline.

"Ms. Evans, I would prefer if you did not question my teaching in front of the class. It shows a lack of leadership and is completely unacceptable. Do you understand me?"

"Yes, of course. Sorry."

His bushy brows lowered, and he went to head back inside.

"It's just—" I started.

"It's just what?"

"I'm Milo's tutor, and I have helped him with his homework and watched him put in the time and effort. So to have his teacher belittling him when he does well can be harmful to his self-confidence. You're supposed to help them be confident. Not berate them when they're struggling."

He grumbled under his breath. "So young, so naive. Please speak to me on the matter after you've been doing this for over thirty years. Until then, Ms. Evans, know your role and do not step out of it. Do you understand?"

"Yes," I said, but I truly meant no. The rage building up inside me from his belittling dismissal of my feedback was enough to make me go to war. That was exactly why I wanted to become a teacher. To help the students who might've run into the Mr. Slades of the world and lost belief in themselves.

We walked back into the classroom right as the bell rang for the session to be over. I stood at the front door, smiling at the students as they exited. As Milo walked past me, his eyes locked with mine. His arm brushed against my shoulder, and he whispered, "Thanks, Teach."

I wanted to say always, but instead, I stayed quiet.

I showed up at the library before Milo that afternoon. Sometimes I worried he might be a no-show. When fifteen minutes passed, a knot formed in my stomach. Thankfully, at the twenty-minute mark, Milo texted me that he was on his way.

When he came walking in, a sigh of relief found me.

"Sorry I'm late," he mentioned, placing his backpack on the table. He took a seat. "Had to stop at the gas station."

"No worries. You weren't that late."

"Don't do that."

"Do what?"

"Lie to keep from hurting my feelings."

I parted my mouth to speak, but before I could, he pulled out a few items from his backpack—a pack of red licorice and a Diet Dr Pepper.

I arched my eyebrow.

He shrugged. "I noticed you snacking on them the past few days in class."

My heart skipped a few beats, which it shouldn't have been doing when it came to Milo Corti. Then again, hearts didn't really care when the mind told them to behave.

"Why did you get those for me?" I asked.

"Because you stood up for me, and I appreciated that. I was going to get you flowers but didn't know if you liked flowers or what your favorite kind was."

"That's sweet. This is perfect, though unnecessary."

"My mom would've wanted me to do it."

"Your mom always sounds like a wonderful woman."

"Why do you do that?" he asked.

"Do what?"

"Speak about the dead in the present tense as if they're still here."

My lips pursed. "Oh. Yeah, that is strange. It's just that when my mom passed away, I'd talk about her as if she were still here, using the present tense, and it stuck with me. I didn't even realize that I do it with others who've passed away."

"I like it."

I arched my eyebrow, surprised. "What? Milo Corti likes something?"

"A glitch in the *Matrix*."

"I love a good Milo glitch. They entertain me."

"Don't get used to it. I'll be sarcastic and rude again in no time."

"Don't rush it," I said. "I kind of like this version of you."

His eyes met mine, and I swore I almost saw a curve to his mouth. Did he almost smile at me? And it wasn't one of his sass-packed grins I'd receive when he realized he was getting underneath my skin. No, it was a genuine one. Milo's genuine smiles were few and far between, so whenever one slipped out, I felt as if I were being spoiled. His almost smile was enough to make my own lips turn up.

He lowered his head, breaking our connection. "I wish you didn't do that, Teach."

"Do what?"

"Smile my way. It messes with my brain."

"And why's that?"

His head slightly rose. His normally intense and cold stare was now soft, gentle, timid even. "Because when I see your smile now, I'm reminded of your smile from the night we met. And when I think about your smile from the night we met, I think about—"

"Milo." I interrupted him.

He tossed his hands up in surrender. "I know, I know. We don't talk about that. But..." He leaned across the table, clasping his hands together. "We do daydream about it, don't we, Teach?"

Yes, we do...

My hands trembled as I tucked my hair behind my ears. My tongue rolled across my suddenly parched lips as I broke our stare. An internal battle raged inside me. I knew my thoughts about Milo were inappropriate. I knew my mind had secretly crossed the line of professionalism, but I couldn't stop it. Sometimes I'd blink and recall my hands on his body...his lips on my chest...my legs dangling against his shoulders... I'd have to shake myself physically to escape the spell he cast over me. I was good at being responsible. I never walked jaded lines...not until him, at least. What kind of wizard was Milo Corti, and why did his magic enchant me so well?

I cleared my throat. "Take out your math book, please. We'll go over the assignment due tomorrow."

His wicked grin came back. I hadn't seen his sinister smile in some time now, and for some reason, it felt a little bit good to witness it. Sarcastic and rude Milo was what I'd prefer over heartbroken and struggling Milo.

After completing our tasks for the afternoon, Milo pulled out a flyer from his backpack. He placed it in front of me, and I looked at it.

"The Apostle Islands are supposed to have cool ice caves. I figured maybe I could do some shoots up there for my photography class."

"Oh, that's way up north, isn't it?"

"Yeah. I figured it might be worth the hike. It's about six hours away."

"Very neat, Milo."

"Do you want to come with?" he asked. "I know you mentioned you used to hike a lot with your mom, and the hike to the caves is about two miles. Plus, it would be nice to have someone help with the gear and set up the shots. There's a cheap boutique hotel we could crash at for a day, then drive back. I can even drive it if you don't want to."

"You want to stay at a hotel?" I commented, a bit flustered by that idea. "Together?"

He smiled. "If you want to share a bed, just say that, Teach."

"Milo, stop," I sternly stated out loud, but inside, my thoughts began to sprint. My face heated as my mind imagined what that situation would look like. Me in his bed, pretending not to feel what I felt. Trying my hardest not to have our arms accidentally brush against one another as we twisted and turned throughout the night. That seemed like a recipe for trouble.

"Separate rooms," he offered.

Why did a sliver of disappointment trail through me?

"Of course, separate rooms," I echoed, hoping he couldn't read my body language. "And you'd want us to drive together?"

"Figured it made sense to save on gas." He raised an eyebrow. "Is that an issue?"

Yes, Milo. Of course it is. It's completely unacceptable.

Instead of saying that, I stumbled over my words. "I mean, well, it is part of your assignment…and I did offer to help you, so I guess that makes sense."

No! No, Starlet! That definitely does not make sense.

"Like a field trip of sorts," I presented, trying to resolve any self-guilt I was battling.

I was hit with a push and pull of conflict in my chest after he asked. Yet most of me wanted to go. I wanted to see the ice caves. I wanted to hike. I wanted to spend a weekend with Milo.

That was the most troubling truth about it all.

"Great. Two weeks from now?" he asked.

"Sure," I replied. I said it so freely, too, as if I wasn't making a terrible decision. What about that man made me want to make bad life choices?

As I stared at him, my chest tightened slightly. His expression had shifted to something I hadn't seen often from him. Did he seem to be...smiling? A real smile, too, slightly bashful even. The dash of anticipation that leaked out from behind his normally sarcastic and mundane expressions made my own lips curve up. Milo was such a professional at using sass to cover up his true feelings, so for me to catch that smile slipping out seemed like a major deal. Was he nervous about the trip, too? And was he excited? Did he get the same kind of butterflies as me? How dangerous were the two of us together becoming?

"I'll book the two hotel rooms," I offered.

"Are you sure you don't want to be cuddle buddies?" he teased.

"Shut up."

He smirked. That sarcastic, crude, annoying smirk that tossed my stomach into a frenzy of butterflies was back from the somewhat timid smile he accidentally shared. I hated it.

Sigh.

I loved it. I hated that I loved it.

The truth was, I loved every kind of smile and every kind of grimace that he shared with me.

"You're never going to stop bringing up the night we hooked up, are you?"

"No, probably not. I like the way it makes you bashful."

"I hate you."

"Good," he said, shoving his stuff into his backpack. "It means you still know how to feel."

I rolled my eyes at him repeating the words I said back to me. How did he even recall that when he was wasted out of his mind?

"What will you tell your dad about being gone for the weekend?" I questioned as I stood and collected my things.

"Trust me. He won't notice."

That made me sad for him.

I already knew my father would ask me a million questions about the trip, and I didn't even live under his roof.

"Have a good night, Milo," I told him as I walked past him to leave the study room.

"What's the answer?" he said.

"The answer to what?"

"Your favorite flower?"

"It doesn't matter."

"But what if it did?"

"Milo—"

He stepped closer to me, the points of his shoes brushing against mine. His head bent down, and his mouth grew wickedly close to my ear. He moved in slow motion, or perhaps his mere existence seemed to slow down time. His breath tickled alongside my neck as he whispered to me. "What if it did matter, Teach?" His words, the cadence, and the timbre of his tone caused goose bumps to erupt along my spine. His nearness, heat, and intentions all combined to make my heartbeats intensify. My breaths grew choppier as he held his proximity to me.

I stood tall even though I wanted to melt into a puddle of nothingness. I wanted to behave badly with the bad boy who turned my world upside down solely with his presence. My tongue lapped over my thirsty lips before they parted, and I murmured, "Peonies. I love peonies."

CHAPTER 14

Milo

The past two weeks moved at turtle speed. I felt like a toddler right before Christmas as I anticipated the journey with Starlet. I couldn't wait to escape my current reality and be locked away with Starlet for the weekend.

When Saturday came, I was beyond ready to be alone with her. I wasn't used to this feeling of excitement. I'd spent so much time not feeling anything, yet now with Starlet, it felt as if every single emotion in the world was creeping back into my spirit. Fear. Joy. Happiness. Anxiety. I felt it all, and I wasn't sure how to comb through said emotions. They just lingered within me. Plus, a part of me couldn't stop thinking about the dirty possibilities of this trip. What if we somehow ended up lost in the woods, and the only way to stay warm was by pressing her skin against mine? What if she came to drop something off at my hotel room, and I invited her in to have her test out the bed?

I tried my best not to reveal my thoughts through my exterior, though it was hard not to react when she pulled up to my house in her Jeep, looking as beautiful as ever.

"You think you packed enough?" I joked. It was pitch-black out still, seeing how we were leaving early Friday morning.

The sun hadn't even begun to rise yet and wouldn't for about another hour or two. Her trunk was filled with suitcases, winter gear, and hiking equipment. It appeared we were going away for a month's time instead of two days based on how much she'd packed.

"Better safe than sorry," she stated. For a split second, she paused and looked at me. She searched deeper than most people did when they studied me. She did that often as if she were seeking secrets to my soul that I'd never shared with others.

Her lips turned up into a smile. "You're a morning person," she stated as if she'd collected that data point from my eyes.

"I am with you," I replied.

A wave of shyness washed over her eyes, but her gentle smile remained. "Well, good morning, sunshine."

Her soft words shot straight through my hard exterior and landed against my soul. "Good morning, beautiful."

There was a slight tremble to her as my words found her.

Do I make you nervous, Starlet?

Her lips parted, and she combed her hair behind her ears. "Let's get on the road."

"Are you sure you don't want me to drive?" I asked even though my night driving was shitty. Everything mostly blurred together when I had to drive at night.

"It's about six hours away," she said. "So I'll do the first three hours, and you can do the second."

"The person not driving is in charge of music," I mentioned as I slid into the passenger seat.

"Deal. But please don't have crappy music taste."

"This could make or break our connection, now that I think about it, Teach."

"We don't have a connection," she corrected.

I smirked.

We had a connection. Even if both of us denied it.

Something about us pulled us closer to one another. And I didn't even think it was the dead mothers aspect. I sensed it the night at the party. Something about her felt so familiar to me—a stranger who felt sort of like home. I didn't know that was a thing until I met Starlet.

Since her, I haven't hooked up with anyone else. I didn't want to. I didn't reach out to anyone I knew, looking to roll around in the sheets to help me forget about my life. I was living instead of being the walking dead I'd been over the past few years. I was working hard on assignments, listening to audiobooks—*for fun*—and finding reasons to talk to Starlet any chance I could get. Meaningless sex or blacking out no longer had any appeal to me. I didn't want to hide from the world anymore. I wanted to feel again. And Starlet Evans? She was a mastermind at making me feel again.

I hooked my phone up to Bluetooth and put on my favorite playlist.

Starlet instantly cocked an eyebrow as she began to drive. "Bullcrap. This isn't your music."

"Why not?"

"It's smooth jazz."

"Yeah, it is."

"You like smooth jazz?" she asked, stunned.

"I do. I like all music like this. Along with folk and slow acoustic."

"Wow. That surprises me."

I arched my eyebrow. "What music did you think I'd be into?"

"I don't know…heavy metal?"

I chuckled. "All that angst in me, huh?"

She giggled and shrugged. "I sometimes struggle with judging a book by its cover. That's on me."

I kicked off my shoes because I hated to wear shoes during long car rides, and then I got as comfortable as I could in her car, which was pretty easy with her heated seats and extra legroom. "I also play the saxophone."

Her eyes widened as she kept her stare on the road. "Bull!"

"I've played since I was a kid."

"Oh my goodness. Well, you must play for me at some point."

"I don't really do it anymore. Not since…" My words faded off. *Not since my mom.*

She nodded in understanding. "I get it."

"I'd like to play for you," I blurted out. I didn't even know where that came from. What the hell, Milo? I really didn't play music for anyone, yet I felt the pull to play for her. I wondered what she'd think of it. If she'd be impressed. If she'd like it. If she'd like me.

Why did I want this woman to like me so damn much? Why did she live in my mind more than most things?

It was as if Starlet was a drug to my mind, yet instead of making me dazed and foggy-brained, she cleared up my thoughts. She made the sad parts of me easier to bear. They weren't completely gone. I knew that wasn't how depression worked. But I felt less alone when I was struggling through them with her around. She saw the heavy load of my pain and offered to carry it with me in the most subtle ways. Plus, she'd do things that temporarily hit me with so much peace, like her smiles.

Starlet and her fucking smiles.

A big part of me was shocked that she agreed to drive up north with me and stay the weekend for this photo shoot. I thought she would've shut the idea down quickly and suggested we do a local hiking area or something.

Don't get me wrong. I wasn't complaining. Being stuck in a car for six hours with Starlet Evans wasn't my idea of torture.

Conversations between the two of us came easy. The first two hours of our drive flew by. I'd learned more about her mind and her humor in that timespan than I had over our few weeks in the library together.

At one point, I asked if we could stop to watch the sunrise. She did it without any question. She exited the highway and pulled over to the side of the road that overlooked the wooded areas below. The trees were all naked of their leaves, covered in the dusting of the latest snowfall. The wind pushed through, shaking said branches, scattering the snow gently to the ground.

We climbed on top of her Jeep and bent our knees into our chests. Her leg brushed against mine, and I hesitated to inch closer to her to feel her more. It only took a small touch to be filled with her warm energy.

The darkness began to fade from above as the illumination of the sky discovered shades of purples and blues. Soon after, pink and orange hues bled over the landscape, peeking through the clouds, finding their placements in the world. The warm glow spread across the sky, growing more intense with every passing second. The higher the sun rose, the more vibrant the tones became before they began to shift to softer, muted pastel hues. Each stage of the sunrise felt like its own personal masterpiece.

I'd never shared a sunrise with another person since Mom passed away. It was my own thing, my secret moment of solitude, but for some reason, it felt even better having her beside me. As Starlet studied the sky, I studied her. Her brown eyes grew glassy as she watched with such awestruck amazement.

"Wow," she murmured in a complete state of bliss.

"Yeah," I whispered, my eyes still on her. "Wow."

Starlet felt like that to me. I hadn't been able to place what it was that she'd felt like since the day I met her.

She felt like the sunrise.

Bright, vibrant, and awe-inspiring with such mind-blowingly satisfying warmth.

Starlet began to allow tears to travel down her cheeks. She seemed unashamed that she let them fall. Without thought, my thumb brushed against her tears, wiping them away slowly. She tilted her face my way, taken aback by my action.

"Sorry," I muttered, feeling foolish for thinking I was allowed to touch her whenever I pleased. She wasn't mine to touch, but damn, how I wished she was.

"Don't be," she said, pushing a few of the tears away on her own. "I'm sorry for being so emotional that I cry at freaking sunrises."

"Don't be," I said, echoing her words. "I like that about you."

She chuckled. "That I cry over sunrises?"

"No." I shook my head. "That you feel. I like that you feel things so deeply." It made me want to feel things, too.

I took a deep breath as I glanced at the now-fading sunrise.

Good morning, Mom.

We got back on the road not long after that. By hour three, the sun was wide awake, beaming through the windshield, so Starlet put on her dark sunglasses, and she asked me what my plan was after I graduated.

If I were honest, I hadn't really thought of my plan.

I wasn't one to have dreams or goals, which left me as a bit of a floater.

"Not a damn clue," I told her.

"Have you considered college?"

"It's too late to apply. Besides, I don't even know what I'd study."

"That's fine. You can always take a gap year to figure things out or not go at all. College isn't for everyone."

"In my dad's mind, there are only two main paths—college or the military."

"Would you join the military?"

"Not a chance in hell."

She glanced over at me, then back to the road. "If you could do anything, what would it be?"

"Anything?"

"Anything in the world."

I narrowed my eyes. "No wrong answer?"

She giggled. "This isn't a test, Milo. There's no wrong answer."

I loved when she giggled. It got me higher than any pill ever had.

"I'd be a wanderer. I'd buy an RV and go across America, witnessing as many sunrises and sunsets as possible. I'd make a vlog about it on YouTube or some shit and show different people the world and all the unique places."

"Oh my gosh," she said. I held my breath, thinking she was about to tell me how ridiculous the idea was. Instead, her eyes widened, and she said, "That's one of my dreams! I've wanted to do that since I was a kid."

"Bullshit."

"Not bullcrap."

I smiled.

I liked how instead of cursing, she used different words like bullcrap. It was cute.

She had the same dream as me. That created an odd sense of tumult in my thoughts. I couldn't stop but wonder if Mom did this. Did she make Starlet for me? Did she somehow force our paths to cross? Did something in the stars bring us together? I didn't believe in destiny, but I hoped for that to be true. That was something new for me, too—being hopeful.

"My life goal was to take a school bus or an old van and transform it into a mobile home," she explained. "I'd spent a ridiculous number of hours looking up videos like that. In my perfect world, I'd have an RV home and go everywhere with it. That or a tiny house. I think tiny houses are the coolest houses. Or a tree house!" she remarked with such excitement.

"Star?"

"Yes?"

"I think I just fell in love with you," I half joked.

She didn't laugh, though. If anything, she grew a bit too somber.

"I was kidding," I said, feeling like a dumbass for making that comment.

"No, I know. It's not that. It's just...I like when you do that. I really like that."

"Like what?"

"When you call me Star. Only the people closest to me call me Star."

That damn muscle in my chest began to beat faster. "And you like it when I do?"

She nodded. "I like it when you do."

"Does that mean we're close?"

She turned her head toward me, her brown eyes locking with mine. It was only for a slight second before she turned her attention back to the road, but it felt forever wrapped in her stare. I hoped she'd look at me like that more often. As if when she met my stare, she saw forever.

"We should pull over and fill up on gas," she said, shifting the conversation. Clearly, I'd crossed a line asking her that question, but to be fair, she walked me toward said line when she mentioned me calling her Star. Plus, each day, it felt as if our lines of appropriate and inappropriate was drawn in the sand, and with one small breath, it could've been blown away.

Blurred lines, Starlet. We were walking on blurred lines.

As she exited the freeway and pulled into a gas station, I hopped out of the car to fill it up.

"Oh, no, you don't have to—" Starlet started, but I stopped her.

"It's cold out here, and you don't need to freeze your ass off. I've got this." One thing I did learn from my father was the fact that you never allowed a woman to fill up the car tank. Honestly, my father imposed a lot of good life lessons on me before he was lost to grief. He always treated Mom like she was his queen, and he was a peasant who was lucky to even exist in her orbit. That was one thing my father excelled at—loving my mother.

I filled up the tank and told Starlet we could switch driving since we were about three hours from our destination. She agreed. I opened the passenger door for her, and she slid into the car. As she situated herself, I bent down over her, grabbed her seat belt, and slid it slowly across her body. My knuckles glided along her chest as I moved the buckle into place. I clicked it in and winked at her. "Safety first." Then I shut the door.

I was thankful for the two-second walk to my side of the car in the cool air. I needed to calm myself down from the slight touch of her chest against my hand.

"I'm a bit shocked that you trust me to drive your car," I said after getting into the car and turning the key in the ignition.

"What can I say? I'm a bad judge of character. Don't make me regret it," she joked as she hooked up her music.

Kendrick Lamar blasted from her speakers, and she speed-rapped the lyrics of the mastermind lyrical genius.

And just like that, I wanted Starlet Evans more than ever before.

* * *

ONCE WE MADE it to the boutique hotel, I was ready to sleep for a few hours before gearing up for our hike and photo shoot. As she went to check in for our rooms, I gathered our suitcases to take inside. When I entered the boutique, I saw the rage on her face as she went back and forth with the receptionist.

"No, no. You don't understand. We have to have two rooms," Starlet argued. "How could you have overbooked? I booked two rooms!"

"Yes, ma'am, but unfortunately, you went through a third-party website, and the other guest went through our site. Therefore the room must go to them. But your room is one of the best. It's our extra-large honeymoon suite."

"Honeymoon suite? I like the sound of that." I smirked as I approached Starlet, but the annoyance in her body language made me realize it wasn't a joking manner.

"Is there another hotel nearby?" Starlet asked the worker.

"Yes, but they're all booked due to the winter festival this weekend."

Starlet slammed her hand against the counter and groaned.

The employee looked at me and batted her eyes. "I mean, I could think of worse-looking men to share a room with," she teased.

Starlet raised her head and made the most dramatic eye roll I'd ever witnessed. "Please don't stroke his ego."

"No, by all means, stroke it. I love being stroked. Tell her, Star. Tell her how I love being stroked."

Starlet smacked my chest as she grew bashful. I caught her hand against my chest. My stare fell to our touch, just as hers did, and I held her hand for a second longer than I should've.

She yanked her hand away from me and combed her hair behind her ears. She always did that when she was nervous or thrown off by my absurd comments. It was cute. There were so many cute things about her. My mind made a mental list of everything I found adorable about the woman.

I smiled at her annoyance as I slid my hands into my pockets. "We'll take the room," I told the employee. Clearly, Starlet was in the middle of an emotional breakdown, so the sooner we got her into a room to have her full-blown freak-out, the better.

The staff carried our luggage to the room, and I thanked them for the gesture. Not long after, a bottle of champagne was sent to the room. They must not have known I was underage, yet Starlet's ID showed she was over twenty-one. I called it a win. Starlet called it a disaster.

"This is bad. This isn't good. This is so, so bad," she muttered, pacing back and forth in the room. It was an impressive space. It was large, with a California king-size bed, a pullout sofa, and a bathroom with a deep soaking tub.

"Don't worry. I'll sleep on the couch."

"Milo." She sighed, walked into the bathroom, and stood in the shower that was blocked off by a see-through wall. "You'll be able to see me showering!" she grumbled. "Why even put up this wall if it was going to be see-through?!"

"If it makes you feel better, I've already seen you naked."

"Milo!"

"Okay, okay, you're stressed out a bit."

She headed back over toward me and collapsed onto the giant bed. "This is the worst day of my life."

"That's funny. I thought it was the best day of my life."

She dramatically flipped her head in my direction, still lying on the bed. "Why are you such a pain?"

"I was born this way. Don't worry. When you shower, I'll head out of the room and give you your space. Scout's honor." I walked over to the bottle of champagne. "Want some—"

"Don't you dare open that, Milo Corti! No drinking this weekend!"

I smiled. "I like when you use my full name. It turns me on."

"Well, turn off. There will be ground rules for this sleepover." She pushed herself to a sitting position, kicked off her shoes, and then crossed her legs like a pretzel on the bed.

"I hate rules."

"Yeah, I can tell. Which is why we need them."

I plopped down on the sofa across from her. "Okay, let me hear it."

"Absolutely no touching."

"Disappointing yet fair. Continue."

"No sexual remarks of any kind."

"I'll do my best. Next?"

"No slipping into my bed."

"What if I slid into it?"

She gave me a stern look.

I tossed my hands up. "All right, no cuddle buddies. Got it."

"And last, we keep things surface level."

"Says the digger who always asks me questions about my mother."

Her eyes softened, and she shook her head. "I know. I'm just adding to the confusion, but I feel as if we are on a slippery slope, especially with us sharing a hotel room. I'm not blaming you for any of this since I've been a willing participant. Yet I think now I realize how many lines we've crossed." She swallowed hard. "I can't lose my job, Milo. This means too much to me."

I sat up straighter, less relaxed. "Star, I know I make a lot of inappropriate jokes, but I would never do anything to jeopardize your career. I'm a dick, but I'm not that big of a dick."

"Thanks, Milo."

I grabbed a pillow from the bed and tossed it onto the sofa. "Take a nap," I told her as I lay down on the sofa, not bothering to pull it out into its bed form. "We've got a long, cold hike to take in a few hours."

She smiled.

I loved it.

But I'd keep that secret to myself. I didn't want to push her buttons unless I knew she'd push mine back.

I tossed and turned on the sofa, trying my best to get comfortable. Unfortunately, my legs dangled over the edge, which made it damn near impossible to get situated.

"Fine." Starlet sighed.

I opened one eye and glanced her way. "Fine, what?"

"We can share the bed. It's clear you're uncomfortable." She took all the pillows on the bed and made a barrier wall right down the middle. "You stay on your side, and I'll stay on mine."

I smirked. "That's quite generous of you, Teach."

"What can I say? I'm a good person." She pointed a stern finger my way after I climbed into the bed. "Don't you dare touch me."

"I'll keep my hands to myself. Unless you change your mind," I teased. "Because if you change your mind, my hands are going straight for your puss—"

She swatted me with her pillow. "Go to sleep, Milo."

I did as she said, hoping my dreams would be of me between her thighs.

* * *

AFTER A FEW HOURS, I was awakened when I felt an arm brush against mine. I opened my eyes and found the pillow barrier was completely gone. Somehow, Starlet moved closer to my side of the bed, and her head rested peacefully against my shoulder blade.

I thought about pulling her closer, wrapping her body in my arms, and allowing our heat to merge. Instead, I left her where she was because I feared that if I moved her, she might wake up and remove herself completely from my touch. Having her sleeping against my shoulder felt like a dash of joy I didn't want to lose.

Therefore, I closed my eyes and went back to sleep, hoping she'd slowly inch closer.

CHAPTER 15

Starlet

I woke up to find my head resting against Milo's chest. Pushing myself up, I almost yelled at him for breaking through the pillow border, but then I noticed his position. He was right where he was supposed to be. I had shifted toward him.

I lowered myself back and let my hands lay against his chest as I listened to his heartbeat. The warmth of his hold sent comforting chills down my spine. I stayed against him longer than I should've, but I couldn't pull myself away. I breathed in his oak trees and lemonade scent, wishing I could've remained there all day.

I stayed for five more minutes.

Then ten.

Maybe twenty.

I wished it didn't feel so right having him beneath me. His arm was slightly wrapped around me, and I fell against him as if I were always meant to be there.

Move, Starlet.

I gently sighed before slowly inching myself back to my side of the bed. I placed the pillow border back in place. I tried to fall back asleep, but I missed his touch too much. I'd keep that fact to myself, though.

* * *

"Heated gloves and heated socks?" Milo asked me as I handed him a backpack filled with essentials. I hadn't been hiking in the winter in a long time, so perhaps I'd gone over and above with precautions, but I always said better safe than sorry.

"You never know what could happen out there," I warned, zipping up my coat as we parked the car in a secluded area to head out for the hike. A few hikers were already on the trail toward the ice caves, and I was packed with a heavy level of anxiety intermixed with excitement. It was the first hike I'd taken since Mom passed away. A part of me thought I wouldn't find myself on a trail again if I were honest. I wasn't used to not having her by my side.

"And granola bars?" he mentioned.

"My mom always packed granola bars. If you unzip that top zipper on the backpack, you'll find Fruit Roll-Ups and trail mix in little baggies."

He did as I said and raised an eyebrow, amused. "I'm impressed, Teach."

I smiled. "What can I say? I'm pretty impressive."

"Yes, you are."

I felt my cheeks flush from his commentary. I didn't think he meant it in a flirtatious way, but that man was a master at making my stomach swirl with butterflies without even trying. Sometimes he'd just be standing still, and my body would react to his mere existence.

I hated how my mind couldn't control my body. If it could, all the attraction I felt toward Milo would've dissipated.

We gathered our gear and camera equipment and set off walking toward the trail. Before we set foot on it, Milo stopped me by placing a hand on my shoulder. "Star, wait."

"What?"

"Are you okay?"

I arched my eyebrow. "What do you mean?"

"I know you haven't been hiking since your mom, and I just wanted to check in to make sure you're really okay to do this."

There he was.

Sweet Milo.

The gentle one who didn't come out to play that often.

My stupid heart and how it chose to beat for him.

"I'm okay," I told him with a smile. He tilted his head, studying me as if he were trying to figure out if I was being honest with him or not. "I'm okay," I repeated.

He nodded. "If there's any moment that you're not, let me know all right?"

"Will do."

We started the hike, and the cold breeze of winter brushed against my slightly exposed face. It was, indeed, one of the coldest winters I'd experienced in some time. Yet the world around us was beautiful. Snow covered the grass and the bare branches of the trees. The sun rays cut through the trees, adding just a touch of warmth every now and again. When we approached a small lake, we stopped to have Milo take a few photographs. I took in a few deep inhales as I stared at the iced-over water. Something was so beautiful about the idea that something so frozen in time would soon flow freely once spring touched it.

I studied Milo as he took his photographs. I could tell by how he set up his camera and how he posed situations that he wasn't simply a good photographer. He was great. I'd learned that about him over the past few weeks—Milo Corti was great.

He was pretty much good at everything when he put in the effort. I knew the main issue for his struggles had everything to do with grief, which was understandable. Grief had that effect on individuals. It could make extraordinary people seem nothing more than uninspired, weak, and frozen over in sadness.

The most stunning thing to me, though, was the aftermath of grief when the frozen hearts began to thaw.

"Look at this one," Milo said, hurrying over with his camera in hand. He had a tiny smile on his mouth, showing pride in the photograph, and the moment I saw it, I understood why.

"Wow!" I expressed, stunned by his artistic eye for detail.

"You like?"

"I love."

His smile grew.

He cleared his throat.

He looked away.

He, too, got bashful.

What did that mean about us? Us? As if that could ever be a possibility.

I rubbed my hand against my chest and shook my head. "Should we keep going? We should almost be at the caves."

"Yeah, for sure. Let's go."

We continued the hike, and once we made it to the ice caves, the mere amazement stole my breath away. "Oh my goodness," I breathed out, feeling my eyes fill with emotions.

"Wow," Milo muttered, just as stunned as I was.

Ice crystals hung from the ice caves over our heads. The walls and ceilings of the cave were polished and smooth, with an opaque tone to them. Various shades of blue, green, and white were found throughout the large caves. It was remarkable. I hadn't even known tears were rolling down my cheeks as I studied the unique formations of the frozen tunnels. You could see where the waterfalls had frozen over, too, which created these intriguing situations that were pure artwork.

When I turned toward Milo, he already had his camera out, and I was taken aback when I saw him pointing it toward me.

I parted my lips to argue with him about taking my photo, but then I smiled and allowed it. A part of me wanted to remember this moment. I wanted to recall today for the rest of my life.

He then walked over toward me and snapped a few photos of the two of us together. We smiled, we made goofy faces, and we laughed. We let go of any worries we carried within us that afternoon. We allowed ourselves to have fun together. I danced in the caves and felt freer than I'd felt in a long time. Milo smiled more than I'd ever seen him smile.

I felt as if that was him. The real him. The version of him that'd been sleeping for so long.

It was an honor to see him awaken. I silently prayed he wouldn't fall asleep again anytime soon.

When it was time to leave, I took a deep breath and stared at the otherworldly beauty of the frozen landscape surrounding us.

"Do you ever wish you could freeze time?" I asked Milo.

"I do today."

I turned toward him to find his stare on me. His eyes were so sincere that I almost cried solely from his gaze.

"Are you happy today?" I asked.

His smile deepened. "I'm happy today. Are you happy today?"

"I'm happy today."

"Good. Let's head back and get you some hot cocoa. I'm nervous that your nose will fall off, Rudolph."

We began the two-mile hike back to our car, stopping every now and again to take in the chilled air. When I told Milo that my mother would've loved the views, he told me he was proud of me for being brave enough to hike again.

Hearing him say he was proud of me did something to my soul. It was as if his pride in me meant more than anything to my spirit.

I was proud of myself, too.

I hope you are, too, Mom.

And I hoped that wherever she was, she could see the ice caves and all of their beauty. I hoped my mother ended up somewhere with hiking trails galore and could explore them all. I hoped she was able to laugh, jump, skip, and run through the wilderness the same way I'd been able to do that afternoon.

"I feel her in the wind," I confessed to Milo when we finished the hike. "I know it sounds stupid, but I feel her in the wind."

"Nothing about that is stupid," he disagreed. "I feel my mom in the sun."

Who knew two opposites could have so much in common?

When we made it to the car, we unloaded our equipment into the trunk. We were parked between trees in a somewhat isolated area. It seemed most of the travelers that day had already headed out since the sun was beginning to set.

Once finished, Milo shut the trunk, and I headed to the driver's side of the car to slide inside.

"I thought about kissing you," Milo confessed before I opened the door. I paused before looking up toward him, thinking perhaps I imagined the words that left his mouth. He took a few steps toward me. "I know we're supposed to pretend that what happened between us never happened between us, but after today, after watching you be the most real version of you, I can't bullshit my way through this."

"Mi—"

"I thought about kissing you so much that it's about all that consumed my thoughts the moment we reached the ice caves."

I sighed because I thought about it, too. I thought about it so much over the past few weeks that the thoughts of him and his mouth, his lips, and his tongue haunted my dreams. Some nights, I'd close my eyes and try to remember what it felt like that night we were strangers, yet it felt like everything for a short period. Some nights, I'd pretend he was lying in my bed with me.

I hated myself for wanting his touch so badly. Why did I crave something so wrong for me? I'd always done the right thing. I'd never misbehaved. I was a straitlaced individual who always walked down the right path. I never faltered. Yet when it came to Milo Corti, all I wanted was more. More of his looks, more of his smiles, more, more, more...

"You don't have to explain to me why I can't kiss you, Star. I get it. I'm not a dumbass, and I'd never want to put you or your job at risk. But after seeing you today, seeing you free, I just wanted you to realize you are everything I'd ever want in a person, and if I could, I would kiss you for the rest of my life without a second of hesitation or doubt."

He stepped closer to me. With each step, my heart skipped a few beats. Whatever. A fully beating heart wasn't a life requirement.

His eyes locked with mine, and I couldn't look away, even if I wanted to. He did that to me. He hooked me in and made me stay.

"I was thinking...maybe I'm not able to kiss you...but maybe, just maybe..." He swallowed hard and seemed so nervous, so timid. "Maybe we can be friends?"

"Friends?" I choked out, my mind spinning to thoughts of only his lips.

"Yes, friends."

My back was against my car, yet he kept approaching me. So close that his tall, broad frame hovered over mine. I felt small yet safe. I was boxed in by the boy who should've never grown that close. It didn't feel like a friendship. It felt the opposite of friendship. It felt...wild. Exciting. Exhilarating.

I shut my eyes. "Milo...I-I don't think I'm supposed to be friends with students."

"But you want to be."

I want to be.

Oh, how I want to be.

"We...I, we can't..." I stuttered, opening my eyes to find his brownish greens on mine. Why did his eyes have to do that? Make me feel everything all at once?

"Secret friends?" he offered.

I laughed but felt the tears behind my eyes.

No part of me wanted to be his friend.

Every inch craved so much more.

"Okay," I agreed. "Secret friends."

He moved in closer. His mouth lingered by my ear, his hot breaths melting against me. "I always wanted a friend like you."

I tilted my head up, and a small smile crept across my lips. "Do friends always stand this close to one another?"

"Secret friends do. It's what secret friends do the best."

"What else do secret friends do?"

135

His stare dropped, and his hands somehow became entangled with mine. "Secret friends hold hands."

"Milo."

"I don't make the rules, Star."

"It sure sounds like you do."

I stared at him as his tongue slightly grazed across his bottom lip as he stared at my mouth. I should've pushed him away. I should've told him how irresponsible we were acting. I should've used my brain. Yet my heart took the lead, completely shutting my brain off.

I pulled him closer.

And closer.

And closer...

My chest lay against his, our bodies so close that I struggled to know where he began and where I ended. So close that his touch felt like my own.

"What else?" I whispered. "What else do secret friends do?"

He placed one hand on the top of my car and inched his face closer. His lips swept against mine as my heart rate intensified. His eyes were dilated, and I was certain his thoughts were as absurd as my own. Packed with wants, needs, and desires. And sins...

So many quiet sins were begging to be unleashed.

"Secret friends do whatever they want, and the world would never know."

"Like this?" I asked, gently sliding my tongue against his bottom lip.

No, Star...

His tongue parted my mouth before he nibbled on my bottom lip. "Like that."

It's wrong...

His eyes closed as he pressed his forehead against mine. "Star, if you don't want this, I'll pull away. If you don't want me, I'll let you go. But if any part of you does, then say yes, and the moment after that yes, I'm going to take all of you inside the back of your Jeep."

I knew what I should've said.

I knew the words that should've left my mouth, but they didn't come. The saint in me was silent as my bad side was released.

"Take all of me," I whimpered.

Within seconds, Milo's mouth crashed against mine. He kissed me as if he'd been waiting decades to do so. His lips on mine were all I wanted, all I craved for the longest time. He opened the back door of my car and pulled me inside. We scrambled, tossing off layer after layer of clothing but leaving our shirts on.

He placed me on his lap, and I felt his hardness brush against my thigh. It was freezing outside, yet all I felt was his heat against me, warming every inch of my being. He scrambled for his wallet and pulled out a condom. I took it from him, tore it open, and smoothed it slowly down over his length while maintaining eye contact the whole time. I began pumping his length in my hands a few times before placing him at my entrance. I hovered over him, not giving him what he wanted just yet. As his lips parted, I wanted to see how much need would build within him. The desperation in his dilated eyes only turned me on more.

He lifted his large hand to the side of my neck and gripped me, pulling me closer to his face. His lip danced across mine before he swept his tongue against them. "Don't tease, Star," he muttered with a wicked grin. "Because I'll tease you back," he ordered before taking his other hand and softly rubbing my clit. A moan of desire escaped me from the act as he took my bottom lip into his mouth and nibbled it. "And I'm a fucking great tease." He slid a finger inside me, and my hips involuntarily rocked to try to make him fall deeper. He paused his movement, tightened his hand around my neck, and pulled me even closer. "You like that?"

"Yes," I replied breathlessly.

"You want more of that or all of me?" he hissed, his intoxicating tone making me high.

"All of you," I whispered. I pulled his finger from inside me, brought it to my lips, and then I sucked it slowly, tasting myself against his skin. My eyes locked with his, and I saw the way the movement turned him on even more. "I want all of you."

The passion and heat of the moment became incendiary after that. We were starving for one another as the windows fogged up from our body chemistry. I lowered myself onto him fully, and he began thrusting harder and deeper as I gripped the rear deck of the back seat. I felt filthy in the most thrilling way as my curly hair dangled in his face. He swept it out from in front of my eyes and gripped the back of my neck, forcing eye contact not to break between us. His warmth and intensity left me feeling as if I were soaring through the world with no fear of falling. The weeks of abstinence between us, the weeks of secretly longing and daydreaming, were all boiling over and now clashing against both of our bodies. Our tongues lapped against one another, starving for each other, our hands explored, and our hips rocked together as if we were one. He delivered faster thrusts, and my nails dug into his back as he ordered me to fuck him harder, wilder, deeper. More, more, more…that was all I wanted from him. More.

My mouth fell against his neck as I cried out in pleasure from the feel of him filling up every inch of me. I loved how he felt inside me. I loved how he'd press me against his body, ensuring I knew he was addicted to every part of my being.

"I love how you feel," he whispered against my neck, licking my skin before moving his mouth to my earlobe. I moaned as my hips rocked against his. My hand fell to the window, and my handprint stayed against the chilled glass panel as I arched my back from the intense ride Milo was taking me on.

"That's my girl," he said, his voice coated in desire. "I love when you moan out for me," he said, nibbling against my neck.

I came against him hard, and at the same time, he let out a tortured groan, his face contorting in ecstasy. The look of somewhat shock in his eyes as we came together showed me exactly what I'd been feeling this whole time. This was different from before. We were different. The way we'd come undone, the way we'd lost ourselves yet found each other, was a new, uncharted territory we wandered.

At that moment, surrounded by trees as nightfall settled over us, Milo and I became something special. Something more.

More, more, more…

"Fuck," he breathed out as he slid out of me.

I was breathless as my body clung to his. He trailed kisses up and down my neck before he found my lips and kissed me slowly. Gently. There was so much care taken with his kisses. There was so much protection in his eyes.

More, more, more...

"I want this," he told me between kisses. "I want you, Star," he swore as he kissed me again. A split second of concern hit me as he kissed my lips. Milo tasted like promises he couldn't keep. Like a promise of tomorrow when we only had today.

Yet I couldn't bring myself to force us back to reality because I wanted him, too. I wanted him more than I'd ever wanted anything before. He felt like the missing piece to my soul's puzzle, and I didn't want that to slip away. Being with him was intoxicating, and I wasn't interested in discovering my sobriety, at least not for the next twenty-four hours.

It felt as if we were in our own twisty fairy tale. Six hours away from reality and from anyone who knew who we were. We were make-believing in a time and place that was solely for us. I, for one, was not ready to wake from our enthralling fantasy. There was only one thing I craved at that time—more, more, more.

CHAPTER 16

Starlet

I had sex with Milo in the back of my Jeep.

Oh my goodness, I had sex with Milo in the back of my Jeep!

And I didn't regret it. I had a tug in my gut telling me that I should've regretted the act that happened between us, but I couldn't bring myself to do so. It felt so good, so right, being in his lap, feeling him inside me.

Once we made it back to our hometown, I knew I'd overthink every single thing that happened between us that weekend, but for the time being, I would allow myself to be wild. To be untamed.

We drove back to the boutique hotel, and Milo carried all of our bags to the room. Before I could even mention that I was starving, a knock sounded on our door.

I walked over to open it and found a beautiful older woman with stunning silky gray hair down her back smiling from ear to ear. "Hi,

Ms. Evans. We noticed your return, and I wanted to stop by to say hello. I'm Emily Turner, the owner of the boutique."

"Oh, it's nice to meet you."

"You too. I was informed about the mix-up with overbooking, and I wanted to express my utmost apologies. We would love to offer you one of our igloos facing Lake Superior for a romantic dinner for you and your partner. On the house, of course."

"Oh, he's not my..." My words faded as I raised an eyebrow. "On the house?"

"Completely. We can book the reservation for you now, and you can come down and enjoy the views. The igloo itself is heated, too, so you don't have to worry about being cold."

"That would be amazing, actually. How about at eight?"

"We can make that work. Thank you, Ms. Evans. We hope you're enjoying your stay."

Emily left, and I shut the door right after her.

As I turned around, I saw Milo standing there with a smirk on his face.

"What?" I asked.

"Your partner? It seems you didn't argue that much."

I shrugged. "You'd be shocked by what I'd do for a free meal."

"Dare I ask what you'd do for a Klondike bar?" he joked.

"You, Mr. Corti. I'd do you for a Klondike bar."

He eyed me up and down with a devilish grin. "Seems you'd do me for even less than that."

I felt my cheeks heat from his comment because he wasn't wrong.

"I'm going to take a shower before dinner," he told me as he pulled his shirt over his head in one quick movement. He unbuckled his jeans and walked past me straight into the bathroom. I listened as the water turned on, and I watched as his silhouette stepped into the water. My body reacted as I watched him step under the stream of water.

Without much thought, I undressed and joined him.

* * *

"ARE YOU HUNGRY?" Milo asked as he pulled out the chair for me inside our little igloo table setting.

"Famished," I replied, taking my seat. That was not shocking based on the number of times we found ourselves entangled with one another that evening. One would think we'd be completely exhausted after spending the day hiking, yet somehow, we'd found a way to go round after round with one another. Maybe it was simply because we both knew that what we did up north couldn't happen when we returned home.

Maybe, just maybe, we were trying to get it all in before our fantasy of the story of us came to an end.

Milo took his seat and smiled my way. "You look beautiful tonight."

A chill raced over me. "I'm not used to you complimenting me like that."

"If it makes it easier, I've thought about it every single day that I've seen you. I've thought about how stunning you are. I didn't say it."

"It's nice to hear."

"Secret friendship is really working out for us."

I laughed. "I don't think this is what a secret friendship would look like. This feels more like a secret…" My words faded off, but Milo was there to finish it.

"Relationship," he said. "It feels like a secret relationship."

I bit my bottom lip. "This is bad, isn't it?"

"Awful."

"We're going to regret this."

"Totally."

"So we should stop it."

"Absolutely," he agreed. "But…"

"But?"

"We won't."

"We won't?"

He shook his head and reached his hand across the table. "Do you know why?"

"Do tell."

142

"Because it feels too good being bad with you."

I smiled even though I shouldn't have because he was right.

We were the greatest mistake that felt so right.

"We're going to crash." I laughed, shaking my head at how irresponsible we were becoming. Whitney would've been shocked by the girl I'd been over the past day.

"And burn, maybe," Milo agreed. "But no regrets."

I bit my bottom lip. "Promise?"

"Yes." He held his pinky out toward me, and I wrapped my finger around his. "Promise," he said. "Now, let's eat our dinner so I can eat my dessert later tonight."

"I like how you do that," I confessed.

"Do what?"

"Dirty talk. When we're hooking up…" I felt my cheeks heating up as shyness crept up on me. "I wish I could do it, too."

He arched his eyebrow. "You're more than allowed to join in," he swore.

"I know, but I get shy. I can't just do it randomly. I'll feel too silly."

"What if I close my eyes while you're doing it?"

I laughed. "Still too shy."

"We can start with phone sex. Then you won't see me, and I won't see you."

"I doubt we'll find a time to have phone sex."

Milo leaned in toward me. "Trust me. I'll make time to have you whisper dirty things to me through the phone receiver, Star."

I didn't doubt that at all.

We'd laughed so much that night that my cheeks hurt from all the smiling. At one point, after our laughter, Milo sat back in his chair and shook his head in disbelief.

"What is it?" I asked.

"I just didn't think I'd be able to feel happy again."

And just like that, my heart slowly began to become his.

We talked more about our moms and our dads. I told him about the pink bike with yellow daisies painted all over it that my mom built for me, with a white wicker basket and purple handlebars. "It was amazing. It fell apart a few years back, but man, I used to ride that thing everywhere."

"I could imagine little Starlet riding that bike around town."

"I had a matching helmet, too." I beamed with joy.

We talked about the heavy things, too.

"What are the hardest days for you?" Milo asked me.

"There's only one, really. My mom's birthday used to be hard, but now it's just a celebration. My dad and I always get together and make her favorite cake. The hardest one for me is Mother's Day. It's like a constant reminder each year of what I don't physically have anymore."

"Yeah, that's a hard one for me, too. They are all still hard for me."

"Some will get easier, and that's okay. Some might not, and that's okay, too."

After an incredible meal, we walked outside and stared at the stars that littered the darkened sky. Milo wrapped his arms around my waist, and I looked up in amazement.

"Look at the constellations!" I remarked, pointing up at the sky.

"I don't see them," he said.

I laughed slightly. "You're joking, right?"

He shook his head. "Not seeing them."

For a moment, I thought he was pulling my chain and trying to tease me. Yet when I saw the serious look on his face, I grew a bit confused. I pointed once more. "Right there. There are dozens of stars."

Still nothing from Milo.

I turned around to face him, placed my hands against his chest, and stood on my tiptoes to give him a kiss. "I think you need glasses, Mr. Corti."

His lips turned into a smirk. "I think I need you more right now." With his finger, he traced the outline of my lips. "And trust me when I say I don't need glasses to explore you."

"Then by all means..." My cheeks flushed a little before I took his hands in mine. "Explore."

* * *

144

EVERYTHING FELT a little different that night compared to the previous times we'd hooked up. The first time at the party was void of emotional connections. The second time, in the back of the car, was quick and packed with so much adrenaline that it happened so wildly.

That night, though, we took our time. A part of us knew we were moving closer and closer to the end of whatever it was we'd been doing with one another, far away from our reality. When we returned to our town, we wouldn't be able to find ourselves intertwined as we'd been for the past twenty-four hours.

I knew I should've been worried about what we'd be when we went home, but I couldn't bring myself to care. I allowed myself to live in the moment. To be there with Milo and not worry about the tomorrows that would soon ruin our awakened dreams.

Milo undressed me slowly, taking off my clothes to reveal my black bra and panties. His mouth found mine as his hands moved to the back of my bra and unhooked it with two flicks of his fingers. It fell to the floor within seconds. I moved to begin taking off his clothes, but he stopped me.

"Let me have you first," he whispered, trailing kisses down my neck. Shivers of wants and desires filled me as I watched his eyes dilate and his mouth began to taste every inch of me. I didn't know it was possible to be turned on by the simple way that another studied you, touched you, and explored you. Milo laid me against the bed and worshipped me as if I were a goddess. His hands roamed over my body as he took his time kissing every single inch of me. And when I said every inch, I meant he did not miss a single spot. His mouth connected to my skin as if he were famished and in need of my existence so he could survive for another day. He pulled me to the edge of the bed. My legs dangled over the side, and he lowered himself to a kneeling position in front of me.

His mouth kissed the silk fabric of my panties as his thumb began to rub my clit through the fabric of the panties.

I moaned in pleasure as the slight touch sent a wave of excitement through my system.

His fingers wrapped around the edges of my panties, and he began moving them down slowly. Once he removed them, he kissed my inner thighs, making my hips arch up in need.

"Part your legs, Star," he ordered. "I want to see all of you."

My legs widened, and he moved right between them. His mouth found my clit, and he sucked it slowly before flicking his tongue against it a few times. I cried out, wanting more and more of his explorations. He pressed the palms of his hands against my thighs, opening me up wider. "I wish you could see how beautiful you look," he whispered before he slid a finger inside me.

Every step of the night felt as if it were moving in slow motion yet moving too quickly at the same time. I savored every second of Milo as he took me in.

What was it we were doing that night?

It wasn't just sex like the first night we'd met. I knew that for a fact. Yet I wasn't sure if it was love yet either. What was the thing between those two realms?

Falling.

That was what we were doing that night.

We were falling for one another.

Falling, falling, falling…

CHAPTER 17

Milo

I woke to an empty bed. Starlet was nowhere to be found. An instant knot of worry built inside my gut as I became concerned that she regretted the night prior. I'd never truly cared about rejection until that very moment.

The night before was one of the best nights I'd had in a long time. I'd daydreamed about tasting every inch of Starlet since the first night we'd met. The only difference between when we first hooked up compared to last night was, well...everything. I felt everything for Starlet Evans. I felt more than I knew a coldhearted person like me could feel for another person.

I rubbed the exhaustion out of my eyes. Whenever I woke up, there were a few seconds of darkness, even when my eyes were fully open. It took a few moments for my vision to reappear, and when I saw Starlet wasn't there, I feared she'd returned to reality and realized what had happened the night prior was a mistake for her.

That was my ultimate fear—her realizing I was nothing more than a mistake.

Before my mind could trauma dump its toxic thoughts of me being unworthy, the hotel door opened, and Starlet walked in with a tray of coffee and muffins.

"Good morning, sunshine." She smiled brightly, bundled up in her winter gear.

A sigh rolled through my system. She came back.

"Morning," I muttered, rubbing my eyes once more as I sat up in bed. "What time is it?"

"A little past nine. You're a good sleeper."

"How long have you been up?"

"Since around six. I figured I'd get an early hike in and watch the sunrise."

"You've been hiking already? This morning?"

She nodded as she placed the tray of goods down. She then took off her coat and shoes. "What can I say? You unlocked my love of hiking. I just needed to see what the sunrise looked like this morning before we headed back to town."

"I would've gone with you. You could've woken me up."

She grabbed a muffin and coffee and approached me. She placed it on the desk beside the bed and leaned in to kiss me. It felt good to know we were still kissing. I somewhat feared that when the sun came up, the kissing between us would stop.

"You looked too cute sleeping. I didn't want to wake you up. Besides, I had to make sure everything was in order for our last activity today before we headed back home."

I raised an eyebrow. "Last activity?"

She smiled widely, and her doe eyes sparkled with excitement. "How do you feel about surprises?"

"Hate everything about them."

She frowned slightly. "Oh. Well, how do you feel about surprises from me?"

I grinned and pulled her into my chest, kissing her on the forehead. "I could become a fan of those kinds of surprises."

* * *

ICE FISHING.

She took me ice fishing.

Not only did she manage to find a spot on the water, rent a four-wheeler to get us on the ice, and get all the equipment necessary for the adventure but she even cut up the bait for us to use.

"I can't believe you did all of this," I said, a tad bit speechless at the thought that Starlet put into this activity to make it come to play.

"There was a fifty-fifty chance you would've hated the idea, and this all blew up in my face, and we had a very awkward, quiet ride home, but I wanted you to have a moment to feel close to your mother the way you made me feel close to mine on the hike."

I understood that a woman couldn't cure a person's depression. But dammit, did Starlet make it a little easier to breathe.

It took everything inside me not to get choked up in my emotions as we sat out there on the ice for a few hours.

We didn't catch any fish, but I caught a whole shit ton of feelings for a woman who came into my life at a time I needed someone the most.

If I had the opportunity, I would've stayed on the ice with her for a million more hours. I would've asked her more and more questions about her life, her dreams, and her goals. I would've laughed at her trying to untangle her fishing rod and smiled at her when she wasn't even looking my way. I would've run my fingers against her cheeks and kissed her dimples. I would've told her how she scared me shitless because she made me feel. That woman made me, the cold soul of winter, feel again.

You would've loved her, Mom.

You would've loved her more than you loved me.

As that thought crossed my mind, a light breeze pushed through, hitting my face. It was as if Mom were replying to me with the words, "Never a chance I'd love someone more."

She used to say that to me all the time when I was a kid. She'd put me to bed at night, tuck me in, and press our foreheads together.

She'd say, "I love you, my Milo Antonio. Never a chance I'd love someone more."

"You do that a lot," Starlet mentioned as we sat in our chairs on the ice.

"Hmm?"

"You mumble to yourself."

I hadn't known she'd noticed. My brows knitted, and I shook my head. "Not to myself. To my mom. I still talk to her."

"Good," Starlet said as she reeled up her fishing rod a bit. "That's good."

That's good.

What an odd reaction to learning that someone still spoke to their dead mother.

"Star?"

"Yes?"

"You're really weird."

She laughed, and I wanted to swim in the sound. "I am really freaking weird."

"Good," I said, nudging her. "That's good." I stared at her closer and narrowed my eyes. She was shivering. "Are you freezing your ass off right now?"

"Oh gosh, yeah. I'm pretty sure I lost feeling in my left butt cheek like thirty minutes ago."

"Geez, Star, you should've said something. Let's get going."

"No, no, it's fine, I'm fine," she said through gritted, chattering teeth. "This is great."

I smirked at how she was trying her best to push through, but I knew it was time to go. I started packing our things, and we headed back to the car. After loading everything up, I walked over to Starlet and pulled her into a hug. I held her for longer than normal because I hadn't had an actual hug in the longest time. The last time my arms wrapped around a person like that was when I held my mother to say our final goodbye. It had been over a year. A year since my arms wrapped around another person. A year since I had true, authentic comfort from a person. I didn't know how much I'd missed that inter-action until it was upon me.

My body engulfed hers as her heat sank into me. The smell of her hair filled my nose as my arms banded around her. My hold was tight enough to matter yet not restrained enough to constrict her freeness. It felt as if her goodness was being transferred into my soul, and I was giving her the best parts of me in equal measure. I didn't know I still had that. I didn't know my spirit still had good parts to share.

"Thank you for today," I told her. "I needed today."

"I think I needed this weekend," she agreed. "I needed you."

I pressed my forehead to hers and closed my eyes. "If there's an afterlife, do you think our moms are friends?"

"Yes," she quickly replied. "And I think they sent us to one another."

I kissed her and felt the reality begin to settle in that I wouldn't be able to do that freely once we returned to town. "Can I tell you a secret?"

"Yes," she softly said, her warm breaths melting against my skin.

"I already miss you, and you're still here."

She inched in closer, pressing her body against mine, resting her head against my chest. "Can I tell you a secret?"

"Yes."

"I missed you before I knew you existed."

* * *

I DROVE the first few hours before nightfall, and Starlet finished up the ride home, pulling into my driveway a little after eleven o'clock. The only light that existed around the house was the front porch light, which always stayed on. Mom was the one who used to shut it off each night, but after she passed away, neither Dad nor I took on that responsibility.

Starlet shut off her car engine, and we sat quietly in the car for a few moments.

Neither one of us talked about what the transition of our return to town would look like. We didn't discuss what was on and off-limits with our newfound secret friendship.

All we knew was that we couldn't do what we'd done for the past two days.

"What now?" she asked, turning to look at me.

Her brown eyes seemed so sad, and I hated that. I never wanted her to look at me with sadness in her eyes. Some people's eyes were built for sadness, but Starlet's weren't. They were built for smiles, laughter, and joy.

"I don't know," I told her. "But I know the second I get out of this car, everything has to change. And I don't want it to change."

She placed her hand against the console between us, and I placed my hand on top of hers. "Maybe we just act normal. Like friends," she offered.

"I don't normally eat my friends out for dessert," I joked.

"Milo," she scolded, growing bashful. "I mean it. We can't do what we've done. It's too risky."

"Yeah. I know." I brought her hand to my mouth and kissed her palm. "So tell me what to do, Teach."

Her lips trembled for a second, and her eyes flashed with emotions, yet she didn't cry. "You'll show up at school and pretend I don't exist. I'll do the same. Then we'll meet in the library, and you'll bring your sarcastic comments like before, and we'll be who we were before we became...who we are."

"When do we get to be who we are again?"

Her breath caught.

She didn't answer.

My heart caught.

I stayed quiet.

"I'm sorry, Milo. I...we have to get you through these next few months and graduation."

"Ninety-three days," I said. "Ninety-three days until you're mine."

She raised an eyebrow. "You've done the math?"

I nodded. "I've done the math."

She bit her bottom lip, and a few stubborn tears rolled down her cheeks. "Everything in my head is telling me this is wrong. That I'm supposed to be smarter and not fall for you, not feel what I'm feeling, but my heart…it feels everything, and I don't know how to shut that off, and I don't think I want to, but I know this isn't supposed to feel so right. But it does. You feel right to me, Milo. And that scares me. And it's not fair of me to expect you to wait these next three months for us to figure out what we can be. That seems like a very selfish thing for me to ask you to do."

I was still holding her hand. I wasn't sure if I'd be able to let it go.

"Starlet…I need you to understand something. Before you, I was sleepwalking through the coldest winter of my life. I wasn't sure I'd be able to make it through. Then you came and saved me. So believe me when I say I can wait until spring to feel you again. I can wait until spring to make you mine."

She leaned toward me and kissed me.

Her lips against mine, her unspoken truths falling into me through her taste.

We tried to kiss in that very moment, yet it felt like goodbye.

I wished it hadn't.

I wasn't ready for goodbye, not with her, at least, never with her.

We stayed connected as long as we could before I opened the door and said good night.

As she pulled away that evening, she didn't know it, but she took pieces of my heart along with her. I didn't mind. I knew if anyone would keep them safe, it would be her.

"She's the one, Mom," I muttered as I grabbed my suitcase.

The wind hit my face as if Mom said, "I know."

CHAPTER 18

Starlet

I valued three people's opinions most in my life—my mother, my father, and Whitney. One thing I was never able to do with Whitney was tell her a lie. She read me like an open book. The pages, paragraphs, sentences, and words of my story always rested right on my face. I was already worried about her finding out about the weekend, and I knew it would be impossible to hold it in.

"How was your hiking adventure?" Whitney asked me after I finally made it back to our dorm room. I was beyond exhausted and emotionally spent as I collapsed onto my bed.

Whitney was still up studying, which I was hoping she hadn't been. I wasn't completely ready to unload the events of the weekend to her, but I knew sooner or later, I'd tell her everything.

"I went with Milo," I blurted out. "I spent the weekend with him up north."

Her eyes widened as she sat up straighter. "I'm sorry, you spent the weekend with who?"

"You can't judge me," I told her, the guilt of the weekend finally catching up with me.

"Did you sleep with him?" she asked. My face told her the answer. "Oh my goodness, Starlet!"

"I know, I know! It sounds so bad."

"Uh, it doesn't sound bad. It *is* bad. What were you thinking?"

"I don't know. I wasn't, I guess. Aren't you the one always telling me I should let loose a little? Be a little bit freer?"

Her eyes bugged out. "Yeah, I am that person. I said to let loose a little. A little, Star. I meant, like, smoke a joint or take a pole-dancing class. I didn't mean screw your student."

I shivered at her words. "I wasn't screwing my student. It's different with Milo."

"I'm sorry, but you sound a little crazy right now. You can't seriously be jeopardizing your whole college career for a man. For a man?! We hardly even like men!" she shouted, tossing her hands up in shock and disgust.

A big part of me was thrown off by my roommate's reaction. She was always so addicted to the idea of me living a life outside of my studies, and now that I had, she was scolding me as if I were the worst person in the world.

"Whitney, let me explain—"

"No, Star. Don't try to explain it to me. You're smarter than this. You've worked too hard to throw it all away for some boy. You've known him, what? Three months? You've been in college for three years. It doesn't make sense to risk so much for a dick."

"He's not just some dick," I argued, getting heated from annoyance because how could she not understand? How could she be so logical at that very moment? I knew my anger was coming from a place of knowing she was right, too. She was one hundred percent right, and if the situation were reversed, I would've given her the same speech.

That annoyed me the most. My brain knew I was playing with fire, but my heart didn't care about the burns. I wasn't angry with Whitney. I was furious with myself. I knew better.

I knew better, yet still...

"He's something different, Whit," I offered. "He's…he's…"

"Your student," she scolded.

My heart began to shatter because she didn't see what I saw. She didn't feel what I felt. How could she, though? Just because we all had hearts didn't mean they beat in the same fashion.

"I'm falling in love with him," I confessed quietly. My chest ached as the words evaporated off my tongue. I felt crazy, ridiculous, and in love, and that terrified me. I felt as if I wasn't even in control of my own thoughts and feelings anymore. I felt as if love was swallowing me whole, and I prayed it wouldn't spit me out because I felt good when I was with him. I felt as if I were floating when Milo was beside me.

Yet when he wasn't, when my mind grew loud and reality settled in, I began to crash.

Was love supposed to feel like that?

Intoxicating and ruthless?

Or was love supposed to be gentler without so many complex emotions attached to it?

"Then stop falling, Starlet," Whitney barked at me, wide eyes and all. "Stand up."

Tears began streaming down my cheeks, and I shook my head in disbelief at her words. "I shouldn't have told you," I muttered, crawling under my blankets. Regret was sinking in quickly.

Whitney stood and walked over to my side of the room. She climbed into my bed and pulled me into a hug, showing me that her words weren't coming from a place of harshness yet a place of love and honesty. "No, you should've told me, and you knew you should've, too, which is why you did. A big part of you knows this isn't right, which is why you came to me. I could be a fake friend and tell you what you want to hear, but that's not us, babe. That's never been us. We are real with one another, no matter what. So this is me being real. It would be best if you stopped any feelings you're feeling for this guy, Starlet. And as long as you keep tutoring him, you'll keep falling for him. You need to stop that. Just focus on your career and your life. This won't end well."

I stayed quiet.

A big part of me wanted to argue with her. A big part of me wanted to call her out and be childish and say she'd never fallen in love. Therefore, she wouldn't understand. But a bigger part of me understood her and knew she was right. She wasn't being cruel; she was being truthful. That was the greatest thing about having a real best friend—having someone who would tell the truth, even when it was hard.

Yet I couldn't stop tutoring Milo.

I couldn't let him go.

No matter how much logical sense that made.

"If it were me, Star, what would you tell me to do?" she questioned.

I hated that question, and I refused to answer it that evening because I knew the answer.

I would've told her to stop falling in love with the boy and focus on herself. It was as if my heart and my head were alienated from one another. As if they were enemies of war, playing for control of my soul.

Later that night, my dad called to check in on things. I walked out of the dorm room and headed to the study lounge so I could talk to him privately.

"How was your weekend getaway?" he asked. "I was a bit worried about you hiking by yourself."

I swallowed hard, feeling guilty for the lie I had to tell. Dad thought I'd gone up north to hike on my own. He'd even offered to join me. "It was great. We'll have to make it up there at some point. You'd love the ice caves."

"Sign me up for next winter. I missed you tonight for dinner, but I packed up some meals for you and Whitney when you come next weekend. You'll have double the food to take back with you."

"Thanks, Dad. You're the best."

"How are you feeling tonight? You doing okay?"

I hesitated and bit my bottom lip. It seemed that the good high I was riding over the weekend was coming to a complete halt. "I'm fine."

"Okay, now tell me the truth."

I sat on top of one of the tables and stared out at the snow falling outside. "Do you think Mom would be proud of me? Of the person I am?"

"Of course she would. She'd be amazed by you, buttercup."

"Even if I made mistakes?"

"I think she'd love you even more for your mistakes. We never wanted you to be perfect, Star. We just wanted you to be you."

A few tears rolled down my cheeks. I wished I were home. I wished I could have one of Dad's big bear hugs because they always made me feel safe.

"What's going on, Star?" he asked. "What's on your mind?"

"A lot. Too much to talk about, I guess."

"How can I help? Want me to drive up there for a visit?"

I smiled as if he could see me. "No, it's fine. I'll be okay. I'm just trying to decide whether I'm making the right choices, that's all. Just a bit of anxiety."

"Well, consider how the choice feels in your body before you over-think. Does it feel good and safe?"

Yes, yes...

He continued. "If it does, it's probably the right option. Even if it looks wrong to the world."

"Thanks, Dad. I needed to hear that."

"Always. I love you."

"Love you, too."

We chatted for a while longer before saying good night. As I climbed into bed, I thought about his words. The weekend with Milo felt good and safe. That was all I knew. That terrified me.

CHAPTER 19

Milo

"Hey, best friend," Tom said on Monday afternoon, walking up to my locker. He'd been calling me his best friend for the past few weeks, ever since I'd accidentally nicknamed him. He was eating that slipup of mine like the Jolly Ranchers he was always shoving into his mouth.

"What's up?" I asked as I shut my locker and swung my backpack onto my right shoulder.

"I wanted to invite you to the best party of all parties in the history of parties this coming Saturday. I'm officially turning eighteen. My parents will be out of town, and I'm throwing a rager."

"Do people still say rager?" I muttered as we began walking toward our next class—English. My favorite hour of the day.

"People still say rager. It's me. I'm people." He pulled out a card from his backpack and handed it to me. "Here's your invite."

"You had invites printed?"

"I'm just that level of extra."

I glanced down at the invitation in my hand and arched an eyebrow. "Choose your own Tom costume party?"

"Any Tom of your choice—except Tom Cruise from *Risky Business*. I claimed it. Be creative."

"I'll do my best."

He paused his footsteps. "Wait, you're actually going to come? And you're going to dress up?"

"Didn't you just invite me, and isn't it a costume party?"

"Yeah, but I mean, you're kind of, you know...anti-social."

"I show up to the hangouts all the time."

"I mean, you're there, but not really there. Plus, the bigger the crowd, the less likely it would be that you'd show."

That was true. The bigger the crowd, the more people I'd have to avoid having conversations with. People loved small talk, but I hated it.

"About how many people are coming?" I asked, now concerned that I agreed to show up.

"Nope! No take backs. You said you'll be there, so now you have to show up." Right before I could answer, Starlet walked past the two of us. Tom let out a low whistle. "She's so fucking hot, man."

"What?" I snapped, taken aback by his words.

"Hey, Ms. Evans! I like your hair today," he said with a singsong tone over to Starlet, making her turn to look toward us.

Her eyes locked with mine briefly before she turned toward Tom. "Thank you, Tom, that's very kind of you."

"It's really nice. Then again, everything looks nice on you, Ms. Evans," he flirted.

Yup.

That was right.

He was flirting with my secret friend that I wanted to be more than a friend with, and rage built inside me that I wasn't even able to act on. Secrets were fun.

Starlet smiled. *Damn.* I wished that smile were against my mouth. "I'm not the one grading your homework this week, Tom. No need to suck up to me. I'll see you both in class."

I'd hoped she'd look back at me one more time, but she didn't. She was too much of a professional for that.

As she walked away, Tom's eyes followed the movement of her hips.

"Dude," I said, shoving him. "That's our teacher."

"Student teacher. She's pretty much our age. You know, after my birthday, I bet I'd even have a shot with her."

"Don't hold your breath," I muttered.

Tom shrugged as we continued on our way to class. "You're probably right. If she were ever going to go for a student, it would probably be you, seeing how I think she has a crush."

The words threw me for a loop, and I almost tripped over my own feet as Tom popped another Jolly Rancher into his mouth.

I narrowed my eyes at him, somewhat trying to convince myself that he didn't say what I thought he'd said.

"What?" I asked.

"I think Ms. Evans has the hots for you," he repeated.

My chest tightened. "What the hell are you talking about?"

He raked his hand through his hair. "I just noticed how she stares at you when she hands out assignments. She lingers."

"That's bullshit," I muttered, walking faster. "She looks at everyone the same."

"Maybe, dude. But if you ever get the chance to unlock that door… please, for the good of all of us guys who have daydreamed about her, walk through it. Because I would screw her in a heartbeat."

"People don't daydream about Ms. Evans," I said, trying to hide my annoyance as my hands formed fists.

"Are you kidding me? Everyone talks about that woman. Even Chris talks about her! Well, okay, he doesn't talk, but he looks. How could he not? She's like a damn supermodel. Her curves…" He bit his fist and rolled his eyes as if he were getting off from the idea of her alone.

"Chill, man. That's our teacher."

"I bet if I had the chance, I'd teach her a few things myself."

Rage.

161

Straight-up rage was all I felt.

I knew we were friends and all, but man…I wanted to punch Tom square in the jaw for talking about screwing my girl.

Well, my secret girl.

My secret friend.

What the hell ever it was that we were.

I was in a shitty mood now.

Fuck Tom. Fuck him and his daydreams about the girl who wasn't openly mine but was…mine. And I was hers. Completely fucking hers.

* * *

"You can't look at me like that," I told Starlet as I walked into our study room after school.

"Like what?" Her eyes were on me, and I felt it all: her gentleness, her care, and her falling for me.

"Like that," I said, gesturing toward her. "Like when you see me… you actually see me."

"I don't know how to stop that. Besides," she confessed, shrugging her shoulders, "you look at me the same way."

I couldn't argue with that fact.

But I was still in a pissy mood. I was annoyed that Tom and other guys were checking her out and talking about how they wanted to screw her brains out. During the class, I watched how all the guys' eyes seemed pinned on her, and it only made me angrier. Could I blame them for their attraction? Of course not. Did it piss me off? Absolutely.

If it had been any other girl I'd previously fooled around with, I couldn't have given a rat's ass about their attraction to said girl. But Starlet was different. She wasn't like those girls. She was my person. Precious, unique, weird, and mine. Solely, undeniably, mine.

She arched an eyebrow. "What's wrong with you?"

"Nothing," I shot out. "I'm fine."

"You're grumpy."

"I'm not."

"You're grimacing."

"I'm not," I growled.

She laughed at me. Yup, she laughed as if my annoyance were tickling her. "You're so weird. What's going on?"

"My friend Tom thinks you have the hots for me."

Her laughter faded off. "Wh—why would he think that?"

"Because of how you look at me. He said if you had the hots for any student, it would be me."

"Oh no. This isn't good."

"Don't worry. I shut it down fast. Lucky for us, Tom has the brain of a toddler and was already onto another topic."

"If that's the case, why are you so upset?"

I grumbled and crossed my arms as I sat back in my chair. "Because, they, shit..." I sighed and tossed my hands up in surrender. "They all know you're hot, all right?!"

She raised an eyebrow. "Come again?"

"The guys at school have been going on about how hot they think you are, how they want to hook up with you, and all this other bullshit. It's as if they have no moral compass."

"Says the guy who screwed me in the back of my Jeep forty-eight hours ago."

I went to shoot a comeback to her comment, but when I saw the smirk and tongue-in-cheekiness of her words, I couldn't help but feel less intense. "Whatever."

"You're jealous," she mentioned.

"I'm not. Psh, I'm not the jealous type." Yes, I was. I was damn jealous. I'd never experienced that before, though, which left me feeling exposed and embarrassed that she was right.

"Oh my gosh, you are the jealous type."

"Let's start on our homework," I muttered, unzipping my backpack.

Starlet sat back in her chair and shook her head. "No. I want to focus on this jealousy thing a little bit. It's kind of sexy."

"It would be sexy if it were true, but it's not. I'm not a jealous guy."

"Don't worry. I get jealous over you, too."

I arched my eyebrow. "Bullshit."

She nodded. "Yup. On the school's lower level, in the girls' bathroom, there's a list of the hottest guys in school. And the girls add tally marks with who they think is the hottest. Guess who the leading man is?"

I smirked, sitting up a bit straighter. "No shit, me?"

"You." She pulled out her cell phone and started scrolling through her photographs. "In the bathroom by the cafeteria, there's a list of names of girls' initials who would like to"—she cleared her throat as she read the picture—"sit on Milo Corti's face."

She held the phone out toward me. The list was massive and completely ridiculous.

"A few other messages talked about how you hooked up with them. You have quite the reputation around these parts."

"Being a manwhore to avoid dealing with my shit was somewhat my thing for a long time."

"That was until me."

I smiled. "Yeah. Until you. I honestly don't understand why the girls are writing that shit in the bathrooms. It wasn't like I was connecting on a deep level with them."

"What can I say? We, girls, tend to like emotionally unavailable men."

I snickered as I glanced closer at the list. "Is that an S.E. I see at the bottom of the list?"

Her cheeks rose, and she pulled her phone back from me. She shrugged. "I didn't want to feel left out."

The thought of her sitting on my face would remain on my mind for the remainder of the evening.

"Can I be inappropriate real fast?" I asked.

She laughed. "You can't be inappropriate real fast."

"But I want to be inappropriate real fast."

"Fine. You get ten seconds to be inappropriate real fast."

"I'll need fifteen seconds."

"Twelve seconds tops."

I narrowed my eyes. "Are you going to time me?"

She pulled up the timer on her cell phone. "And...go."

"Being in this library just makes me realize that I want to fuck you in the quietest places and make you scream so fucking loud." Her jaw dropped open as shock washed over her. No words left her, so I continued. "Oh, and I like your hair when you straighten it like that. It looks very yankable."

"Milo."

"Yes."

She grew flustered and combed her hair behind her ears. "Take out your freaking math book."

CHAPTER 20

Milo

The weekend came fast, and as I walked over to Tom's house, I was slightly anxious. I had avoided drinking since my last blackout situation at school. I also had a big exam in my math class on Monday, and I knew I had to study my ass off the following day to prepare for it.

If you had asked January Milo if he'd skip drinking and drugs so he could study, I would've laughed in your face. But there I was, trying to be a responsible adult. At the same time, I was trying to be a good friend, too. Tom had been good to me over the past year when I didn't even deserve his grace. The same went for Savannah. I was mentally absent from most people who called me their friend, but it was as if they knew I was struggling. They had every right to turn their backs on me, but instead, they stuck by my side. That meant more to me than they'd ever know.

"There was a bet going on that you weren't going to show today," Savannah said as I walked into the house. It was packed with people.

Some I knew, others I didn't, with a wide array of red Solo cups floating around.

I nodded her way. "You bet for me or against me?"

"Always bet for you, brother." She smiled and held her cup toward me.

I shook my head. "Not drinking tonight."

Her eyebrow shot up. "You always drink."

"Trying this new thing."

"And what's that?"

"Being sober."

She shivered. "That sounds awful."

Depends on the day.

"What Tom are you?" I asked her, glancing at her oversized outfit and backward baseball cap.

"I'm a tomboy, duh. What about you?"

I looked down at my outfit—a white T-shirt and black jeans. "Isn't it obvious? I'm Tom from Myspace." I glanced around the living room, then back at Savannah. "Where's the birthday boy?"

"He's in the kitchen, probably dancing on the countertop."

That sounded about right.

I started toward the kitchen but paused and turned back to Savannah. "Hey. Sorry for treating you like crap for the past few years. I wasn't in the best headspace."

She narrowed her eyes. "And you're doing better now?"

"Getting there."

"Good. We all missed you."

"I've been around."

"You've been around but not here. I see it again...the light in your eyes is back. Whoever she is, I'm glad you found her."

"What?"

She grinned and took a sip from her red Solo cup. "A guy doesn't heal like that without a badass girl in his corner." She narrowed her eyes. "Is it Ms. Evans? Tom is convinced it's Ms. Evans."

I shook my head. "It's not Ms. Evans."

"Then who is it?"

"Nobody."

"Liar."

"Maybe."

"You're not going to tell me?"

"Nope."

She studied me, debating how much more she should push for an answer, but then she gave up. "Just treat her well, will you? Like a princess."

I gave her a half grin before heading toward the kitchen to find the birthday boy. In all his glory, he was dancing on the countertop in a white button-down, white ankle socks, and a pair of white briefs. He was taking his Tom Cruise from *Risky Business* seriously.

The second he saw me, he cheered loudly. "Best friend!" he shouted, hopping off the countertop. I was surprised he didn't twist his damn ankle with that leap.

He shot over and hugged me tightly before slapping his hand against my chest. "Are you Tom from Myspace?"

I nodded. "I'm Tom from Myspace."

"Hell yeah, you are." Tom looked around and held his arms out. "Hey, everyone, Tom from Myspace is here!"

Everyone cheered for me as if I didn't just toss on a white T-shirt and call it a day. I was the laziest costume in sight, but they all seemed amused. That was the power of alcohol. It made the most mediocre individuals seem like Superman.

"Let me get you a drink," Tom said, patting me on the back.

"Oh. I wasn't going to drink tonight."

His eyes widened as if I'd confessed that I hated puppies. "What do you mean you're not drinking tonight?!"

"That's exactly what I mean."

"Are you pregnant?"

I smirked at the drunkard and patted my stomach. "Expecting in six months."

Tom turned toward the crowd. "Hey, everyone! Tom from Myspace is pregnant!"

Everyone once again cheered.

Idiots.

"You have to at least take a birthday shot with me," he urged, nudging me.

"I've got a math exam on Monday. I can't get messed up this weekend."

"Uh, news flash, we all have a math exam on Monday, but your best friend only turns eighteen once."

"I'm surprised you're not spending the day with your parents."

"Yeah, well, some parents don't give a shit about their kids." He said it effortlessly and with a smile, but I saw the twitch behind his grin. What the hell was that? Was perfect, bubbly Tom not as happy as he played himself up to be? Did we maybe have something in common? Parental issues?

"But you know who does give a shit about me?" he asked.

"Who's that?"

"Jose." He held a bottle of Jose Cuervo tequila and waved it toward me. "Jose has never let me down, unlike my parents. So let's take a shot to celebrate!"

I wanted to argue with him, but from the split second of truth that slipped out of Tom, I felt guilty for his disappointment in his parents. I didn't want to add another wave of disappointment, so I allowed peer pressure to pull me in.

I took the shot glass from him and patted him on the back. "Bottoms up."

Before I knew it, the shots were flowing and studying for my exam in the morning seemed less likely.

* * *

I WASN'T HAVING a shitty time.

I was having a damn good time with everyone. I found myself laughing more than I normally did, and even though I was drunk, it didn't feel like a depressed kind of drunkenness. I simply felt...good.

People conversed with me as if I were the person I'd once been before Mom passed away. I was talking back, asking how they'd been, too, and I wanted their answers.

What was going on?

The buzz felt good, and Tom had already told me I was crashing here for the night, which was fine. I didn't want to take my drunk ass home to see my dad's drunk ass, which would remind me that my home life was still shit.

I walked up to Brian, who was talking to Chris about video games, and Chris was doing what he did best—listening. I joined the two on the couch in the living room, and they welcomed me into the conversation as if I'd been there the whole time. Chris patted me on the back and gave me a half grin.

I glanced at their costumes. Chris had cat ears on and a collar. "Tom from *Tom and Jerry?*" He nodded and puffed out his chest with a big smirk, proud that he was recognized. I looked over at Brian, who dressed as a train. "And Tom the Tank Engine?"

"Choo-choo, motherfucker!"

The three of us hung out for a while, discussing everything. It felt like the first time we'd sat and engaged in over a year. Or at least, it was the first time I was engaged. Even without many words, Chris interacted more than I'd been over the past year.

"It's good to have you back around," Brian mentioned when we went to get more drinks.

"What do you mean? I've been around every weekend."

"Yeah. You've been there, but not really." He patted my chest. "It's good to have you back," he repeated.

I smiled, knowing what he meant.

He brushed his thumb against his nose before patting down his big Afro. "Maybe someday you can stop by and play games with us guys again like we used to. Tom is an awful gamer, so it would be nice to have some real competition."

"I'd like that," I told him. I meant it, too.

Around one in the morning, the party was still going on, yet I was ready to check out. I knew it was time to head to the guest room I was staying in because all I could think about was Starlet. My drunken mind belonged to her, but that wasn't very different from my sober mind.

After one last shot with the birthday boy, I headed to the guest room and shut the door behind me. Before climbing onto the bed, I removed my shoes, T-shirt, and jeans. I pulled out my cell phone and called her when I got comfortable.

I shouldn't have called her, but I did. I needed to hear her voice. I always wanted to hear her voice. Who was I lately?

"Hello?"

Her voice was soft, as if she were waking up. That wasn't shocking. It was after midnight.

"Hey, Star."

"Hey. Are you okay?" she asked, yawning through the phone.

I smiled as I lay on the bed because she asked if I was okay. "Yeah, I'm good. How are you?"

"Sleepy." She yawned again. "Are you intoxicated?"

"I might be intoxicated."

"Happy intoxicated or sad intoxicated?"

"Happy."

"Mmm. Good. Happy is good."

I turned onto my back and stared at the ceiling. "Star?"

"Yeah?"

"I miss you."

"I miss you, too." She paused for a minute and asked, "Are you alone right now?"

"Yeah. I'm crashing at Tom's. It was his eighteenth birthday party tonight."

"Happy birthday to Tom. Don't tell him I said that, though."

I laughed. "I'll keep it between us. It was a costume party. We were supposed to dress up as different Toms."

"Who were you?"

"Tom from Myspace."

"That's very vintage of you. And somewhat lazy."

"What can I say? I'm a lazy dude." I cleared my throat. "Hey?"

"Yes?"

"I miss you."

She chuckled lightly. "You said that already."

"I know, but it's true. I miss your eyes. And your lips. And your curves and—"

"You're horny." She cut in.

"Only for you. Is your roommate home?"

"No. It seems everyone has a social life except for me."

"I can come over and be social with you."

I listened to her turning in her bed, and I could almost see her bashful smile in my mind. "No, you can't. You're drunk. Besides, you coming to my dorm room is strictly off-limits. It goes against the secret friends rule."

"I don't think that was a rule."

"It is now."

"So we can add rules whenever?"

"Only when they are needed to remind you why you can't come to crawl into my bed in the middle of the night."

I groaned. "But I want to crawl into your bed in the middle of the night."

"Two and a half more months."

"That sounds like forever."

"And some change."

"Star?"

"Yes?"

"I had fun tonight."

"That's good. I'm glad."

"I didn't know I could still have fun until I found you."

"Oh, Milo..." Her soft breaths were heard through the cell phone. "Be careful, or you'll make me fall in love with you."

If only she knew how much I wanted that to happen.

"Say something to make the butterflies go away," she ordered. "Say something to make me roll my eyes."

"What are you wearing?"

She burst into laughter. "That will do it for me."

I smirked because I could envision her smile. Then curiosity hit me. "No, really, what are you wearing?"

"Drunk Milo is so inappropriate."

"Every Milo is inappropriate," I told her. "Now would be a great time to practice that phone sex, huh?"

"That's true." Her voice lowered slightly, and then she said, "A tank top and black panties."

Just hearing the word panties fall from her beautiful mouth made my cock brick up. "Yeah? Are you wearing a bra?"

"No. Just the tank top."

I shut my eyes, envisioning her hardened nipples through the fabric of the tank top.

"I wish I was there lying with you," I told her.

"And what would you do to me?"

"Everything, Star." I slid my hand into my boxers and gripped my cock. "I'd do everything to you."

"Tell me exactly what you'd do. In detail, please."

My hand slowly stroked my cock as my thoughts became more inappropriate. "Before I tell you, you need to slip your hand into your panties and start rubbing yourself, Star."

"What makes you think I'm not?" she replied breathlessly.

That image alone made my cock throb as I quickened my hand movement. I bit my bottom lip before continuing. "I pin you down on your bed and lower myself to your neck, leaving a trail of kisses against your soft skin, allowing my tongue to create small circles before I begin sucking."

"My mouth parts as I whisper for more and beg you to let me taste you first."

Fuck...

"By all means," I replied. "Taste."

"I roll from beneath you and lay you on your back. I remove your shirt and trail my hands down your chest until they meet the top of your boxers. I shimmy myself down so I'm resting between your legs. Then I pull your boxers down your legs, revealing your massive, hard cock. I lick my plump lips as I stare at your thickness, wanting you to fuck my mouth until I gag against you. So I wrap my hand around your cock and begin stroking, up and down...up and down...locking my eyes with yours the whole time I start working you..."

Did sweet Starlet just whisper the word cock on the phone to me?

Did she say she wanted me to fuck her mouth until she gagged?

Well, I'll be damned. Was I drunk, or was she? I'd have to tame myself from getting off too soon solely from the softness of her voice saying dirty things.

I pushed the comforter to the side of the bed, already getting too warm from her words.

"Then what?" I asked.

"Then I lower myself and let my tongue glide up and down your dick while my hand continues to stroke it. I take the tip of your hardness into my mouth and begin sucking it, swirling my tongue around it as if sucking against my favorite lollipop. I go slowly, infusing every inch of you against me while my hand massages and squeezes your balls. My speed picks up as I begin deep-throating your cock, sliding my mouth deeper and deeper with every inch as you gather my wild hair in your hands and take control of guiding me up and down your thick, hard cock, allowing it to choke me, making me gag on how massive you are."

"Shit, Star...you're going to make me..." I murmured, unable to form more words as I licked the palm of my hand and went back to stroking. "Keep going..."

"I place a hand against your lower stomach, pressing gently as my mouth takes all of you in, leaving little room for me to take a breath, but I don't care because I want all of you, Milo. I want you to fill every hole I have, fucking me nice and slow, then nice and hard. Harder and harder as you grow closer and closer to—"

Before she could finish, the bedroom door opened, and in walked Tom. "Hey, man. Everyone's gone. I wanted to see if you wanted to play some video games or—holy shit! Dick! Dick!" he hollered as he saw me lying there with my cock in my hand.

"Oh shit!" I shouted back before saying, "Gotta go."

I dropped my hand from my cock and hung up on Starlet.

Tom instantly shot out of the room, slamming the door behind him. There was nothing but silence for a beat until he said, "Don't worry, Mi-Mi. I didn't see anything. Except, well, everything. That's going to cause nightmares tonight."

"My bad," I pushed out, uncertain what else to say. What were you supposed to say besides "my bad" after your friend caught you jerking off?

"We should probably never talk about this again, huh?" he asked.

"Yeah. I agree. Never again."

"Cool. Okay. Night."

I collapsed against the mattress. My body felt thrown off by the complete transition from almost getting off from Starlet's seductive voice to then having Tom burst in, taking away any desire and causing a flurry of panic. It took my heart a minute to settle down, and when it did, I was left with just a pool of disappointment because Starlet would've easily brought me to completion with her voice alone.

Starlet: Everything okay?

Milo: Yeah. Tom just burst in. Kind of ruined the moment, huh?

Starlet: Haha. Only a little. It's fine. I should be sleeping, anyway.

Damn.

Milo: Talk tomorrow?

Starlet: Of course. Good night.

I sighed and covered my face with a pillow to shout out all my frustrations.

Good night, Teach.

CHAPTER 21

Milo

"Who were you having phone sex with on Saturday?" Tom asked right away on Monday morning as we walked to our lockers.

I gave him a harsh, stern glare. "I thought we were never talking about that again."

"Yeah, but if we were going to talk about it again... Who was on the other line?"

"I'm not doing this," I told him as I approached my locker. I opened it and gathered my books as Tom leaned against the locker beside me.

"Is it one of the twins?" he questioned. "Or Claire? I heard she had the hots for you. Then again, who doesn't have the hots for Milo Corti? The man, the myth, the legend."

"It's not the twins or Claire," I grumbled.

"So it *is* someone. Who? Is it a junior? You dog, I bet it's a junior."

"It's nobody," I said, shutting my locker.

He pushed himself from the locker and slammed his hands to his chest. "It's not my mom, is it? 'Cause if you're screwing my mom, Mi-Mi, we might have some friendship issues."

I let a small laugh slip out and shook my head. "You have too much energy for a Monday morning."

"Not as much energy as you had Saturday night. By the way... Do you eat a lot of protein or something? Spinach? What's your workout routine? Because that was quite the—"

I shot my stare at Tom. "T?"

"Yes?"

"We aren't talking about the size of my dick at seven in the morning on a Monday."

He tossed his hands up in surrender. "Okay. Fair, fair. I'll ask you about it on a Thursday afternoon if that's better for you. I tend to like to talk about my dick closer to the weekend, too."

"Or we could never talk about it. Ever."

"Yeah, or never. That's cool. All I'm saying is I understand why the girls always talk about you. If I had what you had, I'd be a manwhore, too."

"I'm not a manwhore anymore."

Tom got a goofy smile on his face. "Because of her?"

I rolled my eyes and walked off to the principal's office to see Weston for our morning meeting. I didn't reply to Tom, but I knew the answer.

Yes, Tom.

It was because of her.

*   *   *

I SAT across from Weston's desk, slumped in a much comfier chair than before. The space looked renewed, with new furniture and sparkling hardwood floors. There was even an air freshener spitting out a scent every thirty seconds, taking away from Weston's protein smells.

Not so bad, Unc.

"How are you doing today, Milo?" he asked me as he removed his glasses. He leaned back in his chair and smiled brightly.

"I've been worse."

"That's true. I've checked in with all your teachers. It seems you're passing all your classes, which is remarkable. Having Ms. Evans as your tutor seems to work in your favor."

"She's good at what she does."

He raised an eyebrow. "Did you just compliment a person? I haven't heard you do that in a long time."

"What can I say? I'm a nice guy," I dryly replied. I was tired. I stayed up way too late studying for the damn math exam I had later that day.

Weston smiled Mom's smile, and I felt it in my chest. Lately, I have been doing okay. I didn't think about death as much as I thought about the living, and a part of me felt guilty about that. I wouldn't say I was recovering from Mom's tragedy, but the grief grew quieter. Was that what grief was supposed to do? Or was it supposed to stay at the forefront of my mind to remind me how much I loved the person who'd left?

Shit.

I was thinking about death again.

"She'd be proud of you," Weston stated. I guessed he was thinking about the dead, too.

I shrugged, not certain what to say.

"How's your dad?" he asked me. "I stopped by with my spare key and stocked up your fridge the other day. He wasn't home."

And there I was, thinking my father had finally made it to the grocery store. How sweet and naive of me.

"How is he?" Weston repeated.

That was a weighted question. I knew if I told him the truth, Weston would worry. I knew Weston would know I was lying if I told him a lie—a lose-lose situation. So I went with the truth.

"He's worse than me," I confessed. "And I don't think he's getting any better."

Weston rubbed the back of his neck. "Healing doesn't have a timeline."

"So what? He might stay like this forever?"

"I hope not. I truly hope not. But maybe he just needs something that might shake him out of his depression."

"It doesn't help that he's self-medicating with booze."

"No, that doesn't. I'll try to catch him sometime this week. I'll stop by and see how I can help."

I nodded as the bell rang overhead. I grabbed my backpack and slung it onto my shoulder. "Your office looks good. I like the brighter lights."

"Right? The past few weeks, it looked pretty awful during the construction phase. Maybe that's the thing about progress. Maybe it has to look messy for a while before it can look good again."

I rolled my eyes. "Okay, Fred Rogers, slow down. No need for the '90s sitcom heart-to-heart speech."

He laughed and stood from his desk. "Give your dad some grace, okay? If I lost my other half, I would forget how to breathe, too. Maybe he needs his son to help remind him that there's still fresh air to take in."

"It's bullshit," I muttered, feeling a tug of annoyance. "He wasn't there to help me when I was drowning."

"Grief doesn't care about the age of a person. It hits them all differently. I'm not here to back your father up for how he's been handling things. He should've been there for you over the past year more than he had been. But then I think about the shit he's been through—shit we'd never understand. He was in the military and lost some of his best friends. He was overseas when his parents passed away. He lost the love of his life. That's a lot of loss on one person's soul, and it doesn't get easier. It just gets heavier."

I hated Weston's words because I knew they were true. I wanted to resent my father for his grief. I wanted to yell, scream, and shout at how selfish he'd been. But then, sometimes, I'd think back to hearing him sob on the anniversary of Mom's passing. I'd sometimes see the hurt when he'd choke on his words. His whole body moved as if grief controlled his limbs.

It was clear that our griefs weren't equally yoked.

I'd lost my mother.

He'd lost his very best friend, the other half of his soul.

That kind of break was the kind that didn't come with healing.

Maybe showing him grace was the right thing to do. Yet still, it was hard because I wanted him to be there for me when I was drowning, too. That was the issue with life. It never worked in perfect scenarios. If it had, Mom would still be alive.

I brushed my hand on my neck and nodded toward Weston. "I need a late pass for class."

He agreed and scribbled a note for me. "Here you go. And, Milo?"

"Yeah?"

"I'm proud of you."

I smiled slightly.

His words reminded me of Mom's.

* * *

MY DAYS WERE MOSTLY WRAPPED around getting to English class to see Starlet. She was the highlight of my days. A few months ago, I didn't know she existed. Now, I couldn't imagine her not being around.

Sitting in class, listening to boring Mr. Slade and staring at the beautiful Ms. Evans, I felt an odd sense of peace. Starlet and I had a secret that no one in class could know about, making me feel damn good. The only issue was I couldn't stop wondering when my mouth would be allowed to find its way to hers again.

"Take out a pencil, everyone. Time for a pop quiz," Mr. Slade stated. The classroom groaned. I didn't feel as worried about it. I was officially up to date on knowing my shit.

"Need a pencil?" Savannah asked.

I shook my head and held one in the air. Right at that moment, panic washed over me as everything went black. I gripped my desk's sides as adrenaline rushed through my system. When I say everything went black, I mean everything.

"Shit!" I shouted, going to stand from my desk but tripping over my feet. I rubbed the palms of my hands against my eyes, yet there was nothing there. I could hear everyone around me panicking, too. Savannah's voice echoed in my ears, along with Mr. Slade's and Starlet's.

Starlet.

I couldn't see her.

I couldn't see anyone.

I couldn't see.

I can't see, I can't see, I can't see—

"Mr. Corti, stand up at once," Mr. Slade ordered.

I blinked a few times as my chest tightened, and it returned. It was faint at first, but the more I blinked, the more vision returned to me. There those brown eyes were, standing over me with a look of nothing but straight panic. Starlet held out her hand to help me stand.

"Quite a way to try to get out of a pop quiz, Mr. Corti," Mr. Slade rudely stated. He returned to passing out the exams, and Starlet kept her eyes on me.

"Are you okay?" she asked, concern soaked in every inch of her expression.

I didn't answer because I didn't know.

* * *

"WHAT WAS THAT?" Starlet asked, leaping up from her chair as I walked into the library later that afternoon.

She rushed over to comfort me but stopped the second another person walked past the glass panels of our study room. I hated that she had to have that hesitation. I hated that I couldn't wrap her in my arms and hold her.

"Nothing. Everything just went dark for a short period," I explained, taking my seat. "I got the pictures from up north developed and—"

"What do you mean everything went dark?" she questioned, alert and concerned. She took a seat across from me and didn't tear her eyes away from me. I didn't know why I expected anything else from her. I did fall out of my damn desk and have a full-blown panic attack in front of the whole classroom.

"I don't know. That's exactly what I mean. Everything went black. I couldn't see for a while. It's fine now. Everything's fine."

"It's not fine," she disagreed. "You were having trouble seeing when we were up north, too. And I noticed you squinting a lot. You need to get your eyes checked out."

I laughed. "Don't worry about me, Teach. I'm fine."

She reached a hand across the table and placed it on my forearm. "Please, Milo."

The concern in her voice made my chest tighten slightly. "You want me in glasses that bad, huh?"

"It could be something serious."

"It's not anything serious."

"But it could be—"

"Okay," I said, tossing my hands up in the air. "I'll get an eye exam if that makes you sleep better at night."

She nodded. "It will. Thank you."

"Now, can we stop being serious, and can I show you the photographs?"

She sat back in her chair, removing her hand from my forearm. I missed her touch before it fully disappeared from my skin. "Yes, I'd love to see them," she said, combing her hair behind her ears. She did that when she was nervous. She was probably still working through her worry about me, but I'd be fine.

I was always fine—even when I wasn't.

"Star."

"Yes?"

"I'm okay."

"Promise me you'll go?" Her gentle brown eyes stared into me, into my soul, and that was when it happened. They say one couldn't pinpoint the exact moment when they began to fall in love, but I could. It was in the study room at the public library on a cold winter afternoon. I was falling in love with Starlet Evans and knew I could not stop it.

No, it wasn't because of her concern for me that I was falling in love with her. It was her concern with…everything and everyone. I knew I wasn't special when it came to Starlet's gentleness. I'd watched her interact with a few of the other students. I'd watched her extend her time and energy to help whenever others approached her. Starlet was the definition of love, and I was falling into her with every passing second.

When I looked at her, I was filled with light. That was what she did to others. She added light to the darkest corners of their spirit.

I wanted to tell her, but I knew it was too soon.

But it was there.

The love had begun, and I knew it would only keep growing as time passed.

Starlet was the kind of girl where love only grew stronger over time.

"I promise," I told her. "I promise on my mother's heart."

Her lips pursed up, and those doe eyes blinked a few times before she nodded. Her shoulders relaxed as a tiny smile found her lips. "Let me see the photographs."

CHAPTER 22

Milo

*M*y father had been drunk for the past few weeks, but that was nothing new. He didn't even question where I'd been the weekend I'd run off with Starlet. Most of the time, it felt like he was a ghost, more than my mother had been. He'd sometimes walk past me to the kitchen to grab another beer, haunting me with his slight presence.

The bills on the countertop stacked up more and more each day. For a while, I figured he was still going to work and just doing a shitty job at his job, but the more time passed, it became clear that he wasn't in any position to show up to a nine-to-five position.

He was officially losing himself in his depression and alcoholism, and I wasn't sure what his story's next step or phase would be. Some nights, I worried about walking into the house and finding him dead in a puddle of his own piss and beer. I hated those thoughts because I wasn't sure if my heart could take another break like that. It felt selfish to think those kinds of things, but even though we weren't currently close, I had more good memories with my father than bad.

He was the man who taught me how to ride a bike.

He was the person who showed me how to drive a stick.

He taught me to play the saxophone and introduced me to jazz.

He told me he was proud of me every night until Mom died.

Before the tragedy, my father was my hero. The man I looked up to at all times. He was my family's protector, and I was almost certain that he could pull us out of the darkness if anything ever went wrong. And if I lost him...if he lost the battle of depression and lost his life...I was almost certain I'd lose the last small bits of me, too.

When I arrived home that night, he was awake on the couch, eating a burnt pizza and watching the news.

I dropped my backpack on the recliner in the living room and nodded his way. "Hey."

He grumbled a little and gave me a nod back.

"I need my insurance card," I told him. "I have to set up an eye appointment."

"Yeah, okay." He scratched at his messy hair before scratching his beer gut. "I'll get it for you."

"Do you know what eye doctors are covered? I'll call and set up an appointment."

He narrowed his eyes in thought and shook his head. "No. Your mother normally..." It happened again—his words getting tangled up in his grief. "I'll find the card and figure that out," he said.

"Thanks."

I stood there for a minute, staring at a man who hardly resembled my father, and for the first time in a long time, I didn't hate him...I felt bad for him. It was clear that life had raked him over hot coals, and he was barely breathing.

Maybe I'd expected too much from him.

Maybe I'd thought he was stronger than he'd actually been because, for my whole life, I'd always looked up to him.

Yet at the end of the day, our parents were human, too. Their hearts had probably been through a lot more trauma than our own.

I didn't know what it would be like for me if I'd lost the love of my life.

I didn't know how I'd be able to recover.

So that night, I gave him a break. I didn't push for him to be the father I once knew. I didn't tell him how shitty he'd been doing in his parenting role. Instead, I went online and began searching for after-school jobs so I could maybe help him keep up with the bills.

"He'll be okay," I muttered in my room after applying to fifteen different locations. "Just make sure he's okay, Mom," I begged.

I didn't know if I believed in God, but I did believe in my mother. So if I prayed, they'd be sent straight to her. If anyone could've answered my tainted prayers, I knew she could.

* * *

ONE MOMENT.

One situation.

One sentence.

That was all it took for a person's world to turn on its head.

A few weeks later, I was able to set up an appointment to get my vision checked out. I wished it were getting better over the past few weeks, but it hadn't improved in the slightest. At least I had no more blackout moments in Mr. Slade's class. I didn't want to hear more shit from him about how I was faking my sight being screwed up.

"So you've had a few eye issues?" the optician asked me as I sat in front of a table with a machine that was going to blow a puff of air into my eyeballs.

"Yeah. I was looking into glasses."

"Wonderful. You came to the right place. We're just going to run a few tests for you, and then we can have you out on your way."

I'd never been to a doctor's appointment of any kind on my own. Mom always dragged me to them, and Dad wasn't in the best shape to attend an appointment with me. I was still somewhat shocked he was able to find the insurance card for me to use.

The tests were painless. I was certain I'd want contacts over glasses, but they still had me look around at different frames. As I was doing so, I couldn't help but wonder which frames Starlet would like on me. When did I become the asshole who cared what a person thought about his appearance? Shit was getting weird lately when it came to my feelings for Starlet.

Even though we hadn't been able to touch one another, kiss, or do all the things I'd daydreamed about doing with her, I still felt as if our connection was growing more and more. Never in my life did I want to be with another person. We didn't have to do anything at all. Being in the same space as her seemed to be enough to calm the loudest parts of my mind.

"Milo?" the optician called after going over all the tests. "You can come back with me to finish up."

I followed her into one of the exam rooms. She smiled at me, but it felt like a sad smile. The kind of smiles people offered when they were giving condolences.

"How blind am I?" I joked as I took a seat across from her desk.

Her smile fell to a frown.

My gut dropped.

She cleared her throat and turned her computer to face me. "Do you see this photograph? This is what it should look like versus this image." She switched the photo. "Which is yours."

The difference between the images was shocking. I didn't know what it meant, but from her reaction, I knew it wasn't good.

"So how strong a pair of glasses do I need?" I asked her.

Her frown deepened as she clasped her hands together. "Milo, I believe this is a condition called retinitis pigmentosa. It's a rare eye disease that—"

"Eye disease?" I cut in. "What do you mean, eye disease?"

She paused before picking up a pencil and scribbling down some information. "More tests are needed to rule out retinitis pigmentosa, but we are not able to perform them here. Here is a name of a remarkable ophthalmologist. They will be able to run the proper testing such as electroretinography tests, fundus autofluorescence tests, and a variety of others."

She kept talking, but my brain shut down.

Her mouth was moving, and words were coming out, but I couldn't process what was being said to me. The words eye disease were the only things playing on a loop in my mind. I couldn't process what it meant or how to handle that situation on my own.

I should've been asking follow-up questions, but Mom always did that. I should've called Dad, but he wouldn't have answered.

"Am I going blind?" I blurted out as I choked on the words.

Her sad smile returned, but she didn't answer my question. "You'll meet with the ophthalmologist and will be able to get more answers. You'll need someone to drive you to the appointment when you go in since your eyes will be dilated after the tests."

She said some more bullshit, but I was officially checked out.

It was only midday, and I could've driven back to school to finish the afternoon, but my dad called me out for the rest of the day for the appointment. I did text Starlet and told her I'd meet her for our session in the library that afternoon.

I showed up at the study room three hours before she'd arrived. I sat there on my phone, researching retinitis pigmentosa on the internet. The more I searched, the scarier it became. The early symptoms were all things I'd experienced throughout the past few years. Night vision issues. Peripheral vision issues. Temporary blackouts.

The later-stage symptoms were what terrified me the most, though. Loss of vision. Blindness.

I felt sick to my stomach. I wanted to scream, yell, and cuss at the God I didn't believe in. Instead, I sat in the quiet study room of the quiet library and stared at the words on my phone. With each second that passed, I became increasingly numb to the reality set out in front of me.

Blind...

I was going blind.

One moment.

One situation.

One sentence.

That was all it took for a person's world to turn on its head.

CHAPTER 23

Starlet

"You are never here before me. I guess you need to miss out on school more often than not to have you show up on time, huh?" I joked as I walked into the study room to find Milo sitting there. He smiled up at me, but it felt off. The smile didn't eliminate the bleakness in his eyes. Something was troubling him.

That was the thing about falling for a person—you noticed every tiny detail about them. Which meant you could tell when something was off.

"What's wrong?" I asked, setting my bag down.

"Nothing. Just tired, that's all."

"How did the eye appointment go?"

"It was fine," he said with a tiny smile. "How are you?"

I narrowed my eyes. "How are you?"

He laughed, but it wasn't his normal laughter. The sound made me uneasy. "You can't answer a question with a question."

"Sure I can." I took a seat. "Are you happy today?"

His words told me yes, but his smile told me no. Yet, if I'd learned anything about Milo, it was not to push him when he wasn't ready to open up.

"I already finished all my homework for the week," he told me. "I could've told you that via text, but I just kind of wanted to see you."

Butterflies.

A flurry of freaking butterflies.

"Oh. Okay. Well, what are we going to do for the next hour or so?"

"This is going to sound stupid, but..." He leaned forward and clasped his hands together. "Can we just stare at one another for a little while?"

"Milo. What's wrong?"

"Nothing. Everything's fine."

"You're lying."

"I'm lying."

"Tell me what's wrong."

His voice cracked, and he cleared his throat. His eyes grew glassy and became packed with emotions. "Star," he whispered.

"Yes?"

His lips parted, but he hesitated. His brows lowered, and I swore a flash of sadness crossed his stare, but it disappeared so quickly that I wasn't even sure it really occurred.

"What is it?" I questioned.

"I think I'm going blind."

I froze in place for a few moments before speaking. "What did you just say?"

"I think I'm going blind."

He said the same words again, and still, they didn't register.

"I'm sorry, what?" I asked once more.

"I'm going—"

"No, you're not." I cut in.

My voice cracked.

My heart did, too.

Milo grimaced and studied his fidgeting fingers before looking back up at me. "It's called retinitis pigmentosa. I learned about it at the eye appointment. I have to go to a specialist to get it officially diagnosed, but I'm certain that's what it is. And over time, my vision will only get worse."

"So it's not for certain? It's not a guaranteed thing?"

He smiled, but it wasn't a happy grin. It was the saddest smile I'd ever seen. "It's okay, Star."

"No, it's not," I sternly stated.

"Yes, it is," he calmly replied.

I choked out laughter that was soaked in pain. "Shut up, Milo."

"Star—"

"No!" I cried out. "You're fine. You said the eye appointment was fine when you showed up today. You said that! That's what you said."

"Don't cry."

"I'm not."

"You are."

Oh.

How was I not supposed to cry, though? How was I supposed to stay strong when he was telling me the most heartbreaking news I'd ever heard? How was I supposed to be okay?

"Secret friend, new rule," he requested. "No crying when you learn Milo is going blind."

"You can't play the secret friend card on me."

"Yes, I can because I can't handle seeing you cry without me wanting to fall apart, and I can't fall apart. Not today, at least. Please."

I wiped my eyes and worked the best I could to pull myself together. Because once a secret friend rule was created, one was forced to do what was requested of them—even when it was hard.

I sighed. "How many doctors do you have to see about it?"

"Only one more."

"You should see more. You should get multiple opinions."

His smile? Still broken. "One will be enough," he swore.

"But—"

"It will be enough, Star."

I stepped toward him, shaking my head in disbelief. "What did your dad say?"

"He doesn't know. No one does. Only you."

"Milo...you have to tell him. You can't go through this alone."

"I'm not going through it alone anymore. I told you."

I wanted to argue with him. I wanted to tell him how selfish it was to keep this to himself, to keep it between the two of us. But I couldn't fight him because all I wanted to do was be there for him.

I sniffled. "How can I help?"

His eyes flashed with emotions, and he cleared his throat a few times before blinking his eyes repeatedly. When his stare met mine, the smile on his face didn't seem so broken anymore. It seemed gentle and safe.

"Can you sit for another minute and let me stare at you?" he asked. "I want to stare at the most important things in my life a little more often lately. Just for ten minutes or so."

My Milo...my favorite secret friend.

I pulled my chair to his side of the table, placing it directly in front of him, and took a seat. With shaky hands, I smoothed out my outfit, cleared my throat, and then locked my eyes with his. His beautiful deep brownish-green eyes.

We didn't say anything as we locked eyes with one another.

Words weren't needed because all he requested was to see me for ten minutes.

Ten minutes later, we sat still.

I wanted to cry.

I didn't cry.

I wanted to scream.

I didn't even whisper.

My hand reached out toward him, and he took it. We held hands for another ten or so minutes. I saw a slight tremble in the corner of his mouth, but he cleared his throat and pushed away his nerves. I wished I could crawl into his head and read his lonely thoughts. I wished I could lose my sight instead of him losing his.

It didn't seem fair. It didn't seem right.

He was getting better.

He was learning how to breathe again.

How dare the world try to make him drown once more?

After we finished our time in the library, I offered him a ride home, seeing how he couldn't drive at night. He turned down the offer and said he could use the fresh air.

"Plus, how would that look, Teach?" he whispered, sliding his hands into his pockets. "What if someone saw us driving together?"

He was right.

I hated that he was right.

His lips turned into a tiny smile. "Don't be sad, Star."

I laughed, shaking my head as I stood in front of my car. "Don't comfort me when I'm supposed to be comforting you."

"You are comforting me."

"How?"

"Just by existing."

He took one step toward me. Probably too close, yet I didn't step away. The feelings I had for that man only intensified as he grew closer, and I wanted to feel it all. He was like a crashing wave in the middle of a desert. Refreshing and forbidden.

His mouth parted as his hand slightly brushed against mine. His voice dropped an octave as he said, "One day, I'm going to love you out loud, and it will be the best day of my life."

"Milo…"

"I promise, Starlet. I promise."

And that was exactly when my love for Milo Corti began.

After he left, I climbed into my car and sat there for a while, not turning it on. I fell apart for him, crying into the palms of my hands, not understanding why life had to be this way.

I drove home and researched retinitis pigmentosa for the remainder of the night.

I couldn't sleep. My mind ran a million miles an hour. I couldn't even imagine what Milo's thoughts were doing to him.

Around two in the morning, I sent him a text.

Starlet: Okay?

I hoped he was sleeping, but within seconds, I received a message back.

Milo: Okay.

Milo: Go to bed, Teach.

I sighed.

Okay.

CHAPTER 24

Milo

$\mathcal{I}$ wondered what it looked like for others—the world. What did they see that my eyes missed out on? I wondered if I ever saw the world as it was actually supposed to be seen. I never knew I had an issue, which was probably part of the problem. I just assumed everyone saw everything through the same lens as I did.

What did their blues look like? And their greens? How far beside them could they witness? What were their perspectives on life, and how had I gone so long without knowing I was different?

Lately, I felt as if I looked at everything from a new viewpoint. I studied things longer; animals, people, and plants. I zoomed in on objects more than I ever had before. Once you learned you might lose your vision forever, you looked at life through a different set of eyes— cliché as it sounded. The issue was that I wasn't certain that what I was seeing was what I was supposed to be seeing.

I also went through a box of photographs that sat in the back of my closet. They were a collection of pictures of my parents and me. I went through them over the past year every now and again whenever I felt that missing Mom was too strong. Something about seeing her in photos and witnessing her smile was enough to get me through some of the hardest days.

The idea that I wouldn't have that source of connection with her one day terrified me. I didn't want to forget her smile. Her eyes. *Her*. I was terrified of forgetting her.

When it was time for the next appointment for my eye exam, I somehow managed to get Dad to drive me to the doctor's appointment, where he waited in the lobby for me to finish. When I walked into the office space, I felt nauseous. It was as if I'd already known what was coming, yet I was still terrified to hear the words leave the doctor's mouth.

Everything felt as if it were moving in both slow motion and rapid speed. I couldn't get a grip on the situation, and my eyes were tired of being dilated and examined repeatedly.

I kept blinking, trying to shake off the odd sensation taking place.

Then for a while, I was left alone in the exam room.

I sat there, feeling an achingly loud sense of loneliness. I knew when the doctor returned, he'd have the results for me. I wasn't certain I was ready to hear the diagnosis.

He walked back in with a smile that told me everything I needed to know. "Okay," he stated. "The results are back...but first, do you have a family member in the lobby who you'd like to bring in so they hear all the information with you?"

That was his nice way of saying, "You're going blind, so you might need a support system."

"My dad's out there," I mentioned.

He nodded. "If you'd like, you can go get him and bring him back with you."

I felt idiotic for wanting my father to come into that exam room with me. I was grown enough that I should've been able to handle it on my own, but such a big part of me wanted his support.

I wished it were Mom, though. I wondered if I'd ever stop wishing it were Mom.

Without much more thought, I pushed myself up from my chair and headed out to the lobby to find my father. As I glanced around, I noticed he was no longer sitting there waiting for me.

I checked the bathrooms for him, but they were all empty. I shot him a text message but received no reply. I went outside to see if he'd perhaps taken a cigarette break, yet my stomach tightened up when I looked across the parking lot and realized his car was gone.

Before walking back to the office, I pulled out my cell phone and opened my contacts. My finger hovered over Starlet's name for a moment. She was who I wanted at that time. She was who I needed. But she was strictly off-limits for her own good. If I called, she'd show up. I had no questions or doubts about that. Yet I couldn't screw up her world solely because my own was a mess. I'd never add harm to her life if I could avoid it. Still, I wished she was there with me. She was good at making the bad things hurt a little less.

I put my phone away and headed back into the doctor's office, feeling like a complete moron, and resumed my seat. I cleared my throat. "Sorry. Something came up, and he had to leave."

Embarrassment wasn't enough to express how I'd felt.

I felt alone.

I was alone.

And I was on the verge of losing my vision.

* * *

MY FATHER never came back to pick me up. I ended up using an app to order a ride home, and when I got there, Dad was nowhere to be found yet again. I spent hours raging about the fact that the asshole couldn't even manage to be a parent for more than fifteen minutes. When I needed him the most, he couldn't even be bothered to stay.

My rage only built as time passed because for some reason, it was easier for me to be pissed at my father than to deal with the reality of my situation.

I hated him.

I knew I should've given him the benefit of the doubt as Weston told me, but I couldn't muscle up the fuck to give.

Screw him for not being there for me.

The wrong parent died.

That was one of the darkest thoughts to cross my mind, and I felt like an asshole for even thinking about it. But I had. I felt even worse because I believed it. What kind of monster did that make me? What did that say about my character?

When Dad stumbled into the house around seven that night, he was wasted out of his mind. I felt a certain rage build up inside me, looking at the shape he was in. How selfish of him to get behind the wheel like that. It was as if he had no care in the world for the other people on the road. For how his driving could've caused another to lose their life.

That was how Starlet lost her mother. A person got behind the wheel, thinking they were fine, and clearly, they weren't. People like my father were the reason people like Starlet didn't have their loved ones anymore.

He dropped his keys seconds later and scratched at his wild beard. When he looked up, his eyes were bloodshot. He looked like the walking dead.

"You left me," I muttered. I didn't even know why I was talking to him because it was obvious he wasn't in a clear state of mind.

"I'm sorry. I ran out for a drink, and when I got back, I guess you were gone."

"You didn't call me."

"My phone died. Forgot to charge it."

"Where have you been since then? The appointment was hours ago."

"What is this? Fifty questions? Don't forget who's the parent here, boy." He brushed past me toward the kitchen and opened the fridge to grab another beer. That was what he didn't need—more poison for his soul.

Maybe I was a hypocrite, seeing how I'd drink, too, but not like him.

Never like him.

"How did that eye appointment go, anyway?" he asked as he plopped down on the recliner in the living room. He burped as he cracked open the can and took a long swig.

I stared at him for a moment, considering what to tell him.

I'm going blind, Dad, and I'm scared. I'm going blind, Dad, and I need you. I'm going blind, Dad, and I don't know how to deal with this without you in my corner. I'm going blind, and I miss Mom. I miss her so much that it hurts to breathe. And I miss you even more, even though you're right here in the room with me.

Those were the words I wanted to say.

Those were the truths I'd wished I could speak about.

Instead, I said, "Fine. I'm going to do my homework."

"Good," he agreed. "Keep those grades up, will you? Don't be a dummy."

I didn't reply because I knew that it wasn't my father who was talking. That was a man who surrendered himself to his demons. I watched him be torn apart day after day, and there was nothing I could do to help him.

That night, I slept with my lights on. When my alarm went off in the morning, I still felt nothing but darkness.

As I headed to the lake in the morning to watch the sunrise, I was surprised to see a person sitting there on my bench. As I grew closer, they turned to face me, and I felt a tug in my chest. There she was, sitting there in my most sacred spot, waiting for me.

The relief that swept over me felt like a calming balm to my tired soul. How did Starlet know? How did she know I'd need her that morning? My eyes stung, and my knees almost buckled as I walked her way.

I smiled a bit, almost embarrassed to show how much her being there meant to me. "Hey, Teach."

Starlet was bundled up, rubbing her hands together. "Good morning."

"What are you doing here?"

"I hear this spot has the best sunrises."

"I can cosign that fact. It does indeed." I took a seat beside her, so close that our bodies were brushed up against one another. The lake was semi-frozen. Areas had flowing water, while others were big chunks of solid ice. Soon enough, spring would sweep through and melt it all away.

"How did you find this spot?" I asked her, confused by how she'd discovered it.

"You told me it was hidden from the world, and I wandered around for a while. Then I found the bench with your parents' initials. I knew I landed in the right spot."

My fingers traced over the initials slowly. I often wondered what emotions were in my parents' hearts when they carved their names in wood.

"Were you up all night on your search engine?" I asked her.

"No," she quickly stated. "That would be ridiculous."

I arched my eyebrow.

She sighed. "Yes, I was."

"Figured that would happen."

She turned toward me and placed a hand on my leg. "Milo, you're going to be okay. No matter what happens, we'll figure out the best way of life for you."

We.

She said it so effortlessly, as if she had no plans of going anywhere. If there was ever a moment in my life when I needed to hear the word we, it was right then and there.

I snickered a little and nodded. "Everything's gonna work out fine," I said, using the line she told me her father always used on her.

"Yes, exactly. Everything's gonna work out fine."

"I'm scared," I confessed.

"That makes sense," she replied. "I'm scared, too."

I lowered my head and stared at my hands. "I don't want to be an extra burden to your life, Starlet. I don't want you to feel like you have to go researching or anything. I can do this on my own."

"I know you can," she agreed, "but that doesn't mean you have to."

"You're the best thing that's ever happened to me." The words rolled off my tongue so effortlessly as if they were made solely for her ears to hear.

Her eyes glassed over before she leaned in toward me and rested her head against my shoulder. We sat there in the darkness, waiting for the sun to rise. We were quiet for a while until I said, "The doctor recommended I use a walking cane to keep me from running into stuff."

"That's a good idea."

"I'm not blind yet. People will look at me like I'm insane."

"Since when does Milo Corti care what people think?"

I smirked. "Since he found out he's going blind. I don't think I need it. Not yet. It turns out it could take years before my vision fades completely."

She sat straighter and tilted her head. "What scares you the most about it?"

"Currently, there are only two things, really. Not being able to see the sunrise and not being able to see you."

She placed her hands against my face and pulled me in toward her. Her lips fell against mine, and she kissed me slowly. Her forehead fell against mine, and as she shut her eyes, she whispered, "I see you, Milo. Even with my eyes closed."

I shut my stare and sighed. "I see you, too."

We watched the sunrise together, and it felt extra intense that morning.

"Do you know my favorite thing about sunrises?" she asked me.

"What's that?"

"Even when you can't see the sunrise, you can still feel it. It's still there for you. There's a certain tingle in the air, like magic undulating in the atmosphere around you. The warmth of the sun hits your skin after being enclosed in nightfall for so long. Your skin can almost feel the sensations of each color." She shut her eyes and tilted her head up to the sky. "The yellows, the oranges, the blues, and purples. It's as if the sunrise is bursting all over you."

Her eyes opened. She smiled as she turned my way and said, "You don't have to see the sunrise to witness its beauty. You can feel it against your soul."

I placed my forehead against hers and kissed her lips slowly. "You feel like the sun to me," I whispered. She was the thing that kept me warm.

Her lips parted against mine as she spoke. "Can I come back to join you tomorrow?"

"And the day after that," I told her. "And the day after that..."

And the day after that.

CHAPTER 25

Starlet

I got a C on my English paper the other day.

Mom would've been disappointed in me. The Starlet I'd been a few weeks ago would've also been disappointed in my current self. But lately, I felt disconnected from my education and former self. I'd been going back and forth in my mind wondering if my life choices were actually my own. Or was I trying to hold on to my mother's legacy as much as possible? Was I trying to be a carbon copy of the woman I'd loved more than anything because I missed her so deeply? Was I dishonoring myself by trying so hard to honor her? Is that what she would've wanted for me? Would she have wanted me to lose myself in an attempt to try to find her?

That was a complicated conversation with myself because if I wasn't the person I thought I'd been before, then who was I? What were my likes? What were my needs? What made me happy? I thought I'd have a few years before encountering my quarter-life crisis. Truthfully, I figured I'd skip over any life crisis because I had everything planned out to the T. That was all until I met Milo Corti, who turned my world upside down. Or was my world upside down all along, and he was the one who set me right-side up for the first time in years?

Whitney didn't ask me about Milo again. That was because I gave her the impression that he and I were done doing whatever it was we'd been doing. I wasn't lying about what was going on between Milo and me, yet I wasn't sharing the complete truth.

The omission of the truth is still a lie, Starlet.

My mind felt as if it were set in a back-and-forth fight between doing what was wrong and what was right. I tried not to think about it too much because the guilt of it all would eat at me. Some days when I looked in the mirror, I didn't know who stared back at me. I felt like I was in the middle of a massive personality split. I was shifting from the good girl I'd always been into something else, which scared me.

I wondered if my mother would've been proud of my changes or disappointed in how far I was veering off the original path. I wondered if she was ashamed of how I'd been acting. I wasn't behaving like she would've behaved, which created a heavy level of guilt that I wasn't certain I knew how to deal with. When I allowed my mind to slow down from the high Milo gave me, I'd sit with so much remorse and shame when I allowed myself to emotionally sober up.

Mom would've never fallen for the forbidden boy.

She would've never had a one-night stand.

She would've never gone to a fraternity party.

She would've been better than me, and she would've wanted better for me.

Realistically, I knew what I was supposed to do. I was supposed to push Milo away. I was never supposed to let him in as much as I had. I was better than that. I was the responsible girl who'd always done the right thing. Yet it seemed that my mind shut off whenever I was near him. All I wanted to do was be near him. To touch him. Hold him. To help him through his current struggles. It scared me how much I cared about him in such a short period. It scared me that I had a hard time focusing on my own life because I was overthinking the possibility of a life with Milo after he graduated.

When I built up a little courage to push him away, I'd walk into the library and see his stare on me. His lips would smile, and he'd say, "Hey, Teach." And the courage I'd held would slip away. I knew I was playing with fire, but I had no fear of being burned for some reason.

Plus, he made me feel alive. I didn't know I hadn't felt alive since Mom passed away. I'd spent years walking in a daze, moving on autopilot, trying to cover up my grief by becoming a perfectionist. In my mind, I might not have been able to control death, but I could control my life with strict guidelines. Yet somehow that guide was destroyed the second I met Milo.

I didn't know I could feel so deeply for another person. Looking back, I hardly even let John in. He was just a pawn in the chess game I'd been playing with my life. I'd been directing every single move to protect myself—to protect the queen from being hurt again.

Maybe that was why I tried so hard to become my mother—because if I were her, I couldn't get hurt. If I were myself, my true authentic self, I could shatter. I could break. I could grieve the hardest things so deeply, and that frigthened me.

Falling for Milo was terrifying because life didn't promise everything would be okay. It didn't make promises at all. If life made promises, then Milo would've been okay. He wouldn't be going through his current struggles, which seemed extremely unfair.

He's going blind.

My chest ached when I thought about his diagnosis.

All I wanted to do was ensure he was okay, which meant that many of my thoughts were wrapped around him. He didn't speak about it often, but I knew the possibility of him losing his sight ate at his thoughts. It ate at mine, too. The more time we spent together, the more connected we became. The more he hurt, the more my heart crumbled.

I'd spent so much time online researching different specialty centers. Looking into clinical testing they had going on across the United States and reading every article on retinitis pigmentosa. Many individuals described retinitis pigmentosa as if they were looking through the hole of a straw. They only saw so much, with blackness all around them. So many things were adding up, like how he couldn't see the stars when we were up north, how he'd run into things more often than not, and how he struggled with reading novels.

It wasn't fair.

I hated that life wasn't fair.

On a random Wednesday late morning, Whitney walked into our dorm room and arched an eyebrow as she saw me tossing on my winter coat. She glanced down at her watch. "Hey, what are you doing here? Aren't you normally in class?"

"I'm skipping today," I told her as I zipped up my jacket.

Her eyes narrowed. "Skipping? You've never skipped class. You literally went to your psych class when you had food poisoning last semester."

Her words landed in my gut, and guilt began to spiral. She was right. I should've been in class.

I glanced at my vision board beside my floor-length mirror. I shook my head, took it down, and tossed it upside down on my desk. "Yeah, well, I'm not exactly the same Starlet I was last semester."

"Star…" She walked over and placed a comforting hand on my arm. "What's going on?"

I turned to meet her stare, and tears flooded my eyes. I shook my head. "I just need to get away. I just need…" *My mom.* I needed my mom. I felt so weak and lost. I didn't know what to do with myself, and Mom wasn't there to guide me. She'd been gone for years now. How was it possible that I still felt as if I needed her every single day?

I took a deep breath. "I think I'm going to go drive to Pewaukee for a hike."

Whitney's lips parted as she stood slightly stunned. "Is there anything I can do to help? Will you be okay driving up there? You seem upset."

"I'll be fine. Thanks."

"I can come with you," she offered.

"You have classes today."

She gave me a small smile. "Unlike old you, I'm more than fine skipping a class or two."

I let out a small chuckle and then cleared my throat. "Whitney?"

"Yeah?"

"If I told you I was still seeing Milo, what would you tell me to do?" I whispered. "And if I told you he was going blind and was struggling, what would you tell me to do?"

Her hand was still on my arm, the comfort still being delivered. "Depends. Do you want your hard, truthful best friend or your soft, truthful best friend?"

I quietly snickered as tears fell from my eyes. "I thought you only had the hard, truthful version."

"That was until I saw how our last conversation went. Sometimes people don't need harsh reality checks. Sometimes they need someone in their corner to be gentle with them. And I'll always be in your corner, Star."

"No matter what?"

"No matter what." She lowered her head and chewed on her thumbnail. "He's going blind?"

"Yes. He just found out."

"Gosh. That's hard. And you're still falling in love with him?"

"I think I'm already there."

"Like puppy love or real love?"

"Real-real."

She smiled. It was a soft, timid smile, but it was there. "Okay then. Back to your question. If you told me you were still seeing Milo, what would I tell you to do…" She sighed and brushed her hand against her forehead. "I'd tell you to be careful with your heart but still let it lead you."

I smiled. "Thanks, Whit."

"Always. Besides"—she wiped my tears—"you were more than due for a nice plot twist to your life story. I think I was truly just in shock when you first told me. Plus, you, my friend, of all people, deserve to fall in love. Especially with a hot-hot guy."

CHAPTER 26

Milo

When Mom got sick, we were given an unstable timeline of events. Some days moved slowly, and others sped past. For the most part, the good days were the ones that went by in a blink of an eye. The bad ones seemed to last forever. Watching her worsen day after day was the hardest part for me. There was nothing more heart-shattering than witnessing someone you love fading away.

The unknown was the hardest part because some days she seemed like herself again. As if she was going to win her battle.

Finding out that I was losing my eyesight slightly reminded me of that same feeling. An unstable timeline of events. The problem with being diagnosed with retinitis pigmentosa was it could be years before it worsens or days. There was no way to know how soon the progression of the loss of sight would develop. I didn't know if I was being too ahead of the curve, thinking about using a walking cane. I didn't know how much worse it could get. I didn't know what limitations I should place against myself. I felt lost in a cloud of confusion, and scared there was a chance that one morning I'd wake up to a world of darkness. Or that one day, I'd blink and nothing would appear.

Everything felt overwhelming, but I did know one thing. I didn't trust myself driving anymore. What if everything went black as it had in class? What if I'd put others lives in danger by being on the road? I was losing a sense of independence, and that broke me more than I thought it would. I wasn't good at asking for help. That never came easy to me.

"I need you to drive me to school each day," I said. Those words felt ridiculous as they left my mouth. Dad sat on the couch, which seemed to be his norm whenever he was actually home. He'd never slept in his bedroom since Mom passed away. I'd always find him knocked out on that couch instead. Coming to him for help felt crazy, seeing how he could hardly help himself.

"What's wrong with your car?" he asked.

"Nothing. I just can't drive."

"Why the hell not? Did you get a ticket or something? What did you do?"

A twitch of anger hit me, but I tried my best to stay calm. "I didn't do anything wrong."

"Clearly, you did if you're not allowed to drive."

"No, I didn't. You would've known the reason I couldn't drive if you hadn't ditched me at the doctor's appointment."

He grimaced and shook his head. "I came back for you. Your ass just wasn't patient, that's all."

"Whatever. I need you to drive me to school."

He scratched at the back of his neck. "I'm busy. I'll get you money so you can get someone to pick you up. Maybe one of your friends can take you."

"Dad—"

"I don't really have it in me to go back and forth this morning, Milo. It's seven in the damn morning and—"

"I'm losing my sight," I blurted out, feeling annoyed and angry with him. He didn't even ask what was said at the doctor's appointment. He hadn't even questioned the reason why I couldn't drive. He didn't care. Not a single part of that man that cared.

"Bullshit," he replied.

"I am. That's what the doctor's appointment was about. I have this issue with my sight, and there's no cure."

"Can't glasses help?"

"No. It's more serious than that."

He sat up on the couch. "Like you're going blind?"

I nodded.

He cleared his throat. His head dropped, and he muttered something under his breath. I paused to see what exactly he was saying or thinking. Instead, he pushed himself up from the couch and walked past me.

"I'm going to go wash up. I'll drive you in a minute," he told me.

He headed to the bathroom and shut the door behind him. I heard him slam the counter and say "Fuck!" repeatedly.

A few minutes later, he came out of the bathroom, grabbed his keys, and headed out to the car. "Let's go."

I pretended not to notice the bloodshot eyes he'd had when he exited the bathroom. He pulled up to the school and put the car in park. He turned my way. "You got more of them appointments?"

"I have a few, yeah."

"It's that serious?"

"Yeah. It's that serious."

His head dropped, and he shook it. "What the hell am I supposed to do about this? How am I supposed to...this was your mom's role. She was better equipped for—"

"She's gone." I interrupted. "She's gone, Dad. You have to face that fact."

"I know. I know, all right? You don't have to remind me. I know she's..." His words faded off.

"Dead," I finished. "She's dead. Like it or not, you're all I've got, and I need you right now. I need you, Dad, all right? I need you."

Tears began to fall from his eyes, and he sniffled. He wiped at his face. "Okay. All right. I hear you, okay? I'll be there. I got you."

My chest tightened from seeing him fall apart. He normally hid that side of himself from me. I wanted to say something to comfort him, but I didn't think words would be able to do that. Instead, I told him what time to pick me up, and he agreed to be there. There was a chance he would be a no-show again. But I hoped he'd make it.

I prayed he'd be there for me.

* * *

EVERY NIGHT before I fell asleep, I'd receive a text message from Starlet telling me she was in my corner. She was my biggest cheerleader and offered any form of support she could shoot my way. When I felt too overwhelmed, she'd meet me at the lake. We'd watch the sunrise together before I walked her back to her car, buckled her in, and I'd steal a kiss from her. That kiss got me through the rest of the day most of the time. Before, I needed sex and booze to distract me, but now, all I needed was Starlet and her kisses. Starlet and her comfort. Starlet. All I needed was her.

Our tutoring schedule shifted due to all the appointments I'd had in front of me, and the nights I didn't get to see her only made me crave mornings even more.

To my surprise, Dad began to show up for me. Not only did he show up to pick me up from school, but he also took me to my appointments the following two weeks. He'd sit in with me and ask the doctors questions whenever I didn't know what to ask.

For the first time in a while, I felt as if I had a parent again. I had a glimpse of hope for a future between us. Sure, it wouldn't be like before, but we could have a new normal. Like Starlet and her father had.

At least, that was what I thought before the night of my group therapy session.

My doctor recommended I get a therapist and consider group therapy with other individuals who were legally blind or in the process of losing their vision. The idea of it sounded awful to me, but I agreed to it. I knew if I didn't, I'd fall deeper into my depression, and that didn't seem like the smartest thing to do. Plus, the curiosity of it all was there. I'd never met a blind person, and I selfishly wanted to see their life.

The group session happened in a conference room of a warehouse that was used for different businesses. The space was lit up with lights, which made a major difference in my vision. I noticed the brighter the lights, the better I could see a lot of the time.

Eleven chairs were set up in a big circle, and I was one of the first people to arrive. I picked a seat, and it didn't take long for people to fill up the seats beside me. To my left was an older guy, probably in his late sixties. His name was Henry, and he lost his sight due to health issues. To my right was a kid about ten years old named Bobby. Bobby was born blind. Seeing someone that young without his vision made me feel a bit more guilty about complaining about my vision issues.

"Who's to my left?" Bobby asked, nudging his shoulder toward me and bumping it.

I cleared my throat and turned to him. "I'm Milo," I loudly stated.

Bobby snickered. "Not so loud. I'm blind, not deaf," he joked. I felt like a complete idiot, but Bobby rolled on with the conversation. "Are you new here?"

"Yeah, first time."

"What's with your eyes?"

I arched my brow. "I'm sorry?"

"What's special about your eyes?"

Special?

I hesitated before replying with what I thought he was asking me. "Uh, I have retinitis pigmentosa."

"Oh, sweet!" Bobby exclaimed. "My friend Cate has that."

"I don't see what's so sweet about it." I grimaced.

"Yeah, well, you don't see it cuz you're blind, dude," he replied with a snicker.

What was wrong with this kid?

He shook his head slightly. "Lighten up a little. It's not like the world around you is going to do it for you. Everything around us might be dark, but your personality doesn't have to be."

"Okay, baby Yoda," I muttered, not wanting to engage anymore with the burst of optimism sitting beside me. I wanted to wallow a bit more—not make inappropriate jokes about losing my sight with a blind kid.

Bobby didn't care about my desire not to engage with him. He kept on chatting. "I was born without sight. Some people call it a congenital disability, but my mom calls it my superpower. Kind of like Matt Murdock."

I arched my eyebrow. "Who the hell is Matt Murdock?"

"Dude! Are you kidding me? Matt Murdock, also known as Daredevil. Also, also known as the best superhero in all the Marvel worlds. He's a blind superhero. He's amazing."

"Don't listen to the kid," the guy on my left grumbled. "He just talks a lot about anything. I hate the idea of people referencing superheroes when they talk about us being blind. It's like them trying to give us a pity gift or some shit."

I liked his attitude. It was much more in tune with my own.

Bobby sighed. "Don't listen to the old grump, Henry, over there. He hasn't been happy since 1845."

I smirked slightly.

This kid was annoying but funny.

"You'll learn fast that our little group here has a lot of different personalities," a woman said, walking up to me. She held her hand out toward me. "You must be Milo. I'm Tracy, the group leader."

I shook her hand. "Nice to meet you."

"You too, Milo. I'm glad you joined us. I think you'll find out how unique and wonderful this group is. I think it's funny that you somehow were seated between the two most vibrant individuals in our group. We like to call them *The Odd Couple*."

Henry grumbled, "It's a stupid name."

Tracy smiled and whispered toward me, "I'll let you guess which one is Oscar and which one is Felix." She began to navigate herself over to her chair. "Hey, everyone, it's good to have you all back for another weekly session. We have a new individual joining us, so let's try our best not to scare him off. Everyone, welcome Milo today."

Everyone greeted me. I hated the attention on me, so I was thankful when Tracy shifted the conversation from my arrival to the overall discussion. Everyone seemed to have their own strong personalities, and they laughed a lot together, too. I learned about how long they'd been dealing with their sight situations and how many achievements they'd made throughout their lives.

For the first time since my diagnosis, I felt a little less alone and a little less scared. Some of the things those individuals had done in their lives were truly remarkable. Tracy herself had run half marathons, and rock climbed. Another person opened up a bakery shop. Bobby was convinced he was the next Marvel actor in a few years. By his spunk, I wouldn't have put it past him.

When the session came to an end, Tracy had everyone say a word or two to describe how they were feeling about their current situations. All sorts of words were tossed out. Happy. Disappointed. Stuck. Annoyed. Proud.

When it came time for my words, I swallowed hard. "Pissed off."

"That makes sense, Milo. Do you want to talk about why you chose those words?" Tracy asked.

I shook my head. "No."

"Then that's great, too. Thank you for sharing."

The session ended, and I was happy I wasn't pushed to share about why I was pissed off. But I was also proud of being honest at the moment. I was pissed off about my current situation. I knew it was awful for me to feel this because some of the people in that room seemingly had it more challenging than me, but I felt as if I'd been robbed of a part of my life out of nowhere. I didn't get what kind of beef life had against me. I didn't understand why it kept swinging at me, trying to knock me out, but I was pissed off about it. I was pissed off that my sight was already crappy and would only get worse over time. I was pissed off that there wasn't a cure. I was pissed off that others could just get a pair of glasses and be on their way. I was pissed off that life wasn't fair, and I was pissed off that Mom wasn't around to give me some pep talk to make me feel better.

Maybe that was what pissed me off the most.

"You picked good words," Henry said, leaning in my direction as he began to stand from his chair. "Pissed off. I feel like those are my words every damn day—pissed off."

"Yeah. They seem to be mine a lot, too."

"Listen, kid. You didn't ask for my advice, but I'm old and that's what older people do because we've been through enough shit to know enough shit. So listen here. I know today you heard about all this amazing stuff that people did. Running marathons, opening shops, wanting to be superheroes, and crap, but let me tell you something. You don't have to do any of that stuff, all right? You can just be yourself. And if yourself is some asshole who only likes sitting on your front porch and telling people to piss off, well, that's good enough, too. We don't have to be some success story to tell others to be like, 'See? I'm not lesser than you! I can do these things, too!' Because you're not lesser than others. You're human, you're whole, and you don't have shit to prove to anyone. If you want to be pissed off, then be pissed off for as long as you want, all right?"

It was as if Mom knew I needed a pep talk made just for me, so she sent Henry. "Thanks, Henry, I appreciate that."

"Henry's right," Bobby said, joining in. "But you could always be Daredevil, too. The options for us are limitless."

Henry grimaced. "Will you shut the hell up, boy?" he yipped at Bobby.

"Love you, too, Henry," Bobby replied.

I snickered at the two of them. They were definitely the odd couple.

I exited the building to find Dad still parked in the same spot where I had left him. A sigh of relief rolled through me as I walked over to the car and climbed inside.

He gave me a lazy smile. "Are you good?"

I nodded. "Thanks for waiting."

"Yeah, of course, of course." He brushed his thumb across the bridge of his nose. "But you're sure you're good, though, right?"

My chest tightened a bit. "Yeah, Dad. I'm good."

"Good. That's good. All right. Let's get home. I can order us a pizza or something." He turned on the radio, and we rode home in silence, but I didn't feel as pissed off as I had prior to stepping into the car with my dad.

He asked if I was good.

That was more than he'd done in a very long time. For a split second, I felt as if I were getting my father back. Sure, to the outside world, it probably seemed like the bare minimum of what he should've been doing, but to me, it felt like the biggest victory. Finding out your father still cared after doubting it for over a year felt like something to celebrate.

We ate pizza that night on the couch, while watching a basketball game together. We didn't talk much during the game, but sometimes words weren't needed. We'd said a lot that night without words just by sitting that close and eating dinner together for the first time in months.

CHAPTER 27

Milo

*L*ately, it felt as if all my days blended into one. I felt as if I were moving through life at turbo speed. Between school, tutoring, therapy, and practicing using my cane, I felt extremely overwhelmed. I didn't even know if I actually needed to learn to use a cane, but I figured it couldn't hurt. I lost my balance enough for it to be concerning.

I'd spent hours wearing sunglasses and walking up and down my driveway with my cane, learning how to feel the different textures of the driveway pavement and grass. I'd learned that swaying the cane back and forth, along with tapping every now and again, helped me. There was a strap on the handle, which I thought I was supposed to wrap around my wrist. I quickly learned not to do so, seeing how if the cane got hit by a car, I'd be dragged along with it if it were attached to me.

My forearm felt sore at first from holding the cane so tightly. It was a lot harder than it looked, and I felt tired from the learning curves. I updated my friends and Weston on everything going on, and some days, they'd join me for evening walks to help me get used to using the cane.

Weston told me to start bringing it to school, but I didn't feel ready for that. I knew the second I did, the whole situation would become even more real than I was ready for. I wasn't willing or interested in hearing outsiders' opinions on my blindness. Plus, I felt embarrassed. I knew that was stupid, but I did. I didn't want people to know I was different. It was never my plan to stand out, but now I knew I would, no matter where I went. I only had a couple more months of high school to get through. I'd rather stub my toes and bang my legs a few more times in school if it meant others wouldn't know about my issues.

Dad was seemingly handling everything pretty well, up until a Thursday evening after my group therapy session. I walked outside to meet him, and his car wasn't parked where it had been when he dropped me off. I pulled out my cell phone and called him, but it went straight to voice mail. It was pretty cold out that evening, so I headed back inside the building to wait for him to come back.

Hours passed, and I was still waiting.

The security guard of the building came up to me and smiled. "Hey, sorry, but we're locking up the building for the night."

"Yeah, of course. No worries. I'll get out of your hair," I muttered, brushing my hands against my brows. I stepped outside into the chilled air that assaulted my face. I pulled out my phone and tried Dad one more time. Still no answer.

"Hey, what's going on?" Starlet asked when she answered my call. "How was your group session? How are you feeling?"

My left hand fiddled with my coat buttons as I leaned against the building. "It was fine. Look, I'm in a bit of a situation. My dad was a no-show to pick me up and—"

"You're still there? What's the address?" She cut in.

She didn't hesitate to come get me.

I felt humiliated when she picked me up about fifteen minutes later. I climbed into her car, freezing my ass off. "Thanks," I shivered, tossing my hands in front of the vents on her dashboard, blasting out heat. I was in desperate need of defrosting.

"Oh gosh, were you standing outside this whole time? Your face is so red."

"I'm okay," I lied. It felt as if my skin was seconds away from falling off.

"Here," she said, turning me to face her. "Give me your hands. Mine are warm."

"I'm fine."

"Milo. Hands. Now."

I grumbled and turned toward her, giving her my hands. A wave of instant comfort raked through me simply from her touch. I was still in a bad mood, but she made it feel a little better.

"I'm sorry I had to call you," I whispered, ashamed. "I didn't know what else to do when no one else answered."

"Don't apologize for that. I don't mind at all." She frowned as she rubbed my hands between hers. "I hate that I'm unable to be your first call."

"Soon," I swore. "We'll get there."

"I just feel you need me more now than ever, and I hate it. I want to be there for you so bad, Milo. I hate this feeling."

"You're here now. That's all that matters. Let's get moving. I'm exhausted."

She agreed, putting the car into drive. Once we reached my house, I saw Dad's car in the driveway. An instant burst of comfort hit me seeing it. At least he was home and not hurt. That comfort shifted straight to humiliation within seconds.

Starlet cleared her throat. "Um, a guy's pissing in your front bushes."

I looked to my left toward the house, and there he was, Father dearest, pissing in the bushes with his ass out on public display.

"Shit," I huffed, hopping out of the car. I darted over to him, not making it before he stumbled backward and fell to the ground with his damn dick in his hands. "What the hell are you doing, Dad?"

"Fuck off," he muttered, waving his hand toward me. Then he

began singing "Can't Take My Eyes Off You" by Frankie Valli, and my heart shattered because that was his and Mom's wedding song. They used to dance to it all the time in our living room.

"Dad, get up," I urged, pulling up his boxers and pants. I buttoned them as he rolled back and forth, still singing, still drunk out of his mind. I tried to lift him, but he was too heavy to do it alone. When he looked at me, his singing came to a halt, and his already glassy eyes intensified as he said, "You have her eyes. I can't look at you because you have her eyes."

Another fracture to my heart.

"Come on, Dad. Let's get inside," I whispered as my voice cracked.

"Today's our wedding anniversary," he told me before returning to singing his song. There they were—my father's cracks. I didn't even realize what today had been. I didn't hesitate to go on with life that morning when I woke up. But for him, it was a day of hurt. Of struggle. Of pain. Another day, another memory of the woman he loved more than life.

"I'm sorry," I said, my eyes stinging as I tried to get him up.

"Here, let me help," Starlet said, rushing over. I looked at her with such shame on my face, but she didn't say anything. She simply bent down and grabbed Dad's other arm.

"It's their anniversary," I whispered to her, feeling embarrassed that I hadn't remembered.

She nodded in understanding and went to help him stand. "Don't worry. We got you, Mr. Corti. We got you."

"Jacob," I softly told her. "His name is Jacob."

She smiled a little. "We got you, Jacob."

Dad's drunken eyes fell on Starlet as we got him to a standing position. "Dance?" he asked before taking her into his arms and swaying her back and forth.

"Dad—" I started.

"I'd love to," Starlet replied, holding him up the best she could. I stood back, watching the two of them sway. Dad sang his song to Starlet, holding her as if he refused to let go. The situation was odd, heart-shattering, and absurd, but it was happening.

My father drunkenly danced with my secret girlfriend as he sang his wedding song on my parents' anniversary. He leaned against her as if she was the last hope he had left inside of him. Starlet allowed him to do so, to feel what he needed to feel at that very moment.

Then she began to sing along with him.

* * *

AFTER A WHILE, Starlet and I managed to get Dad inside the house. I put him to bed while Starlet grabbed a glass of water and ibuprofen to set on his nightstand. We moved out of the room, closing the door behind us, and I felt an overwhelming need to have her in my arms. I pulled her close to me, and she fell into my body.

"I'm sorry about all of that," I whispered.

"Don't be. I'm glad I was here to help."

I dropped my hold on her and rubbed my hand against the nape of my neck. "I feel like such a dick. I didn't even realize what today was. The whole time I was waiting for him to pick me up, I was cursing him out in my mind. Thinking he was a shit dad for leaving me stranded. When, in reality, he was drowning all day. He was trying his best. I'm an asshole."

"You're not. You didn't know, Milo."

"Which is another issue. I didn't know. I should've known what today was. I should've been there for him or something, but I've been living in my own shit that I didn't even consider how he was doing. Or how many days he had that held importance that I didn't even think of."

"I think you're both just doing your best at every moment. Life is hard, complicated, and tiring. You're both just tired. It's okay to rest. Please don't be so hard on yourself or him. Today's a hard day, and that's okay. We're strong enough to make it through the hard days. Everything's gonna work out fine."

"How do you always know what to say?"

She laughed. "I don't. My dad gave me a pep talk not long ago, and it struck me pretty well. I'm just passing on his teachings. If you ever get an Eric Evans pep talk, count yourself lucky."

"Is there a waiting list I could get on for one of his talks?" I semi-joked.

I held a hand out toward her. She took it, and I pulled her into me. We began swaying back and forth to the music that didn't exist. I buried my face into her neck, breathing her in. I never knew I could need a person as much as I needed her.

"Stay the night," I whispered against her ear, kissing it gently.

"Mi...I can't... What would your dad say if he woke up?"

"He won't be up before sunrise. He wouldn't even notice. Stay the night," I murmured, this time my mouth against her neck.

"Mi..."

"Please, Star," I pleaded quietly as my lips grazed against hers. "Stay with me tonight. I'll let you go in the morning. I promise. But please... stay the night."

She pulled away slightly and studied me. Her head tilted slightly. "Come on. Let's go to sleep."

CHAPTER 28

Starlet

he following morning, I woke up with a trail of kisses down my neck from Milo. I smiled, feeling his skin pressed against mine. He rolled over so he was on top of me, pinning me down to the mattress. His mouth grazed over mine. "Hey, Teach?" he whispered, infusing his warmth against my body.

"Yes?"

"Can we play hooky today from life?"

I looked up at him and giggled. "No, we can't play hooky, Milo."

He grumbled and fell against me, running his mouth across my collarbone. "Please? Just one day. One day with you and me being you and me?" I closed my eyes and lightly moaned from the sensation of his kisses. "We can call in sick."

"We aren't sick."

Cough-cough. He covered his mouth.

I laughed. "Why do I think that was a fake cough?"

"Oh, no. There's nothing fake about this. I'm coming down with something drastically," he groaned as he dramatically flopped back to his side of the bed. He pressed the back of his hand to his forehead. "I think I have a fever, too."

"Is that so?"

"Yeah, come here and check," he said, placing his hands against my hips and lifting me into his lap without any effort at all. I didn't think I'd ever get over how easily he moved me around.

I straddled him and placed my palm on his forehead. "You feel fine to me."

He frowned. "That's probably because you're coming down with the same bug as me." *Cough-cough.*

I placed my hands against his bare chest, leaned in, and kissed his lips. "We're not going to play hooky today, Milo."

"I want to spend the day with you," he whispered, his voice low and timid. His eyes flashed with a splash of tenderness that made my heart skip a few beats.

"Don't look at me like that," I warned.

"Like what?"

"Like you're about to make me agree to do bad things."

He pulled me closer to him and lay me against his body. His lips brushed against my earlobe. "Please do bad, bad things with me, Star." His tongue slipped from his mouth, and he trailed it along my ear. "Please?"

I closed my eyes and rested my head against his chest, listening to his heartbeats. "What would we even do if we played hooky?"

"I don't know…each other?"

I laughed, feeling him harden against my leg. Clearly not all parts of Milo were sick. Some were wide awake and ready to play. "We are not skipping school to have sex, Milo."

He pouted. "You're no fun."

"Story of my life until you."

"We could take the Amtrak to Chicago," he offered. "It would be an hour and a half trip. We could shut off our phones from the world and pretend it's only us and do all kinds of tourist bullshit and laugh and have fun and just be us. Doesn't that sound like fun? Just being us for a little bit of time?"

I pushed myself up slightly and studied his eyes. As I looked at him, I saw it—his need to escape for a little while. Even though he was seemingly playful with it, I could tell he needed a break. I should've been more responsible. I should've told him we could take a summer trip to Chicago when we were allowed to be us fully. I should've told him how important it was that we didn't skip school. I should've told him no.

Instead, I laid myself back down against his chest, listening to his heart once more, and I said, "Now that you mention it, there is a little tickle in the back of my throat."

I could feel his smile, even with my eyes closed, as he said, "We can't go to school. It would be irresponsible to spread our germs around."

"That's true. I guess we'll have to spread them around Chicago."

"That's a really responsible thing to do."

I pushed myself up slightly and locked eyes with him. "Will your dad be okay? Are you sure you don't want to spend the day with him?"

Milo shrugged. "We don't really do that."

"But maybe—"

"We don't do that, Star." He cut in, signaling that I was crossing a line. I didn't bring up the topic again. Clearly, his relationship with his father was complicated, and it wasn't my place to add my input. My only job was to make sure Milo was doing all right, and if that meant playing hooky, then we'd do that.

* * *

I CONVINCED him to bring his cane to Chicago.

He'd been so self-conscious about it that I figured trying to use it in a different city might help him. It was clear that he didn't need the cane as much as he might in the future, but I figured any practice would be helpful.

The moment we stepped off the train, we shut off our phones. I'd never had a day when I completely disconnected from the world, and I was looking forward to it more than I thought possible.

The streets of Chicago were busy with traffic and pedestrians moving around in a hurry. Tourists surrounded one of the biggest attraction sights—the Bean or as it was officially known as, *Cloud Gate*.

"This was going to be one of the stops on my imaginary road trip," Milo mentioned, snapping photos of me in front of the Bean. I smiled widely, posing on one leg as he snapped away.

"You've made up actual stops?" I asked.

"No. Just a few random stops I wanted to see across the states. I'm shocked I've never been here, actually, seeing how it's so close."

"You know what we should do? Make up a road trip map together and mark down all the spots we want to see. I have so many places I'd love to go hiking at."

"And I want to see the burger family!"

I narrowed my eyes. "The burger family?"

"You don't know about the burger family?"

"Should I?"

"They are the A&W Burger Family statues. They are spread across the states, but I know the ones I want to see are Hillsboro, Oregon."

I laughed. "You want to travel to see hamburger statues?

"It's a family of burger people, Star. A family!" he exclaimed, smiling wide. I loved when he slipped into that version of himself— full of joy and light. It looked so good on him. "We need to find a place for lunch and discuss all the places we'd plan to go on for this road trip," he said.

"I could use some food."

"Deep-dish pizza?"

"Do you know most people from Chicago don't eat deep-dish pizza? Down here, we do more of a thin crust style."

"Lucky for me, I'm a tourist. So again, deep-dish pizza?"

Deep-dish pizza it was.

The rest of our time together felt free. We'd laughed more than we ever had and kissed in public places with no worries about who might see us. By the time we headed back to the train station, I was already dreading not being able to hold him the way I had that day. I was dreading not touching him in the hallways of school. I knew summer was only a few months away, but honestly, it felt like centuries when you were falling in love.

When we made it back to downtown Milwaukee, we finally took out our cell phones and turned them back on.

"It was kind of nice to be unplugged from the world," I mentioned as we walked out of the train station and began to cross the street to where I parked my car for the day. Milo's footsteps froze in the middle of the road as he stared at his phone. Cars were coming his way, and I yanked his arm, tugging him to the curbside before he could get hit.

"What are you doing? You almost died," I said, confused by his sudden unawareness.

He was still looking down at his phone with knitted brows.

"Milo? What is it?"

His shoulders slumped forward as his body held a slight tremble.

"Milo?" I questioned.

He didn't look at me.

His trembles intensified.

"Milo. What is it? What's wrong?"

"It's my dad." When his head rose, his eyes were flooded with tears.

True alarm and concern shot straight into my heart. "What happened?"

"There was a car accident. Weston has been trying to reach me. He said it's bad, and well...shit..." His voice cracked as he shook his head. "I need to get to the hospital. I need to get to the hospital. I have to, I have to, uh..." His words faded away as he began to crumple.

"Which hospital? I'll take you. Let's go."

He muttered the hospital's name, and I quickly pulled up directions on my phone. When we arrived, I went to get out of the car, but he stopped me. "You can't come up. Weston is here, so you can't walk in with me."

"I don't care," I told him. "I want to be here for you."

"Star. You can't. It's fine."

My chest tightened as the reality of our situation came back in full force. His father was fighting for his life inside of said hospital, and I couldn't even go up there to be by Milo's side due to my position at the high school. It seemed ridiculous and unfair.

"I'll wait here until you're done," I told him.

"It might be hours," he whispered, his voice tired and cracking.

"I'll wait here," I said once more.

He nodded once, then slid out of the car. As he walked away, I had to force myself not to rush in beside him so he wouldn't have to go alone. Thirty minutes passed quickly. Then an hour. It wasn't long after that that Milo came out of the building and walked toward my car again. He opened the door and climbed back inside.

I sat straighter, waiting to hear the news.

"He's pretty beat up and not doing too great. He's in a coma, and they don't know... They didn't have much information to give me. They said I could call for updates or come back during visiting hours, which I'll do."

"Okay. That's good. And Weston?"

"He left a little bit before me. I told him I'd take an Uber home or something."

"You're not going to stay with him tonight?"

"No. I'm staying at my place."

"Alone?"

"Yes."

"No." I shook my head. "I'm going to stay with you."

"You don't have to. I've already stolen a day of your time. I'll be fine and—"

"I'm staying with you," I repeated.

He looked at me and parted his mouth as if he wanted to argue, but no words left his lips. He simply nodded, completely defeated.

I took him to my dorm room, where I collected a few items in a duffel bag to take over to Milo's. He sat on my bed, quiet. I was certain his mind was busier than ever, twisted with corrupted thoughts that were eating at his spirit.

As I grabbed my phone charger from the wall, the dorm door opened, and Whitney walked in with her headphones. The second her eyes fell on Milo, her jaw dropped open, but she held her composure the best she could.

"Is everything okay?" she asked as I zipped up the duffel bag.

"Yeah. Everything's fine. I'll be gone for a few days," I told her.

"But what about your big exam tomorrow?"

"I don't care," I confessed, feeling my anxiety build as she said all this stuff in front of Milo. Nothing against my best friend, but she was the last person I wanted to deal with at that moment. My mind was focused on Milo and Milo only.

I turned toward him and gave him a tiny smile. "Ready?"

He nodded and stood from my bed.

"Starlet—" Whitney started.

I turned to her and placed a hand on her forearm. "I'll explain everything when I'm back in a few days."

She nodded, maybe not in complete understanding but in solidarity. "Be careful," she whispered, not loud enough for Milo to hear. Then she pulled me into a hug and said it once more. "Just be careful, Star."

Milo and I drove to his house, and he grabbed my bag to carry it inside. He moved as if walking through quicksand, seconds away from being pulled deeper into his own tortured depression.

It wasn't fair, watching him break. He was just beginning to learn to breathe again, and it felt selfish that the world was trying to pull him back down, deeper into the darkness when he'd just begun to feel the warmth of the sun.

I was able to take in his home a lot more than I'd been the night prior when I'd stayed over. His house felt like a time capsule of sorts. I could feel his mother through the decorations of the home. Dashes of feminine touches were scattered through every room. Photographs were plastered on the walls, yet many of them were crooked and covered in dust. A few light bulbs were burned out, and the space was dimly lit.

The home had such a haunting feeling to it. As if it was once so lively, yet it had been stuck in neutral ever since his mother passed away. What was once a warm and inviting home had transformed into a dreary place soaked in sadness.

I moved to the fireplace to study the photographs on the mantel. Pictures of Milo with both his parents. He looked so much like his mother that it almost took my breath away. From the sparkle in their eyes to the curves of their smiles. I now understood why it could be difficult for his father to look at Milo. It was like looking at his favorite dream and not being able to hold it any longer. The living room coffee table was littered with empty beer cans and a half-eaten pizza in the box, and the floor could've used a good vacuuming, but when I looked around, all I really noticed was that two people lived there who were trying their best to make it through every single day. I'd never known a home could feel frozen in time until I'd stepped inside their four walls.

The moment Milo saw my eyes on said table, he grumbled to himself and hurried over to clear it. "Sorry. It's my dad," he tried to explain, pushing down the bit of embarrassment. I walked over and helped him clean it up. "Don't worry about it. I can help."

"You don't have to. I got this," he said before standing and running into the side of the end table next to the recliner chair. "Shit!" he yipped, almost dropping the cans in his hand. "Fuck!"

"Are you okay?" I asked, rushing over to him.

"I'm fine," he snapped, his anger building by the second. The moment he realized his tone, he looked at me and sighed. "Sorry. It's just a lot right now."

"Here, give it to me." I took the items from him and went to toss them into the trash bin. When I came back, I could see how defeated he appeared as he rubbed his leg where he'd hit it. "Can I make you something to eat? Or tea? Coffee?"

He shook his head as his back was turned to me. He stared outside at the falling snow. April was right around the corner, yet snow was still dusting over our town as if it had no plans to vanish.

I was so worried about him but wasn't certain what I could do.

"Milo...how can I help?"

He turned to look my way and then walked over to me. He pulled me into a hug, and I held on tight. We stayed there for a second before his lips kissed my forehead, then my cheeks, then the curve of my chin, then my neck, then...

"Milo, wait," I whispered as his mouth trailed down the nape of my neck. Shivers moved through my system as I fought my wants versus his actual needs. Yes, his mouth against my skin felt good, the warmth of his touch trailing against me. I wanted him. There was no denying that fact because I always wanted him. My brain knew it wasn't right, but my heart didn't care about right or wrong. All it knew how to do was fall for the broken boy who every now and then let me into his shattered pieces. But it wasn't what he needed. He didn't need physical intimacy or a lover at that moment.

He needed a friend.

He needed me to be his friend.

"I want you," he whispered against my skin. His tongue slipped from his mouth and traced along my collarbone. "I want to taste every piece of you," he swore, his hands roaming against my waistline.

"Milo, no," I said, stepping away from him.

The room felt as if it chilled over as confusion flurried throughout his eyes. "What the hell, Star? I just want you right now. That's it."

"No, Mi. You're sad and worried."

"No, I'm not. I'm fine."

My heart ached for him because I could feel his frustration. I could sense his want to disconnect. To unplug and lose himself against me so he wouldn't have to face reality. He was doing everything in his power to avoid facing the truth about his shattered heart.

"You haven't said a word about your father since we left the hospital," I calmly stated. "That worries me. We should talk about it and—"

"Don't," he whispered through gritted teeth. He turned his back to me, and his shoulders dropped as he shook his head. "If you don't want to fuck, you can just leave," he coldly stated.

"Mi—"

"I mean it, Starlet. I don't want to have a fucking heart-to-heart session with you, all right?" he shot at me. He turned my way, and his eyes almost shattered every inch of my being. His eyes showcased the opposite of what his words were stating. I saw it in his stare—the need for comfort. The fear of his solitude. The pain of the possibility of yet another massive loss.

How much heartbreak could a heart have before it simply gave up on beating?

I moved toward him and placed a hand on his shoulder. "Talk to me."

"No."

"Please."

"No."

"You need to let it out."

"There's nothing to say. Okay? My father's a drunk who got himself into this situation. End of story."

"Mi—"

"What?!" he cried out, his voice cracking as he took steps away from me. "What do you want me to say, Star? You want me to talk about how pissed off I am at him? You want me to express how damn traumatic this is for me, not knowing if he's gonna be okay? You want me to dig deep into how messed up my mind, and my thoughts are, knowing that I could get a call any second now saying he's gone? Is that what you want?" he asked. He was yelling, but I knew he wasn't shouting at me. He wasn't angry with me. He was pissed off at the world. At the injustices of it all. At the unfairness. With just cause.

"Or, oh wait, let me guess, you want me to tell you how angry I am with myself, huh?" he asked. His movements stilled as he shut his eyes for a split second. His head slightly tilted to the left as if he was trying to gather his thoughts. As if he was trying to control his emotions.

I wished he wouldn't, though.

I wished he'd allow himself to spill over. To feel it all, every hurt, every ache, every slice of pain.

When his eyes opened, I saw the waterworks seconds away from pouring out. "Because I should've spent today with him like you mentioned. He'd still be okay if I would've helped him instead of running off to Chicago to try to escape this shit." He glanced at the photograph of his parents on his mantel and began to whisper. "I might not get to tell him I'm sorry, Star," he said. "I might not get to make up with him, or have a beer with him, or tell him ten years down the line that he was right and that I was a little shit. I might not reminisce with him about Mom, or get to build a new relationship with him. He's in a coma, and he doesn't know I'm sorry. He doesn't know I'm sorry for being a fucked-up kid with daddy issues. He doesn't know that I forgive him for not knowing how to parent after Mom left us. He doesn't know I love him."

I could've reassured him that his father knew that Milo loved him.

I could've been the person who comforted him and told him that his father could still pull through.

He didn't need that right then, though. He needed to break.

Sometimes one had to break into a million pieces for healing to begin. All Milo needed from me at that very moment was my arms wrapped tightly around him as a physical reminder that he might've felt alone, but he wasn't. I was there and would be there as long as he needed me. No matter how long it took.

CHAPTER 29

Milo

We stayed in bed all night in a darkened room. Starlet tried to get me to eat something, but I couldn't bring myself to do it. I couldn't think straight. I couldn't focus on anything at all except the fact that Dad was currently fighting for his life.

My mind felt sick.

I didn't know minds could feel sick until that very moment.

I couldn't lose him, too.

Hadn't I lost enough?

Hadn't the world stolen enough from me?

Starlet stirred in my bed as she began to wake from the night prior. Before her eyes even opened, her hand reached out toward my side of the bed, and it landed against my forearm.

Still here, Teach.

Her brown eyes fluttered open, and I didn't feel alone for a split second like I used to. I felt sad but not alone and sad, which used to be my default.

"Hi," she whispered, rolling on her side to face me.

"Hi," I replied, combing away the hair falling in front of her eyes.

"You didn't sleep."

"No."

"You should've woke me."

"We both don't have to suffer."

As I said that, her eyes softened with a sense of deep sadness. It was as if she remembered what reality had been for me after her dream state. If I were honest, I hadn't realized the truth. I was walking in a state of delusion. Part of me was thinking that Dad was off drunk somewhere, being a damn fool, and I'd hear his car pulling into the driveway anytime now. Not that he was in a hospital bed debating between life and death, debating between finding Mom or coming back to me.

"I'm so sorry, Milo," she said.

The words made me twitch. I pressed my forehead to hers. "Please stop saying that. It's just a reminder that there's something to be sorry about."

"Okay, sorr—" She stopped herself and pushed out a smile. "How can I help you today?"

I kissed the tip of her nose before pushing myself up to a sitting position. "Can I cook for you?"

She raised an eyebrow. "What?"

"I want to cook for you. Breakfast, then lunch, then dinner. Can I cook for you, Star?"

"What? No. Don't worry about me. I can cook for you—"

I swallowed hard and shook my head. "No, you don't understand. I just...I need to cook today, and I want to cook for you."

She stared at me, a bit perplexed, but nodded in agreement. "Okay, yes. I would love that."

I stood from the bed and walked over to my dresser, where my mother's recipe box was sitting. I hadn't opened it since she passed away. I was too scared to look at the recipes she left for me.

Moving back to the bed with the box, I opened it and placed it in front of us both.

"These were my mother's recipes. She left them to me after she passed away. She said whenever I felt extremely lost, I should make one of the meals. I haven't had the nerve to open the box yet, but I'd like to today," I told her.

She sat up and pulled her knees into her chest. "I think that's a beautiful idea."

I gave her a broken smile as I proceeded to open the recipe box. Inside were dozens of memories crafted by my mother. I paged through the recipe cards, some dusted with flour, others with drops of oil. Cacio e Pepe, ricotta gnudi, mushroom frittata, carbonara. Just seeing her words made my chest tighten. My first thought was how idiotic I was to wait so long to look inside that box. The thought that followed was how long would my sight allow me to see my mother's handwritten cards. It was odd how somehow, I looked at life with a different set of eyes ever since my diagnosis. I'd never cared before how people wrote words against paper. How they dotted their i's and crossed their t's. But now, knowing that maybe someday I could lose all connection to those little things, I took them in more, especially when it came to Mom's recipe cards.

As I pulled out one of the cards for a loaf of dutch oven baked bread, my chest tightened a bit. On the left side of the recipe card were the ingredients and directions to make said bread. Then on the right side was a note from my mother. I pressed my fingertips to the words, following the indentations where her pen leaned heavily on the paper. Her words were created with such tender love and care that I could almost feel her through the curves of her penmanship.

My world,

Making bread takes time. A lot of resting.
Humans are like bread, too. Sometimes we just need a little rest to rise.

Con amore,
Mama

Notes.

She left me notes on the recipe cards.

I flipped through the deck and pulled out another. Pasta alla norma.

My world,

Perfect for a sunny day with French bread and a side salad.

Even better with a glass of red wine. (Once you're of age, of course.)

Con amore,
Mama

I felt as if my world was spinning faster as I flipped through more and more. Each card had a little note. Each card held a message to me from her. Even when she was at her weakest, she took the time to write out a personal message on every single recipe for me, signing each one with con amore. With love. Leave it to my mother to know when I'd need her love the most.

Who knew love could still exist in the afterlife? I felt as if Dad was trying to race off to meet her. A part of me couldn't blame him.

"She left me little notes on each card," I explained to Starlet. "I didn't know that until right now."

"Sometimes life brings you comfort when you need it the most."

If that were true, I supposed that was why the world brought me Starlet.

"I'll set up a grocery order to be delivered. Then I can start cooking. If you want to shower, I set out some towels and whatnot in the bathroom for you," I told her. "I'll give my uncle a call, too, to see what I need to handle today."

"Sounds good." She placed her hands against my kneecaps before leaning in and kissing me gently. She whispered against my lips. "You're not okay."

I shook my head. "I'm not okay."

She kissed me once more. "And that's okay."

I kissed her back, and I was so thankful she existed. I'd never been more grateful for a person's existence before.

She pushed herself up from the bed and held her hand out toward me. "Before you order that food, come take a shower with me. It will feel good against your skin."

I hesitated for a moment, thinking of a million things I needed to do, but then I locked eyes with her, and an odd sense of calmness washed over me. The same kind of calm I'd received while reading the recipe cards. A sense of not being alone.

I took her hand into mine, and she pulled me toward the shower. We removed one another's clothing after I turned on the water. The bathroom steamed up quickly as Starlet and I stepped inside. Water raced over our bodies as I shut my eyes. Something about the shower brought forth emotions I hadn't known I'd been suppressing. Tears began to stream down my face, intermixing with the water crystals as Starlet began to wash my body. She started at my scalp, shampooing my hair. Then she washed my back and my chest, moving down to every piece of me. As I opened my eyes, I stared into her browns, feeling less and less alone as her body washed mine and I washed hers.

Her hair was soaked, showcasing her natural curls as they fell down her back. She'd never looked more beautiful to me than at that moment right there.

My hands fell to her hips, and I pulled her body against mine. I pressed my forehead to hers as I shut my eyes. The water was hot, yet for some reason, chills raced throughout my whole system.

"Thank you," I whispered.

"Always," she replied.

* * *

AFTER THE SHOWER, she put on a pair of her panties and one of my T-shirts that was oversized on her. She looked perfect. As she went to slide into a pair of pants, I gave her a tired grin. "Pants are overrated."

She laughed. "So today's a comfy day? No pants needed?"

"No pants needed whenever you stay with me."

I cooked her breakfast. A bacon, red pepper, and cheese frittata. As I set her plate in front of her at the dining room table, I felt a pull of nerves hit me. "Just so you're aware, I'm not a cook like my mother was, so if you hate it, that's fine."

She breathed in the aromas and moaned. "There's no way I'm going to hate this."

I sat down beside her, and before I began eating, I mumbled a prayer under my breath. I wasn't a praying kind, but Mom always prayed over our meals whenever we'd sit at that table, so I took up the task for her. It was odd, but that was what fear did to a person. Fear makes a person do things out of character.

I rolled my shoulders back when I finished and began eating. To my surprise, it tasted like Mom's used to taste. "Oh my god," we said in unison.

I looked up at Starlet as she shot her stare toward me. "Bravo, Mr. Corti," she said, applauding. "This is fantastic."

"Not so bad at all."

We ate until we were stuffed, and when lunchtime came around and we ate some more.

I took a break and went to the hospital to sit with Dad for a few hours. Nothing changed, not for the better and not for the worst. I headed back home after visiting hours ended.

Starlet helped me prep dinner, which was an enjoyable experience. We moved around one another as if we were made to run a kitchen together. We'd prepped the dutch oven bread a few hours prior to going with dinner that night—bucatini with lemony carbonara.

My world,

It's not the most authentic version of carbonara, but when life gives you lemons...make pasta.

Con amore,

Mama

As Starlet made the salad, I walked behind her and wrapped my arms around her waist, and kissed her neck. I paused a moment as a memory flashed back toward me. Dad used to always hug Mom from behind when she was cooking, and he'd kiss her neck.

Grief hit me like a wave. I stepped backward, trying to shake it off.

Starlet turned and noticed my sudden shift.

"What is it?" she asked.

"Nothing. Everything's fine."

"You're lying."

"No, I'm not."

"Yes, you are. Do you know how I know?"

"Do tell."

"Because when you lie, your eyes look cold."

I chuckled, amused. "And when I tell the truth, how do my eyes look?"

"Alive," she replied. "They look alive."

I wanted to shoot off a witty comment, but my sarcastic ways were messed up due to my sadness. So instead, I told the truth. "My parents used to cook together. Mom called Dad her sous chef. They'd play music and dance around the kitchen, hugging and kissing and laughing. As a kid, I thought it was so annoying, but...I don't know. I just got a flashback of that as I held you."

"Oh." She nodded. "The tiny ones hurt the most sometimes."

"The tiny ones?"

"The memories that seem so small and minuscule. It's as if you almost forgot they existed until they show up again and knock you backward."

I nodded. "That was exactly it. But it was odd because...it triggered me, but at the same time, I realized I had what they had with you. I felt what they felt when I held you…" I pulled her into me and kissed her forehead. "I realize that it's you," I whispered.

"What's me?"

"You're the something that makes me feel better, even on the worst days."

Her eyes glassed over, and she kissed me slowly. Or perhaps I'd imagined it was slow. Whenever I was around Starlet, it was as if time slowed down in the best possible way.

I smiled at her as my arms wrapped around her body. "You know, I really like seeing you in my T-shirt. It's almost as if it were made for you."

She stepped back and spun around. "You think so? Maybe I should've put on pants instead of just my underwear."

I moved over to her and pulled her into a hug. "Oh no. The panties are what makes the look complete."

I kissed her forehead, and she snuggled into me. "Are you okay, Milo?"

"I am right now." I always felt better when she was in my arms. I smiled and kissed her. I couldn't wait for the day we could do that in public. I'd kiss her in front of every single person. We'd be that annoying public displays of affection couple who made people gag.

We stood in the middle of the kitchen holding one another, with no goal of letting go anytime soon. That was until dinner was ready. Then we moved back to the dining room for the third meal of the day.

I grabbed a bottle of wine from the liquor cabinet. "I would say my parents would have a problem with me drinking this, but seeing how one's dead and the other's in a coma, I doubt I'll get grounded."

Starlet's eyes widened, shocked by my words, but then she narrowed her stare. "Does dark humor help you?"

"It does, and there will probably be a lot of it these next coming days."

"Good to know. Very good to know."

I glanced around my dining room, noticing how brighter it

appeared than the days before. I couldn't exactly put my finger on why it seemed that way, though.

"Did...did you change the light bulbs in here?" I asked her.

She nodded. "I ordered some while you were at the hospital a few hours after lunch. I read online that sometimes brighter lights can help with retinitis pigmentosa. I changed them in all the rooms." She paused and shook her head. "I'm sorry. I should've asked you if that was okay. I noticed a few bulbs burned out and figured I should change them. If you hate it, I could switch them back. It's not a problem at all."

I stood stock-still, not moving an inch as I stared at her. She was remarkable in every possible way. From her messy hair, her stunning eyes, her kind smile, and her heart. Her heart... I didn't know why she'd come into my world, but I knew she was my miracle. The thing that made my hard days more bearable. The person who reminded me how to breathe again after years of holding my breath underwater. She was the next act of my play after the interlude that I'd seemed to be stuck in for years. I couldn't believe that I was lucky enough to know her. To feel her. To fall hopelessly in love with her.

How did a bastard like me end up with someone like her?

"I love you," I blurted out. It wasn't how I'd planned to tell her. It wasn't attached to some big romantic gesture or said with a softened tone of admiration. I blurted it out. Almost aggressively, even. It was as if my body physically couldn't hold the words in any longer. As if my body needed to expel that truth as soon as possible.

"I love you," I repeated, this time slower, softer. "I love you. I love you. I love you."

Starlet's doe eyes widened as she tilted her head up to meet my stare. "You love me?"

"I love you." How could I not? She was the warm summer nights to my cold winter days. She was my person.

I never thought I'd have a person.

I thought it would always only be me.

My stomach tensed up as she stared at me. I cleared my throat, feeling a bit foolish for blurting it out. A tinge of self-doubt hit me as I realized she might not say it back. Why would she, honestly? I was a mess. I knew about my scars and often wondered how another could ever love them. I swallowed hard, reminding myself that I didn't say the words to hear them back. I said the words because they were true. I loved her. I loved her in a way that I didn't know my heart was able to love, and I thought she deserved to know that. A person like her deserved to know they were loved. It would be a shame if the most loving individuals never had a chance to hear those words spoken their way.

I brushed the palm of my hand against the side of my neck. "Listen, you don't—"

"I love you, too." She interjected, making my heart stop. Or was it beating faster? I couldn't tell.

"You love me?"

"I love you."

I kissed her because that was all I could think to do at that moment. She kissed me back because she loved me, too. Lately, my emotions never knew where to land. It was as if I had felt a million different things in such a small period, unable to get my footing, but as she kissed me, I felt as if I were finally back on solid ground.

That night when we went to bed, I was able to hug the woman who loved me as much as I loved her. As she lay in my arms, she turned to me and said, "Have you thought about telling your dad everything you told me last night? Maybe telling him how you need him here? I've read some articles about how sometimes those in a coma can hear you. I think he might need to hear how you really feel."

I took her advice into consideration. At that point, I was willing to try anything to see him open his eyes again.

CHAPTER 30

Milo

The following morning, I showed up at the hospital to sit with Dad. I hadn't been sleeping the best. I'd been running into nightmares more often than not, leaving my mind exhausted by the time I'd wake. Starlet mentioned speaking to Dad from the heart, and that messed with my mind because my heart was pretty fucked up as of late. Starlet made my heartbeats a little tamer at times, but that didn't stop the fact that I was still struggling day in and day out. I wished love was enough to erase the hard parts of life. Instead, it worked as a calming balm. It didn't fix the cracks in my heart, but it soothed it every now and again.

I didn't know how to speak to Dad.

I didn't know where to start or where to end. I didn't know if he could even hear me, honestly. I felt a bit ridiculous doing it but watching him hooked up to those machines was enough to make me want to try anything at least once. I wasn't good with words. Mr.

Slade would probably agree with that fact. Still, I was going to try my best.

"I'm pissed off at you," I told him, staring at all of the wires hooked up to his body and the tube sitting down his throat. The echoes of the machines in his room were sounds that haunted my dreams. "I'm so damn pissed at you for ending up here. I needed you," I whispered, pulling my chair to his bedside. "I needed you, Dad, and you weren't there. And that pisses me off."

I sniffled before clearing my throat. "Mom would've been by my side. If it was the other way around, she would've sat with me and told me we'd be okay no matter what. She would've been on top of every angle of my life. She would've noticed something was off with my vision before I even considered it an issue. She would've been there for me. So, screw you," I told him, wiping the tears that fell down my face. "Screw you for thinking we had to drown alone instead of together. Screw you for falling apart and not thinking I could help you. And screw you for trying to leave me now. You don't get to do that, okay, Dad? You don't get to check out from here and find Mom because I'm not done being mad at you yet, okay? I'm not done with you. I'm not done with us. So, wake up. Please? Please, Dad? Will you wake up? Please wake up now, so we can be broken together. Get up, Dad," I cried, placing my head against his shoulder. "Wake up, wake up, wake up."

The machines kept beeping, but Dad didn't open his eyes. He didn't come back to me at that moment, but I kept cracking. I mourned the man he once was and the man he'd become. I regretted our missed opportunities to heal together. I mourned the pain that both of us had suffered. Then I came back the following morning and spoke to him again.

* * *

ON DAY TWO, I held his hand as I talked. "They're talking about getting me a guide dog," I told him. "It would be way down the line. You'd be amazed at the process it takes to get one. It's kind of funny to think about. I'd been begging you for a dog since I was a kid, and now I get one while you can't say no." I leaned my chin against his shoulder and looked up at his closed eyes. "So how about you wake up and tell me no, Dad? How about you tell me how you don't want to deal with dog shit?" I nudged him slightly. "If you don't wake up soon, I might mess around and get two dogs for the hell of it."

I jumped somewhat when I felt a slight squeeze of my hand. My eyes shot to his hand in mine, waiting to see if I felt it or if my delusions were becoming too strong.

"Come on, Dad. Wake up."

Nothing.

I said good night and came back the next morning for day three.

* * *

ON DAY THREE, they removed his breathing tube and replaced it with an oxygen mask. That felt like a forward movement. I really needed forward movement.

"Her name's Starlet. You might not remember this, but you slow danced with her on your anniversary. She's everything good in this world, Dad," I mentioned as I paced his hospital room. "She's smart, kind, and beautiful. She's so damn beautiful, but oddly enough, that's the least interesting thing about her. She's driven in a way I'd never been. She makes me want to be a better person and watches over me when no one else is around. I try to do the same for her, but it seems she has her life together much better than I ever have. She knows what she wants from life, and I have no doubt she will achieve all her goals. Sometimes, a lot of times, I think I'm not good enough for her, especially with all my issues. I don't want to be a burden on her life with my sight issues. At my group therapy session, they talked about the extra burden that falls on their loved ones sometimes. I don't want that. I don't want her to lose herself as she tries to help me. Anyway, that's Starlet. I love her. I love her so much, Dad. You would too if you met her. I think everyone falls in love when they meet her. Oh, but here's the kicker." I moved over to him, bent down near his ear, and whispered, "She's an employee at the high school. My student teacher. Wild, right? Weston would lose his shit if he found out, and I'm sure you would have a field day cursing me out if you could. So here's your chance. Cuss me out, Dad. Wake up. Tell me how much of an idiot I am."

His eyes fluttered, but then nothing.

* * *

ON DAY FOUR, he was breathing on his own.

I sat in my chair and stretched my feet onto the railing of Dad's hospital bed. "You know how you were convinced someone dented your car at a grocery store when I was fourteen? That was Savannah and me. We were playing in the garage, and I knocked it with my bat. I was shocked you didn't notice, but when you came home from grocery shopping and were convinced someone did a hit-and-run, I figured, why come out with the truth? Oh, and when I was eight, I was mad at you for punishing me, so I put your toothbrush in the toilet and called you poop breath to my friends for two weeks. Oh, and when you were deployed when I was in the first grade, I told the whole class you were actually in Hollywood filming a movie with Brad Pitt. I didn't want them to know you were off at war. I didn't want to think about it in case something bad happened to you."

I stared at him, hoping for anything. Any sign of him getting closer to waking.

I kicked my feet off the railing and pulled my chair closer to him. "Come on, Dad," I murmured, staring at his face that held so many of my features. "Give me something, will you?"

"Some are just a bit more stubborn," a nurse said as she walked into the room with a smile on her face. "I'm sure any day now, you'll be talking to him, and he'll be chatting back."

"It's been five days of nothing," I told her.

"That's not true," she said. "He doesn't have that big tube down his throat anymore—progress. And he's breathing on his own—progress. And he's listening to you."

"What? How do you know?"

"Right there." She pointed at him. "When you speak, his head moves slightly in your direction. He's just tired, that's all. He needs a little rest."

"Like bread," I murmured, thinking about Mom's recipe card.

"I'm sorry?"

"Nothing. Thank you. I should get going. I know visiting hours are almost over." I stood from my chair and squeezed Dad's hand. "See you tomorrow."

It could've been my imagination, but I swore he squeezed my hand back.

* * *

WESTON FORCED me to attend school the following two days, which was the last thing I wanted to do, but I also knew I couldn't fall behind again.

After the sixth period, I started feeling a bit better about being at school because that meant I'd be able to see Starlet in the next hour. That always made the days a little better.

On the way to English, I ran into Bonnie and Savannah, who were chatting it up with one another as always. Bonnie gave me a big grin and nudged me in the arm. "We have good news for you."

I grimaced. "Should I be nervous?"

"No. You should be excited, my friend. We know you've been going through a lot, especially since your dad is in the hospital," Bonnie explained.

"Why do I feel like you're about to say something crazy?"

"Because she's about to say something crazy," Savannah replied.

"We think you need to get laid," Bonnie said matter-of-factly.

I arched my eyebrow. "Come again?"

"I know we voiced how we wished you'd use therapy over your sexcapades techniques throughout the years, but desperate times call for desperate measures. Guess what we overheard in the girls' bathroom this morning."

"Why do I feel as if I don't want to know?" I murmured.

"It was the twins Beth and Amanda. They were bickering about who could get you in bed first," she told me. "You have two of the hottest twins frothing at the mouth for you."

Savannah agreed. "You can definitely use it to your advantage, especially with everything going on with your dad. We know you use sex to disconnect a bit. So—"

"I don't do that anymore," I confessed.

The two girls stopped in their tracks. "What?" they said in unison.

I shrugged as I approached my locker. "I said I don't do that anymore. I don't hook up with girls like that."

"Oh my gosh," Savannah said in shock. "You're in love!"

"What? No, I'm not," I lied as I opened my locker.

"Yes, you are. Why in the world won't you tell us who she is?" she asked me.

"Savannah has been convinced that you've been in love with some secret girl for a while now. She keeps going on and on about how different you've been," Bonnie said.

I grabbed my books from my locker. "There's no one."

Just then, Starlet came walking by. I met her stare and gave her a small smile. She smiled back at me and then at the girls. "Good afternoon, ladies," Starlet said before she let her eyes fall on me again. "Good afternoon, Milo. See you in class in a few," she said before walking off, my eyes following her the whole time she walked away.

Bonnie's and Savannah's jaws dropped. "You're dating Ms. Evans?!" they whisper-shouted.

My eyes widened at their comment. I slammed my locker shut, turned to them, and whispered, "Shut up, ladies."

Savannah placed her hands on my shoulders and narrowed her eyes toward me. "Milo Corti, I've known you since you were in diapers, so don't think you could lie to me for a second, okay? Are you, or are you not, in a secret relationship with Ms. Evans?"

I blinked a few times. I blinked a few times more. "It's...complicated."

"OHMYGOSH!" they shouted in unison.

I was fucked.

The bell rang, so I headed toward my next class. Bonnie had to go in the opposite direction, but Savannah kept her pace beside me. "You need to tell me everything," she whispered. "Everything!"

"No, actually, I don't."

"Milo! I'm your best friend. I deserve every single detail." She narrowed her eyes and forced me to stop walking. "Is she good in bed?"

"I'm not answering that."

"So, you've had her in your bed."

"I'm not answering that, either."

"Oh my gosh, she's the best sex you've ever had, isn't she?"

I sighed. I pinched the bridge of my nose and shook my head. I knew I wasn't going to get out of that. "Yeah, she is...but that's not all it is...I... I love her, Savannah. You can't say anything to anyone. But I love her."

Savannah's eyes glassed over as she flew her hands over her chest. "OHMYGOSH!" she cried out.

For fuck's sake.

I didn't know how much more I could take of this.

We headed to English class, and I didn't look at Starlet. I didn't need to make the situation more obvious than it'd already been. Savannah passed me a note as class started.

Does she love you, too?

I read the words and crumpled up the paper.

She passed another one.

Are you going to marry her?

Crumpled.

Can I be your best woman when you get married?

Crumpled, crumpled, crumpled.

Oh my gosh. You're screwing our teacher!

Crump-fucking-crumpled.

Tom has been convinced that you two have been screwing for a long time.

"Stop it," I whisper-shouted, tearing up the last piece of paper.

Savannah seemed unfazed by my shortness with her. "This is just like the soap operas my grandma watches every day. Scandalous. I love this for you. You needed a better story arc outside of the sad stuff. I think it's good for you. I think she's good for you."

I grumbled and ignored Savannah's commentary.

She wasn't wrong, though.

I knew Starlet was good for me, too.

For the next few minutes, I overthought how I'd have to tell Starlet that my friends had found out about us. I'd also have to hammer it into said friends that if they spoke a word about it to anyone, I'd rip them in half and toss them into the lake where no one would ever find them. Halfway through class, Weston showed up to the class with a look of dismay on his face.

"Sorry for the interruption, Mr. Slade, but I need to borrow Milo from class," Weston said as he straightened his glasses. He turned to me, and a small smile found his face. "He's awake."

He's awake?

I shot up from my desk, grabbed my backpack, and started in Weston's direction. When I passed Starlet, I noticed her eyes on the verge of tears as a smile stayed plastered on her face. My sweet, sensitive Star. She mouthed, "He's awake."

I felt her words roll through my soul, and I nodded and continued to head out with Weston.

He's awake.

* * *

WESTON and I flew to the hospital, and the moment I walked into Dad's room, I saw his eyes. I could still see him, and he could still see me. I worried for so damn long that I wouldn't be able to see his eyes ever again if he hadn't chosen to wake up. Yet there he was—awake.

"Hey, Son," he whispered, his voice hoarse and tired.

I rushed over to him and wrapped my arms around him. I began to sob against his shoulder as he fell apart against mine. All the fighting we'd done over the past year didn't seem to matter at that moment. All of the hurt and struggles we'd faced seemed to evaporate right then

251

and there. Nothing mattered except for the fact he was okay. He was alive. He was awake.

"Don't ever do that again," I scolded him, feeling as if my heart would fly out of my chest from how hard it pounded against my rib cage. "Don't ever fucking do that again, Dad," I repeated.

Once I let him go, his tears kept falling. He brushed the back of his hand beneath his nose and sniffled as he looked toward Weston and me. "I think I need to get help," he confessed. "I can't stay this way. I want to get better. I need help."

Hearing him say those words felt like music to my ears. I hugged him again and softly spoke. "Okay, Dad. We'll get you help."

"Okay." He sighed.

I sighed, too.

Okay.

CHAPTER 31

Milo

We found a rehab center in Chicago that fit Dad's needs. He stayed in the hospital for a week to recover, and on a Sunday morning, he came home for a short period, packed up some of his clothing, and Weston drove him down to the center to get him checked in.

I offered to go with them, but Dad said he'd rather not have me see him checking into a place like that. I wanted to be there, but I respected his choice. I couldn't argue with him when he was on his way to get help. He'd be there for at least four weeks, which felt like a reasonable amount of time to help him get back on his feet.

The moment they left the house, I called Starlet to come over, and she was there within thirty minutes. We talked for a while, then spent hours working on our homework. We cooked one of Mom's recipes for dinner, and as we set the table for the meal, we were interrupted by the sound of a car engine outside. I froze for a second after hearing keys jiggling in the front door. Then in walked Weston.

"Okay, Milo. Your dad is all settled in. I know you said you wanted today to be on your own, but the idea of you sitting here alone killed me. So I got us some dinner."

Starlet stood in the dining room, frozen in place. I didn't move an inch, either. It felt as if everything around us slowed down.

"Ms. Evans," Weston stated, stunned by Starlet standing there. In my T-shirt. In her panties.

Fuck.

"Oh my goodness! Principal Gallo, hi," Starlet blurted out, growing flustered.

I saw Weston's nose flare as the rage he was witnessing hit him at full speed. "Are you kidding me?" he shouted. He pinched his nose and turned his back on us both.

"I can explain," I said as Starlet began to tremble uncontrollably beside me. Her mind was probably in an instant meltdown. My gut hurt just thinking about what was happening within her body.

"How about you not?" Weston snapped. "Ms. Evans, perhaps you should go find your pants and leave this house."

Starlet's mouth parted, but no words came out. Tears rolled down her cheeks, and she hurried to the bedroom to collect her things. When she walked out with her duffel bag, Weston huffed in amazement.

"Were we having sleepovers? Is that what we were doing?" he snarled at her.

"Take it easy, West," I told him.

"Don't," he barked, pointing a stern finger my way. "Don't, Milo."

Starlet moved past Weston with her head staring down at the floor. Her body was trembling at a speed that made me nervous. Her lips parted once more. "I'm sorry," she whispered. "I'm so, so sorry." I wasn't sure if it was an apology for Weston or me, but before I could tell her not to apologize, she was out the door, in her car, and driving away.

Weston's hands were on his hips, and he looked at me as if I were insane. "Are you shitting me, Milo?"

"You didn't have to react like that," I told him.

His eyes widened with anger. "Oh, I'm sorry. Was I supposed to be oddly cool with one of my teachers screwing her students? Screwing my nephew?! Gee, my bad. I forgot that that was how I was supposed to react to that situation!"

"Student teacher," I muttered as if that made a huge difference.

Weston stared at me as if I had grown two heads or something. "Un-fucking-believable, Milo. Truly. With everything going on right now, you thought this was the right next step."

"You think I don't know what's going on? It's all happening to me, okay? I get what's happening. And if it wasn't for Star—"

"Ms. Evans," he corrected. "Her name is Ms. Evans to you."

"I love her," I said, standing tall but feeling as if I were a little kid being scolded for acting out. "I love her, West."

For a moment, his eyes glassed over. For a moment, I thought he might understand. For a moment, I thought he'd heard my words and was looking past the flaws in how Starlet and I found our way to one another. But then his stare turned cold. "Well, stop loving her. Now."

He turned and walked out of the house, leaving me standing there alone.

The first thing I did was rush to my phone to call Starlet.

She didn't answer.

I shot off a handful of text messages. I called her a dozen more times.

Still, no reply.

CHAPTER 32

Starlet

On Wednesday afternoon, I was summoned to the principal's office.

I hadn't slept a wink the night prior. I was physically ill for most of the night, unable to do anything other than throw up everything inside me. Whitney was worried I had the flu, but I was too ashamed to tell her what happened.

I knew she'd hit me with an "I told you so," and I wasn't ready to hear that. I wasn't prepared to hear anything. I was simply terrified about how I'd screwed up my life. Everything I'd been working for over the past few years was about to be wiped away because I decided to fall in love with a man who loved me, too.

As I walked through the halls of the high school, I noticed Milo, and he caught my stare and came rushing toward me.

"What are you doing here? You should be at home, Milo. You shouldn't be at school dealing with what you're going through," I told him.

"I needed to check on you. What's going on?" he whispered, stepping closer.

"Don't, Milo," I softly spoke back.

"You didn't answer my messages."

"I can't do that," I told him, biting back the tears fighting to fall.

"Star—"

"*Don't*," I whispered-shouted. I locked my eyes with his, and instantly, I felt the tears seconds away from falling down my face. His eyes were packed with concern, with care, with the gentleness that I'd learned to love from him. *I love you. I love you so much it hurts.* "Don't call me that, Milo. Please. I can't talk to you. I have a meeting with your uncle."

"I can come, too."

"No. That would just make things worse. I knew what I was doing, and I went into it with my eyes wide open. Now I have to face the music. It's not your fault or your responsibility to deal with this. I have to face the consequences."

I rounded the corner into an empty hallway. Milo followed me and glanced around before grabbing my arm and pulling me into the janitor's closet. The same closet I had pulled him into weeks prior when he was wasted.

"Are you out of your mind?!" I whispered, shoving my hands against his chest. "You can't do this, Milo."

"I know, I know, shit!" he shouted, raking his hand through his dark hair. "Fuck. I fucked up, Star. I'm sorry. I just...I can't stop thinking about you and wondering if you're okay." He took a step toward me and shook his head. His hand fell to the side of my cheek, and those eyes I loved locked in on mine. "Are you okay?"

Those three words made the tears begin to fall. I shook my head in disbelief at what was happening. I wanted to tell him that I wasn't okay. I wanted to pull him against me and cry into his shoulder. I wanted him to protect me from the world that was imploding around me. But I couldn't.

I couldn't hold him.

I couldn't touch him.

I couldn't love him.

What was worse about the whole situation was that I wasn't the one who truly needed comfort at that moment; it was Milo. He was the one whose world had been set on fire. He was the one who was watching everything fall apart before him. He was the one who needed to be held. To be touched. To be loved.

My body trembled slightly as I stood tall. "I'm going to walk out of here, Milo, and you'll wait a while to exit after me."

He grabbed my arm, sending a wave of electricity through my body. "Star, please. Let me hold you for a second."

I ripped my arm from his touch. "No. No. Don't you see? This is wrong. It's been wrong from the beginning, and I allowed it to spiral into this mess. This was a massive mistake, Mi."

"You think we were a mistake?"

The pain in his voice broke my already shattered heart even more.

"No, of course not. That's not what I mean." He was so far from a mistake. He felt like the first thing ever since my mother passed away that felt right. Milo Corti felt like home to me. Yet that still didn't make it right.

"Do you regret this?" he questioned.

I shook my head and placed a hand against his cheek. "I could never regret you. Even if I tried." His face tilted slightly, and he kissed the palm of my hand, sending chills through me. I lowered my head. "I have to go meet with the principal."

"I'll come with you. We'll face it as a team."

"You can't do that."

"I can. It's fine. He's my uncle. He'll understand. He'll—"

"Milo." I cut in and shook my head. "You can't fight this battle for me. I have to be a grown-up and accept my fate. I'm sorry. I have to go." Before he could reply, I slipped out of the closet and hurried away. I didn't look back out of fear that he'd follow me. Or out of fear I'd crack and rush into his arms. Even though that was all I wanted.

* * *

MY STOMACH SAT in knots as I stood in Principal Gallo's office. He instructed me to close the door behind me, and I did as he said. He gestured for me to take a seat, and I did that, too. My body trembled as he sat across from me, his desk being the only barrier that separated us.

My head stayed down as I fumbled with my fingers. My nerves were at an all-time high, and I still felt nauseous even though I hadn't had a single thing to eat in over twenty-four hours.

He didn't say anything for a while, making me feel like he was waiting for me to take the lead.

I couldn't manage to look him in the eyes as I sat across from him. "Principal Gallo—"

"How did this start?" he cut in.

My head rose, and I met his stare. "Excuse me?"

He removed his glasses and pinched the bridge of his nose. "The situation between you and my nephew. How did it begin?"

I swallowed hard, debating how truthful I should've been about the whole situation. Then I realized it truly didn't matter. The truth was all I had, and no matter how I told it, it would still result in the same outcome. So I gave him every piece of the story. "We met at a college fraternity party before I began student-teaching here. We..." I paused, feeling a bit of embarrassment hit me. "We connected."

"You slept with him," he dryly stated.

I nodded. "Yes, sir."

His brows knitted as he clasped his hands together. "And then you showed up and noticed that he was a student here?"

"Yes. Exactly."

"And so you continued doing what you did at said party."

"No," I shook my head. "Not at all. For a long time, I set boundaries with him. It was strictly professional, and well, then, well, I, well, he, well...we..." I began stuttering over my words. Unable to untangle my jumbled thoughts. Before I could push out another syllable, the door to his office flung open, and Milo shot into the room, shutting the door behind him.

"It's not her fault," Milo barked at his uncle, rage shooting through his words. Or perhaps it wasn't rage. Maybe it was fear of what would happen to me. I felt bad for that, too. For making Milo worry about me when his whole world was up in flames.

"Milo, you were not invited to this meeting," Principal Gallo said. The vein in his neck was popping out, making me more and more nervous about the intensity of his emotions on the subject at hand.

"No, fuck that, West. Come on. You know this is bullshit," Milo shouted. "She's too good at what she does to be punished for—"

"For what?!" Principal Gallo whisper-shouted. "For screwing around with a student? With my nephew?! You can't be serious right now, Milo. I have a job to do, and I need you to leave my office so I can handle this now."

"She saved me," Milo blurted out. His eyes glassed over with emotions as he stared at his uncle, leaving all of himself right there in that office. He was raw and real as he spoke. "I didn't want to be here anymore," he confessed. "I didn't want to exist. I was dying, Weston, and she saved me. She saved my fucking life. So don't do this to her. Don't ruin her life because she chose to save mine."

"Milo. Leave my office," Principal Gallo ordered.

Milo stood tall. "No."

"Milo. Leave. Now," he repeated.

"No."

"Mi—"

"I've lost everything," he said as his voice cracked. "I've lost every-thing, West. I can't do this, okay? Please. I can't lose her, too."

And just like that, my heart shattered into a million pieces for the one I loved.

I went to place a hand on Milo's arm but stopped the moment I saw the principal's stare follow mine. I didn't touch him. I couldn't touch him. "Milo, please go," I whispered as my voice cracked. "Please. Everything will be okay."

Milo's eyes softened with confusion as he studied me. I was thankful for him trying to stand up for me at that moment, but I knew I had to stand on my own. Life was about choices. I'd made my bed, and now it was time for me to lie in it. I couldn't have Milo trying to lie beside me in the mess I'd made.

He blinked a few times toward me before turning toward his uncle. "If you ruin her life, I'll never forgive you."

"It's not his fault, Milo," I swore. "It's not his fault."

I thought that was what pained Milo the most, because he knew it wasn't his uncle's fault. Milo and I made choices. We made decisions that we shouldn't have made, and now we had to deal with the consequences of said decisions. There was no one to blame except for ourselves.

After he left the room, shutting the door behind him. Principal Gallo somewhat deflated in his chair as he pinched the bridge of his nose. "He shouldn't have even been in here. This was supposed to be between you and me, Ms. Evans."

"I know, but he came because he knew I'd be here," I whispered, staring down at my shaky hands. "He came because of me." The realization of that settled in for me as I sat in that chair across from the man who held my whole career future within his hands.

Principal Gallo stayed quiet for a moment. His eyes were heavy with emotions, and I couldn't figure out what exactly he was thinking. I couldn't figure out where his mind was going, and what he was about to say to me.

All I knew was that he, too, was going through the motions of grief, trying to figure out what the next proper steps were to take. He was drowning just as his nephew had been.

"I'm sorry," I said to him, shaking my head slightly. "I'm sorry for all of this. I mean that from the bottom of my heart, Principal Gallo. I am sorry for it all."

He cleared his throat, still not looking toward me. "Perhaps we should follow up with this conversation next week. Until then, please keep your distance from the school. I'll be in touch once everything is handled. Also, please keep your distance from my nephew. He has enough going on in his life. Your involvement isn't going to make anything easier for him. Trust me."

I heard his words, but my heart didn't want to listen. Because in the middle of Milo's storm, he still showed up for me. What kind of monster would I be to not do the same for him?

"I won't stop seeing him," I confessed.

Principal Gallo raised an eyebrow. "Excuse me?"

"I know how this looks to you, Principal Gallo. I know how unprofessional it is, and how awful of a human being you think I am, but I am in love with your nephew, and all I can think about is how he doesn't deserve to be alone. I'll step down from finishing my teaching degree. I'll pivot directions, seeing how I tainted my character, but I do not regret a second of what happened between Milo and me—"

"Starlet—"

"Wait, let me finish. I know you are here to tell me why this is wrong, and why I screwed up, and I want you to know that I see all of that. I get it, and I accept blame, but Milo means the world to me. He means more to me than anyone ever has before, and I cannot leave him. I cannot let him go. He's the best part of my days. Even when he's sad and broken, he's still so good. And I want to be that for him, too. I want to be his good. So go ahead. Tell me how awful I am. Tell me what a shame of a human being I have showcased myself as...but please know that this thing between him and me is real. It's the realest kind of love I've ever felt, and I'll never apologize for that feeling."

Principal Gallo's brows lowered. "Are you done now, Starlet?"

I nodded. "Yes. I think that's it."

He removed his glasses and sat back in his chair. "Good. Now it's my turn." He stared at me with such an authoritative look. As his mouth parted, my fears of what words he'd create grew more and more. Then he said, "Stay."

"I'm sorry, what?"

"Understand that this isn't me as the principal of this school, this is me as an uncle. I've been with my wife for forty years. Longer than both you and Milo have been alive. Milo's parents were together thirty-some years. My sister Ana and I both lived epic love stories with our soulmates. We've lived love stories that people would make movies about. I didn't understand when I first saw you two together.

Hell, I probably didn't understand up until you said no to me. Maybe I still don't understand, but I saw it, Starlet. I saw what you two have, so all that I ask from you is that you stay.

"My nephew is drowning, and I haven't been able to figure out how to help him in over a year. Nothing seemed to work, and I was at my wits' end. Then you showed up, and everything began to shift. He laughed more when he came to my office. He smiled more, too. I didn't think that I'd ever see him do those things again. Now, I realize why he was able to do those things. It was because of you. You brought Milo back to life, Starlet. So please...stay with him. You're saving his life."

I took a deep breath and released it slowly. "I think he's saving mine, too."

"I hope you understand that I cannot allow you to keep teaching here. If anyone else received wind of you and Milo..."

I nodded. "I understand."

"But I won't report you. We'll come up with a reason for your teaching semester to come to an end."

"Thank you, Principal Gallo."

"No. Thank you, Starlet."

* * *

LATER THAT NIGHT, I pulled up to Milo's house with my duffel bag in my hand. I rang his doorbell as my heart skipped a million beats. My mind was spinning at a rapid speed as I waited for him to come to the door, yet the moment he did, the moment he opened the door and stood in front of me, everything slowed down.

I found my grounding.

I found my peace.

He leaned against the doorframe. His eyes were bloodshot, and he looked exhausted. "Hi."

"Hi," I whispered. I gave him a small smile. "Okay?"

He sniffled a bit and pushed out a smile and nodded. "Okay."

I crashed into his arms, and he pulled me in tight, holding me as close as he could. I refused to let him go, too. I'd stay in his arms as long as he needed.

"Okay," he repeated, resting his chin on the top of my head.

Okay.

CHAPTER 33

Starlet

*M*y world had turned completely upside-down, leaving me feeling more lost than ever before. I knew I needed help to get my life back on track, but I wasn't sure if my path was made for me anymore.

"I don't know what I'm doing with my life," I stated as I sat across from my college adviser's desk. "I feel as if I don't even know who I am anymore." It had been a week since Principal Gallo found out what had been happening between Milo and me, a week since Milo's dad went off to rehab.

For the past week, my focus had been getting Milo to all his appointments and helping him out the best I could. At times, I felt as if he saw himself as a burden, but I didn't want him to feel that way. Being able to be there for him felt good, finally. But I'd be lying if I said helping him seemed like a good reason to avoid my own issues.

It was time I faced the music with feeling so lost as of late, and saying those words out loud felt like I finally released the breath I'd been holding for months.

Mrs. Marvin had been my adviser for the past few years, and I'd never found myself sitting in her office. I had to go digging through my paperwork to even recall who my adviser was. I'd never needed guidance on my life choices before because I was so convinced that I was on the right path. Clearly, I'd been misguided for some time now.

"That's okay," Mrs. Marvin said, smiling my way as if I didn't just tell her that I was having a complete identity crisis.

I arched an eyebrow. "Did you not hear me? I said I don't know what I'm doing with my life."

"Yes, I heard you. And that's fine. You're young and learning the ins and outs of yourself, Starlet. You're not supposed to have it all figured out yet."

"I'm a junior. I only have one more year of college. No offense, but I feel like the clock is ticking louder and louder each day."

She kept smiling.

That annoyed me a bit.

"I looked over your records, Starlet, and it appears you are a great student. You have stellar grades—"

"I did get a C on a paper this semester."

"I have students who come into my office thrilled by their C papers."

I sighed. "You know the crazy part about it? I didn't even care that I got a C. It felt good not to have to be so perfect for once in a while." I groaned and rubbed my hands over my face. "What's happening to me?"

"Burnout. It happens to the best of us. The problem is you students have so much pressure put on you to have it all figured out right at the age of eighteen. That's a crazy concept if I'm honest. You'd be shocked by how many people come in freshman year thinking they want one thing and leaving senior year with a completely different plan of action."

"What advice do you give them?"

"Pivot. Change directions. That's more than allowed."

"Even this late in the game?"

"I have people sitting where you are a semester before their graduation. It's never too late to change the life you're living. It's the bravest thing you can do. So what do you want, Starlet?"

"That's the thing. I don't know. I don't have the slightest clue what I want."

"What a fun place to be because that means the sky is the limit. I think it's about time you start trying some different things or writing out a list of things you're into."

I don't even know what I'm into, I thought to myself.

I felt as if my life was a blank canvas, and I had no idea how to paint.

"Here's some homework for you," Mrs. Marvin said. I sat straighter. Homework was good. I was great with homework, minus that dang C. "I want you to make a list of fifteen things you like. Fifteen things that make you happy. Then I want you to come back to me."

"Oh. That's easy enough. Okay. I can do that."

Fifteen things that made me happy? That would be a walk in the park.

"I'll have the list to you by next week," I told her confidently.

* * *

SPOILER ALERT: naming fifteen things that made me happy was not a walk in the park. I'd been staring at my notebook with the page numbered one through fifteen with no progress at all. The only thing that saved me from the despair of my nonexistant list was Whitney calling and asking me to go out for lunch with her.

I hadn't been back to our dorm room very much, and I needed best friend time. Whitney didn't scold me for not being around as much. She simply seemed happy to see me. It amazed me how far one person's jaw could drop after I filled her in on everything going on in my life.

"Well, you're definitely not Cheerios anymore," Whitney breathed out. "What are you going to do?"

I shook my head. "I don't know. The counselor says a lot of people change their majors along the way. And with my communications degree, I could find a job in a different field. On top of that, I have my two minors."

"I guess you being an overachiever paid off," she joked. Then a frown found her. "You really are considering giving up your teaching career for this guy?"

"It's not just about Milo," I confessed as I picked at my fingernails. "I think it has less and less to do with him and more to do with me. I went into this wanting to be a teacher simply because I wanted to make my mom proud. And sure, maybe I do end up still wanting to teach, but where my head is right now, I don't know if I can make the right choices. I don't know my likes or dislikes. All I know is that I'm good at learning things. I'm a great student, but that doesn't mean that it makes me happy. For the first time in my life, I want to be happy, Whit."

"I want that for you, too, Star. It's funny, though. I thought I'd be the one going through a college life crisis way before you."

I snickered. "I'm just full of surprises this year."

"The things we do for love..." she somewhat joked.

"You think I'm crazy."

"Yes," she quickly stated. She reached across to me and held my hand. "But I also think all the best women in the world had to be a little crazy to get what they wanted. You're brave, too, Star. And besides, even if this all blows up in your face and your life spirals downward, you'll have a good story to tell in the nursing home one day."

I began fidgeting with my hands as I sat back in my chair. "Whit, do you think you could name fifteen things that you love to do?"

"Fifteen?" she asked, then she waved a dismissal hand my way. "I could easily name thirty."

She'd named forty-two by the time lunch was over.

CHAPTER 34

Milo

Starlet and I began spending almost all our time together. We showered together, cooked together, and watched movies together. We'd been listening to the same audiobooks for fun before bed. It was as if our worlds were emerging the way we'd hoped. But something felt off. She felt off, which left me unsettled.

One night after I finished my homework, we took a shower together and tossed on some sweats to be comfortable.

"You need to eat something. I can cook for you or order something in," Starlet said, going through the fridge as I sat on the barstool in front of the island, staring her way. She was wearing my oversized sweats, and all I could think about was how much I loved her.

"I'm not too hungry."

"You still have to eat. It's important to eat. I'll grab my phone and—"

"Hey."

She turned to me, and her shoulders dropped. "Hey."

"Come here." She walked over to me and stepped between my legs. I wrapped my arms around her. "Are you good?"

"Yeah, I'm fine. Everything's okay. I want to make sure—"

"Star."

Her eyes were glassed over. She shook her head. "I'm just mentally working through some things."

"You want to work through them out loud with me?"

"No. It's fine. I don't want to add more pressure to your life."

I arched my eyebrow. "Now you're worrying me. What's wrong?"

Her eyes flashed with emotions, but she blinked them away. That was the opposite of who I'd known her to be from the beginning of time. Starlet never hid her emotions. That was one of the many things I loved about her.

"Star," I whispered, brushing my mouth against hers. "Talk to me."

"I will. Soon. Just not tonight, if that's okay? I just need to process things first."

"Did I do something wrong?"

Her eyes widened, and she shook her head. "No. Of course not. Honestly, you're the only thing that really makes sense in my world right now."

"Well, when you're ready to talk, I'm ready to listen." I kissed her cheeks. "But in the meantime, just know that everything's gonna work out fine."

She pointed a stern finger at me. "How dare you use those words against me?"

"Sorry, Teach. You should've never taught me those words."

Her head dropped a little. "You probably don't have to call me Teach anymore. That's not something I see coming to fruition in the foreseeable future."

I arched my eyebrow. "What do you mean?"

"Nothing. It's nothing. I'm just figuring out some things, that's all."

"Did Weston come down on you hard?"

She narrowed her eyes and shook her head. "No. Quite the opposite, actually."

"What did he say to you?"

"He told me to stay."

That made my damaged heart skip a beat or two. I placed my forehead against hers.

I was so damn happy she'd stayed.

At least, that was how I'd felt at first. As the days went by, Starlet stayed by my side even though I told her it was okay to get back to her life and her world. I was keeping up with my homework. I couldn't say the same about Starlet.

She seemed so worried about me being okay that she was willing to jeopardize her own education. Whenever I brought up the teaching situation, she'd tell me it was fine and she was figuring it out. She told me not to worry about her, but it was almost impossible not to. On Sundays, when she'd generally visit her father, she'd end up staying at my place. Her whole life was being turned upside down due to me, and I couldn't stop feeling the heaviest level of guilt surrounding that. I knew that my stuff was heavy, but it was never meant for Starlet to carry that load.

Usually, when I went to group therapy, I was more of a listener. I wasn't one to speak up about my issues. Maybe that was why my problems took so long to get better. But that afternoon I felt as if speaking up wouldn't only help me, it would help the person I cared most about.

I sat in the metal chair with a knot in my stomach when it came time for me to share.

"I think my girlfriend is giving too much of herself to me," I confessed.

"Go deeper with that thought, Milo," Tracy said. "Dig some more at what you mean."

I brushed the back of my neck with the palm of my hand. "My dad is currently in a rehab center. He'll be there for a while, so my girlfriend moved in with me temporarily to make sure I wasn't alone. Don't get me wrong, I love her. I love having her around but...she gives so much. She worries about my eyesight more than I do. She's been bringing in these new tech systems, too, to help me read and I'm not even at that point in my journey. And while she's doing all of this, she's losing herself. She's so focused on me that she's not taking good care of her."

"I've been there before," another person said. His name was Greg. He was much quieter than the others, but added in to the conversations whenever he saw fit. From what I was learning, he wasn't the most positive guy around. "She's going to give and give until it's too much and she'll resent you."

"No," I disagreed. "She's not like that at all."

"That's what you think now. Just wait and see," he bitterly replied.

And there I was thinking Henry was the grump of the group.

"Greg, let's make sure we don't project our situations on others. Milo's situation isn't the same as yours," Tracy urged.

Greg grumbled. "Okay, but don't blame me when I end up right."

"Oh, shut it, will you, Bitter Betty," Henry scolded. At least my favorite grump was on my side. Henry cleared his throat. "What Milo is getting at, and correct me if I'm wrong, is that he feels like his life is a burden on hers."

I nodded. "Yes. Exactly. I know this is a long, slow journey for me. It could be years before I'm legally blind and even longer before I lose my vision completely. If she's already this hyper-focused on me, then what would the rest of her life look like? What would happen to her world when I physically need her more? Or if my mental health worsens? There will be days that I can't pretend to be happy. I already feel awful having bad days because it makes her feel sad and I hate making her feel sad."

"This is part of the journey," Tracy explained. "It's a hard part, and it's tricky. Because we deserve love in all its forms, just as everyone else does. Then there's a slippery slope of knowing how much is too much to request from another person. How much are you willing to place on another's plate?"

"I don't want to waste her time," I whispered.

"Then be a real man and let her go," Greg said.

"Greg, I swear I'll throat punch you," Bobby called out.

"Bobby, no throat punching," Tracy scolded the kid.

"But some people deserve throat punches," Bobby argued.

"He's not wrong," Henry muttered.

I smirked a little but still felt the knot in my stomach.

"Stop trying to sugarcoat it for the kid. You know I'm right," Greg grumbled. "They'll look back in twenty years and will both be miserable."

That was my biggest fear. I didn't want to be the reason Starlet lived with regrets.

After the session, we all said our goodbyes. Henry and Bobby called out to me and invited me out for ice cream the following Sunday.

"You two hang out outside of the sessions?" I asked, somewhat surprised.

"Well, he is my grandfather, after all," Bobby mentioned.

"*Step*grandfather," Henry corrected. "His mother married my son a few years back. They met at one of the family gatherings the group did. Now, this kid is stuck in my life forever. Anyway, we get ice cream every Sunday at Taylor's Ice Cream Parlor at noon. You're more than welcome to join."

"I'd like that. Thanks."

"And, Milo? Don't pay much attention to what Greg was saying. He can be a real jerk. And I should know, seeing how I'm the biggest jerk."

"Yeah, thanks." I heard Henry's words, but Greg's were louder that night. I headed out of the building to find Starlet sitting in her Jeep, waiting for me.

I climbed into the passenger seat, and she smiled. I wished she didn't do that. It made it harder for me to think straight.

"Hey, how was the meeting?" she asked.

"Good. It was good," I lied. I felt awful.

"I'm glad. While you were in there, I was looking up some different apps that can help with your vision."

I arched my eyebrow. "I thought you were going to be working on your homework."

She shrugged. "I'll get to that later on."

That was enough to push me over the edge that Starlet didn't even know I was dangling from.

That night we'd stayed up too late watching yet another movie, but my mind was everywhere but on the film.

"We should go to bed," I said, standing from the couch.

She held her arms out toward me, and I picked her up. I carried her to the bedroom and laid her down. She pulled me toward her and kissed me. I kissed her back. First slowly, then deeply, then as if it were the last kiss the two of us would share.

She began to remove my clothes, and I let her. She began sucking my earlobes and licking my neck, and I welcomed it. I wanted her that night. Probably more than I'd ever wanted her before.

"Should I shut off the lights?" she asked me.

I shook my head. "Can we leave them on? I want to see all of you." Every inch, every piece, every curve.

This time as we slept together, it was different from all the times before. We were making love that night. I'd never made love before her, and I knew I'd never do it with another soul. Love was something so new to me. I didn't expect her love to travel to so many areas of my world. Her love lived within the small moments. The quiet ones. The gentle easing of harsh storms. It was in her soft embraces and slow kisses. It lay upon my skin pressed against hers. It was the indulgent caresses of our souls. It was in her eyes, and I knew it was in mine.

True love.

I took in every move she'd made against me that night.

At that moment, I should've felt nothing less than bliss. I should've found solace in the fact that the most genuine form of love was lying against me. When I looked into Starlet's eyes, I saw forever. I saw my heart and how it was forever becoming tattered to hers.

That realization terrified me. Because the only thing I'd ever known about love, true love, was how it could break a person. How they could shatter and lose themselves to said love. My father loved my mother, and then she was gone. When she'd left, a part of him died that very same day. I was watching it happen with Starlet, too, with her dreams and her ambitions. She was letting them die all in the name of love. All because of me.

The saddest truth about true love was at the end of the day. It could only lead to true heartbreak.

As we made love, as her brown eyes locked with mine, I felt it in my chest. The aching that would one day come. The hurt that would one day develop within either me or her soul. Because even though it was true, love couldn't ever beat death.

While my mind should've chosen to live in the moment, to flourish in the minutes, in the seconds of my time with Starlet, I couldn't allow it.

My heart was breaking because I loved her too much.

My soul ached because there would come a day when our love would have an ending.

I was so tired of endings. Endings made me never want to begin anything again.

My head turned slightly, and I closed my eyes. I felt tears forming as I tried to slow down my mind. To not let my fears, my anxiety, and my panic overtake something that was supposed to be so beautiful.

Fuck you, Milo, I told myself.

Screw my messed-up brain and its inability to live quietly in the moment.

"Hey," she whispered, placing her hand against my cheek. "Look at me," she requested.

I hesitated to turn my head back toward her because I knew when I met her stare, the tears would fall. I knew it would change everything because I was about to mess this thing up. I was about to take a well-soaring plane and make it crash.

"Milo, please…"

I sighed, obsessed with the sweetness of her voice and the softness of her touch on my face. The tears fell without warning. I turned to her, my eyes burning with emotions, some I hadn't even known how to decipher.

Her expression wasn't confused or judgmental, though. It was gentle. She pulled my mouth to hers and kissed me. "I love you," she swore against me. "I love you so much."

She saw it, too—the love.

"I love you," she echoed again, and again, and again...

I kissed her harder as my tears fell against her cheeks. Her beautiful cheeks, with her deep dimples and loving eyes. She kissed me with love, and I kissed her with the same. Her love felt like poetry to my uneducated mind. It felt effortless and timeless. I wondered what my love felt like for her. Was it soft? Was it gentle? Was it raw and free?

Was it poisonous? Did it hurt?

We made love that night.

The only problem?

She made love to me as if it would last forever.

I made love to her as if it would end come morning because it would.

Come sunrise, I'd say my goodbyes.

Because love couldn't last forever, therefore we'd only have that night.

CHAPTER 35

Starlet

$\mathcal{I}$ woke up the following morning in Milo's bed and reached out to place my hand against his chest as I had the previous few days. When I didn't find him in the bed, I sat up and glanced around the room. He stood there in his gray sweatpants, wearing no shirt, staring out of the window with a coffee mug in his hands.

"Good morning." I yawned, rubbing the sleep from my eyes.

He turned my way with a tiny smile on his face. "Morning."

"How long have you been up?"

"Not that long. Figured I'd drown myself in coffee for a while."

I glanced at my watch and noticed the time. "Oh, it's later than I thought. We should get going if we are going to catch the sunrise. Let me get dressed fast and—"

"I love you, Starlet." His words were so calm and confident that they made my heart do a few backflips. "Do you know that? Do you know that I love you?"

"Of course I know that."

He walked over toward me and set his coffee mug on the night-stand. He then placed the palm of his hand on the back of my neck and pulled me in for a kiss. He kissed me long and hard, harder than he'd kissed me in some time. I felt it vibrate throughout my whole system, sending me into a flurry. It felt different. Something was off about the way he kissed me. I didn't know kisses could taste like goodbyes before he laid his lips against mine.

I pulled away slightly and narrowed my eyes. "What's going on?"

"Nothing, I just needed to kiss you. That's all."

"Milo—"

He stood and held his hand out toward me. "Let's go watch the sunrise."

I lightly swatted his hand away. "No. What was that?"

"What was what?"

My heart was racing, and I placed my hands against my chest as if that would soothe its wild beats. "Tell me what's going on."

His head lowered, and my heart dropped right when he said, "Star, I think you're amazing..."

"No." I shook my head. "What are you doing?"

He rubbed the palm of his hand against the nape of his neck. "I just feel as if we...with everything going on in my life right now, I don't think we should..." His words kept fading off, so I went ahead and finished them for him.

"Are you breaking up with me?" I asked, my voice shaking with the nerves pushing their way from my stomach to my throat. A wave of nausea crashed into my nervous system, rocking my whole world upside down.

His head stayed staring at the floor instead of looking at me. "Listen—"

"No." I cut in. "No. If you're trying to break up with me, you don't get to stare at the floor, Milo. If you're going to break up with me, look me in the eye and do it like a grown-up."

Please don't look up. Please don't look up...

He looked up.

He locked his eyes with mine.

He broke my heart.

"I can't date you anymore, Starlet."

He said Starlet instead of Star.

He used my full name. He hadn't done that in weeks.

That felt like a betrayal I wasn't ready to face.

I was going to be sick. Everything in my head began to spin, and I felt as if I were going to pass out any second now. I stood from the bed, but my vision blurred. What was he doing? Why was he saying that? There was no way he was breaking up with me. Not after everything we'd been through. Not after everything I walked away from.

I shook my head. "I left everything behind for this. I want this. I chose to walk away from my job for us. I'm giving up my career because I want this. I want you. I want us. You can't do this to us, Mi. This is our first chance to really be an us, and you can't throw that away," I cried out.

I was confused, hurt, and shattering. Months ago, I walked in on my ex-boyfriend cheating on me and it hurt me. Not because of him cheating but because it threw a wrench into what I thought my life was supposed to be. But looking back, everything had to happen as it had. Otherwise, I would've never met Milo. We were meant to be, and I knew it. Because if we weren't, I wouldn't be feeling the overwhelming pain I was facing. It wouldn't hurt this bad if he wasn't the one for me.

I needed Milo to hear me. To listen to my words, to hear my pain. "Please, Mi...please. We're doing so great." I pulled his hands into mine so he could feel me. He needed to feel my warmth, feel my soul seeping into his.

How could he do what he was doing? How could he turn his back on me when we were finally able to be who we wanted to be, what we wanted to be—together.

"I know, I know," he whispered, shaking his head. "I just...I don't think I'm good for you."

"You don't think you're good for me? What? Of course, you're good for me. You're the best thing that's ever happened to me."

"You don't see yourself, Star. I do, okay? I do. I see you throwing everything away because of me. You aren't acting like yourself anymore. You hardly do your homework, and you don't go to class. Half the time, you act like you don't want to be a teacher anymore."

"So what if I don't? That's fine. I'll become something else."

"See what I mean? You're not thinking straight. You're so focused on making sure I'm okay that you're forgetting about your whole life."

My mouth parted to respond, yet my mind was too jumbled to form my next words. I felt insane as I stood in front of him. The number of tears falling from my eyes sent a wave of embarrassment through my system because he wasn't feeling the aches of heartbreak as deeply as I'd been. He wasn't falling apart in the same fashion as I was.

You idiot, I thought to myself.

How could I have been so naive? I thought what was between us was real, but clearly, it was a one-way street of true feelings, and I was the driver behind the wheel.

He didn't feel for me the way I'd felt for him. It wasn't possible.

If he had, he wouldn't have been able to let me go so easily.

"You made love to me last night, Milo," I cried as I shoved my hand against his chest. "You made love to me knowing you were going to break my heart in the morning, didn't you?" He paused. I shoved him again. "Didn't you?"

His voice cracked. "Starlet..."

"No!" I shouted, shoving him again. And again. And again. He took every shove as if he deserved it. My tears fell relentlessly, my pain causing my body to want to quit.

"I'm sorry," he whispered, grabbing my wrists to stop my swings. I didn't even care because I didn't want to hit him. I wanted to love him and him to love me back.

"I'm so sorry, Starlet," he softly said.

He used my full name again.

He wasn't going to take it back.

He wasn't going to change his mind.

He didn't want to be with me, so he let me go.

I pulled my wrists away from his hold, realizing that the story I thought we were finally beginning wouldn't be a full-length novel. We were nothing more than a short story; he wrote the end before we explored our first chapter.

"Please don't," I begged. "Please don't throw me away."

"I hope one day you can understand where I'm coming from," he pleaded, those brownish-green eyes staring deep into my soul.

I looked him dead in the eyes, too, hoping he could see how he hurt me and understand the words that were about to fly from my mouth. "Fuck you, Milo Corti. I hope I never see you again."

*　*　*

I WALKED into the dorm room, feeling like my heart had been ripped from my chest. I didn't know love could do that...slice open every piece of one's soul and still allow them to continue through life as if they weren't the walking dead.

"Hi, roomie," Whitney stated from her bed, glancing over her shoulder. She was wrapped in a blanket, watching a reality show, which she quickly shut off.

"Hi, roomie," I replied, dropping my keys on to my desk.

Whitney frowned. "Heart?" she asked.

"Broken," I replied.

"Hug?"

"Yes."

She held her arms open wide. I dragged my feet over to her and collapsed into her arms. Whitney didn't ask me anything else. She didn't question what went down when I went to see Milo. She didn't inquire about our final words. Mainly because she knew none of that mattered. Nothing that went down between him and me would've changed a thing because two facts remained the truth: Milo left me, and I let him go.

Now, both of us had to pick up our own pieces.

Both of us had to learn how to live without each other.

It was an odd feeling—how one day, Milo was a stranger, and another, he was my everything.

I loved him, and he loved me. I didn't question that at all.

Still, we had to let go.

I guessed the rumors were true. Love wasn't enough to make something last forever. Sometimes life got in the way. Tomorrow, I'd pick myself up. Tomorrow, I'd try to exist in a world where he no longer belonged.

Yet tonight, I'd cry.

* * *

I SHOWED up at the tattoo parlor without giving my father a heads-up. The moment I walked inside, the crew cheered excitedly to see me. Dad was in the middle of a session and couldn't come out for another hour to meet me in the front lobby.

The second he saw me, though, he said, "What's wrong?"

I stood from my chair and parted my lips to speak, but no words came out. I burst into uncontrollable tears. It only took a few moments for him to step forward and wrap me in his embrace.

"It's okay, kiddo," he whispered as he held me tight. "It's okay."

But it wasn't okay. Nothing was all right. My whole life had turned upside down, and I had no idea how to get back on track. I'd fallen behind in school, lost my student teaching position, and lost Milo.

I had nothing.

I didn't even know who I was anymore.

Mom would've been so ashamed of the woman I was becoming. So embarrassed by the choices I'd made that winter, which made my life come to a sudden crashing point.

Once I managed to calm myself down, Dad took me into his office and shut the door behind us. I sat down and told him everything. Every single piece of the story, not leaving one drop of information out of the equation.

I wasn't even brave enough to look my father in the eyes as I told him everything. My stare was focused on the carpeting as a million words I'd never imagined I'd speak out loud to my dad came rolling off my tongue.

Once I finished, I sat back in the chair, feeling like a complete fool. I raised my head to find my father's stare, and with one exhalation, he said, "Well, damn."

"I messed up, Dad. I messed up everything. My whole life is ruined, and I don't know what I'm going to do."

"Let's take a step back, kiddo." He brushed his hand against his beard and narrowed his eyes. "You're in love?"

What?

That was what he decided to focus on?

That was the piece of my messed-up story that he fixated on?

"What does that have to do with anything?" I asked.

"It has to do with everything, Star. You were dating that one boy for years, and you never mentioned love. It felt like you dated him just because you thought that was what you were supposed to do. You've always done what you thought you were supposed to do until now."

"Yeah, I know. And look at what I've become."

"Yeah. Something beautiful."

I narrowed my eyes at him, annoyed and confused by his reaction. "Why aren't you yelling at me? Why aren't you cursing me out and telling me I need to do better and that I ruined my life, and that I made terrible choices? Tell me how much I suck, Dad."

"But you don't. If anything, I should scold you for not screwing up more." He chuckled.

"Dad."

"I'm serious. You're hardly in your twenties, Star. Do you know what your twenties are for?"

"What?"

"They are made for fuckups and mistakes. That's the best part of your twenties—the missteps. Then in your thirties, you somewhat discover who you are until your midthirties when you rediscover yourself because, well, the early thirties are a bit odd. By your forties, you only have like ten more fucks to give about anything, which is kind of cool. Then there are your fifties. And let me tell you, I love it here because, well, fuck it all. Do you understand?"

I knitted my eyebrows together. "I think so?"

He smiled and patted my shoulder. "Sweetheart, what I'm saying is, you're not even a third of your way through your fuckups. Embrace it. Besides, you're in love, so that's a win."

"What's that supposed to mean?"

"It's love, Starlet. And from the sounds of it, it's real love with this one. Which means it's not supposed to make sense. Real love is messy and hard, and it takes a lot of ups and downs to make it work."

"It wasn't like that with you and Mom," I said, slightly deflated. "You two were perfect."

He huffed out a burst of loud laughter. "What?"

"You were. You two were soulmates."

"Yeah, sweetheart, we were. But we were far, far from perfect."

"From the outside looking in, you were. You two never even fought."

"In front of you," he corrected. "We were really good at taking our screaming matches into our cars while you were in the house."

My mouth dropped, leaving me completely stunned. "No way."

"Total way. And plus, the first night we met, we randomly hooked up, and ta-da! She was pregnant."

"What?!" I gasped. "With who?"

"With you, bonehead."

I pressed my hand to my chest. "I was a one-night stand baby?"

"You were completely a one-night stand baby. Your grandparents were pissed about that one. Yes, we were married young, but we felt pressured into doing that by society and our parents. I thought proposing to the girl I knocked up was what I was supposed to do. The first few months of marriage, your mother and I hated one another. We bickered like no other and fought day in and day out. Then after you were born, it got harder and harder until it got a little bit easier. We weren't officially happy, probably until you were two years old."

I sat there completely dumbfounded about the story I was being told. "How have I never heard about any of this?"

"It's not every day you tell your kid that she was a one-night stand accident. Besides, you forget the rocky beginning when you have the most beautiful middle and ending to your story."

"But how was it a beautiful ending? She died, Dad."

"Yes, she did, Star, and that was hard. But she died with our love, and we were left with hers. You can't convince me that that's not a beautiful thing—to love one another until the very end. And if I had the opportunity to relive our story, knowing how it would end, I would do it in a heartbeat. Because I will always choose to relive love when presented with the chance."

Those words made my eyes tear up.

Dad smiled. "Star, we come into this life with only one promise—that someday we will leave it. Death is the final act of everyone's story. We all know this. The problem is so many people live life as if they are already dead, going through the motions of what they think they are supposed to do instead of living their most authentic lives. I don't want you to be perfect. I want you to be real, and I want you to live. Fall in love and live. Screw up and live. Find yourself, Star, and live."

I glanced down at my fingernails and began picking at them. "I do love him, Dad."

"I'm glad you let that love in."

"But he doesn't want me. He pushed me away."

"Why?"

"Because he thought he was ruining my life."

"And why would he think that pushing you away would be the best option?"

"Because he..." I sighed as the realization settled in. "Because he loves me."

"Exactly. I get that it's raw and new right now. You are allowed to be hurt and pissed off at him for that choice. But also be thankful you found a guy who cares so much about your well-being that he was willing to walk away."

"I just wish he had stayed."

"Yeah, but you know what? Sometimes it's not the ending of a couple's story. Maybe you're just on a time-out. Just give it time.

Allow both of you the space to figure yourselves out, then see if your puzzle pieces still fit together."

"Thanks, Dad," I said, feeling a little better about the wildness that was my current life.

"Always, kiddo. Now come on. We're going to go get you some ice cream."

I chuckled. "Dad. Buying me ice cream won't fix my problems."

"You're right. Maybe it won't, but at least you can be sad with Oreo cheesecake custard. It's a bit easier to be sad when you have Oreo cheesecake custard."

Fair point.

"Don't worry, baby girl." Dad smiled at me as he stood and held a hand out to help me stand. "Everything's gonna work out fine."

Everything's gonna work out fine.

"What was this guy's name again?" he asked me.

"Milo."

"Last name?"

"Corti."

"Milo Corti. That's a badass name."

"Why are you asking for his name?"

"Because I'm going to find him and cuss him out for making my daughter cry," he replied matter-of-factly.

I laughed but then saw the serious look on his face. "Dad. Don't you dare stalk my ex-boyfriend."

"Not stalk. Just…follow."

"Dad!"

He grumbled. "Fine, fine. I won't do that."

"Swear?"

He held his hand up. "Scout's honor, Star. Scout's honor."

CHAPTER 36

Milo

"So you're the guy who broke my daughter's heart?"

It was early morning, before sunrise. I stood in my driveway when I saw a tall, buff man covered in tattoos staring my way. He wore black sunglasses, and the moment he took them off, I knew he was Starlet's father. They had the same eyes.

My stomach knotted up as he walked toward me. There was no doubt he could whoop my ass with a single punch based on the size of his biceps alone. The stern look on his face, paired with his grimace, almost made me want to break out into a sprint. I didn't run, though. If anything, I deserved what he was about to lay on me.

"Yes, sir," I replied. "If it's any consolation, I broke my own in the process."

I doubted that took away from the fact that I still broke Starlet's heart.

"I'm Eric," he stated, walking toward me. He unbuttoned his long sleeves and rolled them up his arms. I didn't even know forearms could be solid muscle. What did this guy eat for a living? Whole chickens? "And you're Milo, huh?"

"That's me," I replied, trying not to sound intimidated.

"Where are you heading?"

"I was just going to go sit by this pond my parents and I used to fish at."

Eric narrowed his eyes. "Is your dad still in rehab?"

I nodded, feeling a knot in my gut. "Yeah. For a few more weeks."

"How is it going for him?"

I shrugged. "It's hard to tell. I'm just happy he's getting the help he needs."

"Good. I'm glad. Life is tough. It takes courage to ask for help." He glanced around and then met my stare again. "You want a ride to the lake?"

"Oh no, it's not that far and—"

"Milo." He cut in and stepped closer. "Do you want a ride to the lake?"

I guessed it wasn't a question as much as it was an order. My palms were sweating, and I was almost certain I was seconds away from pissing my pants. "All right, thanks." I climbed into the passenger seat of his car and closed the door gently. The last thing I was going to do was slam the door of a man who could snap me in half with one stern look.

Eric climbed into the driver's seat and asked for directions to said pond. I told him, and within a few minutes, we were parked and walking out to sit on one of the benches. A good amount of time passed without us exchanging words. I didn't know if I should've felt comfort or unease, yet somehow, I felt a wave of both things as I sat beside Eric.

When I finally found enough courage, I said, "I'm sorry about what happened with Starlet."

Eric kept staring out at the iced-over lake. "Which part are you sorry for?"

"What?"

"What I mean is, which part are you apologizing for? Are you sorry for falling for my daughter?"

"No. Of course not." That was the best thing that ever happened to me. I honestly didn't think I would've been able to keep going on with life over the past few months if it wasn't for Starlet entering my life. I'd never apologize for how I felt for her.

"Are you apologizing for ending things with her?"

I hesitated at that question. I was sorry that things ended, of course, but I didn't regret my decision. That was what hurt the most, I thought. I ended things because I wasn't going to be able to give her the kind of love she deserved. I felt my depression settling in more lately, especially with my recent health issues and Dad being in rehab. I wouldn't be able to be the person for her in the way I'd want to be. She'd already lost her position at the high school and was spending more time with me than she should've. I couldn't be the one to ruin her life.

"No," I whispered. "I'm not apologizing for that."

"Then what is the apology for?"

"Her teaching at the high school. It's my fault she was let go from that. I feel awful about it."

"Oh." He nodded. "That." He picked up a small rock and tossed it at the pond, hitting the ice. It cracked slightly. "Did you know that Starlet's mother was a teacher?"

I nodded. "She'd mentioned it during our talks."

He clasped his hands together and rested them in his lap. "Yeah. She was an English teacher. One of the best ones out there, though I might be biased. Do you know what Starlet wanted to be before her mother passed away?"

"What's that?"

"Anything but a teacher." He glanced my way before picking up another rock and tossing it toward the water. Another crack was created. "Her whole life, Star has done the right thing. She never spoke back to me. She always did her chores and excelled at school. She doesn't even cuss."

"Yeah, I kind of make fun of her because of that."

"You and me both." He chuckled before growing somber. "When her mother passed away, she followed in her footsteps and decided she wanted to be a teacher. For a long time, I wondered if that was what she truly wanted or if she felt it was a way to hold onto her mother."

"She's a great teacher."

"Of course she is. She's a great everything. I could not have dreamed of a better child. She's done everything right for twenty-one years. And then came you."

"I feel shitty about it."

"Don't," he said. "I'm thankful for you."

I arched my eyebrow, confused by his words. He gave a slight grin and threw another rock. Another crack.

"Just because a person always does the right thing, doesn't mean it's the right thing for them. The last time I saw my daughter break down was when we lost Rosa. That was until she showed up at my house completely heartbroken after you ended things with her."

That made me feel like utter shit.

"Thank you for that," Eric said. "For making her break."

"Why do you say that?"

"My daughter has been a perfectionist her whole life. Even more so after Rosa passed, and that scared me a bit. I believe we don't need to live a perfect life to be happy. We only have to live a real one. We aren't searching for perfection...we are searching for truth. You, Milo, have made Starlet finally reveal her reality. And even though it hurts right now, I know she'll be able to grow from this. So I thank you."

I picked up a rock and tossed it into the water.

Crack.

I picked up another and threw it again.

Crack, crack.

"I love her," I confessed.

"Yes," he acknowledged. "Kind of hard not to."

"Can I ask why you came to meet with me, though? Especially since Starlet and I ended things."

He smiled before clearing his throat. "Because when she fell apart, she told me you would come and sit here to think a lot since your mom passed away, and she was nervous that you'd have to sit alone while you're going through everything you're going through. I didn't want that. I didn't want you to have to sit alone."

Well, shit.

What a good person.

"I see where Star gets her heart from," I told him.

"Nah. She got that from her mother." He waved me off. "But her good looks? I like to take credit for that."

I snickered a bit before growing quieter. Even during Starlet's heartbreak, she was worried about me. I didn't know love for a person could keep growing, even when you were separated from them. It felt unfair because I knew what was about to happen to me. I would spend the remainder of my life falling in love with Starlet Evans, even if I never saw her again.

I wasn't yet certain if that was a blessing or a curse.

"I'm sorry about everything you're going through, Milo."

I stared down at my hands clasped together. "How did you do it?" I asked. My voice was shaky and timid. "How did you get over losing your wife?"

Eric's brows knitted together. He rubbed his right hand against the back of his neck and contemplated my question for a moment. "You don't get over it," he started. "You get under it." I raised an eyebrow, confused by the answer, so he continued. "You get under the grief, you feel the pressure, and you begin to drown in the sadness. People say to do things and put yourself back out there into the world, but I think that's bullshit. You can't outwork grief. Sometimes healing comes from the allowance of darkness."

"The allowance of darkness?"

"Yes. Think of grief as a beast. A strong, big animal that you think you're supposed to defeat. So you fight against it, push and pull to try to regain some normalcy back in your world. Because that's the messed-up part, right? Everyone else around you will move on a lot faster than you. Everyone else will smile when they think of the person while you still want to cry. Everyone goes back to their mundane everyday lives as if the person who passed was never there, to begin with. They are able to do it so effortlessly, too, because the person who passed wasn't their person. The person who passed was yours. They were your heartbeats, and it feels like they were robbed from you. You're angry and pissed that everyone around you gets to move on while you're still drowning. So you try to act like them and fight grief. You push against it. You kick, you scream, you punch, and you fight until all you have left is depression."

Yes.

That's it...

Every word he said rang true. It was as if he crawled into my mind and read my list of greatest fears.

I lowered my head.

I felt Eric's eyes on me. His stare didn't feel judgmental, though. It felt familiar, as if he were staring at a person he once used to be. "Are you depressed, Milo?"

I nodded. "Yes."

"Okay," he said. "Now, sit with it. Stop fighting."

I glanced up as I fidgeted with my hands. "What do you mean?"

"You asked me how to get over losing a person, and I said you don't get over it. You get under it. That means instead of fighting the monster, you sit with it. You invite it to join you for tea. You mourn, cry, and scream but don't fight it. You don't swing. You drown in it for a while and allow your emotions to take over. You don't shut off your feelings. You dig deeper into them. You keep going, too, because your loved one wouldn't want you to stop. The only thing more terrifying than feeling all your feelings is feeling absolutely nothing at all. Trust me. I know."

"What if it becomes too much? What if I can't get out of the water?"

"Don't worry," Eric calmly stated. "You'll grow gills."

Don't get over it. Get under it.

"I feel as if I'm not only grieving my mom but my dad, too, even though he's still living," I said.

"That's the thing about grief. Sometimes, the worst cases of it are when it's dealing with those who are still breathing. You'll get through this. I hope you both do and end up with a stronger bond."

"Thank you, Eric."

"Let me make sure I'm getting everything straight. You're figuring out your life, yet pushing Starlet away because you think it's the right, noble thing to do."

"I can't be what she needs or what she deserves. I don't deserve her. I don't deserve her care for me or her love. I'm depressed." Saying those two words almost made me choke. It was the first time I'd expressed the truth behind what I was dealing with. It was the first time I said it out loud. Something about hearing it vocalized from my own mouth felt raw.

"Yes," he agreed. "You are. But let me ask you a question. Who told you that those who are depressed are not deserving of love?"

Me.

My mind.

My thoughts.

He tapped the side of his head. "Every thought that comes in here, young man, is not an honest one. Learn to filter out the bullshit, even if it's loud. You deserve to be loved. The truth of the matter is we're all a little broken. We're all a little cracked. But those cracks are what make us who we are. And every shattered person is still worthy of love. Maybe even more so than others."

"Thank you."

"Of course. Now, don't get me wrong. I find it noble that you stepped away from my daughter while you figure out your stuff and allowing her to figure out hers. You can't pour from an empty glass, and while Starlet might not understand that right now, as she's hurting, it's the best choice for you both. But do one thing for me."

"Sure, anything."

"Hold onto your love for her and her love for you, even from a distance. Starlet's love got me through my heartbreak from losing my wife. Her love is what saved me, even when I was sometimes distant. Use that love, that feeling, to help you through the currents of your

293

grief. Then once you begin to swim again—and you will, Milo—swim home to her."

"What if I'm too late?"

"That's possible, but what if you're right on time? That's the scariest thing about life—it makes no promises. But do you know the most exciting thing about life?"

"What's that?"

"It makes no promises."

Eric smiled, a smile that mimicked hers. I wondered how much of his daughter lived in his face and how much of Starlet lived within her mother's.

We finished our talk, and he drove me back to my place. As he parked the car in the driveway, he said, "I think I'm going to visit that lake on Friday mornings if that's okay with you. I liked the view."

"That's fine by me."

"And bring your backpack. I might not be the best tutor, but I'm damn sure I can help you out with a few equations to get you to graduation."

I gave him a half grin. "Thanks, Eric."

"Welcome. And, Milo?"

"Yes?"

"Swim."

CHAPTER 37

Starlet

*L*ate one Saturday night, I stood on Milo's front porch. It took everything in me to ring his doorbell, and when I had, I almost darted into the bushes to hide. My nerves sat in my throat, but I stayed still as stone. I couldn't leave things the way we had. After talking to my father, I felt as if I had to speak to Milo one last time from my heart.

I didn't know what words would come out once he stood before me, but I was ready to try to find said words.

When he opened the door, I saw the look of shock on his face.

"Hey. What are you doing here? Are you okay?" he asked, alert. "Come inside," he said, stepping to the side of his door. The care in his tone told me all I needed to know. He loved me more than any person had ever loved me before.

"It felt off to me," I whispered as I stepped into the foyer of his house.

He raised an eyebrow. "What felt off?"

"The last time we had sex. Looking back, I knew it was different. I could see it in your eyes, too, and I couldn't pinpoint it, but now I get it."

"Listen—"

"No," I cut in. I took a step toward him and placed his hands into mine. I stared down at our intertwined fingers. I missed his touch so much that his warmth almost knocked me backward. "I need you to listen first. I need you to know that I understand why you pushed me away. I get why you think I need to refocus myself. You're right. I am lost and need to figure myself out before I can be with you. But I will be with you, Milo. So I have an issue with how you made love to me the other night."

"What do you mean?"

"You made love to me as if it were goodbye. That's not sitting well with me because that's not the end of this story. We aren't saying goodbye to one another. We are taking a pause to figure ourselves out before coming back together, okay?"

He pulled me closer and rested his forehead against mine as he closed his eyes. "I can't ask you to wait for me to figure my stuff out. Plus, the journey with my vision is only at the beginning stages. I don't want you to give up your life so you can care for mine."

"I know what I'm signing up for, Milo. Trust me, I do. I'm not asking that you allow me to wait for you." I grazed my lips against his and whispered. "I'm asking for you to wait for me."

His eyes softened. "I'll wait for you forever, Star. You're all I've ever wanted."

"Promise?"

"Promise."

"Good." I stepped away from him and smiled as I removed my coat and dropped it to the floor. "I'm staying the night. In the morning, I'll leave and journey to find myself. In the morning, I'll begin again. But tonight, I need you to make love to me as if you're promising me forever instead of saying goodbye."

His eyes flashed with the same passion I saw the first night he took me in. He reached forward, wrapped his fingers around my white T-shirt, and pulled me back to him. My hands fell against his chest, and my heartbeats intensified as I stared into those eyes I loved so much.

"You want me to show you how I promise forever?" he whispered against the edge of my ear. His hot breaths sent tingling sensations down my spine.

"Yes," I breathlessly sighed, feeling emotions racing through my system. I wanted all of him that night. No rules, no limitations.

"No reigns?"

"None."

"And I have until sunrise?"

"Yes."

His voice dropped an octave. "You've made a mistake, Star," he warned.

My heart skipped a few beats as he said those words. "What do you mean?"

"What I mean is…" His mouth moved to the nape of my neck, and his tongue glided against my skin, creating tiny circles as he spoke. "I hope you're not tired because this will take a while."

I parted my mouth to respond, but he lifted me into his arms and took me to the kitchen, where he sat me against the countertop. "Take off your shirt and lay backward," he ordered as he unbuttoned my jeans.

My fingers wrapped around my T-shirt, and I pulled it over my head, exposing my black bra. I laid backward, feeling the chill of the marbled countertop as Milo removed my jeans down my thighs, and I lifted my hips to wiggle them off, watching the look of sweet discovery find him as his eyes fell on my black lace thong.

His hands wrapped beneath my ass cheeks as he lowered himself between my legs. "Mine," he whispered as his tongue swept against the thin fabric of the panties. "All mine."

A pool of heat fell to my stomach as his tongue began lapping up and down. The palms of his hands sat against my thick thighs, and he pushed them apart as he gripped the thong between his teeth and moved it to the side. His hot breaths melted against my clit right before he licked it so subtly, so teasingly that without any thought, my hips arched, needing more attention.

"Please," I whimpered, tossing my arms to the sides of the countertop and gripping the edges. My legs quivered as he swept his tongue against it again, making my thighs move closer, trying to hold him in place to force more pleasure from his mouth.

He took a finger and moved the panties further to the side, then began circling his thumb against my clit. "I missed you, Star, so please forgive me as I take my time to taste every inch of you," he said before his face fell against my core. My hips rocked against his face as his tongue moved up and down my lips slowly, then picked up speed as if he were starting to feast on his favorite meal. I cried out for more, feeling every inch of my body heating up from his pleasure as he slid a finger inside me.

I spread my legs wider, giving him more room to breathe me in, and with that freedom, he added another finger. I stared down at him, my heart racing faster as the man of my dreams made love to my pussy as if he'd been dreaming of doing so for the longest time. I fell back on the countertop, twisting and turning as his hand speed quickened. He worked my body like I were a goddess, and he came to my temple for worship. His voice groaned against my core as his tongue intertwined with the movements.

"Look at me, Star," he ordered, pulling his face away, still working those fingers nonstop, holding eye contact. "*Con amore*," he whispered. "*Sempre.*"

With love always.

My breaths were panting as his eyes locked with mine. My heartbeats intensified as his words filled me with a peace I didn't know I could find. I pushed myself onto my elbows and kept his gaze as he worked his magic within me. My back arched as I grew closer and closer to losing myself entirely from his words.

With love always.

He meant it.

I felt it, too.

"I...it...you..." I stumbled over my words, no longer able to form sentences. I fell into a euphoric state as he brought me closer and closer to my climax.

"That's it, Star, keep your eyes right here," he said, his voice dripping with sex appeal and love. I liked when he did that. I liked when he took control of my body and my soul.

"I'm going to…Milo, I'm going…"

He picked up his speed, sliding in deeper and harder, working me as if his only goal was to make me come repeatedly. My body quivered against his fingers as I cried out his name. My thighs throbbed against the countertop as he took his free hand and thumbed my clit in circles, working more and more to bring me to the most earth-shattering orgasm I'd yet to discover.

"Oh my gosh." I gasped.

Aftershocks raced through me as he slowly pulled his fingers from me. He kept eye contact as he removed his pants and slid his hardness inside me.

"Milo," I breathlessly panted, slamming my hands against the countertop.

The love in his eyes, the small part to his lips as he groaned out in a torturous pleasure, made me fall for him even more than I had before. This didn't feel like goodbye. He was making love to me with a silent promise that he'd be back for more.

Mine.

All mine.

Con amore sempre.

He leaned in and rolled his tongue against my lips before placing his hand against my back pulling me closer to him. My hand fell to his chest as he began thrusting harder, more profound. The feeling of him entering me repeatedly made my breaths manic and untamed. The wildness of his lovemaking made my legs tremble against him as his hands fell against my hips.

He cursed under his breath as he closed his eyes and pressed his forehead to mine.

My mouth parted to speak, but words were a mystery that I couldn't obtain as he brought me closer and closer to another orgasm.

Each thrust felt as if it were signed with forever, and each touch was marked with always.

I wrapped my arms around his neck. He lifted me, allowing me to place my arms around his waist as he moved us to the refrigerator. My back fell against the steel, cool fridge, and he thrust even deeper, making the entire appliance vibrate with us.

"Yes, yes, please," I begged, feeling my thirst for more of him building with every intense thrust. His mouth landed against mine, and he parted my lips with his tongue. Our tongues swirled together as we kissed like hungry animals, not wanting to miss a drop of one another's tastes.

"Bed," I pleaded, feeling the quivering of another orgasm building more and more.

"Bed?" he whispered against my mouth.

"Bed," I replied, wanting to bring him to the same place of wonderment he'd brought me multiple times.

He carried me to his bedroom and laid me in the bed, keeping the lights on so he could see every inch of me. He climbed over me and tangled his hands in my wild hair. Slowly, he pulled me closer to him and rested his forehead against mine. "I love you so much, Star. I hope you feel that, too. I hope you feel my love," he whispered as his hardness sat against my entrance.

He wasn't as wild as he'd been in the kitchen. No, his movements were steadier and tamer as he kept eye contact with me the whole time. I felt my chest tighten as emotions swept over me.

Milo wasn't saying goodbye at all. As he entered me, each thrust was him telling me he'd wait. Every deepening second was him locking my heart with his key. He made love to me in that bedroom as our bodies intertwined and became one system, one rhythm, one love story.

As we were drenched in love, I arched toward him, and he quickened his pace. My fingers dug into his back as I pressed myself to his body. We kissed hard, but we made love harder repeatedly that night. When he came inside me, I fell apart along with him, feeling our bond only growing.

At one point, we fell against the mattress, exhausted. I closed my eyes as he trailed kisses across my whole body, making me feel loved, safe, and free.

As he laid beside me, I moved closer, fitting against his body as if he were my missing puzzle piece. My head fell to his chest, and I listened to his heartbeats. He held me in his arms for hours, making love to me spontaneously throughout the night. Filling me up with his passion and sealing said love with kisses all over my body. He loved me in all ways possible that night. Hard and intensely. Slow and romantically. He laid every version of love against me, making it impossible for me to doubt said love.

I didn't feel like we were saying goodbye when the sun rose. I only felt closer to him. We imprinted on one another's souls, and the promise of forever was preserved for us both.

Milo was slow to get out of bed. He collected my clothes and dressed me. His hands caressed my chilled skin, feeling every inch of me.

After he stepped into his sweatpants, we moved to the porch, and he wrapped his hand around my neck, pulling me closer. His kiss was long and slow, and I wished it could've lasted for the remainder of my days. A part of me was afraid to pull away, but then I remembered what he had shown me the prior night and what I'd be coming home to later.

"Can you make me a promise?" I asked.

"Anything."

"Can you not stay by yourself? Let your friends and family care for you when you need them, okay? When things get hard, don't face those issues alone."

"I promise," he said. "Can you make me a promise?"

"Anything."

"When you're done finding yourself..." He placed his lips against my forehead and gently kissed me. "Please come find me."

CHAPTER 38

Milo

Don't get over it. Get under it.

Eric's words stayed with me as I went into the week ahead. I missed Starlet so much that it was hard to focus on anything else. But I also knew if I ever wanted to be the man she deserved, I had to focus on myself, on my life, and on getting it back together the best I could. I first had to be my best self for myself so I could be my best for her. I also had to give her space to become the person she was meant to be, too.

Still, missing her didn't get easier. I allowed myself to drown a bit in that sadness. I realized how lucky I'd been to be able to miss a person like her. It was a damn honor to even know a love like hers.

"I can give you the letter now," Weston mentioned as I sat across from him in his office on a Monday morning.

I stared at my uncle, a tad bit confused. I hadn't slept in a while, and the few hours I did sleep weren't the greatest. I'd been tossing and turning most nights. Staying in the house where my parents raised me without said parents felt bizarre. I hadn't even known how quiet the house could be. I missed the small sounds of Dad walking around. Him opening and shutting doors while cursing at the television. Now, there was nothing but silence. I didn't know that silence could be so painfully loud. I couldn't wait for Dad to come back.

"What do you mean?" I asked.

"The letter from your mother that she wrote you for your graduation. I can give it to you now if you want."

I narrowed my eyes. Was he really offering me that? Was the letter on him now? I could've really used a letter from Mom at that very moment. I felt so distant from her lately. Not even the sunrises and recipe cards seemed like enough to push me through.

I could've said yes.

I could've ripped open the letter from her and fed on the words she crafted to try to give me a sliver of hope.

But she said it was meant for graduation.

How could I go against her wishes?

"I'm okay," I told him, surrendering the opportunity. "But thanks."

Weston grimaced. "If you change your mind, just let me know. I know you have Starlet to help you get through these issues, but—"

"We broke up."

He paused, stunned. "What?"

"I ended things with her. I figured I have too much going on in my life, and I had already ruined hers a good amount. Therefore, I thought it was best to go our own ways."

"Is this about me finding out? Because I told Starlet—"

"It has nothing to do with you, Weston. It was my choice. Our lives are just in two different places right now. My focus has to be on school and getting better. Hers has to be on her life. We couldn't figure it out."

"Yet." He cut in. "You couldn't figure it out yet."

I snickered. "Weren't you the one who was against us when you found out?"

"Yes," he agreed. "And then I heard your story and saw how you two cared about each other. What you two had was different. It's what your parents had."

That made me pause because I felt that, too. A stupid part of me felt as if Mom knew I needed love, so she sent Starlet my way. But I couldn't jeopardize her life because I craved having her around. Plus, she felt like a safety blanket of sorts for me—something to work as a distraction to my depression. If I really wanted to heal, if I wanted to get better, be better, I needed to learn to stand on my own. I had to sit with my demons and allow them to tell me their side of the story as I told them mine.

Weston smiled a sad grin my way as the bell rang.

I placed my hands on the chair arms and pushed myself to stand. "I guess that's my cue to get to class."

"Yeah. I guess so." He stood, too, and slid his hands into the pockets of his slacks. "Hey, Mi?"

"Yeah?"

"Are you doing okay?"

My mouth parted, and my first thought was to lie, but instead, the truth slipped out. "No. I'm not." I was in a sea of bullshit, struggling to remember how to breathe most nights.

"Should I be worried about you?"

"No. I have to be not okay for a while. I'll check in if it gets too much, but otherwise, I'm looking forward to that letter in two months."

His smile seemed less worried as he nodded. "I can't wait to give it to you."

"And, Weston?"

"Yeah?"

"Can I stay at your house for a while? I don't want to be alone. Plus, I might need help getting to some of my appointments for my eye issues and whatnot."

"Are you kidding me? Of course. We'll have a room ready for you in no time. Let me know when and where you need to be for your appointments. Your aunt and I have you covered. Milo…you're family. You're not alone."

* * *

"YOU BROKE UP WITH HER?" Bobby asked as we sat in the ice cream parlor on a Sunday afternoon. The weather outside showcased spring peeking through. Everyone was now out of their winter coats and wearing hoodies and light jackets.

"We didn't break up, per se. We're just on a break."

"Like Ross and Rachel from *Friends*?" he questioned. "Do you both know you're on a break? Because that didn't work out too well for them."

"Why the hell are you watching *Friends*?" Henry yipped toward his grandson. "Shouldn't you be watching *Blue's Clues* or something more your age?"

Bobby leaned toward me and whispered. "Don't mind him. He doesn't know really know how to be cool. All he watches is old episodes of *Matlock*."

"It's a great show," Henry chimed in. "Back to what matters, a break, huh?"

"Yeah. We figured it was the best option," I said, picking up a scoop of my chocolate ice cream.

"Is she hot?" Bobby blurted out.

I arched my eyebrow. "What does that have to do with anything?"

"I'm just asking. Is she? I bet she's hot."

I snickered a little. "She's very hot."

"Wow. I can't believe a guy like you gave up a very hot girl," he commented.

"What's that supposed to mean?" I griped.

He shrugged. "Don't take this the wrong way—"

"He's about to offend you," Henry said.

Bobby continued. "But you're kind of ugly."

"What?" I laughed. "You can't even see me!"

"Yeah, but you have an ugly voice. I can tell that your looks match," he joked.

Leave it to Bobby to humble a person fast.

"Does your mom know she's raising a little shit?" Henry asked his grandson.

"Does your son know a big shit raised him?" Bobby countered.

"Language," Henry scolded.

"Sorry, grandfather," Bobby mockingly replied.

"*Step*-grandfather," Henry yipped.

I smiled at the two. I was grateful they crossed my path when I needed some guidance in my life. We spent a few more hours chatting before I headed off to Savannah's house to meet my other group of friends.

Even though I missed Starlet, I was keeping my promise to her. I wasn't alone.

Not by a long shot.

CHAPTER 39

Starlet

I missed him.

I missed Milo and worried about him so much that I could hardly focus on anything other than him. Sometimes I'd find myself reading old text messages between the two of us. It amazed me how a chain of messages could showcase the point when two people began to fall in love with one another.

My focus went back to my schooling and keeping my grades up for the remainder of the semester. Principal Gallo clarified that he wouldn't report me due to the extremely rare situation between Milo and me, but I still wasn't sure if I was moving in the right direction with my life.

Every choice I'd made with my career was built around my mother's. I wanted to walk in her footsteps and see things through her eyes, I thought. Maybe a part did still want to be a teacher, but I also wanted to explore other things to make sure I was making choices for myself instead of living solely in my mother's shoes.

"Okay, roommate, I have an idea," Whitney said one day, walking in with a basket full of random items. There were markers and glitter and stacks of magazines along with poster boards.

I raised an eyebrow. "What's all that for?"

"We're going to figure out your life, one thing at a time, and make a board for it."

I laughed. "I don't know if that's a good idea. I ended up tearing the last vision board I made into pieces."

"Lucky for you, this isn't a vision board. It's a try board. We'll try a million different things each weekend and see what sticks. Like rock climbing, painting, or recording a podcast. We're going to make a list of things to do."

I smiled at my friend, amazed by how outstanding she'd been throughout the toughest semester of my life. She was the true definition of a ride-or-die friend. No matter the mistakes I'd made, Whitney was always in my corner. "You're the best person I've ever met, Whit. I don't deserve you."

She smirked and shrugged. "You're right. You don't. But most people don't deserve me. I'm remarkable. Now, come on. Let's make this damn list."

* * *

As the weeks wore on and spring awakened through the budding tree branches, I still missed Milo every day. Nothing grew easier about that fact, either. While everything was beginning to feel normal again, life didn't feel whole. It felt as if a piece of me was missing, and there was no way for me to get it back any time soon.

I tried to keep busy, and my try list with Whitney made that easier. I'd learned a few different things about myself along the way, too. I tried a spin class and signed up for painting lessons. I wasn't a painter, but still, I tried. I tested different types of coffee. I fell deeply in hate with matcha. I cried sometimes, but I found many reasons to laugh, too.

Getting to know myself felt like the wildest journey I was

partaking in, but it also felt right. It was as if I were supposed to meet myself at that very special moment in time.

When May came around, I was doing a little better. That was until Mother's Day, the most challenging day of the year for me. I kept busy, trying not to overthink it. Dad sent me a message telling me he loved me, and that was nice to see. He was making me dinner that night to celebrate Mom, which would be great. I just wished I'd received a text message from Mom, too.

Whitney: You need to get back to the dorm room, stat.

Starlet: Why?

Whitney: Bring your ass here now.

Starlet: I have a class in thirty minutes.

Whitney: Now, Starlet!

I grumbled and walked across campus back to the dorm room. I usually never went back to the dorm during the day because I had classes back-to-back and walking to the dorm was out of my way. As I took the elevator up to our floor, I got another text from Whitney telling me to knock before entering the room, which was odd. Then again, Whitney was strange, so it was on par.

I knocked on our door, and she opened it just enough to shimmy her body out of the room. She shut the door behind her and smiled at me.

"Hi," she breathed out.

"Uh, what's going on?"

"I owe you an apology."

"What?"

Her eyes glassed over as she shook her head. "I was wrong about him. I was so worried about you getting hurt that I missed the most important part. I know I normally hate men but—and believe me, I can't believe I'm about to say this, but maybe it's not all men. Maybe some are decent. Maybe some are good, even."

I narrowed my eyes. "Whit. What the hell are you talking about?"

She took a deep inhalation and breathed it out. "You have a present."

"What?"

"A present. You have a present. In the room."

"You got me a present?"

She shook her head. "Nope. Not me. But dammit, it made me tear up. Are you ready?"

"You're freaking me out. Move."

She smiled and stepped to the side of the hallway. I placed my hand on the handle and twisted it, opening the door. My eyes instantly teared up as I saw the item in front of me—a pink bicycle with yellow daisies painted on, purple handlebars, and a white wicker basket. A matching helmet was there, too, and inside the basket was a bouquet of peonies and a card.

Milo.

I hurried over and opened the card to read the words.

My world,

I know today's a hard day for you, so I thought I'd give you something to make it a little less difficult. I built it with a new buddy of mine. It's not as perfect as your mom's, but I hope you like it.
I hope you take a ride today and feel your mom in the wind.

Happy Mother's Day to your mother.
She raised the best one of the best ones.

Con amore,
Milo

"So…" Whitney walked into the room and caught me as tears rolled down my cheeks. She patted me on the shoulder and sighed. "Is he your person?"

I nodded. "He's my person."

But I wasn't sure what it meant. I wasn't sure how to feel about everything. It had been weeks since I'd seen him, weeks without a single word, yet this reminded me exactly why I loved that man so very much.

He wasn't only my person, but he was my heart. He was my spirit. He was my light.

"Well?" Whitney asked. "What are you going to do?"

I shook my head, confused. "I…I…I don't know."

"You have to go to him!" she ordered.

My stomach was knotted up thinking about that idea. I couldn't just go to him. I couldn't…could I?

Oh gosh.

I was going to be sick.

"I need air," I told her, shaking my head in disbelief as I stared at the bicycle in front of me. "I need air," I repeated.

I took the bike, put on my helmet, and I went for a ride to talk to the wind.

After taking the ride and still being filled with confusion, I took the bike back to the dorm. Then I hopped into my car and drove the two hours to my dad's place for dinner that night. Within seconds of walking into his house, I poured out everything about what Milo had done for me with the bicycle. Dad listened to every detail as he cut up carrots for the stew he was making.

"Wow. Sounds like a winner to me," he said.

"A winner? Dad! He sent me a custom-made bike after not talking to me for weeks."

"You have to admit, it's kind of really damn thoughtful," he urged.

Yes. It was. But still. I was confused. "I don't know what it means."

"I think it means he loves you."

"Please tell me what I'm supposed to do. Tell me how I'm supposed to respond to this."

"I don't know, babe. It's your life."

I grumbled. "I know. But if it were yours... What would you do?"

He shrugged. "I don't know, but personally, I like him."

"What's that supposed to mean?"

"Milo. I like him."

I snickered. "You don't know him."

"I mean, I did help him build the bike, so we have had a nice connection over the past few weeks."

"What are you talking about?"

"We've been hanging out a few times for the past few weeks, so I'd like to think I know him pretty well."

My eyes narrowed. "I'm sorry, what?"

"Remember when I gave you Scouts honor that I wouldn't stalk your ex-boyfriend?"

"Yes."

"Well, I was never a Scout, baby girl. So, I stalked your ex-boyfriend. I've been visiting him once a week since then."

My eyes bugged out of my head. "No way!"

"Sorry, kiddo. I couldn't stand the idea of that guy being alone after everything he went through. Especially when he put your life's comfort ahead of his during his hardest times."

"You drove over two hours back and forth each week to come to check on him?"

"Yeah."

Tears flooded my eyes as I took in my father's words. "You were there for him? He wasn't alone?"

Dad placed the knife down, picked up a dishrag, and cleaned his hands. He turned to me and smiled. "No, baby girl. He wasn't alone."

Without thought, I rushed into my father's arms and pulled him into a tight embrace. Emotions spilled out of my eyes and rolled down my cheeks. "Thank you, Dad."

He kissed my forehead and held me back. "Always."

When I let him go, I wiped my tears away. "Is he okay? How is he?"

"He's a strong young man. He's still moving forward. He's about to go into his finals at school, but from what I can tell, he's passing all his classes. I haven't been much help in his math class, but my Spanish isn't half bad."

My eyes widened. "You've been tutoring him?"

"*Sí, mi hija*," he replied, making me smile. "Your mother might've been the teacher, but I wasn't half bad at studying."

"You're the best person I've ever known," I told him.

He pulled me into a side hug. "To be fair, you're pretty antisocial, so that's not saying too much," he joked.

I laughed. "Should I reach out to him? Or should I wait a while?"

"Well, I actually have an idea. But you might hate it because you'll have to wait a little bit longer."

CHAPTER 40

Milo

"You'd be happy to know that I passed my math exam," I said to Eric as I heard footsteps behind me as I sat on the bench on Friday morning. I was getting better at using my other senses to tune into my surroundings. As I turned around to see him, I paused, seeing who was standing beside him. "Dad. What are you doing here?"

"I finished my last day in the rehab center, and Eric was kind enough to offer me a ride home from Chicago."

I narrowed my eyes and looked at Eric. "You've been talking to my dad?"

"Yeah. We've become pretty good friends. Had some great heart-to-hearts." He walked over to me and patted me on the back. "He's a good man with a great son. I figured you both might want to watch the sunrise together. I've gotta get back to town."

Eric squeezed my shoulder before walking off.

"Eric," I called out.

"Yeah?"

"Thank you. For everything," I said.

He smiled his daughter's smile, which only made me miss Starlet more. "Anything for my daughter. Which means anything for you."

He walked off, saying his goodbye to Dad before leaving us standing there alone with the sound of the woods and flowing water.

Dad rubbed the back of his neck. "I'm currently debating if Eric's real or if he's that damn angel from *It's a Wonderful Life.*" He snickered.

I gave him a half grin. "That was Mom's favorite Christmas movie."

He frowned and nodded. "Yeah. It was." He gestured toward the bench. "Can I sit?"

"Of course. It's your bench, after all."

He took a seat, and I sat beside him. I watched as his fingers traced the initials he and Mom carved into the wood. He sniffled a bit and cleared his throat. "Thirty-four days." I raised an eyebrow. "Thirty-four days sober. I know it doesn't sound that impressive, but—"

"It's impressive. I'm proud of you."

His eyes glassed over as he took in my words. He shook his head and glanced up at the dark sky slowly beginning to yawn awake. "I didn't think I'd ever hear you say those words again. Not after how I'd been over these past few years. I owe you an apology, Milo."

"It's fine, Dad."

"No, it's not." He flicked his thumb against his nose. "When you needed me the most, I dropped the ball time and time again. I wasn't the parent you needed or deserved, and I apologize for that, boy. You deserved more. Your mother would've given you more."

"Maybe," I said, shrugging my shoulders. "I mean, don't get me wrong. For a while, I thought that, too. I was so pissed at you. I was convinced that Mom would've done better. But who knows? If the tables were turned and you were gone, I don't know how Mom would've handled losing you. Death is hard on people in different ways. We never know how it will change us until it does. I owe you an apology, too. I should've realized how hard this was for you. I had Mom for seventeen years; you had her for thirty-two. That's a lot more to mourn, and I'm sorry I didn't lean into you more. I'm sorry I didn't check in."

Tears began to flow down his cheeks as he sniffled and kept his stare to the sky. Deep blues and maroons were beginning to emerge. The soft clouds moved slowly to the right as the sunbeams began to peek through the landscape. Dad fiddled with his fingers as he took in the sights.

"Your mother told you to look for her in the morning skies," he said. "She told me to find her in the sunsets. I think her point for that was to try to get us to come together and share the beginnings and endings of each day."

"That sounds like something she would've done."

"I messed up, Milo. I've dropped the ball a million times this past year, and I apologize for that. I'm looking into therapy and other things to help with my grief. I don't want to live like this. I don't want to feel this way forever. I want to be there for you. I want to figure out how to be stronger for you."

"I don't need you to be strong, Dad. I get it…this sucks and it's hard, but I don't need you to be strong. I just need you to be here. Mom would be okay with us breaking every now and again. I just don't think she would've wanted us to break alone."

He brushed his thumb beneath his nose as he stared out at the water. "Be broken together?"

"Yeah, be broken together."

"You're a great son, Milo. You always have been, and I'm sorry for not telling you that enough."

"It's okay. I'm going to force you to for the rest of our lives, though," I joked.

He smiled and batted his tears away. "Yeah, well, I deserve it."

"You're great, too, Dad. I want you to know I won't judge you for a bad year when there were seventeen great ones. Someone once told me that we weren't our worst moments. I like to believe that that's true."

His hands clasped together, and he nodded. "I heard you, you know."

"What?"

"When you came to visit me in the hospital and asked me to stay each day. I heard you every single time. I think that was the reason I was able to come back. I think it was because of you, Milo. It was you, and it was always going to be you that brought me back. It was you that saved my life."

* * *

DAD MADE it back home just in time for graduation. A day I wasn't confident I would've made it to on my own. I knew damn well I wouldn't have been there without Starlet. If I were honest, I didn't know if I'd even be alive still if it weren't for her. Yet because of her, I'd made it out of the winter, and I'd discovered spring with summer right around the corner.

Graduation caps and gowns were the most uncomfortable thing I'd ever worn. They didn't look good, either. It was as if it was the school's final way to jab their students in the side with some form of annoyance.

The tassel kept dangling in front of my face as I sat on the football field, staring toward the stage. The bleachers were packed with people, families and friends all there to celebrate the graduates. The fact that Dad was in those bleachers meant the world to me.

The sun beamed down overhead, and I felt as if I was melting into a pool of sweat. It was wild to me how just a few months ago, everything was covered in snow, and now the sun had me wanting to go skinny-dipping.

I'd take the hot days over the cold ones, though.

Weston was in charge of calling the students' names as we received our diplomas. Lucky for me, I'd be one of the first to walk the stage, thanks to my last name. When I was called up, I stood from my chair and headed across the stage. To my surprise, a burst of cheering was heard, not only from my friends who were graduating but from the stands, too. I glanced over at them, and my chest tightened.

Star.

My Star.

My heart stopped for a split second as I froze in place, unsure how to move forward.

Her lips turned up into a big smile, and I felt my whole body warm. Shit. Even from a distance, she still controlled my every move.

"Milo," Weston whisper-shouted, snapping me out of my daze.

I shook my head and cleared my thoughts the best I could. I glanced back at Starlet one more time before walking toward my uncle. I shook Weston's hand, and he pulled me into a tight hug. As he held on, I felt his tears falling. "I'm so fucking proud of you, kid," he whispered.

He almost made me cry on that damn stage, too. I hugged him back, took the diploma, and headed back to my seat. I looked back to the bleachers, and she was gone. I shook my head a few times, feeling as if I were crazy. Had I imagined her being there? Was it all in my head?

I looked down at the diploma and opened it to see the certificate inside. Instead, I found an envelope. A letter with the words "My world" written across the front of it.

Mom's letter.

Without thought, I opened it. Everything around me slowed down. Everyone went mute as my eyes darted across the words written in ink with nothing less than love.

My world,

Today's a special day.
Your graduation day.

This is probably one of the hardest letters I've ever had to write. I have tears falling down my cheeks as I listen to you and your father watch sports in the living room. There's a pot of tea on the stovetop, and I'm waiting for the whistling sound to alert us all. You will rush over to said teapot, pour me a cup, and ask if I'd like sugar or honey in it.

Always both.

You know this, but you always ask.

I want to thank you for taking care of me these last few months. I know it hasn't been easy on you, Son, but you've been the most heroic individual throughout all of this. Thank you for loving your mama when she was too weak to love herself. The greatest part of my life has been, and will always be, you.

If you're reading this letter, that means I'm gone from the physical realm, but I want you to know that I'm right beside you through every step you take.

Especially on today. The day you're walking across that stage, accepting your diploma to start the next chapter of your life.

I want you to know that I understand if the past year was hard for you. I want you to know, no matter what, I'm proud of you. You've could've messed up a million times. You've could've failed over and over again. You could've done drugs, and drank, and fallen apart repeatedly, yet I'm so proud of you, Milo, because you still made it here. To this day.

I do not know what your next steps are. I simply know you're going to be okay, because I know you, Son. I know your heart and how it beats. I know the good in your soul and the kindness of your spirit. You're going to be okay. You're going to be more than that. You will be great.

So now I would like to give you some motherly advice to help you through your years to come. And oh, how I hope they are the most colorful years of your life, filled with so much comfort and joy.

Tips from Mama:

Eat your vegetables. I know Brussels sprouts are gross, but they are good for you. And make sure you floss every single night. Okay, every other night. I don't want to push it.

Forgive your father. I know how soft his heart is, so I worry that it will harden when I'm gone. Take care of each other when you can, and still love him when you can't. Being human is a messy thing and hardships will show up, but do know that even on his weak days, his love for you is strong. Please remember his best days when he's showing you his worst.

Make new friends and hold on to the old ones who were patient while you healed. Hold them a little tighter than others. And when they need you, show up for them. Be their pillar as they were yours.

Fall in love. Please, do this and allow it to be messy. Fall in love fast, and deeply. Fight for said love and be love's anchor. Allow yourself the space to feel things deeply. Say the words I love you as much as you can. You never know when it will be the last time, and I'd rather you drown a person in love than let the moments quietly pass you by.

This might be the most important part of it all. Love yourself, Milo. Please, please, please love yourself. There is no one more deserving to witness your love than the person who's staring back at you in the mirror.

Attached is the last recipe card I have for you. I hope they have brought you comfort in some of your most trying times. All that I ask is that you make this one on a Sunday and sit in a room filled with all the people you love. I want you to eat, and enjoy the meal, and laugh, and joke, and be alive.

Be alive, Milo. Live.

I want you to make your own life recipes. Create unique memories in your own special way. Expand yourself. Try new things. Fail. Try again. You're the most remarkable son I've ever had the blessing to know, and I know whatever you do with your life, it will be delicious.

Con amore, figlio mio. Con amore,
Mama

I opened the recipe card and pulled out the one for Mom's famous Sunday gravy sauce. The sauce she used to cook for hours to feed all our loved ones. My chest felt tight as I muttered to myself. "Thanks, Mom."

The ceremony felt as if it was taking forever, and we were only through the letter M. How many damn people had last names that started with M? I kept looking back up to the bleachers to see if

Starlet was there, but I couldn't find her again. It must've simply been my imagination playing tricks on me.

* * *

"So you're telling me you graduated today, think you saw your hot ex-girlfriend, the love of your life, in the crowd after building her a bike with her dad, and you decided you wanted to come to eat ice cream with grumpy Henry and me instead of going to see her?" Bobby asked me as we sat in the ice cream parlor.

"Yeah, pretty much."

"That's stupid," Bobby said matter-of-factly. "You make bad life choices."

I chuckled a little. "I thought Henry was the brutally honest one."

"I am," Henry agreed. "But the kid's right. You're a dumbass."

"Harsh," I said, shoving ice cream into my mouth.

"We're just your honest friends. Everyone needs honest friends," Bobby explained.

"Okay. Lay it out for me. Tell me like it is."

Bobby cleared his throat. "Okay, but you asked for it. I think it's stupid that you thought you had to push someone away to figure out your crap. My mom always said that the point of love was so people didn't have to do the happy or sad stuff alone. And here you are, choosing to do it alone. That's stupid."

I parted my mouth to give him a rebuttal, but nothing came to mind, so I kept stuffing my mouth with ice cream.

"The kid's right, you bonehead," Henry agreed. "I don't even know why you're still sitting here."

"My dad had to run a few errands before he picks me up from here for my graduation dinner, so I'm pretty much stranded. Plus, if I was daydreaming about seeing her there, then she's already back in Chicago staying with her dad for the summer."

"Uber, Milo. Take a freaking Uber," Bobby said as if it was the easiest thing in the world.

I laughed. "To Chicago?"

"Yeah. And leave a good tip," Henry ordered.

"It's really easy. Are you sure you graduated from high school today? You're acting dumb," Bobby said.

"Like *really* dumb," Henry agreed.

"Besides," Bobby stated, adding more and more sprinkles to his ice cream. "If I could still see and had a girlfriend I thought was hot, I'd spend every day looking at her face."

He was right. I'd wasted enough time already.

"Shit. I have to get to Chicago."

"Duh!" Bobby and Henry said in unison.

As I pulled out my phone, my dad walked into the ice cream shop, smiling my way. "Hey, Mi. Are you ready to go? I've got everything ready for dinner. Even got your graduation gift waiting outside."

I arched my eyebrow. "A gift? You didn't have to do that. Can we also shift the dinner plans? I was hoping you could drive me down to Chicago."

"Chicago?" he asked, confused.

"There's a hot girl," Bobby said. "And Milo's in love with her."

Dad arched an eyebrow. "A girl, huh?"

"A hot girl," Bobby explained. "Trust me. She's the one."

Dad scratched at his forehead. "Well, I was looking forward to dinner, but if it's real love..."

"You'll take me?" I asked, somewhat surprised.

"Today's your day, Son. I'll do anything you want. But first, let me show you your gift. Come on outside."

I said my goodbyes to the guys and followed Dad out of the ice cream parlor. He gestured toward a massive RV in front of the ice cream shop when we stepped outside. "Ta-da! Happy graduation, Son!"

I narrowed my eyes. "I'm sorry, what?"

"I got you an RV. I know you talked about wanting to see the states and travel a lot as a kid, so I figured it was a good time to get you the opportunity over these next summer months."

Don't get me wrong, it was a thoughtful gift, but it had one major problem. "I can't drive it, Dad. I'm not allowed to drive. Unless you were going to come with me."

"Crap…no, Son. I can't do that. I just started that new position and didn't even think about that. I'm sorry. I guess it's a pretty crappy gift."

I shrugged and patted him on the back. "It's the thought that counts."

"If you need a driver, I'm pretty open this summer," a voice said as they opened the door to the RV. I looked up to see Starlet standing there with the biggest smile. "That's if you're okay with my driving skills."

My chest tightened as I froze in place, staring at her. Her natural curls were blowing in the wind as she stood in the doorway of the RV.

My glance shot back and forth between Dad and her as I tried to gather what was happening. I didn't know if I was daydreaming again or not. "She's here?" I asked Dad.

He nodded. "She's here. So you'd better go greet her."

I rushed over to her and took her hands into my shaky grip. My forehead fell against hers as I closed my eyes. "Hi," I breathed out.

"Hi," she replied. "Happy graduation day."

I opened my eyes and placed my hand against her cheek, caressing her skin with the back of my hand. I took in every inch of her. Her eyes. Her dimples. Her smile. Her cheeks. Bobby was right. I was an idiot.

"I've missed you, and I've missed you in every way possible," I told her. "And I'm sorry for pushing you away for a while."

"It's okay. It was good for me. I'm still learning a lot about myself, but the greatest thing I've learned is that I want to learn those things with you."

"I thought we couldn't work if we didn't know ourselves fully. But I realize that change is the only constant thing in life. I don't know how long it'll take to figure out my stuff. I don't even know what better is for me or my new normal, Star. But all I know is that I want you. I want you to know that I want to spend every day I have left looking at you."

"Milo," she whispered, a slight tremble to her tone. "I've spent my whole life trying to be what I thought my mother wanted me to be. I tried to be perfect in every single way to make her proud. But then I met you and realized I no longer want to be a fake perfect. I want to be real. I want to get messy with life. And I want to be messy with you."

I pulled her into me, kissing her deeply as my arms wrapped around her.

From that point on, I refused ever to let her go again.

CHAPTER 41

Milo

"I cannot believe you've been cooking this sauce for eighteen hours," Starlet said as she stood behind me in the kitchen. She'd wrapped her arms around my waist as I stirred the sauce.

"My mom's homemade gravy is a slow and steady kind of recipe," I told her.

It had been a week since we'd reconnected, and we hadn't spent a second apart. It was the most rewarding week of my life, waking up each morning with her in my arms and falling asleep in the same fashion. We'd be off on our road trip starting tomorrow, but first, Dad and I worked on throwing a farewell Sunday dinner for Starlet and me.

"Taste?" I asked, holding Mom's wooden spoon up to Starlet's lips. I hadn't cooked with it since Mom passed away, and it only felt suitable to use it for Sunday's family dinner.

She parted her mouth and tasted the sauce. I knew it was perfect when she moaned more than she ever had with me between her legs. "Oh my gosh, that's everything good in the world."

I smirked and kissed her lips. "Not bad for my first time, huh?"

"You're going to have to make this for me every Sunday. I hope you know that, right?"

"I'll make it for the rest of your life if it keeps you moaning like that," I joked. "You look beautiful, too. I love your natural curls."

She patted her hair and grinned. "I'm falling in love with it, too. One day at a time."

That was how we took everything—one day at a time.

I was still working through my issues with my sight and rebuilding a relationship with my dad. Starlet reentering my life didn't resolve those issues. But it was more manageable, and it was lighter. I still had to learn how to swim through my grief and trials and tribulations, but somehow, I was beginning to discover my gills as my friends, family, and Star began to swim beside me.

"Can you slice the bread?" I asked. "Everyone should be here in a bit. The pasta's pretty much done, and we can set the table now."

"Of course," she replied, kissing my cheek before she moved on to the following tasks. Dad had a pork shoulder on the grill that he'd been smoking for a few hours and was beginning to slice up.

Within a few minutes, people began to arrive. Starlet's dad showed up with his employees from Inked. Whitney brought a Jell-O poke cake. Weston's family came with a salad, and my friends all came with their appetites. They brought a few of their family members, too.

Mom would've loved how packed the house was with people again. With laughter, with love, with friendship.

After he'd finished talking with Eric for a few minutes, I stepped outside with Dad, feeling the warm breeze sweeping through the night.

"How are you doing?" I asked.

He crossed his arms and smiled at me. He smiled. Over the past few years, I'd been making a collection of memories of his recent smiles. For a while, I thought he wouldn't be able to do that again.

Now, all I wanted was for my father to find at least one reason to smile daily.

"I'm doing okay. I decided to join the gym," he told me. "Someone mentioned I should meditate, but I don't think that's for me. Then Eric told me his favorite form of meditation was lifting heavy shit, and I figured that was something I could get behind."

"That's good, Dad. I'm proud of you."

He grinned and placed a hand against my shoulder. "I'm proud of you, Son. The person you are...the person you're becoming..." He sniffled and shook his head slightly. "She would've been so damn proud of the man you are today. I'm just trying to take a page from your book, and make her proud, too."

I narrowed my eyes. "Are you sure you'll be okay this summer with me gone? I don't want you to be alone."

"Don't you worry about me. I'm going to be fine. Besides, Weston and Eric already informed me that they aren't going to take their eyes off me for too long," he joked. "Did you know I'm going to Chicago to get inked by Eric?"

I arched my eyebrow. "Tattoos, huh?"

He snickered. "Some would call it a fifty-year-old life crisis."

"Others would call it healing," I said. "So keep doing that, Dad. Keep healing."

We stood on the back porch for a little longer as the sun set over our heads. The sky bled with bursts of oranges and maroons, strings of purples intertwined with the blues, and we breathed it in.

"Not so bad, Ana," Dad murmured.

Not so bad at all.

The meal was a hit. We could send everyone off with leftovers, just like Mom had done. Starlet even made everyone care packages with chocolate chip cookies to take with them. That was a thing she'd learned she loved to do—bake.

While she was still on the mission to find out who she was and what she'd become, I was proud of her for being patient with the process.

After everyone left, we tossed on comfy clothes and cleaned everything up. We packed the RV for the following day. Then we went over our road map one more time. "This is going to be the best trip ever," Starlet stated as she crawled into bed with me that night.

"I can't believe we are doing this."

We fell asleep in one another's arms. When we woke up, we watched the sun rise over the lake again before going on our adventure to see more sunrises. We sat on the bench Dad made for Mom and stared toward the sky as the colors of the sun painted the landscape right before our eyes.

Starlet rested her head against my shoulder as I wrapped my arm around her waist.

"I love you," I swore.

"I love you," she promised.

As the sun rose over us, I couldn't help but feel our adventure was only beginning.

* * *

One Month Later

"HOW IS THIS EVEN REAL?" I asked Starlet as we finished reaching the top of the Grand Canyon. We'd been on our road trip for thirty-two days and witnessed thirty-two sunrises together, along with our fair share of sunsets. The trip had been packed with beautiful sights and weird stuff, too. Starlet wasn't the biggest fan of Doll's Head Trail in Georgia, where muddy, creepy doll heads and body parts were displayed through the dark, patch woodlands. Even though she was helping guide me through the trails, she held my arm tighter in that park. Dinosaur World in Kentucky was another highlight.

At one point, I was sure she was getting annoyed with me for making her stop at every single dinosaur statue on the roadside, but we'd managed to take a million pictures with T-Rex and his friends.

Watching her dance in the streets of the French Quarter of New

Orleans was one of the highlights of the whole trip for me. Seeing how free Starlet became when she joined a random marching band traveling down Bourbon Street was the best thing in the world. She might not have known precisely what she would do with her life, but she knew how to be free that summer.

"Did you see me dancing with the drummer?" she asked me, wide-eyed with joy.

I smirked and pulled her to my side, kissing her forehead. "I saw you." And I did. I saw her. I saw every piece of her with my eyes open and shut. Starlet's aura was so bright that I couldn't have missed it if I had tried. I felt her in every piece of me. Something about her just made the dark days that much brighter.

She never once fussed about needing to help me at some of the attractions. She never complained about driving the whole trip. She showed up with a grace I didn't think I deserved and gave me her love without limits.

I paused as we sat atop the Grand Canyon, staring at the most breathtaking scenery I'd ever seen. The wind brushed against us, and I was almost sure it was Starlet's mother saying hello. I quickly learned that that was how she liked to communicate—through the wind.

I wished I could've known her. I wished I could've met the woman who'd brought me the best gift I'd ever had. I didn't know how to thank the universe for someone like Starlet. All I knew was that my gratitude was overflowing.

"Here, stand up and let me get a photograph of you facing the canyons," I said as I waved my camera.

Starlet hopped up, turned her back toward me, and stretched her arms wide.

"That's perfect! Keep standing there. Strike a few poses," I directed. She did as I said, and I snapped a few more photographs before placing the camera down. "Okay, now turn back to me so I can get a few shots of your face."

She spun around on her heels and gasped when she met my stare. "Oh my gosh, Milo," she whispered, her hand flying to her mouth.

There I was, down on one knee, with an engagement ring in my hand. My body was shaking nonstop as I stared at Starlet. Every nerve in me was a wreck as she stayed frozen in place. I parted my mouth to speak, and my voice cracked the second the first word came out. "I love you, Star. I love you in a way that I didn't even know love existed. Within a few months, you came into my world and turned my upside-down life right side up. You saved me from despair, taught me what unconditional love was, and you are the best person I've ever met, and I want to spend the rest of forever loving you fully. I want to be yours for the rest of my life, and I want you to be mine. So..." I nervously chuckled, shaking my head to try to stop the tears from falling down my eyes. "Marry me? Marry me, Star, and let's chase the sun for the rest of our lives."

She moved closer and reached toward me, touching my arms. "Yes," she cried, tears rolling down her cheeks. "Of course, I'll marry you." She didn't even look at the ring as she pulled me to a standing position. Her lips locked with mine. I saw it all as I closed my eyes and kissed the woman of my dreams. I saw my future, I saw my past, and I saw my destiny. I was destined to love Starlet Evans, and she was destined to love me back. We were written in the stars—or, more so, the sunrises.

Life wouldn't always be perfect, but I knew it would be safe with us together. I realized that was all I needed from life. I didn't need perfection—I needed safety, which Starlet had been for me. She was the safest place to land, and my only goal was to be hers, too. On the good days, we'd find joy. On the bad days, we'd discover comfort within one another. I was thankful for that and for what Starlet taught me throughout our time together. That no matter what, everything was gonna work out fine.

EPILOGUE

Starlet

Two Years Later

"*I* cannot believe you're getting married," Whitney said as she finished pouring us mimosas. I sat in the hotel room with a stomach of butterflies, knowing I'd be saying "I do" to the love of my life in a few minutes. Whitney, of course, told me that prosecco would make all the nerves disappear.

I yawned once as I stood there in my wedding gown, making Whitney point a stern finger my way. "No! No yawning. I told you you should've taken a power nap as I did."

"I know, but I was too nervous. I couldn't sleep."

"Fair enough, seeing how today's the biggest day of your life." She grinned from ear to ear. "Today's the biggest day of your life!"

The sky was still pitch-black outside as we stood in the hotel room. It was only four in the morning, and I only had a little time left before walking down the hidden path to the lake to meet Milo.

Morning ceremonies might not have been everyone's idea of a

perfect wedding, yet how could we ever get married without the sunrise looking over us? How could we get married without the wind brushing against our cheeks? We needed our mothers there on the best day of our lives.

There was a knock on our hotel room door, and Whitney headed over to open it. To my surprise, Jacob was standing in his suit with a big smile. "Hi, sorry to interrupt. I was wondering if I could get a few seconds with the bride-to-be?" he asked.

"Of course. Not a problem at all. I'll make sure everyone else is ready to go," Whitney said, walking out of the room and shutting the door behind her.

Jacob smiled my way and shook his head. "Wow, Starlet. You look remarkable."

I glanced at my gown and smiled as my hands smoothed over the lace fabric and crochet top. "Thank you. It was my mother's. My something old," I joked, then I kicked up my shoes, which were navy. "And my something blue. Whitney gave me her heart necklace for something borrowed."

Jacob reached into his back pocket and pulled out an envelope. "And maybe this can work as your something new." He walked over to me as I stood a little puzzled. He waved the envelope in the air. "Ana left another letter with Weston to deliver on this special day, too, and I asked him if I could be the one to deliver it to you."

My heart began beating quickly as realization set in that in his grip was a letter from Milo's mother—a letter crafted for me.

"Don't cry yet, Star," Jacob warned. "You can't ruin your makeup this early." He handed me the envelope, kissed my cheek, and hugged me. As he pulled back, his eyes were glassy, too. "She would've loved you, sweetheart, and she would've prayed for a woman like you to find our boy."

I lightly chuckled, feeling a wave of emotions hitting my chest. "You can't say don't cry, and then tell me things like that, Jacob."

"Sorry. It's just a great day. For a long time, I thought it would only be Milo and me moving forward. Thankfully, the world brought me a daughter, too. Enjoy the letter, and I'll see you soon."

He turned to leave the room, and I called out to him. "Jacob?"

"Yes?"

I smiled. "Save me a dance today?"

He smiled back, the same warm, welcoming smile that his son held. "I promise."

After he left, I took a deep breath. My hands were shaky as I went to sit on the couch. I opened the envelope, and my makeup was screwed because the tears began flowing as I read Ana's words.

My world's world,

Hello there, it's nice to meet you. Today's an exceptional day, and I'm sad that I'm not there physically to witness my son deliver his vows to the love of his life, but I am so grateful that I will be there in the spiritual realm, looking over you both.

I owe you many thanks. Thank you, my daughter. Thank you for loving my son. Thank you for being there for him when it's easy and hard. Thank you for being his best friend and his other half. My son is filled with so much love in his heart, and I know he'd pick the best one of the best ones to share his love with.

My love for you both is infinite, and I hope you feel it long after the "I dos."

Welcome to the family, mia figlia.

Eat an extra piece of cake for me, and make sure your life with Milo is just as sweet.

Con amore,

Mama-in-law

I read the letter repeatedly, studying how Ana dotted her i's and crossed her t's. I studied the curves of her penmanship and the love she left in every single word. It amazed me how you could feel someone's love so much when it wasn't physically there.

Whitney came back into the room, grinning ear-to-ear. "Okay, Star. It's showtime. Everyone else is already down by the water, waiting for the bride to arrive. Are you ready to head over to the lake?"

I'd never been so ready for something in my life.

We reached the lake, and I met my father's eyes. He was seconds away from crying when he first looked at me. "My baby's all grown up," he whimpered, walking over to me and pulling me into a hug. "You look astonishing, Star."

I smiled and wiped Dad's tears away. "Do you see her in me?" I asked, speaking of Mom.

He let out an emotion-packed laugh and nodded. "I see her in every piece of you. You are our greatest dream come true, and it is an honor to be your father and to deliver you to the love of your life today." He held me tight in his embrace. "Do you feel her?" he whispered. "Do you feel her in the wind?"

I did.

I felt her every day, even more so during the dawn.

"Are you ready?" he asked.

"I am."

Dad looped his arm with mine, and after Whitney handed me my bouquet of peonies, we began to take the trail toward the lake.

The music began to play as my father and I walked toward Milo, my happily ever after. He looked so handsome in his navy-blue suit with brown suede shoes. A peony flower sat in his pocket, and he was smiling the whole time as Dad and I approached him.

When we reached him, Dad shook his hand and then pulled Milo into a hug. Dad whispered something into his ear that made Milo smile widely and hug Dad even tighter. When they let go, I took Milo's hand and stepped forward.

"Hi," I whispered.

"You're the most beautiful thing in this world," he softly replied, giving me the same butterflies he had since the beginning. Our lives over the past few years have been quite the journey. After our epic road trip, we decided we weren't ready to let go of our adventure. I finished my college degree, yet I didn't go into teaching afterward. Milo and I decided to give our true dreams a shot, and we started our vlog of our travels. We showed up to the world, sharing our ups and downs in life. Milo shared his most authentic self with the world, bringing awareness to blindness and showcasing how his diagnosis wasn't a death sentence. It was simply a new chapter to his story. His story was one hundred percent his, and what a beautiful story it was becoming.

I wasn't too mad about how my life had turned out. It turned out I still loved teaching. The only thing that shifted was how I taught my lessons through our vlogs. On our adventures, we'd cross historical monuments, and I'd do episodes on the backstories of said places. We'd spent the past two years seeing the world, exploring, and somehow, we'd managed to make a life out of it—a life built around our dreams and passions. I might not have officially been a teacher, but I was sharing my knowledge with hundreds of thousands worldwide. Dad called Milo and me his favorite educators.

I knew it probably seemed crazy to others, the two of us traveling in an RV and making a living from uploading videos online, but we felt more like ourselves than we'd ever had.

And now, as we stood there, seconds away from saying, "I do," I couldn't help but smile at the idea of all the adventures before us.

As Milo held my hands in his, the sun rose as he said his vows. "My favorite Star... There was a point in my life when I never thought I'd get here. Most days felt like harsh, cold nights. I was frozen in despair, unable to find my way out of the darkness. I struggled with the idea that love would find its way to a damaged heart like mine, but then you came and whispered your love into my soul. You taught me how to breathe again. You taught me that even broken hearts like mine could someday heal and beat even stronger.

"While my eyesight might be worsening, my vision has far from faded. Because I see it all. I see you, I see me, and the many years of love and joy before us. I hear your laughter in the darkness and your heartbeats in the silence. Loving you is the greatest gift ever bestowed upon me, and I will do it until my very dying day. I will love you forever, Star, because loving you comes easy. I'm forever grateful for you and your love. So today, on the best day of my life, I say I do. I say I do to protecting you. I say I do to providing for you. I say I do to forever. You are my forever, and I promise you today that I will remain yours always. I love you as wildly as the wind blows and as peacefully as the sun rises. Thank you for your love. Thank you for being so patient with me. And thank you, most of all, for existing in the same world as me."

And just like that, I fell even more in love with my best friend.

Milo Corti was the man who stirred my world awake after years of sleepwalking. He brought me closer to myself by allowing me to fall apart at times. He comforted me during the hard parts and laughed with me during the soft ones. He was my person. My one and only.

From that day on, all I wanted was a little more of him every day for the rest of my life. I wanted his rainy springs and his crisp autumns. I craved his summer days and his winter nights. I wanted more of him and more of us.

That was it, and that was all I needed from now until forever.

More, more, more.

ACKNOWLEDGMENTS

Hi, there!

Thank you for giving The Coldest Winter a read. I hope you enjoyed this emotionally-packed read. This novel was a labor of love, and it wouldn't have happened without the support and talent of many individuals who lent their ears and eyes to help me while I crafted this story.

First and foremost, I want to thank Nicole from Emerald Edits for her amazing talent in developmental editing. She went above and beyond to help me craft this story into what it became, and I am amazed by her skills.

Next is my loyal and trusted team of editors. Ellie, Jenny, Virginia, and Emily: Thank you for helping me clean up this novel through rounds of edits. Sorry about the commas. Also, sorry about lay, laid, laying, ugh. I should've had you proofread this part of the book, too. Next time!

A thank you to Renita McKinney, owner of A Book A Day Author Services, for being a sensitivity reader for me on this book. Thank you for your guidance!

Murphy Rae: Thank you for my favorite cover ever. It's stunning, you're stunning, and I'm so freaking happy and blown away by your talent and skills. Thank you!

A big shout out to my beta readers Sarah, Christy, Maria, and Talon for giving me feedback and helping shape this into the book it is today. I am forever grateful to you all.

To my amazing PA, Tina, for being on top of everything when I'm dropping every ball known to mankind. Thank you for being a million steps ahead of me. I am the luckiest girl in the world to have you on my team.

Thank you to Valentine PR and Good Girls PR for helping me build my brand, showing me the ropes, and bouncing ideas off me.

A huge thanks to Nasha, my social media manager, who shows up daily to make my life easier so I can focus on my writing.

To my beautiful agents, Flavia and Meire, thank you for all that you do for me every step of the way. You are extremely talented women with a gift this world needs—I know I did.

I'd love to thank my family and friends for always being in my corner and understanding when I disappear for a few months to crawl into my writing cave. I would be unable to write characters packed with so much love without being surrounded by a love like this. You all are my world, and I love you more than words.

To the readers around the world: Thank you for giving Starlet and Milo a chance. Thank you for picking up this book and diving into the world of The Coldest Winter. I hope you know how much you all mean to me, even if I cannot always reply to your messages. I hope you know how much your words touch my heart. Without you all, I am just a girl scribbling words on paper. Thank you for bringing those words to life.

I am so excited about what's to come! I am so excited about all we have left to explore together in this crazy, wonderful world of books.

It's you and me, readers, taking this ride into the sunrises and falling in love repeatedly. That's what I want for us. More stories. More love. More community.

More, more, more.

-BCherry

ABOUT THE AUTHOR

Brittainy Cherry has been in love with words since she took her first breath. She graduated from Carroll University with a bachelor's degree in theater arts and a minor in creative writing. She loves to take part in writing screenplays, acting, and dancing—poorly, of course. Coffee, chai tea, and wine are three things that she thinks every person should partake in. Cherry lives in Milwaukee, Wisconsin, with her family. When she's not running a million errands and crafting stories, she's probably playing with her adorable pets.

* * *

CONNECT WITH BRITTAINY:

WEBSITE: www.bcherrybooks.com

Printed in Great Britain
by Amazon